ERIC AMBLER was born in London in 1909. Between 1937 and 1940 he wrote six classic novels, including *The Mask of Dimitrios*, which many consider his masterpiece. He then spent six years in the British Army, followed by several years writing and producing motion pictures.

Since 1951 he has written fourteen more highly-acclaimed books. Two (*Passage of Arms* and *The Levanter*) won the coveted Gold Dagger of the Crime Writers' Association. *The Care of Time* is his latest novel.

Mr Ambler now lives in Switzerland.

ERIC AMBLER

The Care of Time

FONTANA/Collins

First published in Great Britain by Weidenfeld and Nicolson Ltd 1981
This continental edition first issued in Fontana Paperbacks 1982

Copyright © 1981 by Eric Ambler

Made and printed in Great Britain by
William Collins Sons & Co. Ltd, Glasgow

THOSE wives of our great thinkers who tend to guard their husbands' sensibilities and reputations too jealously are generally disliked. They are also sometimes feared. The wife of A.I. Herzen, according to Michel B., was notable in this respect. Gossip about any young man with some trifling new thought in his head which might cause her husband intellectual discomfort would disturb her profoundly. Condemnation of the upstart would instantly follow. She always used the same words and they always sounded like an evil spell.

'Time,' she would say venomously, 'will take care of *him*!'

Time, of course, will take care of us all, but one sees why she could arouse fear. And not only in the young. Our older men fear the hand of time striking at the causes in which they have believed as they fear the hand of death reaching out to claim their children. For those complacent optimists who have not yet learned to live, as we do, in the kingdom of despair, that first quick glimpse of failure must always seem like a vision of death itself.

From a memoir attributed
to S.G. NECHAYEV (1847–82)

ONE

THE warning message arrived on Monday, the bomb itself on Wednesday. It became a busy week.

The message came in an ordinary business envelope that had been mailed in New York but had no return address on it. Inside, folded in three, was one of those outsize picture postcards that are offered to tourists in some places nowadays. This one was of a hotel with palm trees and carried an ornate caption proclaiming that it was the *HOTEL MANSOUR, Baghdad, Republic of Iraq*. On the back had been pasted a typed strip of paper.

Dear Mr Halliday,

On its way to you by post there is a parcel wrapped in ordinary brown paper. However, in order to distinguish it from any other parcel you might happen to receive at about the same time, this one is sealed with black electrical tape. The consequences of your trying to open this parcel yourself would be disastrous for both of us. You would die instantly and I would lose someone I hope soon to call a friend and to meet as a collaborator. You should take the parcel to the nearest police bomb-disposal unit and let them deal with it. Providing that they are thoroughly experienced in the work, they should have no difficulty.

Why do I send a bomb to a man whose friendship I seek and whose services I need? For three reasons. First, to make it clear that I am someone to be taken most seriously. Second, to demonstrate my personal integrity. Third, to ensure, with my unorthodox initial approach, your careful consideration of proposals that will be put to you later on my behalf.

I sign myself with a nom de guerre. It is one that I have used rarely in the past, but still sufficiently, I believe, to have earned it a place in any newspaper morgue cross-reference index to which you are likely to go in search of further information about me. You will not find much of that, but

i

what you may find should whet your appetite for a whole and larger truth, as well as the taste of sweeter things.

Yours sincerely,
KARLIS ZANDER

He hadn't in fact signed it, but printed the name in block letters with a felt-point pen.

Use of the term 'ghost-writer' to describe the job I now do for a living always irritates me; not, though, because I find it disparaging but because it is inaccurate. There are times when I wish it weren't. When, for instance, I am reading the publisher's proofs of one of my 'autobiographies' after the subject has revised them and incorporated his, or her, second thoughts and personal syntax. Then, the state of ghostly anonymity enjoyed by some of my colleagues can seem very appealing. In my case, the name always appears. It is put after that of the supposed author and in smaller type. 'As told to Robert Halliday', or 'With Robert Halliday' are the standard credits; and they are there not just to satisfy my ego, but to record the fact that I am part-owner of a copyright. They may also act, incidentally, as advertisements for my professional services. Some publishers have even assured me, with apparent sincerity, that my name on a book may, by serving as some sort of guarantee that it will not be wholly unreadable, actually help to sell the thing in hardcover and raise the paperback ante. I doubt that myself. If the books with which I am concerned usually sell well, I think that is because I choose my subjects carefully. Light non-fiction tends to be ephemeral; but, since I nearly always get a percentage of the royalty take as well as a fee for the initial work, I try to choose subjects with at least some promise of staying power.

Motion picture stars I take on only if they have had very long careers, are still working and remain in sufficiently good shape, mentally as well as physically, to be interviewed about the book on television. I have learned to stay away from comedians. Too many of them are manic-depressives; and their recollections of the past are often drenched in self-pity. Musicians, though, can be good value; as can captains of industry, retired generals and politicians. With the generals some caution is necessary. Most have axes to grind and they can be disturbingly generous with classified information. Generals also tend to feel that, once they have retired, they have automatically become free to ignore the laws of libel. On the whole I like politicians best. True, there is usually trouble with them over the credits. They really do want their books ghosted. Even men who have been openly employing speech-writers all their political lives seem to find it demeaning to admit that they cannot write publishable books without help. There are, of course, accepted ways of overcoming this difficulty. 'Editorial assistance' can usually be acknowledged without serious loss of face. And for the one assisting there can be long-term compensations. If plenty of hitherto unpublished letters and documents, however trivial their content, are included in the book, there will be a substantial hard-cover sale to libraries as well as listings in bibliographies. Political memoirs have been known to stay in print for years. Moreover, as I happen to find politics and politicians interesting, I usually enjoy the work.

However, I do have some hard and fast general rules about choosing my subjects. I will, for example, have nothing to do with pop stars, boxers, baseball managers or persons claiming to have belonged to secret intelligence agencies. Those with drink or drug problems I avoid because, however distinguished they may once have been, or may even still be, for me they will always constitute an unacceptable risk. And not only because they are likely to waste a great deal of time. The major occupational hazard of my trade is the temptation to practise amateur psychiatry. If the opportunities for doing so are to be reduced to a minimum, you have to make rules for yourself and stick to them.

At that time, though, I had no rule – hard, fast, or of any other kind – about jokers who claimed to have mailed bombs to me. I had had no need of one before.

My first impression of the message was, of course, that it was a hoax perpetrated by some acquaintance with a defective and unpleasant sense of humour – that postcard of the Hotel Mansour was a nasty little touch – but I couldn't think of anyone to fit. Next, I began to wonder what kind of man it would be who could think that the way to establish his personal integrity and a friendly relationship with a stranger was to mail the stranger a bomb and then warn him not to open the package. If there was a bomb, such a man had to be totally deranged.

Totally? After a couple of re-readings, I began to have doubts. There was nothing deranged and something curiously confident and knowledgeable about that end paragraph. He knew enough not only to guess rightly how a person with my newspaper background would go about checking him out, but also enough about his own record to choose an alias that would show up if I did check. *When* I did rather. He was in no doubt about my curiosity. Well-informed, then, and all too cute, but not totally deranged.

Suddenly, reading the first two paragraphs again, I understood. The style was the man. This was the message of a vain man, a racketeer of some sort or other no doubt, but one who liked the sound of his own voice and had pretensions to gentility. A simpler man would have said: 'Halliday, I could easily kill you. Instead, I'm telling you how to avoid getting killed. But, in return, I want something from you. So, when you hear what it is, don't try to argue. Just do as I ask, and at once.'

On the assumption that there was in fact a live bomb addressed to me in the mail – and not a tape-sealed package containing some prankish object put there to make me look foolish when I took it to the police – I had to regard that chatty little warning as a threat.

Curiosity, not unmixed with anxiety, promptly triumphed over my plans for the day's work and I began calling New York. Before long I had found out a little about Karlis Zander, but, as his message had predicted, not much. Moreover, the little there was had not come easily. The news agency librarian I knew best had at first been unexpectedly reluctant to oblige an old friend from way back.

'Bob,' he said plaintively, 'this is what some of your spook pals might call sensitive material.'

'I don't have any spook pals. You mean someone upstairs at your place once took an interest? It's his baby?'

'No, that's not what I mean. It's nobody's baby at the moment, but that doesn't mean that I can give it away for free. Why the sudden interest in Zander? What's the story?'

'He's just sent a letter making a package-bomb threat. Okay?'

'Can't you give me more than that? Threatening whom? The Mayor? The President?'

'Me.'

'You?' He coughed up a laugh. 'When did this happen?'

'This morning. He says he needs my friendship and collaboration.'

'Bob, someone's putting you on.' When I said nothing to that he went on. 'All right, so how about reading me the letter?'

I read him the letter, but without giving the last eight words of it and without mentioning the postcard to which it was attached. There was a long silence. Finally, he sighed. 'Bob, will you believe me if I tell you that you're the last person in the world this guy Zander would want anything to do with?'

'I'll believe you. But why?'

'Well, to begin with, Zander only exists now as one of a bunch of old aliases.'

'He's dead?'

'No, he's not dead, but I'll bet he'd like us to *believe* he was. When he was an up-and-coming undercover fixer in a revolutionary cause he didn't care who or how many knew what a clever one he was, how smart and how quick. Nowadays it's all different. Now he's all for heavily-protected anonymity.'

'Doing what?'

'Acting as a contract management consultant. Yes, that's what it says here and that's how his clients are advised by him to describe his services when the government auditors come around. To put it less delicately, he's a high-level go-between, a slush-fund manager with a multi-million-dollar business run out of three briefcases and permanent luxury hotel suites in all major capitals. You want the contract to build a new port facility east of Suez? You want your group to supply those excitable Third-Worlders with that brand-new air-defence system they seem to think they need? Well, he's your man. Or, rather, he's your middleman, the one who has everyone else's private set of game rules and religious prejudices all in his head. He's the one who knows exactly who has to be paid off and exactly how much each of them rates. What's more, he'll handle every last one of those payments in such a way that no Congressional Committee yet invented can ever point the pudgy finger at you and say "bribery". Get the idea?'

'What's he call the consultancy and where's his base?'

'Bob, he has so many different corporate names in so many places that I won't bother listing them. He travels on a number of passports, mostly Lebanese but that was a while ago. As for his base, that's wherever the briefcases happen to be. You see why that bomb-threat has to be a put-on? You're the last person an operator like that would want to know. You don't want to know him either. There's nothing in him for you. Forget it.'

'You say that Zander is an old alias of his. It sounds northern European. Do you know where he's from?'

'Sure. Born in Tallinn, Estonia. A German-speaking family though. When the Soviets invaded the Baltic states after the Nazi attack on Poland he was a university student. The records are either destroyed or unavailable, of course, but he'd have been about eighteen. They grow up young there, and tough too. Though the Russians netted his family he managed to get away. He was one of a party of refugees who made it by sea to Danzig. There he volunteered for the Wehrmacht and after boot camp was sent to a special infantry training school, then to a signals outfit. No field-force posting of the ordinary kind though. He was a fluent Russian speaker as well as having an anti-Soviet background. They were saving him. When Hitler invaded Russia young Zander was transferred to the Abwehr as an interpreter. You know about the Abwehr?'

'Army intelligence and contra-espionage weren't they? Not to be confused with the Gestapo.'

'That's right. Good guys, or goodish anyway. All the same, the Russian-front Abwehr wasn't the sort of outfit you boasted about having served with, certainly not in March forty-five. Besides, at war's end he was a displaced person without a home state to go back to. Estonia was in the Soviet Union for keeps. So he used some of the know-how he'd picked up in the Abwehr and bluffed his way out via France and Spain to Algeria.'

'Very resourceful. Why Algeria?'

'All he knew was soldiering. Would you believe me if I tell you that he enlisted in a para unit of the French Foreign Legion?'

'Why not? A lot of the Legionnaires who fought the battle of Dien Bien Phu were German.'

'Dien Bien Phu, yes. That's where he was wounded. But he was lucky. It was in the early weeks of the battle that he got hit. He was one of those evacuated. His last year in the Legion he spent back in Sidi-bel-Abbès as a weapons instructor. He'd enlisted, by the way, as Carl Hecht.'

'When did you open a file on him?' I asked.

'Oh, not until later, not until . . .' He broke off and I thought that he might be wondering again whether he was giving away too much for too little. But no; it was just that he was an archivist who liked things set out in chronological order.

'We're *reasonably* sure,' he went on, 'that the two years following were spent in either the Lebanon or Jordan or both. With his hitch in the Legion, his wound and honourable discharge, he was entitled to apply for French naturalization. So he changed his name again. He became Charles Brochet. As a French weapons instructor, with some kitchen Arabic picked up in Algeria, he'd have been welcomed with open arms in the PLO training camps.'

'You say you're reasonably sure. Only reasonably?'

'Well, that was just his subsequent story. We had no simple way of checking it out. He's a skilled liar apparently. Good at figuring out what you hope or expect to be told. You asked when we opened this file on him. It was later, in fifty-nine, when he began to make a name for himself in Tunisia. A conspiratorial, partisanish name I mean.'

'Doing what?'

'Running an import-export business for the FLN. The French had effective trade embargoes operating in North Africa on pretty well everything the Algerian rebels needed to go on fighting. Zander's office, which he called C. Brochet Transports SA, acted as a secret purchasing agent for them and ran the stuff overland to the Tunisian border.'

'Arms?'

'Chiefly medical supplies – drugs, antibiotics. That was what made him important. To evade the French embargoes he bought through a dummy corporation called Zander Pharmaceuticals that he set up in Miami, Florida.'

'Using Arab money?'

'He wasn't using his own, that's for sure. His backers had to be Arab, though we never found out exactly who they were. We tried, naturally. The French were internationally unpopular at the time and every item coming out of Algeria was considered important. We had a guy there who spent a lot of time on the Brochet-Hecht-Zander story. One of the first things he did, of course, was to look Zander up in the reference books. Guess what.'

'He found *zander* in the dictionary. It's some sort of fish. Like *Hecht* in German and *brochet* in French?'

'You got it. Zander is a variety of wall-eyed pike.'

'Not very smart of him, was it, to use cover names which were that easy to blow? I'll bet he didn't pick up that habit in the Abwehr.'

'Our man said much the same thing at the time. Monsieur Brochet told him he didn't understand the Arab mind. A respected hero figure boldly defying threats of death and torture was safer than a nonentity. In fact, he said, French intelligence knew all about him and had tried more than once to have him killed. The gallant and well-loved El Brochet had always been given ample protection by solicitous Arab friends. A deep cover John Doe type wouldn't have lasted a week. Which thought brings me back, Bob, to this quaint little letter you've received. Twenty years ago in Tunisia, maybe, the head of Zander Pharmaceuticals could have used your image-building skills to rewrite Robin Hood for the North African Market. Now? No way. What did you say he *says* he wants from you?'

'Friendship and collaboration. If he makes me a firm offer for either, I'll let you know. What about his sex life?'

'Our story speaks of catholic tastes, but there's nothing recent on that.'

We talked a bit more before I thanked him and hung up. Almost immediately the phone rang. It was Barbara Reynolds, my agent, calling.

'Robert, your phone has been busy all afternoon.'

'The changes on the Williams typescript are in hand and I'll be delivering this week.'

'They'll be glad to hear it, but that's not the reason I'm calling. We've had rather an interesting approach from an Italian publisher. Some people named Casa Editrice Pacioli in Milan.'

'Which book is it they want?'

'None in particular. I mean they're not after translation rights. That's what's interesting. They want to talk to you about doing a book for them on a subject of their choice. Not in Italian, of course. They'd take care of the translation later. They want world rights and their first deal would be for English language publication here, then British, Italian, German, Spanish and all the rest. It's rather unusual.'

'What's the subject?'

'They want to put that to you personally. I gather they don't want it talked about in the trade until the deal's set and the book's in work. If it's the sort of idea that can be stolen, you can't blame them. They won't even tell me. They just want to talk to you.'

'In Milan?'

'No, right here in New York. They're represented by a law office.' She mentioned the name of the firm. It was one of those respectable Wall Street partnerships with three or four impressive surnames on the shingle and a string of a dozen or more somewhat younger, but still distinguished, members listed in a column on the letter paper. The member who handled Casa Editrice Pacioli was a man named McGuire. He was, according to Barbara, number three on the list of active partners.

I noticed that I felt reassured by that information and wondered why. It took me a second or two to get the answer. You didn't find men like McGuire acting for the likes of Karlis Zander. I pulled myself together sharply.

'Have you dealt with Pacioli before?'

'Through our Italian sub-agent, of course. Well-established publishers with a healthy educational department and a good back list. They're owned by a conglomerate now, I seem to recall, which may explain their readiness to make this kind of an offer.' Her voice took on the tone of studied calm she always used when speaking of money. 'Robert, they are offering a flat fee, *plus* eighty percent of paperback, *plus* forty percent of serializations. The fee would be fifty thousand, dollars not lire, and would be payable half on signature and half on delivery. Now get this. The fee would *not*, repeat *not*, be an advance against royalties. You earn it simply by doing the job. The half not paid on signature would be paid into escrow here along with five thousand more against your travelling expenses. It's a dreamy deal.'

'Dream-like anyway.'

'Robert, the only way you're going to find out whether the subject's for you is to let Mr McGuire tell you what it is. I said I'd call him back by Wednesday at the latest.'

'What's the hurry? I'm not doing any more of those marathon rush jobs.'

'My dear, I know alimony is deductible, but you have to have something to deduct it from and there are no other irons in the fire. That fifty thousand would be practically found money.' She always calls me 'my dear' when she feels that I am being unco-operative. I guessed that my accountant had been talking to her. The Internal Revenue had been auditing my last three years' returns and were thought to be about to slap a supplementary assessment on me.

'I'll think about it.'

'My dear, you think about it while you're finishing those Williams changes, and then you call me Wednesday morning so I can set up a date for you with Mr McGuire. All right?'

'All right.'

I didn't call her Wednesday morning because that was when the bomb arrived.

It was about the size and weight of a hard-cover book of average length. The brown paper wrapping had been neatly sealed with black electrician's tape of the kind that can be bought in the hardware section of a supermarket. My name and address on the label were typed, as was the address of the sender. He gave himself a PO box number in Miami, where the package had been mailed, but no name.

When the delivery man who had brought it had gone, and I had finished standing there stupidly looking at it as if I were waiting for it to start talking, I very carefully put it down on the nearest table. I sat down then and was surprised to find how cold and sweaty I had suddenly become. The daily who takes care of me was due any minute. I waited there by the front door until she arrived, told her not to touch the package and then went back to my workroom.

There can't be a big demand for bomb disposal in our part of Pennsylvania. Anyway, I could find nothing under that heading in the phone-book police department listings so I called my part-time secretary, who takes an interest in local politics, and asked her for the name of our senior lawman. I didn't tell her about the package. I said that I wanted to check on some aspects of police procedure for the Williams typescript changes. As Williams was an acquitted murderer, the excuse was convincing. She told me that I should talk to Captain Boyle who was new and the most helpful of men.

After a tussle with a protective desk sergeant I managed to get through to Boyle, who began by sounding hostile rather than helpful. He refrained pointedly from asking what he could do for me and had clearly assumed that I was hoping to get a traffic ticket fixed. No doubt he was all set to tell me that, with his coming, times had changed in the county. So I said, calmly, that I didn't know whether I should be calling him or the FBI, but that I had received a bomb-threat. That seemed to interest him a little so I read it out to him. Then, before he had time to comment, I reported reception of the bomb itself.

'This morning, you say, Mr Halliday?' He was now quite affable.

'That's right. It's ticking away in the next room.'

The facetiousness was a mistake.

'Ticking, you say?'

'I was speaking figuratively, Captain. It's not making any actual sound. Look, I don't want to make too much of this, but I'd just like someone from a bomb-disposal unit to find out fairly quickly if it's a hoax or not.'

'We don't have a bomb-disposal unit, Mr Halliday, not here, but I think there's one in Allentown. Give me your number and I'll get right back to you.'

He was back in five minutes. 'Allentown has a police bomb-squad manned by detectives, Mr Halliday, and they're sending a couple of men over with all their equipment right away. They'll want to see the letter as well as the package. Now, this package came to you through the mail, right?'

'That's right.'

'Is it in good shape or is the wrapping paper torn?'

'The wrapping's okay. Why?'

'Well, what I mean, Mr Halliday, is this. Do you want us to send a patrol car all the way out to you, or do you want to save time and drive the package and the letter in to us yourself?'

I considered rejecting this unhelpful suggestion, but, short of declaring that I was scared stiff of the package, could think of no reasonable way of doing so. 'Okay, Captain, I'll drive it into town. But just in case anything unexpected happens on the way, you'll find the letter on my desk here. I'll make a photocopy and bring that.'

He chuckled. 'If it came safely through the mails, Mr Halliday, it'll travel safely in the trunk of your car.'

It did, though I noticed that the bomb-squad detectives who removed it from my car in the police parking lot an hour or so later were less casual in their approach. They wore massive body protectors that came down to their knees and slit-eyed steel helmets that rested on their shoulders like medieval tilting casques. They carried the package in a padded metal basket slung between them on a long pole.

We watched from a distance as they took it to the armoured truck they had brought with them. Then I went with Boyle and one of his detectives to an office. There, I made a simple statement to the effect that I had received both message and package through the mail before turning them over to the police.

After that, I was given a cup of coffee and asked if I minded waiting until the bomb-squad men had used their portable X-ray and come up with some kind of preliminary finding. It seemed that, in cases where bombs were sent through the mail across state lines, the FBI as well as the Postal Service had to be informed. Then both of them, as well as the police, could become involved in investigating the surprisingly large number of felon ies and misdemeanours that Zander would have committed. And I would be a material witness to them all. Graciously, I agreed to await the bomb-squad's verdict. There was no point in telling them that, until at least some of the mounting pressure of curiosity I was suffering had been relieved, they would have had to use force to persuade me to leave.

After nearly an hour, negative reports began to come in. The PO box number in Miami did not exist. The FBI had no record of any Zander. Shortly afterwards, Captain Boyle sent for me so that I could hear the bomb-squad report.

The man in charge of the squad was Detective First-Grade Lampeter. A tall, black, melancholy man, he nodded in a perfunctory way when Boyle introduced us. He was holding an X-ray picture by a pair of clips and seemed to be as disgusted with himself as he was bored by the rest of us. I wondered if that could be a state of mind that went with his job. He had a white partner whose name I didn't catch.

'There's your bomb, Mr Halliday,' Boyle said with a wave at the picture.

All I could see on the X-ray was a lot of grey fuzz, a slightly darker rectangular shadow and something that looked like the silhouette of an old-fashioned mouse-trap.

'Was there any explosive in it?' I asked.

Lampeter pointed to the dark rectangle. 'Regular dynamite,' he said, 'the sort farmers use for clearing tree stumps. Six sticks taped together. No fingerprints on the tape or anywhere else. Standard blasting caps. It's a highly professional job done by, or on the instructions of, someone who knows about bomb-disposal techniques. See that?' He tapped the mouse-trap shape

'Looks like a mouse-trap.'

'It is, more or less. The idea is that when the package arrives the person it's addressed to opens it up by tearing off the wrapping. That takes the pressure off the piece of cardboard holding the spring down underneath. So, snap it goes like any other mouse-trap. Only what it snaps into isn't a mouse but a detonator. So, bang, you've lost both arms and an eye or worse. So, the moment we see an X-ray with that sort of break-back gadget showing, we know how to open the package and render it harmless. We do it like this. Excuse me, Captain.'

He took a law book out of the case behind the Captain's chair and put it on the edge of the desk.

'That's the package, say. Now, I put the flat of my left hand right on top of the place where I know the break-back spring is and I press down firmly. Then, with my right hand, I take a knife with a sharpened hook at the end, like you can buy for cutting linoleum or shoe-leather, and I slit open the package around the edges of the long narrow side. Then, I can gradually slide out what's inside while continuing to maintain pressure on the break-back to stop it flipping over. When it's far enough out for me to see, I can get hold of the break-back itself. Then, all I have to do is remove the detonator. When we had that miners' union trouble and people were sending package bombs to each other by every mail, we dealt that way with a dozen or more in a week.'

'So that's how you dealt with this one, eh?' Captain Boyle had been fidgeting and now seemed ready to skip any further instruction in the rudiments of bomb disposal.

Lampeter shook his head emphatically. 'No, Captain, that's how I was *allowed* to deal with this one by the son-of-a-bitch who sent it or arranged for it to be sent. I told you it was put together by someone who knows the score, someone who knew that it would be X-rayed and opened up like I've shown you with a hooked knife. So, what he does is put in a little extra gizmo to fool me. In the army, where I was trained, that was standard operating procedure with stuff like mines and delayed-action bombs. As soon as the guy who'd designed one of those items had figured, or been told by Intelligence, that the enemy knew how to defuse it, he put in a modification. As a result, the next time some smart-ass enemy tried defusing it by the book he blew his stupid head off.'

'You look all right to me, Lampeter,' said Captain Boyle. 'I take it you spotted the modification.'

'No, Captain, I missed it completely. What he's done is put in an electric detonator as well as the regular one. It doesn't show in the X-ray because it's in there behind the main spring of the break-back. The wiring from the little pen-light battery runs around the outside edge of the whole package. When I put the knife in and started cutting the side open, that should have set if off by shorting the twin flex he used, either straight away or when I began to pull the hook along.'

'Why didn't it? Luck? Some defect?'

Lampeter breathed in deeply before answering. 'No, Captain. No luck and no defect. The bomb-maker had the detonator connections neatly taped back out of the way so that I should know that this time he was just kidding. He could have blown my head off, but he didn't. He's a sweetheart. The FBI lab people are going to love him too.'

The white bomb-squad man spoke for the first time. 'If I ever get my hands on the mother,' he said quietly, 'I swear to God I'll kill him.'

'Aren't you gentlemen taking this a little personally?' I asked. 'After all, I'm the nearly injured party. The bomb *was* sent to me. I'm delighted he was kidding.'

Lampeter's melancholy eyes took me to pieces for a moment before he answered. 'You're a civilian, Mr Halliday, and he hasn't made a monkey out of *you*. They tell me you're a writer. Movie stars' biographies they say. Right?'

'Among other things.'

'Yeah. I think I've seen your name on drugstore bookstands. All that "truth-about" stuff. In that line of work you must have gotten to know where quite a lot of bodies are buried. And I'll bet you've made quite a lot of enemies too.'

'The sender of this bomb says it's a friendly gesture. He wants to convince me of his personal integrity.'

'Ah, shit.'

'It's true, Lampeter,' said Boyle.

'You said he'd had a threatening letter, Captain. It told him to call in the bomb-squad. Received Monday. Right?'

'Right, but I didn't get a chance to show you the actual letter. You were already all suited-up for the bomb when Halliday brought them both in. But it's like he says. Look.'

He had the photocopy of Zander's letter in a plastic folder and pushed it across the desk. Both bomb-squad men read it together. When Lampeter had finished he looked almost cheerful.

'Well, Captain,' he said, 'sooner you than us. When you said threatening letter I thought you meant one of the normal kind. What you've gotten here is a nut-case. And a nut-case who can package bombs as good as this should be able to give you and the Postal Service a whole lot of trouble.' As he got up to go he showed me a friendlier face. 'Know what I'd do in your place, Mr Halliday? For the next six months I wouldn't open any mail at all that I can't see through when I hold it up to the light. And, if the Captain here would let me, I'd take a long vacation as far away from home as possible. Been nice meeting you. Captain, that package is defused and safe now. Do you still want us to deliver to the FBI or will one of your men take care of that?'

When the business was finished and they had gone, Captain Boyle looked at me again.

'Think of taking some of that advice he gave you, Mr Halliday?'

'About taking a vacation?'

'I'd prefer that you didn't take it so far away that we couldn't reach you by phone. The FBI just might want to talk to you so that they have their own record of what you've already told me, and they can turn sour if witnesses aren't always there at the ready. Naturally, you'll be careful to look at mail before you open it. You have a secretary I suppose.'

'Part-time. She gave me your name as a matter of fact.'

'That so? Well, you'll warn her, I guess. Although the Postal Service will be running a check for a while on all packages addressed to you. Did you notice, by the way, that this Zander says parcel when he means package? That's British usage.'

'Yes, I'd noticed.'

'You'll be letting me have the original of this letter, eh Mr Halliday? There's always a chance that the forensic lab people may come up with something we didn't know already.'

'I'll put it in the mail to you.'

He was re-reading the photocopy. 'What's your thinking about this last paragraph?' he asked. 'He knows you're a news-paper man. Have you followed up on his suggestion about newspaper morgues?'

It was simple enough to lie. 'I used to be a newspaper man, yes, but I'm out of touch these days. I'll probably call around, but if the FBI say they don't know this Zander it's unlikely that I'm going to be able to come up with anything.'

'But you'll try all the same?' he persisted.

'Oh sure.'

'And be letting us know when Zander makes the next approach?'

Captain Boyle was a big, handsome man with an old-style politician's smile. It had been a mistake on my part to under-estimate his intelligence.

'I see that you don't accept the nut-case diagnosis, Captain.'

'Of course I accept it. Anyone who sends bombs through the mail has to be some kind of nut. But in this case, I think, not Lampeter's kind. What do you think?'

'I agree. This bomb is a one-off, a show of muscle if you like. I don't think he's going to send any more. Dammit, I don't even think he sent this one, I mean not with his own hands. I'm inclined to think, as you seem to, that the writer of that letter means exactly what he says. He wants something done. He thinks I can do it, that it's something that would specially appeal to me. He just has a funny way of asking.'

'And what's your reaction to it, Mr Halliday? I mean now that you know what was in the package. Are you laughing?'

'No, Captain, I'm not. I'm as mad as Detective Lampeter. But I'm also intensely curious, and quite determined to know more. Unfortunately, that makes me even madder because curiosity and a desire to know more on my part are, I believe, among the various reactions Zander hoped to get from me. Still, if and when he makes his next approach, I won't refuse to listen. I couldn't.'

The Captain nodded. 'See what you mean. Well, if you do find out more, I'm sure you'll fill us in. I know you people have to protect your sources and all that, but here we like to close a case out whenever we can.'

'I'll remember that.'

'One other thing, Mr Halliday. Call it friendly advice. If Lampeter says that job's professional, I believe him. So that means this letter-writer is professional too, in his own way of course. So watch it, eh Mr Halliday? I've had you checked out. You've had bad times that you don't like talking about. Maybe the time's come now to forget about them altogether. No, it's none of my business. Just friendly advice. You're not as young as you look, and the sweet taste of some things can be bad for your health.'

I drove home from town as I had driven into it, slowly and carefully as if I still had the package in the trunk of the car. I had had a beef sandwich and several cups of coffee while I had been at the police headquarters. Now, two hours later, they began to give me indigestion.

When I opened my front door the phone was ringing. I ignored it and poured myself a drink. As soon as the ringing stopped, I sat down and wondered how best to warn my secretary and the daily not to attempt to open any packages addressed to me.

If I told them the truth they would tell their husbands, and they, most sensibly, would instruct or advise their wives to quit working for me. I tried to invent a lie to cover the situation, but couldn't think of one that didn't require the dread word 'bomb' to make it convincing. But did I really need to warn? Boyle had said that the Postal Service would be checking all packages addressed to me. Even if Zander did send another bomb – and neither Boyle nor I really thought that he would – it would be intercepted. So what was I worrying about?

The phone rang again and this time I answered it.

Barbara was angry. 'As you very well know, my dear, because you're not a *stupidly* forgetful person, I promised to call Mr McGuire this morning and you promised to call me. When you fail to call and I call you, your daily woman tells me that you have suddenly driven off saying that you were going into town and that you might not be back. No reason given. Since I am doing my level best to represent you effectively in a deal with a company which I now find is a member state of the Syncom-Sentinel financial empire, I think that the least you can do, my dear, the very *least*, is to spare me enough of your time to make a single phone call.'

'I'm sorry, Barbara. I lost a filling and had to go to a dentist, even if he wasn't my own and forty miles away. I was in pain.'

'Does it take all day to get a tooth filled?'

'I've said I'm very sorry, and I am. What's this you say about Syncom Oil?'

'It isn't about their oil, it's about their publishing interests. I find that Pacioli is a Syncom-Sentinel subsidiary. Burrowing still further on your behalf, I find out that Mr McGuire's firm are Syncom-Sentinel's legal representatives in all their arm's length operations, the diversified as well as the oil interests, from the Persian Gulf to the Arctic. So, not wishing to irritate, or even slightly inconvenience, a high-powered lawyer with fifty thousand on the table and several billions more behind him, I called him back as I had promised. My story was that you were a bit unhappy about the preliminary ground rules. Okay, you understood that the publishers wanted the matter treated confidentially, but you were at present busy completing the final editorial work on a new book. You were reluctant to break off and battle your way in from the country to New York City merely to discuss a project about which you knew less than nothing and in which you could very well have no interest at all.'

'Beautifully put, Barbara. Superb.'

'As a result, my dear, and after a show of reluctance on his part, I was given the following. The book – I quote – is to be in essence the history of a political movement. It will consist partly of a hitherto unpublished nineteenth-century memoir and partly of an informed commentary by a modern expert on the movement and its development over the years. Your function would be mainly editorial. The proposed title is – again I quote – *Children of the Twilight*.'

'Doesn't exactly grab you, does it.'

'It may sound better in Italian. Anyway, titles can always be changed. The point is that, having screwed that concession out of him I felt bound to concede something in return.'

'Such as what, Barbara?'

'I have made a date for you to meet Mr McGuire in his office at three tomorrow afternoon. And before you start belly-aching, let me remind you that you will be listening to a proposal which you can accept or reject. If you fail me by not turning up, you will not be forgiven. Still, for the sake of old times, I hope that if you decide that you can't be bothered you will be so kind as to call Mr McGuire's secretary in good time and tell her so. Then, when you feel like it, you can let me know what happened, one way or the other. Goodbye, my dear.'

I finished my drink and went to see what the daily woman had left for me in the refrigerator.

Later, when I had completed the Williams changes for my secretary to fair-copy, I tried saying *Children of the Twilight* aloud. After I had said it several times I found that it became a tongue-twister. Only as I was getting ready for bed, though, did I wonder what the phrase was supposed to mean.

What kind of human beings were there, or had there been, who could sensibly be called 'children of the twilight'? A political movement? Surely not. They sounded more like the members of some remote Amazonian rain-forest tribe discovered by an anthropologist with a taste for journalese. My mind's eye could see their pictures in the *National Geographic*. Fragile little creatures they were with lank hair, blankly terrified stares and willowy spears clutched in their hands. If the spears were used for killing anything larger or more dangerous than guinea pig, the heads would have to be tipped with poison.

As sleep came it occurred to me that the postcard picture must have been taken quite recently. Those big oleanders beneath the palms around the driveway of the Hotel Mansour had only just been planted when I had last been there.

TWO

Not many of the old Wall Street firms live very near that street nowadays. I found the one of which Mr McGuire was a member located almost eight blocks away in the new Syncom-Sentinel building off Fulton. The firm occupied two entire floors and, by some miracle of the decorator's craft, and the expenditure of vast sums on dyed leather, had managed to give them an appearance of old-world cosiness.

McGuire was in his early fifties, a dark, thick-set man with rosy cheeks, bushy eyebrows and a beak-like upper lip that allowed him to give only very small smiles. I had looked him up in the books. He was a Princeton graduate, had been to Harvard Law School and had served in the Judge Advocate General's department during the Korean war. He was an officer of the American Bar Association and a member of several professional bodies concerned with insurance. An authority on legal aspects of the international insurance business, he had lectured at Columbia on the subject and often read papers before the Investment Bankers Association and the Society of Chartered Life Underwriters. His qualifications as a commissioning editor (even in an acting capacity) for a serious Italian publisher seemed, unless the proposed book were to be a technical treatise dealing with insurance law, to be virtually non-existent.

If he was aware of that fact, however, he was undaunted by it. His self-confidence appeared total. His manner was relaxed, genial and patronizing.

He had a conference table as well as a desk in his office. 'I am told,' he said breezily as he waved me to a chair at the table, 'that I must be very careful, in putting this Pacioli proposition to you, not to offend your professional sensibilities.'

'Told by whom?' I asked. 'Not by Mrs Reynolds, I'm sure.'

'Naturally, I am interpreting what she said. What she actually said, I think, was that you were very "choosy" – would that be her word? – about the kind of assignments you accepted. I gathered that you have certain strict rules and some prejudices. In my own choosy way I call them professional sensibilities. Isn't that what they are?'

I was getting the small smile and its message was plain. *Halliday, we both know that what I'm doing is hiring a hack for fifty thousand bucks to do some scribbling for an important client. Let's not waste time analysing your literary conceits.*

So, I answered the unspoken appeal as well as the spoken question. 'I have prejudices against some things, certainly, Counselor, and imprecise language is one of them. That's a prejudice I would have thought we might have shared.'

I was pleased to see him wince at the word 'counselor'. When you have had as much to do with lawyers as I have in my work, you get to know that quite a lot of the good ones, even the good trial lawyers, don't like being addressed as Counselor. One of them told me that it always made him feel like a character in a TV series. As an honorific it has become debased.

McGuire changed his tune slightly, but without noticeable loss of countenance. When people proved touchy, he was reminding himself, you just let them think that they had scored a point.

'Obviously,' he said, 'there's no need for *me* to tell *you* that I haven't had much occasion to do business with authors. Shall we just take it as understood, then, that you always have, in making your choice of a subject, a set of criteria to apply and that fifty-thousand-dollar fees aren't going to change the fact?'

'That's about it, yes. All I've heard so far is that the Pacioli book is to be the history of a political movement. It is to be organized around a hitherto-unpublished nineteenth-century manuscript with an informed commentary by a modern expert on the movement. I assume that this expert is not a scholar.'

'Why should you assume that?'

'A scholar wouldn't accept the kind of editorial assistance that I have to give. He would believe, rightly or wrongly, that he could do the whole job himself.'

'Then you have no objection to the basic proposition?'

'I find the proposed title meaningless and a bit off-putting, but I'll be able to judge better how valid that objection is when I know whose memoir we're talking about and which political movement.'

'Cards on the table then. I must put it to you as best I can and then attempt to answer the questions that your experience will prompt you to ask.' He had a file on the table in front of him and he smoothed down the cover of it before he went on. 'As you may know, we in this office have among our clients a multi-national corporation with extensive interests in some of the more politically conservative and stable areas of the Middle East such as Saudi Arabia and some of the Gulf states. Obviously, our client likes, when it can, to oblige its friends in those countries. So, when word came through that there existed a book which a high personage considered to be not merely worthy of publication in the West, but of potential importance to the West's policy-makers, our client took notice. Are you with me so far?'

'I think so. When your client had its people at Pacioli look into the matter, they came back with the bad news that much of the memoir and most of the commentary existed so far only as disjointed fragments. In other words, the book is at present little more than an idea.'

He chuckled. 'I hear the voice of bitter experience. But no, it's by no means as bad as that.' He opened the file and from then on referred to it steadily. 'Have you ever heard of a nineteenth-century terrorist by the name of Nechayev? Sergei Gennadiyevich Nechayev?'

'I've heard of an anarchist of that name.'

'You've probably heard of him as such because he was the anarchist who gave anarchy a bad name. I know it's true to say that classical anarchism believed in the possibility of changing society for the better by demolishing centralized government, but it also held that man was essentially a reasonable being who could be improved by means of peaceful persuasion. The early anarchists were cranks, but they were idealistic cranks. It was Nechayev who hung the label of terrorism on the movement and handed to nineteenth-century cartoonists that symbol of anarchism that has lasted right into our own time – that round, black, sinister-looking bomb with a burning fuse sticking out of it. As for the man himself, he was a crook as well as a fanatic, a thief, a liar and a murderer. Nowadays, I dare say, we'd call him a criminal psychopath.' He glanced at his file. 'However, it is his relationship with Michael Bakunin of which I must now remind you. If you've heard of Nechayev, I don't suppose you need telling about Bakunin, eh?'

'I think I'd better hear what your brief there has to say.'

He smiled approval of my caution and then began to read directly from the top paper in the file.

'From eighteen-sixty-five, after the death of Proudhon, Bakunin was the foremost anarchist thinker and writer. Like Herzen before him, he chose Geneva as his first place of exile. Unlike Herzen, though, he was an activist as well as a thinker, a militant and also something of a romantic. He was, for example, a friend of Garibaldi. So, he became the rallying point not only for exiled Russian intellectuals but also for adventurers with intellectual pretensions. The judgements he made were often too hasty. You can't really blame him. In Switzerland at the time there was always a steady flow of refugees from Czarist prisons and the Czarist police. In eighteen-sixty-nine Nechayev arrived.'

McGuire's beaky mouth pouted his distaste for the event and he slapped the file irritably as he looked up.

'You can see how it was, Mr Halliday, eh? Nechayev must have been the archetypical brooding boy-wonder revolutionary. With his con-man tales of secret rebel networks back in the old country, his fanaticism and his flatteries, he soon had the great man in his pocket. While still in Russia the boy-wonder had collaborated in the writing of a frightening Revolutionary Catechism which Bakunin admired, and now they worked together on a series of manifestos putting forward what was in effect Nechayev's own programme of revolution through terror. You see, Nechayev believed in violence for its own sake.'

'And the great man went along with him?'

'Until he saw where the manifestos were really taking him and came to his senses, yes. Then he tried to dig in his heels. He said that passion must be allied to reason and complained that Nechayev was like a man in a dream. But what a dream! It was Nechayev who invented the modern terrorist doctrine of "propaganda by deed". Not that anything that Bakunin said could have made any difference by then. It was all too late. In a movement like that there will always be the lunatic few who have been waiting for, *longing* for, violence. And without even knowing it. No matter what anyone says, the hopeless cases will always respond. Michael Bakunin and Professor Marcuse may have had their second thoughts, but it was too late for both of them. It's always the same. When that sort of damage has been done, it can't be repaired with more talk.'

'How did Marcuse get into this?' I asked.

The question was rewarded with a fleeting smile. He tapped the file. 'I have notes here of some catch-phrases and slogans coined by the terrorist New Left when Marcuse was their guru. Material prosperity, for instance, becomes "consumption terror" when you want to justify the fire-bombing of a department store. And when you can think of no better excuse for an act of violence than your wish to commit it, you simply declare that "talking without action equals silence". That's the rubbishy kind of pseudo paradox that Nechayev liked to invent. But we mustn't dismiss such nonsense too lightly. Half-baked idiocy can be dangerous. That first great terrorist wave which began moving in the eighteen-seventies was carried along by those who thought that they could destroy European society with the weapon of assassination. And at Sarajevo in nineteen-fourteen one tiny group of terrorists almost succeeded. There *are* historians who say that they *did* succeed.'

'They weren't trying to start World War One, Mr McGuire. They weren't anarchists. Their cause was the liberation of Bosnia and Herzegovina.'

'And the cause of the PLO is the liberation of Palestine. Those people could still start World War Three by mistake.' He rode over my attempts to enter further objections by raising his voice. 'Yes, I know. The official leadership of the PLO would regard such a mistake as the ultimate catastrophe. But that's beside the point. The real power lies with those who have the catalytic ability to provoke over-reaction. What we have to face now, as this second great terrorist wave starts to break, is a threat to our civilization of a wholly different kind and on a wholly different scale from anything we have experienced before. And the West will continue to be peculiarly helpless in the face of it. Unless Western political institutions are prepared to pay yet again the dreadful price of moving towards fascism and the corporate police state, they will very soon be finding themselves unable to function. They will have been *provoked* into impotence.' He was, of course, again reading directly from his script, but he had enough of the ham instinct in him to raise a hand aloft and wag a warning finger as he swept on. 'You think I'm overstating the case or even joking? Listen again then to the founding father of the movement. I quote. "We have", Nechayev wrote, "a uniquely negative plan that no one can modify – complete destruction." That's plain enough, isn't it? Well, we know what his followers of the first wave did. Can you imagine what may be done in the near future with the technical facilities now available to those fine young lunatics of the second wave?'

Even a McGuire has to draw breath occasionally and this time I interrupted firmly enough to secure his attention. 'Mr McGuire,' I said loudly, and then waited until I had his full attention before continuing. 'Mr McGuire, I'm sure that both you and your clients feel very strongly on the subject of international terrorism, but I have to tell you that so far you haven't said a thing that hasn't been said before a dozen times. There have been a lot of books published about it, many of them just as indignant as your brief seems to be. The Entebbe and Mogadishu shoot-outs even started a movie bandwagon. As a subject for serious study, international terrorism must now be regarded as, at best, suspect. As far as I am concerned, the subject is old hat and rather boring.'

With a real commissioning editor that would certainly have been the end of the matter. His reply would have been polite but crisp. If terrorism bored me so much that I wasn't even curious to know how and why a few weeks' editorial work from me could suddenly be valued at fifty thousand dollars, then he wouldn't waste any more of my time. It had been good of me to stop by.

Mr McGuire, however, capitulated. For an instant he stared hard at me, then nodded. 'You're right,' he said. 'I allowed myself to get carried away. Let's go back to Nechayev.'

'Is the memoir his?'

'I'm coming to that. You won't be surprised to hear that, where women were concerned, he was poison. One affair he had has become notorious. You may know about it. No? Well, Alexander Herzen the doyen of the exiled Russian intelligentsia had a daughter. After his death in Paris she returned to Geneva to live on the small fortune she had inherited. Nechayev, who was always broke, tried to get his hands on the money by seducing her. He failed, but it was such an ugly story that it has been well remembered. What has *not* been remembered, mainly because there was a family cover-up, is that he had another affair around the same time. It was with the daughter of an Italian doctor named Luccio. Dr Luccio was a member of Garibaldi's corps of volunteers. He had fought beside the Liberator in Italy and attended him between campaigns. When Garibaldi made his new home on the island of Caprera, the Luccios set up house there too. Now misfortune strikes. In eighteen-seventy Garibaldi goes to Switzerland to attend the Congress of Peace and Freedom in Berne. Dr Luccio takes his family along. Enter Nechayev. He is attending the Congress and that's where he meets and woos the doctor's daughter. When Garibaldi suddenly takes off again with his volunteers to fight the French, the doctor naturally tags along. The wife and daughter linger, unwisely maybe, in Berne before returning to their home on Caprera. That's off the north coast of Sardinia, you know, small and isolated. Anyway, it is there, in eighteen-seventy-one, that Nechayev's illegitimate son is born.' He raised his bushy eyebrows at me. 'Where was Nechayev? We can't be certain. There were undoubtedly letters exchanged, but they have been lost. All we do know for certain is that during the following year, 'seventy-two, the Swiss extradited Nechayev to Russia. The charges were technically criminal, not political. He was wanted in Russia for the murder of a student. Tried for and convicted of the murder, he later died in a dungeon of the fortress of St Peter and St Paul. He left behind him as his legacy to the world the doctrines of modern terrorism, an illegitimate son and a memoir of his life and thoughts – written in Geneva apparently – which he had handed or sent to the girl for safekeeping. It has survived and is in the hands of his great-grandson. A copy of it is now with Pacioli.'

'What language is it written in? Russian?'

'A mixture of Russian and French mostly. That would be the way most of that circle wrote. Some of the French is in a nineteenth-century shorthand. There is a little Italian too. The memoir ends with a dedication to the girl in expectation of a marriage in Caprera which could never have taken place.'

'The great-grandson owns it?'

'Yes, he inherited it. In fact, until it came into his hands nobody quite knew what it was because nobody could read it properly. It survived, I guess, as one of those family heirlooms with no intrinsic value that gets passed on as a sort of keepsake with romantic associations. This one was valued, perhaps, because it had belonged to the foreigner who, supposedly, had married great-grandmother in Switzerland and then been spirited away to Russia by the Czar's wicked secret police.'

'Does the great-grandson read Russian?'

'Enough, I gather, to figure out the Russian passages in the memoir and grasp the importance of it. His name, too, is Luccio and he is the person who has suggested the form the book should take. I'll come to his actual contribution in a moment. The Nechayev memoir is short, less than thirty thousand words, but it is of obvious importance as an historical document. Incidentally, the phrase "children of the twilight" about which you have reservations, Mr Halliday, happens to be one of Nechayev's own. He applies it in the memoir to those who share his thinking on the subject of purification through atrocity.'

'Are you sure that the memoir's genuine? Has there been an independent vetting?'

'The process of vetting is still going on, but I understand that those experts on nineteenth-century Russian manuscripts who are outside the Soviet Union seem unable so far to agree on all the relevant issues. Those inside Russia to whom extracts from the work have been submitted have yet to give an opinion. Presumably they will have sought ideological guidance from the authorities there before deciding whether or not it would be wise to give opinions at all. Dr Luccio is naturally disposed to regard the provenance of the manuscript as in itself conclusive. He had heard of its existence when he was a young man. The difficulty is that he never actually saw it until a few months ago. An aunt in Sardinia died leaving him the little she had. That was in compliance with Italian inheritance laws. The manuscript was found among her personal effects.'

'You say he's a doctor too. Of what? Medicine, like his great-grandfather?'

'It happens to be civil engineering in this case. They have doctors of everything over there. But that's unimportant. The thing about this Dr Luccio is that he is senior defence adviser to a highly influential Persian Gulf ruler. He's at present on vacation in Italy. I understand that he went out to the Gulf originally on an airfield construction job and became involved in counter-insurgency and intelligence work more or less by accident. It seems that he discovered in himself a talent – if that's the word – for the craft. Anyway, he has made it his business to gather intelligence on all the various terrorist gangs now operating and, above all, on their sponsors and protectors in the various governments concerned.'

'And now he's feeling that this inherited talent of his should be publicly recognized and deployed on the side of the angels?'

'Why not? He has the ear of an important person in the Gulf. So, when Dr Luccio says that he can, from his own knowledge of the terrorist international, predict beyond all doubt that the next fifty years are going to be a re-run of the last hundred only ten thousand times worse, we listen. When he reminds us that we can no longer think in terms of those old, round, black bombs because the new wave will certainly go nuclear, we are entitled to ask him what he, the expert, suggests that we do about it. Agreed? Well, his reply is that the only solution, the Luccio solution, is exposure of the governments involved to world opinion. The governments he indicates as peculiarly responsible for the international terrorist training camps include, of course, those of Libya and South Yemen, but Iraq is also high on his list. Names of what he calls the "terror-masters" in those countries' secret police services would be given along with detailed accounts of their crimes against humanity.'

'He really believes that exposure to world opinion would actually trouble men like that?'

'More, it seems, than we might think.'

'You make him sound very innocent, Mr McGuire.'

He huffed a bit. 'How I may make, or fail to make, him sound is beside the point. How can I know or appreciate the quality of the revelations he has to make? You must form your own judgements.' It was back to the brief. 'He has one final statement of importance to make. To those doubters who may question the relevance of Nechayev to the problems of dealing with the Baader-Meinhofs, the Red Brigades, the Black Septembers and all their modern counterparts, he offers Santayana's reflection that those who refuse to recall the past are condemned to relive it.'

'He seems to have thought of everything.'

'Almost everything, yes. Though I doubt if Pacioli was his idea. I think that if our client Syncom-Sentinel had happened to own an American publishing house you would have been having this conversation a bit farther up town and with someone who knows more about books than I do.'

The smile he gave me with that was nearly coy, inviting compliments.

'Just talking about books calls for no special skills, Mr McGuire,' I said. 'Do you know who this Gulf ruler is, this high

Arab personage who believes so touchingly in the power of the printed word to make secret policemen blush and change their ways?'

'We've been given no name. We're instructed simply to ask you to work with Dr Luccio in putting the book into shape so that it can be published world-wide.'

'Me specifically?'

'That was the word from the Gulf via Rome and Milan. I don't know why you specifically. No doubt inquiries were made and you, with your Middle East experience, were considered exceptionally qualified. If you accept and go to Milan you could ask them yourself.'

'Yes, I could. Meanwhile, Mr McGuire, I am going to have to disappoint you by making my acceptance subject to conditions, and they will have to be written into the agreement that I think I see there in your file.'

For a while there we had grown quite friendly. Now it was, on his part, back to the snotty smile. 'Well, there can be no harm in your telling me what sort of additional conditions you are hoping to impose. As far as I can see, your rights, all those your agent insisted upon anyway, are fully and thoroughly protected already.'

'My agent didn't know what was involved. The first condition concerns the Nechayev memoir. You may not know it, but forgery is a cottage industry in Italy. My acceptance has to be conditional on proper authentication of the memoir.'

'I told you. There is a measure of disagreement among the experts.'

'There always is a measure of disagreement among experts when it comes to appraising holograph manuscripts. A few years ago there was a measure of disagreement among those experts called in to pass judgement on a manuscript purporting to be Mussolini's personal diary. One lot said that it was absolutely genuine. No doubts at all. In fact, it had been forged by two elderly Italian ladies living in a country village. They and their front man got away with a great deal of money paid out by a newspaper publisher for exclusive rights before they were found out. I know that you can't guarantee in advance that this memoir's genuine, but I can't afford to have my name linked with a forged memoir, no matter whose. I have to reserve the right to pull out if there's no valid authentication forthcoming.'

'Before publication?'

'Of course. Equally, I would not in those circumstances expect to be paid the second instalment of the fee.'

He sighed. 'Well, I suppose it's not unreasonable.'

'The other condition is not so simple. I want it written into the agreement that, once the draft has been approved for publication by its authors, it may not be changed.'

'By the publishers, you mean?'

'By anyone *except* the publishers. I don't want there to be any second thoughts on either Dr Luccio's part or that of his patron.'

'I would have thought that in writing a book of this character with the declared object of influencing international policymakers, an author ought to be allowed to think not just twice but a great many more times.'

'As long as the thinking is all done before the typescript is made ready for the publishers, he can do as much of it as he likes. It is the period between then and publication that concerns me.'

'You'll have to explain. I know nothing of these matters.'

'In this projected book there are to be in effect two works, one of which, we hope, is a document of some historical interest. That will be translated but not edited, except possibly to take out obvious repetitions or to clarify slipshod passages. We can forget that then. But what about Dr Luccio's contribution? He, apparently, is going to tell all, straight from the shoulder. He's going to be commenting on his great-grandfather's role in the original terrorist movement as he goes, no doubt, and drawing modern parallels, but his main effort is going to be put into spilling the beans on the direct involvement of certain governments in terrorist activity. And he's going to do this in a way that shakes the civilized world to its foundations. Agreed?'

'You're exaggerating of course.'

'Not all that much. If, as you said, the book is expected to influence government policies, it's going to have to shake *somebody's* foundations first. I realize that you were giving yourself a blurb-writer's licence when you stated the case for the book, but if it is to have any real impact at all, that has to be delivered by Dr Luccio's contribution. Nechayev's memoir, if genuine, will give the book a measure of academic respectability that will attract some critical attention, but if the only real meat is

Nechayev on Nechayev, the attention will be no more than polite. So, how good is Dr Luccio? How sensational are the revelations he has to make and what's the quality of his evidence?'

'That remains to be seen, surely.'

'Then, I'll put the question more baldly. How do we know that Dr Luccio's motives and those of his patron are those you have described? In my work you come across all sorts of reasons for writing books. Some of them are very strange.'

'Vanity would be a common motive, I suppose. Or exhibitionism. The writer wishes to display himself or herself to the world?'

'Yes. Also common as motives are self-justification, vindication and the need to make converts to some oddball view of a religion. Sometimes the thing's written in the hope of making money, or of shoring up a sagging career with publicity, or even of starting a new career altogether. Then there are the needs, real or fancied, to establish a truth or perpetuate a falsehood, to make saints or fulfil moral obligations to history. There is the need, as there is here apparently, to set the world to rights by prescribing courses of treatment. Those are some of the commoner motives. Also common as a motive is the simple desire for vengeance.'

He was almost grinning at me. 'What fun you must have in your work! I hadn't understood the possibilities. Which out of this galaxy of possible motives is the one that is troubling you where Dr Luccio is concerned?'

'One that I haven't mentioned. It goes like this. I write a book of memoirs or reflections. In it I include facts, half-truths or anecdotes about you that could, if published, seriously discredit you, or even threaten your life. I then let you know that I have done this and that for a consideration, usually though not necessarily financial, I will omit the passages in question.'

He nodded affably. 'Ah yes. Harriette Wilson.' He didn't wait to see whether or not I had understood the allusion before explaining it for me. 'She was a nineteenth-century English lady of easy virtue. Later on in her life, when her clientele had thinned, she made a business out of writing her memoirs and naming names. One of those she attempted to blackmail in that way was the great Duke of Wellington. His reply was "publish and be damned" if I remember correctly.'

'That's the reply attributed to him, yes. But quite a number of her other old friends did buy their way out of her memoirs. Harriette made a good thing out of them. She went on for years.'

'The libel laws are stricter now.'

'But victims of that sort of blackmail have always been reluctant to use the law, Mr McGuire. They still are. The memoir threat is still effective, believe me.'

'Why should you suppose that Dr Luccio is a blackmailer?'

'I don't suppose anything about him. I only know what you've told me. He is some sort of expert on terrorism. Presumably, then, he knows a lot of terrorists personally. As I said, the consideration or favour asked need not necessarily be financial. His price for not naming some names could be that he is given protection against those whom he *does* name. I don't know. I'm not making accusations. I am merely saying that, while I am prepared to be employed, I am not prepared to assist in the operation of a racket. As my agent will tell you, I have asked for and received undertakings to take care of this hazard quite often. Usually the publishers are more than willing to co-operate. My agent will, if it would help, give you the wording of a clause that both sides have found acceptable.'

He made a note in his file. 'Very well. We will see what Pacioli has to say. I gather that I may tell them that, subject to the inclusion of these two escape clauses you have asked for, you are ready to enter into an agreement?'

'Oh yes, I think so.'

My car was in a parking lot a few blocks from the Holland Tunnel, but instead of setting off at once for home I took a cab up town to Barbara's office. It wasn't only that I felt guilty about her. There was something else I had to do that couldn't be postponed.

She was reasonably pleased to see me and cheered up a little when I described the meeting with McGuire. However, as I had expected, my concession of the second instalment of the fee in the event of an adverse report on the Nechayev memoir did not please her.

'I take your point about the authenticity of this Russian memoir. Can't afford to have you mixed up with anything that's not according to Hoyle. But why, if it turns out to be phony, should *you* be penalized?'

'It slipped out. I was trying to make him feel ungenerous.'

'That kind of man never feels ungenerous.'

'Can't you fix it by pointing out that I could very easily have done all my work in good faith *before* the experts finally got around to blowing the whistle?'

'Maybe. But you do sometimes tend to make things unnecessarily difficult, Robert.'

'I'm sorry.'

'Well, how was it left?'

'He'll talk to Milan first thing in the morning because it's the middle of the night there now, and then, if they're agreeable as he expects them to be, he'll call you about the draft wording on the additional clauses.'

'All right. If you want to give me a few minutes to clear my desk, I'll buy you a drink.'

'I have to go into Brentano's anyway.'

'Meet you downstairs in a quarter of an hour then.'

The reference section in most large bookstores is generally one of the quieter areas. You rarely find more than the odd browser or two there. On that occasion, late in the afternoon, I had it all to myself.

What I was looking for was an Italian dictionary; not one of those pocket-size glossaries designed for tourists, but the real thing. I found what I wanted immediately.

I also found immediately the word that I had been half-hoping not to find there. It was in the Italian-English part of the book.

lùccio m. pike (*Esox lucius*) or other fish of same family.

I decided not to buy the dictionary. Zander wrote very good English. I was sure that he spoke it too.

THREE

I had been told that I would be met at Milan's Linate airport, but assumed that this courtesy would be delegated to some junior in the Pacioli offices. To my surprise I was greeted by their senior editor.

His name was Renaldo Pacioli and he was a board director as well as a son of the founder. Having identified himself to me, he asked me to show him my passport. He examined it carefully before handing it back.

'Thank you, Mr Halliday,' he said; 'I will explain the reason for that curious discourtesy on our way to your hotel. There is a suite with a small sitting room reserved for you at the Duchi. It's a little away from the centre out of the restricted traffic zone. If you need to rent a car you may find that useful. Now, if you will let me know when you see your bags coming off we'll get a porter.'

I had spoken to him on the telephone two days previously and, foolishly, tried to draw a mind's-eye picture of a person from the sound of a voice. As usual I had failed. The voice had seemed to me dark and on the plump side. The man himself was straw-coloured, tall and thin. The weight I had imagined came from the quiet baritone assurance with which he spoke. He was in his forties and, according to Barbara, the father of six children.

There was a large car with a beefy young driver waiting for us. As soon as we were installed in the back seats Pacioli pressed the button which raised the glass partition behind the front seats.

'This is one of our special drivers,' he said, 'and I have never heard him utter a word of English, but we shall pretend that he might understand. How was the flight?'

'I slept as far as Paris. The plane change there was a bit tiring.'

'Well, I don't think that you will be disturbed this evening. I can't be sure of course. The intermediary preferred not to inform me in advance of her plans. You will be hearing from her direct.'

There were thunderclouds still overhead and it had been raining heavily. The fluorescent lighting along the airport exit road glared on the wet pavement. His head was only half-turned towards me, but there was light enough for me to see that he was waiting intently for my reaction to what he had said.

'Intermediary? Dr Luccio has an agent now?'

'No,' he said, 'an intermediary, and you may well raise your eyebrows. I will be frank with you. If I had had my way you would not be here.' He held up a quick hand. 'Please, that is no reflection on you. We know and respect the quality of your work. But the house of Pacioli are serious publishers. We would not in former days have accepted to do this Luccio book under the proposed absurd conditions, or perhaps any conditions at all, not absurd. You must excuse me. When I am angry my English becomes confused.'

'I understand you perfectly. But you haven't yet told me what the set-up is.'

'No, I haven't. When my father originally proposed to us that we accept the participation of Syncom-Sentinel in the affairs of our house, we all of us agreed that it was a wise move. With the new electronic machinery, we have been able to produce our intermediate-format educational books in our own plant. We have also earned good profits from what you call trade books. At the Frankfurt Book Fair these last two years we have made good showings and been much complimented. We are leaders in the field. Now, suddenly, we are obliged by Syncom to behave in a most undignified as well as a most unbusinesslike manner.'

'They pressured you?'

'I would not call it pressure. That can be resisted. No, they simply gave us orders. They had Arab friends whom it was necessary to oblige by publishing a book. So, we had been chosen. May we read it? No, because it is not yet completely written. What you will do is commission it from Dr Luccio and employ an American editorial adviser, Robert Halliday, to assist in the work. May we meet Dr Luccio and discuss the proposed book with him? No, that will not be necessary. You will be sent a synopsis of the book in due course. It concerns the phenomenon of terrorism and will include a hitherto unpublished memoir of the nineteenth-century terrorist Sergei Nechayev. Your immediate task will be to secure expert appraisals of these old papers which must establish conclusively that they are indeed Nechayev's work. No expense will be spared in securing favourable appraisals. Our lawyers in New York will act for you in hiring Mr Halliday. Acting for Dr Luccio will be an intermediary, Miss Simone Chihani. She is authorized to make day-to-day decisions on all matters of detail, particularly where security is concerned. Dr Luccio is a very private person and Miss Chihani's security orders must be obeyed at all times and without question.' He paused. 'In asking to see your passport, Mr Halliday, I was obeying orders, as I was when I reserved a suite for you at the Duchi.'

For a moment I considered telling him about Karlis Zander and the package-bomb incident. Then, luckily, I decided to hear first the rest of what he might have to say.

'But in the beginning, Mr Pacioli, when all those peculiar orders about the book were given, how did you react?'

'Very strongly, I assure you.'

'But what sort of Syncom-Sentinel executive was it who could behave in such a clumsy way? If, in order to please their Arab friends, they needed to use the Pacioli name, surely they would have done better to ask apologetically for your help in a way that you would have found hard to refuse. Why give orders? Who could be so foolish?'

'Their man in Rome. We know him well and had always liked him. He is very far from being foolish, but where this book was concerned I think that he was for some reason frightened. In the conversations we had, very angry conversations they were, he seemed to me to be saying only what he had been told to say.'

'Can a corporation as big as Syncom-Sentinel be frightened?'

'I think the man was personally frightened.'

'For his job, you mean?'

'It was possible. I thought that at first anyway.'

'But you changed your mind?'

'We responded to these demands, these orders, reasonably I think, but firmly. We said that when we had read the book we would be able to decide whether or not we would publish it. If Syncom wished to make use of our experience in commissioning non-fiction works by asking us to make the preliminary arrangements, we would gladly help. If, in the end, we decided not to publish the work ourselves, however, we would expect to be reimbursed by Syncom for all expenses incurred on their behalf.'

'And, with provisos about security measures, they accepted that?'

'I don't know whether Syncom accepted or not. Our letter has still not been answered. But someone, Dr Luccio's Arab patron perhaps, objected strongly to our disobedience. Whoever it was, the method chosen to punish us for our independence was cowardly and vicious.'

I watched his face flickering in the lights of oncoming traffic and waited for him to decide how best to tell me. Finally, he tapped the door window beside him. 'A new kind of plastic,' he said. 'It is supposed to be nearly bullet-proof. Not quite, but nearly. The body of this car is armoured too. Why? Well, our family is not what in America would be called rich, I think, but here in Italy we could be thought of as rich. In other words, we the family, and the part of our family business that we still own, could together raise enough cash from our bankers, and Syncom, to make the kidnapping of one of us worthwhile to a professional gang. So, we are all very careful and we buy as much security as we can afford. Our household staffs have been specially vetted. We retain the services of a security organization and we employ drivers expressly trained not only in bodyguard work but also in counter-ambush car-handling techniques. They have been to a school which teaches nothing else. Alfredo is driving us tonight. If he were to see anything even remotely like a roadblock ahead, we would have to hold on very tight because we would either find ourselves suddenly going backwards almost as fast as we are now going forwards, or we would be ramming the obstruction. As there is armour built into the front fenders we would have nothing to lose but a little paint. We have two other drivers like Alfredo and they work in turn to a roster. The men of the family are taken to their offices, the children to their schools and so on. The routes are changed constantly. My wife has been on this madman's driving course herself so that she can have a little independence in her own car. But mostly it is Alfredo, Franco and Bernardo who do the driving. That is, it was until two weeks ago.'

He paused to stare out at the city we were entering as if he expected to see something new in the rain. Then he shrugged slightly and went on.

'From here to Rome we use a courier service for our mail, so we know exactly when Syncom received our letter about the Luccio book. It was on the Tuesday. On the Friday, three days later, Bernardo was on the day shift that ended at seven o'clock. At that time it was his turn for the weekly thirty-six-hour break that they all have. So he picked up his Lambretta from my garage and took off. Near the apartment house block where he lives with his wife and family, he was knocked down by a car. He was only slightly hurt then, but as he began to get to his feet two persons ran over to him from the car, which had stopped, and proceeded to beat him. The attack was witnessed by neighbours who said that the attackers used heavy sticks and their feet. They also said that one of the attackers may have been a woman, a girl. It was quickly over. One of the attackers was seen to put something in a pocket of Bernardo's anorak just before they ran off. Bernardo was still unconscious when the ambulance arrived. His injuries included a broken jaw. We must hope that he will make a complete recovery.'

'What was it they put in his pocket?' I asked.

He looked at me sharply. 'You don't want to know who did it, or if any of them has been caught?'

I could have answered that I was becoming used to Zander's quaint little ways of capturing attention when he had a message to deliver. He might send you a bomb from Miami, or he might give himself a see-through alias for an unsuspecting Wall Street lawyer to pass on to you, or he might put one of your employees into hospital. I didn't answer so callously, though, because just then I was feeling not only sorry for Bernardo but thankful that I had not regaled the man beside me with my now most unfunny bomb story. Instead, I said: 'That sort of thug is almost never caught. The car used was probably stolen and later found abandoned. It's a nasty story but not unusual.'

He sighed, 'I note that you automatically assume that the attackers were not personal enemies of Bernardo's. The police took longer to reach that conclusion. You are right, of course. The car was stolen. What they put in his pocket was an envelope. Inside was a sheet of the Syncom internal memorandum paper used by them for business regarded as confidential. It is a pale yellow colour. On this sheet was typed a single sentence in capital letters. It said: "DIRECTIVES WILL NOT IN FUTURE BE TREATED AS NEGOTIABLE REQUESTS."'

'In English?'

'No, in Italian. The police took charge of it and sent it to Rome. The Syncom offices both there and in London co-operated fully with the police. England was involved because Syncom's European division happens to buy all its stationery there. They reported that, although the sheet of paper used was quite genuine, it was of a quality that hadn't been used for two years. Executives had complained that it was too flimsy. The last batch of it had gone to the Syncom office in Mozambique. The trouble the police had was with the wording of the message. Who would say such a thing to Bernardo? Why the elaborate bureaucratic language? Who could it have been that Bernardo had offended? It was very difficult to convince them that the message had really been for us.'

'Did you ask the intermediary, Miss What's-her-name, why she herself hadn't delivered it on the great man's behalf?'

An attempt at a smile quivered for a moment in one corner of his mouth. 'Miss Chihani, you mean? As you will soon be finding out for yourself, that young woman is very well able to deal with inconvenient questions. She simply ignores them. By the way, she claims to be Lebanese. One of our staff, though, who knows some Arabic and heard her speaking on the telephone to Luccio in that language says that she sounds Algerian. It seems that there is a big difference between the two accents. But you would know all about that of course.' He peered forward. 'Ah, nearly there.' He pressed the button to roll down the partition between us and the driver. 'Please let me know personally, won't you, if you are not absolutely comfortable here?'

I don't believe he really thought that I could be so easily brushed off. He just disliked talking about the work I was there to do. Anyway, I persisted.

'About the Nechayev manuscript, Mr Pacioli. There must surely be some preliminary findings by now, and it's really quite important from my point of view.'

'Because of the clause in your contract that entitles you to leave at once if it's a fake?' He said it without reproach but a little wearily.

'I should have thought you'd be fairly interested too.'

'You're forgetting, Mr Halliday. Fake or not, we have had our orders. In any case, I am going to have to disappoint you. We have had two opinions about the material so far. Each completely contradicts the other in almost every respect. And, as I can already see another unanswerable question trembling on your lips and certain to be asked before your baggage is out of the car, I will save you the trouble of asking it. No, I am afraid that I *don't* know, any more than you do, why they were so insistent on having you in particular to work on this book.

You would be the first to agree, I think, that there are other qualified persons in the field.'

'Sure there are. But in that case ...'

'I can only say,' he said firmly, 'that when I put the question to Miss Chihani she replied that Dr Luccio had seen you on television.'

'I beg your pardon.'

'Yes, it surprised me too. She must have misunderstood him. You have my office number? Good. Then we must keep in touch.'

It was not among the more auspicious first meetings that I have had with a publisher.

A few minutes later, when I had been installed in the suite and was waiting for my bags to be brought up, an unpleasant train of thought arrived to spoil the moment of discovery that I had a marble bathroom. It was the word 'television' that had started it running.

My brief career in television is among those misfortunes of my working life that I try hardest to forget. It began, deceptively, with a petty triumph. In the course of promoting a book in which I had a half share, I appeared on a number of local late-night talk shows of the 'open-ended' kind then in vogue. Produced in imitation of their big-city, big-name counterparts, they went out live, were easily interrupted for commercials and cost less than the batch of old movies then on offer. The moderators were usually local news anchor-men eager to demonstrate that they possessed wit and wisdom as well as good looks and the ability to read from a teleprompter. With one of them I lost my temper and for nearly a minute, until a hastily inserted station-break cut me off, said exactly what I thought of him. What I said in that minute, however, was trenchant enough to be reported, and a current-affairs programmer for the network to which the local station was affiliated became sufficiently interested to call for a tape of the incident. He liked my display of bad manners and I was offered a deal.

It was an election year and he needed a current-affairs show to fill a late-evening slot during the campaign doldrums of the summer months. It would go out on Mondays and be called *First of the Week*. The official idea was that I would interview party leaders in certain key states where the pollsters were predicting upsets. But that was only the official idea. The unofficial one was that I would be as offensive and unpleasant to these respected party leaders as I had been to the moderator of the talk show. That way, it was thought, I would cause my victims to lose their cool, answer back and commit indiscretions. Thus, the network would appear to be serving the public by educating and informing while, at the same time, be doing its higher duty to its advertisers by providing entertainment for morons.

What the programmer had failed to understand, and I in my ignorance of the medium had failed to perceive, was that the sarcasms with which I had assailed the moderator of the talk show had merely been my last-ditch desperate response to a chattering, maddening imbecile who didn't know that 'literary' and 'literacy' are words with different meanings. The trouble with *First of the Week* was that none of the men and women I interviewed was an imbecile, all had been interviewed many times before by radio and TV people who really knew their jobs and most were practised debaters who could run rings around me. The fact that their arguments were very often specious and their supporting evidence plainly dreamed up on the spur of the moment seemed never to matter. They always scored. None of my experience with politicians had prepared me for that sort of rough-and-tumble and my wild attempts to assert myself were brushed aside with careless ease. They were as used to swatting hecklers as they were to scoring phony points.

After the first three shows had been taped, the producer held an inquest. 'Bob', he said, 'you're letting these guys walk all over you. You're letting them come on strong and stay that way. You've been fully briefed. Most of these people are crooks and at least a couple of them are heading for perjury indictments. You know things that they don't want anyone else to hear. You've got to get in there and catch them off balance, put them on the defensive. We know what's going to sell this show – plenty of blood on the floor. Right? But let's make sure it's their blood, not yours. Okay, killer?'

But it never was okay. I was trying to do a job for which I had no talent, and all the clever editing that was later done couldn't conceal the fact. What you saw was a series of affable politicians humouring an ill-tempered and at times impertinent interviewer who never seemed to have any facts to back up the irresponsible allegations he was making. The politicians all came out looking good. The interviewer, of whom you saw less as time went on, tended to come out looking either petulant or sheepish. The blood on the floor was always mine and I supplied pints of it.

I didn't waste time wondering how Zander-Luccio could have seen any of those interviews – if he could recruit bomb-makers in Miami he could, presumably, watch tapes of American network television – but there was no escaping the likeliest reason for his interest in them. My incompetence as a TV interviewer could very well have appealed to someone thinking of hiring a collaborator dim-witted enough to be used later as a scapegoat.

I heard a knock on the sitting-room door and then the sound of the door opening. A voice said, 'Prego,' and something bumped. I gathered that my bags were being brought in. I was in the bathroom drying my hands and admiring the veining of the marble around the washbasin, so I called through, 'In camera da letto, per favore,' hoping to convey that I wanted the bags brought into the bedroom. When there was no answer, I put the towel down, picked up my jacket which had in it the Italian money I would need for the tip and went through into the sitting room.

There, in addition to my bags stacked on a porter's trolley, stood a big hotel linen wagon and two persons in porters' workcoats with the hotel name and crest embroidered on them. The pair could have been Italian but did not look like hotel porters. One was a slim, smiling young man, the other a husky teenage girl. A third person was locking the door to the corridor on the inside. She was tall, dark, and strikingly handsome. As she turned away from the door I saw that she was pointing a revolver at me. With the gun and in her unisex black sweater-and-pants outfit she looked like the lead character in a comic strip to be called SUPERPERSON.

'Good evening, Mr Halliday.' She spoke faintly-accented, elocution-class English. 'Do absolutely nothing, please, and you will be quite safe.'

As she put the gun away in her shoulder bag the other two began to move. They were very fast. Before I could open my mouth to ask a question, the young man had me bent double with an arm-lock and was forcing me to lurch forward so that the husky girl could kick my legs from under me. I hit the floor face downwards, the impact converting the cry of rage that I had been about to utter into a muted yelp. The arm-lock expert, sitting on my back, at once grabbed one of my feet and did something with one of his knees that immobilized me completely. I knew that the woman was now kneeling beside me on the floor because she had started giving orders to the girl They were in a language that sounded a bit like Arabic but wasn't, though I have to say that I did not listen very carefully. I was preoccupied by my awareness of strong fingers busily rolling up my left shirtsleeve.

A final explosion of orders, then the shoulder bag appeared on the rug about eighteen inches from my left eye. She began to take things from it. A disposable hypodermic syringe pack was followed in my field of vision by a plastic vial with a printed label on it and her fingers unscrewing the cap from a small bottle. As the cap came off there was a smell of surgical spirit.

With an effort I managed to get enough air into my lungs to make speech possible. 'What the hell's this?' I croaked.

'This, Mr Halliday?' She picked up the vial. 'Thiopental sodium.'

I said: 'If it's kidnapping you'd better know the score right now. Nobody's going to pay a cent for me.'

She produced a cotton-wool swab from the bag and tilted the spirit bottle against it. 'My name is Simone Chihani,' she said, 'and you have a choice. You know who I am because Mr Pacioli will have told you. Now, you can either come with us quietly, walking for yourself, co-operating, or we can put you to sleep and take you downstairs covered with dirty sheets before driving you to keep your appointment with Dr Luccio. But we have no time to waste. So, make up your mind please. Co-operation or dirty sheets. Which is it to be?'

FOUR

CO-OPERATION meant walking between Chihani and her arm-lock specialist to the service elevator, descending to the basement area and then walking to the door where the hotel staff clocked in and out. On our way we passed a room-service kitchen, then a laundry before we came to the time-card rack. Just beyond was a little glassed-in office with a fox-faced doorman inside to check the comings and goings. He had his radio tuned to a soccer match commentary and, though he looked straight at me as we approached, all he did when I glared at him was to give Chihani a blank stare.

'Friendly or blind?' I asked.

'One of several paid helpers here. His wife is in charge of the room maids on your floor. His brother is a senior porter.'

'And *you* chose this hotel for me. I begin to see.'

'I'm glad of that, Mr Halliday. The more security-conscious you become, the easier things will be.'

We were outside now in a delivery area. Ahead there was a steep ramp up to street level bordered by a narrow sidewalk for pedestrians and a parking bay for motor scooters. Blocking the sidewalk immediately in front of us was a beige Volkswagen minibus with its nearside wheels up on the kerb and a sliding side-door that was open.

'Get in quickly, please.'

I did as I was told and she followed. A dim roof-light showed that all except one row of the rear seats had been removed, the windows covered with flowered cretonne curtains and a screen of the same material stretched tightly across the space behind the driver. No one travelling in the back would be able to see where he was going.

'You sit in the middle, Mr Halliday.'

She took the seat by the nearside window. The boy slid the door to behind him and sat across the aisle from me. There was to be no chance of my peeking around the corners of the curtains.

'How long is this going to take?' I asked.

'The journey? Less than an hour. If you are tired you could have a little nap.'

I didn't bother to reject that idiot suggestion. I was still acutely aware of the bruising on my knees and shins. The pain in my right shoulder hadn't eased either. The expensive scent she used was beginning to give me a headache. Delayed shock can produce odd side-effects.

The door slid open again and the teenage girl climbed in. She had my raincoat with her and tossed it to me before shutting the door and saying something to the invisible driver. He said something back and started up. Moments later the minibus bumped down off the sidewalk and ground up the ramp. As it turned into the traffic on the street above, the two junior thugs took off their porters' coats and dropped them on the floor behind. Their own clothes were matching flower-patterned shirts and plastic wind-breakers. The boy produced candy bars for them both and they began to chatter quietly in their own language as they chewed. About what? About how easy I had been? About how good they were? Or about the greater job satisfaction they experienced when the assignment was more straightforward, as the attack on Pacioli's driver must have been? Hard to tell, but they both had that peculiar wide-eyed impassivity so often to be seen on the faces of those for whom violence is easy. It is an expression that tends to sweeten with age, eventually giving its wearers an appearance of kindliness and good humour that can be danger-ously misleading.

I looked at Chihani and held up the raincoat. 'What's this for?'

She seemed pleased that I had asked. 'Who knows how long you may be away from your room, Mr Halliday? Someone might ask for you. Pacioli perhaps. So, your bags have been unpacked for you and your suits hung in a closet. Your toothbrush is damp. One of the beds looks as if you may have tried to sleep. Your room key is there in your coat pocket. Perhaps you went for a walk. You see, I try to plan for all eventualities.'

The delayed shock was turning now into anger. 'I'll bet there's one eventuality you didn't plan for,' I said.

'What is that?'

'Really having to use thiopental on me. You weren't prepared to do that.'

'What makes you think so?'

'You were all set to swab my arm with spirit, and yet you hadn't loaded the syringe. You hadn't even taken it out of the pack. You were bluffing.'

She looked pleased. 'Very good. Hindsight is beginning to work. And why didn't you call the bluff? Let me tell you. Isopropyl alcohol has a very distinctive smell which you associate with injections. So, you smelled, you believed and you were frightened, as I intended you to be. Why? Because I didn't want to make you unconscious unless it was absolutely necessary. It would have been inconvenient. Something could have gone wrong. Supposing you had swallowed your tongue while we had you in the linen basket. Such a happening would be dangerous.'

'Very. You might have had a corpse on your hands. Better to bluff. That way you get a live-and-kicking, free-breathing writer to take to your leader. I hope he won't mind when I tell him, very politely of course, to get stuffed.'

She shrugged. 'Naturally, you are upset at the moment.'

'Upset, yes, and even more, surprised.'

'Surprised? You are an experienced person. What could there be to surprise you?'

'Odd as it may seem to you, Miss Chihani, I am not used to being assaulted on arrival in a strange hotel by thugs masquerading as bellhops. What's more, the only reason I've come here is to assist Dr Luccio in the writing of a book to counter terrorism. When I find that he has a terrorist gang of his own working for him I think I'm entitled to be surprised.'

That drew a light laugh. 'Have you been terrorized, Mr Halliday? How terrible! But is it true? I would myself say only that what you call your dignity has been a little injured. Yes, that's it; eh? You will calm down.'

'You think so? Where are we going?'

'To meet Dr Luccio in a safe house.'

'Safe house is a jargon term used by intelligence services. Does Luccio belong to one?'

'Safe houses are used by all organizations and groups engaged in covert and clandestine operations, and especially by organizations with a particular need to defend themselves against enemy penetration.' She sounded as if she was quoting from an instruction manual.

'In Dr Luccio's case, which enemy would that be? The anti-terrorism people, the kidnapping specialists or the bunco squad?'

She fielded the insult with another shrug. 'Oh, we have nothing to fear from the police. Our enemy is far more dangerous.'

'Who is this enemy, then? The PLO, the Red Brigades, the PFLP? Who?'

'If you need to know about them, Dr Luccio will tell you.' She gave a sharp order in their private language and the driver switched off the roof-light.

Obviously she was also trying to switch me off. I stayed on. 'Was this enemy the reason why I couldn't leave the hotel by walking out through the front doorway? Would he, or they, have tried to stop me?'

'They know you are here and they know why. They would certainly have followed you, whether I was there or not. The safe house would have been compromised. By acting immediately, the moment you arrived, we gave them no time to complete full and effective surveillance. In all covert or clandestine work every opportunity to forestall and confuse the opposition is always to be taken.' Another quotation.

'Is writing a book in Italy clandestine work?'

'The writing of Dr Luccio's book will be done under conditions of the most strict security, Mr Halliday. Didn't Pacioli make that clear to you?'

'He explained that you, Miss Chihani, acting as an intermediary, would be issuing orders on the subject of security, yes. I didn't say that I would obey them. And you still haven't given me the shadow of a reason why you had to attack me physically. If you needed my co-operation why didn't you just say so and ask for it.'

'It would have been necessary to explain.'

'Isn't that what intermediaries are supposed to do? Communicate and explain? If you'd asked me nicely I'd have gone down with you in the service elevator. Why *didn't* you ask? Because you like using muscle? Because you enjoy it?'

'You're answering your own questions, Mr Halliday,' she replied calmly. 'If I had asked you would have argued, objected and demanded explanations. You would have done, in fact, just what you are doing now. Then, I had no time to spare for your games. Now, it doesn't matter what you do or say. The operation is going according to plan.'

'*Your* plan?'

'Yes, but I am only carrying out Dr Luccio's orders. The orders are to take you to the safe house without compromising its security. Later, after Dr Luccio has talked with you, learned

47

how you respond to operational stresses and made his own assessment of your reliability, more convenient security routines may be established.'

We were in heavy stop-and-go traffic. The minibus jolted forward again jarring my shoulder painfully.

I said: 'Supposing I decide that I've already had more than enough operational stress for today, and that unless I'm taken back to my hotel immediately I shall consider my contract to help Dr Luccio write a book null and void? What do your orders say about that, Miss Chihani?'

She had just put a cigarette in her mouth and had a lighter raised. So that I could have the full benefit of her thinking and feelings about me, she removed the cigarette and lowered the lighter before answering. 'I would say several things, Mr Halliday. First, that you have already been paid a lot of money without having yet done a thing for it. Second, that Dr Luccio wishes to see you this evening and may not be disappointed. Third, that you are an experienced person and must know that it is no use blustering. You will, of course, accept the situation.'

It was, I noted, the second time that she had called me an experienced person. I thought for a moment of asking what she had meant, but she was by then puffing away at her cigarette and clearly determined to say no more.

One thing I do know from experience is that estimates of the passage of time and of distance travelled made while sitting in darkness are usually inaccurate. So, under that particular set of circumstances, my guess that in the next hour and a quarter we covered almost seventy miles was a good one. It was my sense of direction that went haywire. After about twenty minutes in heavy traffic we began to go faster and then, following a brief stop and the sound of a voice from outside, very fast. I assumed, correctly, that we had gone through a toll-gate on an autostrada and stopped to pay. Confusion began when, after thirty minutes or so at high speed, the same thing happened again. We came to another toll-gate. There was no mistaking it. As our driver approached he slowed and wound the window beside him all the way down. I knew because of the changes in the background sounds and because I could feel the cooler air coming in. A second or two after we had stopped completely another voice spoke up from outside. It was a second toll collector telling us how much *he* wanted for that little stretch of road. What sort of an autostrada was it where you had to pay to get on and then pay all over again to get off? Had we managed to do a U-turn somewhere along the way? *Another* of Chihani's security precautions? Could it have been done without my noticing it?

From then on I was lost. I had been sure at first that we were heading north, then maybe a trifle west of north. Now I began thinking east. Monza maybe? The Bergamo area? Or were we about to double back to central Milan and one of those permanent luxury hotel suites that Zander maintained to house himself and his three briefcases on their journeys around the world?

We went through a small town and then turned slowly on to what felt like one of those corduroy roads that army engineers used to build for transport needing firm going across mud. Only this one seemed to have been made of utility poles instead of four-inch logs. Our speed dropped to a crawl. The minibus's suspension thumped protestingly. Then we were on smooth pavement again and starting to make good time through a series of left and right bends that had me holding on to my seat to keep from lurching against Chihani. She had a grab rail to hold on to. After ten minutes of this we stopped again, at some traffic lights in a village I thought. When they turned green and our driver started up through the gears again Chihani reached into a TWA flight bag that she had pulled from under the seat and produced a hand-size CB radio. She extended the antenna, glanced at her watch and then began calling.

She said ' 'allo, 'allo,' twice before an answer came. It sounded like 'Qui batula' and the voice was a woman's. Chihani replied with a couple of short sentences that meant absolutely nothing to me, repeated them both very distinctly and then switched off. I assumed that she had been making a progress report.

Minutes later we entered yet another small town. There was more stop-and-go work and I waited for another run-up through the gears. Instead, we turned left on to cobbles and began to climb a steepish hill. After only a few yards, it seemed, we bore left, made a sharp right and slowed. The minibus lurched up over something that felt like a kerb and came to a standstill. Chihani stood up and pushed past me.

'We have arrived,' she said, 'but I think you had better let me guide you out, Mr Halliday. A little caution is necessary.' She took a heavy flashlight from a bracket by the door.

Because of the darkness inside I could at once see well in the semi-darkness outside, but she had been right about the need for caution. We were in a small flagged courtyard at the foot of a semicircle of stone steps leading up to an entrance. Overhead there was a lantern, but the low-wattage bulb in it did not shed nearly enough light to show up the uneven surface of the flag-stones and a large break in one of the steps.

Chihani went ahead guiding me with the flashlight. 'Follow me, please.'

'What is this place?'

'It used to be a hotel.'

Inside, I could see that for myself. It had been one of those old, shabby, small hotels of the kind favoured, before the coming of the motel, by travelling salesmen on per diem expense accounts, and it still looked like one. Behind what had been the reception desk, and beneath an array of empty mail boxes with brass key-hooks numbered from one to twenty-two, sat a fat girl with long black hair and blue-tinted glasses. The foyer smelt strongly of old soap and carpet dust with just a hint of some carbolic-based disinfectant. The radio in a nearby room was tuned to a pop-music station. The fat girl looked up from the book she was reading as we entered and then, when Chihani snapped her fingers at her, pressed a switch on the wall beside her.

Opposite the desk there was a stairway. As she led the way over to it, Chihani glanced back at me. 'Here also one must be careful,' she said. 'One could easily fall.'

One could indeed. In that kind of hotel almost everything except the outside walls has been modified over the years by owners trying, usually without success, to keep pace with changing standards of comfort and convenience. The quest for space in which to install more bathrooms and utility ducts has always been hard on stairwells. This one seemed to have been re-modelled for the use of mountain goats. The staircase in it was spiral, and constructed with risers too high for the narrow treads. The carpeting was threadbare and slippery. You went up cling-ing to a strip-metal balustrade as you felt for toe-holds and tried to disregard the sharp cracking noises that accompanied every move you made. You reached the top with a relief tempered by the knowledge that it would be worse going down. It was no surprise in such a place to find that, a yard or two away, the passage zigzagged and that, right in the middle of the zigzag, a door had been set. The room number on it was 17.

Chihani tapped on it lightly with the buckle of her shoulder bag.

When I had asked my news-agency friend for a physical description of Zander he had replied that he couldn't really help me much there. Sure, they had pictures; but only some that had been taken in Algiers at the time of the independence celebrations in 'sixty-two. Zander had been identified as one of the smiling faces in a group of politicos posed against Air France boarding steps by the door of a DC3 on the tarmac of Maison Blanche airport. How, or by whom, he had been identified God alone knew. The pictures were of poor quality and, in black-and-white anyway, most smiling faces tended to look very much alike. More useful maybe, after all this time, would be a verbal description. One of the stories about the Zander-Brochet operation had described him as having a head like an Easter Island stone figure.

If all you were talking about was a shape, the man who now opened the door of room number 17 did have that kind of head. The tanned face was long and narrow with a jutting chin and thin lips. There was, though, nothing remote or severe or forbidding about his appearance, nothing, that is, at first sight. He was short, broad-shouldered and dressed in nothing but a blue terrycloth robe and a pair of sandals. He had a good head of hair, thick and white, and a triangle of grey fluff on his chest. The line of a mouth that could so easily have conveyed warnings was here permanently set in a wry little simper that only vanished when the lips were needed to make vowel sounds. It took me several minutes to realize that the mask told you nothing of what was going on behind it and that you had to learn to read a pair of pale, grey-green eyes.

They were smiling along with the mouth as he greeted me. 'Welcome, Mr Halliday, welcome.'

He stood aside, motioning me in. Neither of us made any move to shake hands. Chihani took my raincoat.

I could see more of him now. He was of an indeterminate but well-preserved middle age, a man who watched what he ate and drank, took plenty of exercise, went to a good dentist, had pedicures as well as manicures and used rather too much of a toilet water that smelt expensive. Also noted was the fact that his English, though slightly accented, told you no more than that English had not been the first language of his childhood. The voice was a light tenor.

'Do you mind, Mr Halliday, that I dress informally for our meeting? Do you object?'

The tone was arch. What he meant was that if I was hoping to express my displeasure with him just by standing there staring I would be disappointed.

'How you choose to dress,' I said, 'is the only thing so far about this meeting to which I *don't* object. Does that answer your question?'

'Ah yes.' He nodded amiably as if my response had been both polite and helpful. 'But please come in and be comfortable.'

As I entered I saw that beyond number 17 there was a connecting room that could be closed off with a pair of double doors. This other room had been fitted up as a gym of sorts with an exercise mat, a set of barbells, a stationary bicycle, a massage table and an adjustable couch covered with towelling beneath a big sun-lamp. Number 17 itself was furnished with an office desk, comfortable pull-up chairs, a telex machine and a drinks cabinet. The rug on the floor looked and felt expensive.

'Sit down, Mr Halliday. Sit down, please.'

As he ushered me to a chair I noticed for the first time a curious mannerism he had, a way of moving with his hands and forearms held in the air as if he were a surgeon who had just scrubbed up for an operation. When I was seated he peered down intently at my face. I wondered if he could be looking for signs of a communicable disease. A health and fitness worshipper who practised weight-lifting at his age might well have a phobia about germs brought into his safe house from the world outside. But no, he was just curious.

'You look younger than I had expected, Mr Halliday. Television made you look older, and that was two years ago.'

'Television made me *feel* older.'

'Naturally. You gave so much of yourself to it. Do you realize that of those you interviewed on *First of the Week* no less than three have since been indicted on serious charges?'

'No thanks to me.'

'But how beautifully you cross-examined them! How clumsy and how crude you showed them to be! How splendidly you used the power of words against them! This Halliday, I said to myself, is a man of words.'

'That, according to the critics, was why the show flopped.'

'Critics!' He brushed them away with the edge of a hand.

'Have you never had the experience of reading totally contradictory reviews of a book or a play and finding it hard to believe that the same work is being discussed? Of course you have. You do yourself an injustice.' He beckoned to Chihani who was still standing in the doorway. 'You may come in, Simone. Make yourself useful. Be our hostess. Serve drinks.' He sat down facing me, his robe opening to reveal muscular thighs with a deep scar running up towards the left groin. 'I am informed, Mr Halliday, that your preferred drink is whisky. Which shall it be? Scotch or bourbon?'

'I've already refused your thiopental. Why should I accept your whisky?' I no longer troubled to contain my anger. 'And let's cut out the jokes, shall we?'

His hands made a little gesture of surrender. 'You object to being complimented?'

'When the compliments insult my intelligence, yes. So let's forget all this nonsense about a crappy television show and get to your name. What do you like to call yourself at the moment? What do *I* call you if we ever get as far as my having to call you anything? Which is it? Zander, Hecht, Brochet, Luccio or Pike? Or do you have one of those exotic Arab names with some cute handle to it that you like to use?'

He blinked and suddenly the eyes lost their good humour. That was the first time I saw the transformation take place and it was disconcerting. The simper on the lips remained exactly as it was but the meaning of it changed completely. From being an amiable grimace it became, with that blink, part of an unmistakeable warning sign. An animal was ready to attack.

His verbal response, however, was no more than a reproach. 'I am afraid, Mr Halliday, that you are displeased with us.'

'That surprises you?'

'It causes regret. Mistakes have clearly been made. But I would have expected a man of your experience to have had more understanding.'

'Understanding of what? Judo?'

He sighed. 'Simone, my dear, kindly give our guest some scotch and water with plenty of ice. I will have the same.' To me he said: 'It seems that there has been a little crossing of wires. Permit me, please, to ask you a couple of questions. First, you received both my letter and the bomb itself quite safely, yes?'

'Yes.'

'And you reported to the police and FBI without delay?'

'I reported to the police and they brought in the FBI, but there was no delay. If you wanted to make an impression on me you certainly succeeded. I became intrigued. That much must be obvious. Otherwise I wouldn't be here.'

'But first you checked out the Zander name. With whom?'

'A friend in a news agency. I'm not telling you which one.'

'If it was a news agency I know which one you would go to. Names don't matter. You learn that I am rich and infamous. You are given other information.'

'Which I'm beginning to find was highly inaccurate. For instance, I don't call this a luxury hotel suite.'

He waved that aside. 'This is a safe house. Let us stay with you, Mr Halliday. Titillated and intrigued, you could not refuse to accept the financially rewarding Pacioli deal. Is that how it was?'

'That's *almost* how it was,' I said.

'Had you by then heard again from the police or the FBI?'

'No.'

'How about other persons? Who else were you in touch with?'

'Naturally I talked to my agent.'

'Mentioning me?'

'Only as Dr Luccio. If I'd mentioned Karlis Zander I'd have had to tell her about the bomb. She'd have had a fit and killed the whole deal. So, all we discussed was the Pacioli agreement as a normal piece of business. What is all this? What do you want to know?'

'The bomb, the letter and the postcard were delivered to you three weeks ago, nearly four weeks. If you have heard no more on the subject from the police, the FBI or other official sources, Mr Halliday, you must have been avoiding them.'

'Why the surprise? Of course I've been avoiding them. I'd given them what I thought they should have – the package with the bomb in it plus a photocopy of your letter to me. That's all. I promised to let them have the original letter, but I didn't do so because it was stuck to the postcard. Nor did I tell them about your follow-up through Pacioli and McGuire. I'd promised to let them know if there was a follow-up, but decided not to bother. Instead, I told my agent that I'd call her again in a couple of weeks to see if the agreement was ready for me to sign. Then I took off for a little vacation.'

'A vacation?' He looked quite startled. 'Where?'

'Nowhere you'd know.' But he was still staring at me disbelievingly so I went on. 'A friend of mine has a house on Long Island. He's away quite a bit. I called him in London. I've borrowed the place before. We have an arrangement. It's very simple. My agent didn't get the Pacioli agreement for signature from McGuire's office until three days ago. As soon as I knew she had it I went straight into New York, signed, bought some travellers' cheques and Italian money from the bank and took off. There's been no time wasted.'

'But you hid yourself. You also concealed the Hotel Mansour postcard from the FBI. Why did you do that?'

'Two reasons. Where officialdom is concerned I've learned to keep my distance. That's one reason. The main reason, though, is this, Mr Zander. I regarded that picture postcard as something in the nature of a private message from you to me. Was I wrong?'

'No. Certainly not. You were right. It was very much a private message.'

'A message saying that there was more in this proposition for me than a fifty-thousand-dollar fee? More than just money? Right?'

The eyes became wary. 'You are under contract to help me write a book, Mr Halliday. If there are fringe benefits to the assignment you will undoubtedly discover them,'

I considered him for a moment. He was stalling suddenly and I couldn't see why he should. If he didn't want to level with me for some reason, why didn't he put me off with a lie? Fatigue swept over me and my temper began to go again. 'Mr Pike,' I said, 'the fact that I've reported for duty shouldn't be misinterpreted. I mean don't, for instance, run away with the idea that the enriching experience of being kidnapped by Miss Chihani and her team of juvenile psychopaths is going to persuade me to vary the terms of our agreement.'

'Simone's action was a mistake. It had my approval, however, and I apologize.'

It was said coldly and without conviction. My reply was equally cool. 'That makes me feel a whole lot better. But while we're still on the subject of our agreement perhaps I'd better remind you that there's nothing at all in it about my having to take orders from anyone. So, in future, when Miss Chihani feels like issuing orders about security, or anything else, I'm going to want more than her mere say-so to convince me that they should be obeyed. I'll want to know *why* they should be obeyed.'

Chihani gave a harsh little laugh. 'And I can tell you the answer you'll get now,' she said. 'For your own safety and for ours. That's what you will be told, Mr Halliday. Here' – she shoved a tray with a drink on it in front of my nose – 'calm yourself with whisky.'

'That's enough, Simone,' said my host firmly. He waited until I had the drink in my hand, then took his own and waved her away with it. 'Go and make some sandwiches.'

She put the tray down and went instantly. The distance around the desk to the door was long enough for me to notice that she had the heel-and-toe walk of a dancer or an athlete.

As the door closed behind her my host raised his glass as if to say that we were now free to drink. The eyes were smiling again. 'What is your impression of her?' he asked. 'I mean leaving aside for the moment your present hostility and dislike.'

'My first impression at the hotel was that she looked like an actor in drag. That is to say ...'

'I am familiar with the expression.' He sipped his whisky. 'What I am interested to know is how you evaluate her operational efficiency?'

'As leader of a team of muggers operating in a hotel where the help isn't going to lift a finger against them, I guess she's okay. She seems familiar with the technical problems of giving injections to patients who won't believe that doctor knows best. If she's had nursing experience, though, it would be in the kind of hospital I hope to avoid. A bit paranoid herself, I thought. She spoke darkly of mysterious enemies threatening your lives, Mr Pike. What was all that about?'

'You astonish me.' He sipped his drink. 'Crossed wires there may have been. I've admitted it. But surely you cannot have so soon forgotten the briefing given you by Mr McGuire in New York. Surely you realize that any book exposing the inner workings of the terrorist international is a great threat to these criminal conspirators. They will do anything to prevent its being written. And how better to do so than by killing its authors?'

'One of its supposed authors is already dead. How do they know that it's being written? I'm sure you wouldn't tell them.'

The eyes snapped at me. 'By "supposed author" you mean Nechayev?'

'Of course, Mr Pike.'

'There is nothing "supposed" about the Nechayev memoir. The fact of its existence is widely known and its significance well understood. Full and final authentication is due at any moment. Didn't Pacioli tell you this? I have the English translation here for you to read. Meanwhile, please do not address me as Mr Pike. It is not my name.'

'When I asked you what I should call you, you were offended.'

'Because your manner was offensive.'

'Very politely then. How do I address you?'

'You could address me as Doctor, or as Zander.'

'Okay, Doctor, Zander it is. But you have to understand my problems too. For instance, in your letter to me on the Baghdad postcard you sign yourself Karlis Zander.'

'That was for your benefit, Mr Halliday. So that you could check on me a little, follow leads.'

'I understand that. For instance, Zander Pharmaceuticals was registered in Miami and that's where the package bomb was mailed. Interesting. But which of your names is going on the book? Doesn't it *have* to be Luccio?'

'Oh no.'

'Then what happens to the story McGuire gave me on the memoir, I mean the one about Luccio inheriting it because he was Nechayev's great-grandson? Was that also dreamed up for my benefit? Do we just forget about it?'

'Oh most certainly no.' The eyes were narrowed now, almost turning the simper into a leer. 'That part of your briefing by Mr McGuire should be considered as true.'

'What do you mean by "considered as true"? That it *is* true or that you want us to *pretend*, just for the hell of it and because it might make me feel better, that it's true?'

'For the purposes of this discussion, let us say simply that the memoir came to a descendant of Nechayev and that I have bought the manuscript from him.'

'And the right to publish it? Did you buy that too?'

'Yes, yes certainly.'

'Then you *could* be writing your commentary as the discoverer and legal owner of these long-lost and historically important papers. Well, that's something. Let's try building on it. You're hiring me to edit the book. How about putting your real name on it? No, Mr Zander, hear me out. According to McGuire you hope to influence government policies with this book. You're not just aiming for the bestseller lists. You want to be taken seriously. Right? I have to tell you that hiding behind a pseudonym with this sort of subject kills any chance of achieving the kind of success you want. If you're hoping even to be *heard* on the subject of organized international terrorism, much less listened to and believed, you are going to have to tell all and name names.'

He stared for a moment or two, then reached for the intercom on his desk, flipped a switch and spoke. The only word of what he said that I understood was 'sandwiches'. Having switched off, he considered my half-empty glass and pushed aside his own. Several more seconds elapsed though before he finally decided how best to reply.

He spoke as if for the record. 'Mr Halliday, it is precisely because I *am* prepared to tell all and name names' – he raised his hands into the scrubbed-up position – '*and because this has become known*, that my enemies want to kill me.'

'In other words, Doctor, you're prepared to name *their* names but not your own. Would I be right in thinking that your problem is also one of self-incrimination?'

There was another pause as he prepared himself for more eggshell walking. The hint of melancholy that he succeeded in putting into his simper was impressive. 'Mr Halliday, even the little, the marginal facts, that you were able to find out about me in America must have told you that I have to be prudent.' The raised hands slowly fell. 'My place,' he said, 'is in the shadows.'

'Let's put it on a severely commercial basis then. Whose picture do we see on the book's jacket? To whom does our publisher turn for support and comfort when his libel lawyers advise him that a whole lot of the telling all and the naming of names is actionable? Who comes forward to support his pleas of justification with sworn testimony?'

He brightened up at once. 'Now you are talking, Mr Halliday. Brass tacks, eh? Well, let me tell you. First, none of those named will dare to show his nose. Second, if our publisher is of the type to be frightened by what his own lawyers tell him, then we should get another. Are there not other publishers with stronger nerves?'

'Mr Zander, there are always other publishers, but .. '

'Good. Now, here is something to eat.'

Chihani had returned with a plate of bread-roll sandwiches that looked as if they were stuffed with salami. I passed on them but raised no objection when Zander directed her to refill my glass. There were several bad tastes in my mouth for which another strong drink could probably have done something. I thought, too, that the business of mixing and serving the drink might divert their attention from me while I made a decision. Should I say something that would blow the whole deal there and then, or should I wait and tell Pacioli so that he could handle my defection in his own way?

However, Zander was giving me no chance of deciding anything. As he began to munch a sandwich he made his surprise announcement. 'Mr Halliday,' he said, 'has come up with a clever suggestion.'

'He is a clever person.' She almost made it sound as if she meant it.

'Yes, he is indeed. He has suggested that we postpone all decisions about the book's publication until we have done our work and have the manuscript complete. That is a very professional approach I think.'

'Excellent.' She put his freshened drink down in front of him and turned back to prepare mine. I wondered why she was suddenly looking so relaxed.

Zander bit into his sandwich again. 'What sort of work plan do you have in mind, Mr Halliday?'

'Obviously, the first thing to be done is for me to read the Nechayev memoirs. If they are to be our basic text, the sooner I get to know them the better. How about your own preliminary work, Doctor? I should be studying that too.'

He pretended to consider the proposal before shaking his head. 'Mr Halliday, I think it will be better if we come to my work later. It is mainly in the form of notes and not well organized. Better that we begin at the beginning.'

I have heard a great many variations on that airy theme from indolent or phony clients and a reference to non-existent notes is nearly always in there somewhere. The client has often written nothing at all, of course, just day-dreamed a little. The genuinely shy or over-modest ones are rare. Still, Zander was able to make the lie sound remarkably convincing. Work on a book with him would have had its entertaining moments.

'I quite understand, Doctor. Now, you say you have an English translation of the memoirs.' I noticed that my freshened-up drink was mostly water.

'Pacioli had one made. It was not very good, but I have worked to improve it myself. You should know that it was the habit of the old anarchist groups in Geneva, even when they were writing mainly in Russian, to use French also. It was a lingua franca with them. Some also used shorthand for writing, perhaps for secrecy. The Nechayev memoirs have passages in Fayet shorthand. This was a system invented in France.'

'I see.'

'And the French passages have been left in French.'

'That's all right. I can read French.'

'Simone, it is in the centre drawer of the desk. The envelope marked with the number three.'

She took a fat, page-size envelope from the drawer and handed it to him.

He weighed it in his hands thoughtfully. 'Mr Halliday, we come back again to the problem of security.'

'All right.'

'The enemy forces who think that they have you under surveillance at your hotel do not yet know that you evaded them this evening.'

'I guess they don't. You want me to go back up by the service elevator, the way I came down?'

'There would be no point. They will have all access to the building covered by now. The point is that when you return, however you return, they will realize their mistake.'

'So?' For one nasty moment I was wondering what I could do or say if they had decided to maintain security by keeping me in their safe house on ice.

'So, from the moment of your return you will be considered hostile. They will step up their counter measures. The risk for us here will greatly increase. I must accordingly ask you if you are now willing to obey security orders for your journey back to Milan tonight and for your return here tomorrow. Are you willing?'

'Of course, now that I have been given reasons.'

'Then let us say that we will meet again tomorrow at a time to be arranged by telephone but following a procedure to be determined in advance.'

He nodded to Chihani who reached forward and took the

glass out of my hand. 'No more whisky tonight,' she said, 'and we will go as we came.'

'In the minibus?'

'Yes, but not all the way. There is a service station area on the autostrada near Milan. From there we can get a taxi to take you to your hotel. You have enough Italian money I think.'

'Yes.'

'Arrangements for your return will be as follows. At twelve tomorrow morning you will be telephoned at your hotel and questioned about your reading of the Nechayev memoirs. Then, depending on your replies to my questions you will be told whether or not it is safe to leave the hotel. If it is not yet safe you will be telephoned again at a stated time. You understand?'

'Yes.'

Zander snickered. 'Very ingenious, Simone.'

'Upon being told that it *is* safe for you to leave, you will immediately go down from your room and take a car or taxi to Malpensa airport. Not Linate, where you arrived, but Malpensa. Understood?'

'Yes.'

'On arrival at Malpensa you will go to the Milan bus-ticket counter in the main hall. There can be no mistake. The sign above is in Italian and English. You will then wait until the girl who was with us tonight walks by. Go with her and obey all her instructions. She will lead you to transportation. Understood?'

'It all seems fairly clear.' But they were both looking so pleased with themselves and with my humble obedience that I changed my mind about leaving it at that. 'Clear, that is,' I added, 'except for one thing.'

'What?' demanded Chihani.

I looked at Luccio. 'Doctor, you must know that most major American publishers are owned by other, bigger, diversified corporations. Syncom, for instance. Now you must know that people like Syncom aren't easily pushed around. Do you really believe that you can persuade them to publish something that their lawyers tell them is plainly and criminally libellous?'

'For me, they will do anything,' he said airily.

'Doctor, who is this patron of yours?'

'Patron?' The eyes had become stony and the tone colour of his voice had changed in an odd way. I knew that I had gone too

61

far but also guessed that it could be more dangerous to back down than to persist.

'That's what I said, Doctor. I'm talking about that high personage in the Gulf who gives orders to Syncom on your behalf.'

'Who has been putting such absurd thoughts in your head? Pacioli?'

'The statement that you enjoyed the protection of a high personage in the Gulf was made during the briefing I was given in New York.' It was unlikely, I thought, that McGuire employed a driver who could be beaten up, but I took out a little insurance for McGuire himself against package bombs designed to work. 'In fact,' I added, 'that was one of the aspects of the whole proposal that I found most intriguing. Naturally I was curious about his identity. Is it supposed to be kept secret?'

He sat back, looked down at his whisky and then drank some. Several seconds went by before he looked at me again. Then he said slowly: 'You may now be in a small way committed to me, but you are not yet *trusted*, Mr Halliday. Don't forget that, please.' He seemed to remember the envelope with the memoir in it that he was still holding and handed it to me. 'You had better get started back. Have you sleeping pills?'

'Yes, thank you.'

'Take several tonight. You must be well rested tomorrow.'

With that he stood up and walked through into his gym.

'We have our orders,' Chihani said. 'Time to go.'

As she led the way out I glanced into the gym. The master was naked and preparing to sunbathe. The long jagged scar on his thigh looked like the result of a shell-splinter wound.

The return journey was made in silence. To pass the time in the darkness I tried going through my Pacioli contract from memory, clause by clause, to see if I could spot the one that Barbara would use to get me into the clear and on to a plane for New York. Oddly, the exercise had the effect that counting sheep is supposed to have on the sleepless. I dozed and, when we eventually stopped, Chihani had to wake me.

'Jet lag and whisky together,' she commented.

She ordered the minibus lights switched off and then went with me to the gas station to call a cab. When I went to the men's room she waited outside. She also waited until the cab came. As she was careful to point out, this was no mere courtesy on her part. Security procedures must never neglect matters of detail or make easy assumptions. At that stage, perhaps, it probably did not much matter if I saw and memorized the number plates on the minibus, but, on the other hand, it might matter a great deal.

'Go to your hotel and stay there until I order you to leave,' were her parting words as she slammed the door of the cab on me. Even if I had felt like saving her the trouble of issuing orders that I had no intention of obeying, she gave me little chance of doing so.

It was nearly eleven when I arrived back at the hotel. At the desk I asked for an Alitalia timetable and was told that I would find one in my sitting room.

What I found in my sitting room instead was a fog of panatella smoke and a delegation of three.

FIVE

THE smoker was a fellow countryman whom I had not seen for several years. As the surprise of seeing him there faded and memories of our last meeting began to flood back, I realized that, as far as I was concerned, time had not been a healer and that, judging from the look on his face, our mutual dislike was as lively as ever.

Also present were Renaldo Pacioli and a man wearing half-glasses and a tweed suit who looked all set to play the family doctor in an aspirin commercial. Of the three, only Pacioli was looking troubled by the possibility that I might not be pleased by their dropping in unannounced. While they were still getting up out of the armchairs and clearing their throats, I walked over to the windows and opened them both as wide as I could.

The smoker said, 'Hi, Bob,' and stubbed out his cigar in an ashtray already overflowing with butts. As I tossed my raincoat and Luccio's envelope on to the desk, Pacioli came towards me with his hands spread out in a curious gesture of surrender combined with apology.

'I beg you to forgive this intrusion,' he said, 'and I hope that you will find the reasons for it understandable. You have evidently recognized in your compatriot here a familiar face. He is at present, he tells me, a political attaché at your country's embassy in Rome. I found him with this other gentleman, Herr Schelm, in my office when I returned from meeting you. They both flew up from Rome this afternoon expressly to see you. When we could not reach you by telephone to explain the urgency, we came here at once. Herr Schelm was already concerned on your account. When we found that, although a bed appeared to have been slept in, you were not still here, we were even more concerned. On the advice of Herr Schelm, however, it was decided not to call the police but to wait.'

'Well,' I said, 'I can tell you *what* I've been doing. I've been having a meeting with Dr Luccio. The meeting wasn't my idea and I wasn't consulted about it in any way. I was just taken to it. *Where* I was taken I can't tell you because I don't know. As I was hired to meet with and listen to Dr Luccio, I guess I can't complain and risk being told that I'm a sorehead.' I stared at the familiar face. 'Was that what you wanted to see me about? The work I'm supposed to be doing here?'

He pretended, as he always had, to be indifferent to my hostility. 'Bob,' he said, 'there are two reasons for my being here. The first is to tell you that back home a couple of weeks ago your personal file was pulled.'

That stung me, as he had known it would, and I snapped at him. 'What the hell for? I have nothing to do with you people and I mean to keep it that way. If they're pulling names on the sucker list, they can forget mine. I'm not available.'

'Easy, Bob. That mail-bomb caper created quite a lot of interest. You couldn't expect that some word of it wouldn't get to us. And when we hear that you've been asking round about Zander, well naturally we have to start asking questions too.'

'You know Zander?'

'We've known him for a long time, but not always as well as we'd have liked. Nowadays, he's what we call a handle-with-care package.'

He had always had a taste for trade jargon. 'Meaning what?'

'Meaning that he's one of those individuals with whom we prefer not to have direct dealings of any sort. The reasons can be operational or, as in this case, chiefly political. We prefer to keep some characters at arm's length. It's nothing new or very special. When Dieter Schelm's outfit has that particular problem he calls in us or maybe the British. On this one we've asked Dieter to help out.'

'To deal with a book?'

'Not just any book, Bob. Have you read these memoirs?'

'Have you?'

'Not me personally, but apparently that nice Mr McGuire had a photostat of the original Russian that he didn't mind our people seeing back home. What he told us about your deal with Zander, though, had them worried. So did some other things.'

'What things?'

'Things like you concealing evidence, Bob. The FBI and Captain Boyle were concerned about you too. Your agent's office didn't know where you were. We had to get your secretary to help us find that Zander letter in your workroom. She said you always put papers you didn't want her to see in the bottom right-hand drawer of your desk. That's where we found the postcard from Baghdad they tell me. So, realizing that you've unwittingly involved yourself in something you can't fully understand, we decided to offer you the helping hand.'

'Bullshit.'

He went on with the faintest of smiles. 'We also hope, of course, that in return for our good offices in taking care of the FBI's understandable displeasure at your efforts to obstruct justice, we get a small measure of co-operation from you in respect of Zander.'

'Thanks, I'll take the FBI's displeasure, if any. I'll also apologize to Captain Boyle. He's a reasonable man. As for your helping hand and your good offices, I don't have to tell you what you can do with them. You'll think of some place suitable.'

He rolled his eyes at Schelm and sighed heavily. 'As I told you, Dieter, little old Bob here is a hard man.' He looked at me again. 'The second reason I'm here is that your personal file gives you a suspicious nature and a long memory for bad breaks. So, having assured our friend Dieter Schelm that you are indeed the Robert R. Halliday we all know and love, I will also vouch for his credentials. He is a very senior official of a West German intelligence service, though at present on loan to Nato as director of their Combined Intelligence Services Liaison Bureau. Dieter Schelm is a civilian with the assimilated rank for Nato admin purposes of a two-star general. He speaks Oxbridge English so you needn't worry. Your jokes will be understood.'

Schelm offered his hand. 'How do you do, Mr Halliday.'

The family doctor impression that I had of him went the moment our hands touched and when I really saw him. He could have been a doctor, but not the kind traditionally associated with good bedside-manners, childbirth and house calls. The disqualification was in his eyes. There was great intelligence there and even humour, but no hint of compassion. It was only the half-glasses that gave him, now and then, an odd look of professional benevolence.

He glanced at the familiar face and said, 'Thank you, my friend.'

It sounded like a dismissal and evidently was. The face said something to him in German that I didn't quite understand and then turned to me. 'Well, Bob,' he said, 'this is as far as I go. It's good to see you looking in such great shape. I hear you've given up pretty well everything the health nuts don't recommend. It shows. If there's anything you want from us, you know where to find me.' He gave us a comprehensive farewell wave, gathered up a canvas tote bag along with his topcoat and left.

As the door closed I went to the telephone. 'The first thing I propose to do,' I said, 'is to call room service and find out what they have in the way of food at this time of night. You may be thirsty too. What can I get you to drink?'

They both asked for Pellegrino. While I waited for room service to answer, I scribbled ROOM PROBABLY BUGGED on the phone pad and held it up for Schelm to see.

He smiled pleasantly and nodded. When I had finished with room service, he said: 'You're right. It was bugged. But your acquaintance from the American embassy brought along a portable detection device they have now and the bugs were dealt with while we were waiting. Otherwise there could not have been so much plain speaking. What made you think that this room might not be secure?'

So I told them how I had been taken out of the hotel and gave them a run-down on my evening with Chihani and Zander. I stopped while the room-service waiter delivered the drinks and snacks, but the only other interruptions were those caused by Pacioli's outbursts of indignation.

I did, though, find out from him about the autostrada on which you paid twice.

'That would be the A8 and A9 going north,' he said. 'They start as one. You pay entering that first section because there are several free exits from it along the way. But if you go on as far as Varese, say, on the A8 or to Como on the A9 you must pay more. You could also on the A8 have taken the left branch that goes nearly to Arona. Did you see nothing at all of the route you took?'

'Nothing, Mr Pacioli. That's what I keep trying to tell you. Inside the minibus I couldn't see outside, either coming or going.'

'I am sorry. It is all so disgraceful and you are our guest. Please continue. You say the man calling himself Luccio received you wearing only a bath robe in this hotel to which you were taken?'

Schelm was a better listener. He did not interrupt once.

'I think it is only fair to tell you,' I said finally to Pacioli, 'that, although I don't much feel like having another wrestling match with this hotel's night operator, I'm now going to put in a call to my agent in New York. And I'm going to tell her that our deal's off.'

His long face grew longer. 'May I know what reasons you will be giving, what justification for trying to break our agreement?'

'Misrepresentation will do for a start. I'm not saying you were responsible, but, according to McGuire, my job, the main job that is, would be to edit Luccio's material. There is no Luccio material. All I've had from Dr Luccio is violence, double-talk and his personally-edited English translation of the Nechayev memoirs. They're in that envelope over there, all two hundred pages of them, quadruple-spaced. Only get this, please. McGuire told me that Luccio's belief in the authenticity of the memoirs rested on his personal knowledge of their provenance. Luccio, he said, had inherited them. Luccio himself says that's wrong. He bought them. That I can believe. He bought them from whoever faked and forged them.'

'You have not yet proved faking and forgery, Mr Halliday.'

'I don't think I have to prove it,' I said. 'You haven't met this man. You told me so yourself. I have met him and I say that the burden of proof is now on you.'

'I don't think that either of you is going to have to prove anything,' Schelm said cheerily. 'You say, Mr Halliday, that he gave you his personally-edited translation of the memoirs? May I look at it?'

'Help yourself,' I said. 'I'm still curious to know why the CIA and Nato intelligence get themselves all excited over some phony nineteenth-century memoirs and a wheeler-dealer from Estonia, but I guess that's all going to turn out to be classified information.'

He smiled politely but gave no reply as he went over to the desk and picked up the envelope. 'I take it,' he said to me, 'that Luccio hasn't yet been told of your decision to break your contract to work with him?'

'No.' But I had hesitated and he pounced at once.

'Did you perhaps hint? Please be very frank. This is important.'

'I was trying not to sound too chicken. Okay, I'll be frank. I thought of telling him, but I didn't. For one thing, he and his little entourage scare me. Two, I didn't know where I was, where they'd taken me. For *me* that was scary as well, believe it or not. Third, my agreement is with Casa Editrice Pacioli, not Zander. Fourth, Syncom-Sentinel is in a better position to get police protection for Mr Pacioli while he's telling Zander that the party's over than I am. Fifth – do you need a fifth reason?'

Pacioli shook his head but Schelm fluttered the envelope he was holding to regain my attention. 'Mr Halliday, I would like to hear all your reasons please. It will help, when I start answering your questions, not to be telling you things you already know.'

'Okay. Fifth reason. I've met a lot of people wanting to get into print or have their names on books, and I have a pretty good idea by now of the various ways in which their minds work. Now, I'm not claiming that I know how a weird mind like Zander's works, but I'm sure of one thing. Whatever he wants, it isn't a book.'

'Quite right. Anything else occur to you?'

'It wasn't easy to read in the back of the cab, but coming into the city the street lighting and neon signs helped. That copy of the Nechayev memoirs you're holding is supposed to be an English translation with only the French passages left untranslated. That's not what it is. There are several long passages of untranslated stuff that doesn't look like Russian or French. Could be one of these computer languages, I guess. I marked one or two of them by folding the pages in.'

'Those,' said Pacioli, 'must be the French shorthand system pages. Our experts could not decipher them into any familiar language.'

'They're not in shorthand here,' I said.

'And the language has nothing to do with computers.' Schelm took the script out of the envelope and flipped through to one of my folded-in pages. 'Excuse me please.' He smoothed the page out and stared at it thoughtfully.

'What language is it?' I asked.

He ignored the question but glanced at his watch. 'I think, Mr Halliday, that it is by now after office hours in New York.'

'I have my agent's home number.'

'Would you consider postponing your decision to call her for a few more minutes?'

'What for?'

'I'm told that you were curious to know why Zander insisted on you and no one else being employed to work with him on this book. I have the explanation. Would you still be interested in it?'

'For a few minutes, yes.'

69

He sat down again, shifting his chair slightly to face me, and peered at me over the half-glasses. 'Do you mind if I smoke?' he asked.

'Not a bit. Go ahead.'

He nodded as if he had won a bet with himself. 'Thank you, Mr Halliday. The reasons for personal antagonisms can sometimes be quite trivial. It was very obvious that the sight of your old acquaintance from the American embassy gave you no pleasure. He smokes a lot. You don't. It was just possible that . . .'

'No, Herr Schelm. There's nothing trivial about my reasons for disliking him. All that cheap cigar smoke just reminded me of them.'

'I see.' He leaned forward. 'I should explain that we and his section in your embassy often exchange information.'

'Then he must be a CIA chief of station now.'

'When I asked him about you, Mr Halliday, he told me that although his people would not object to my asking for your co-operation I was unlikely to get it.'

'That doesn't surprise me.'

'You were, of course, formerly a newspaper man, a foreign and a war correspondent.'

'Yes.'

'You may say that it's none of my business, but I do know that, once upon a time, the Agency used now and then to ask correspondents to help out in small ways.'

'Now and then it did.'

'Forgive me for asking these very personal questions, Mr Halliday, but I suspect that this cigar-smoking person whom you dislike may have been your case officer when you had that unfortunate experience.' He was peering at me intently. 'Am I right?'

'Unfortunate did you say?' But I was beginning to like him, so I hesitated and the sarcasm I had been about to utter was left unsaid.

He understood though, 'No, Mr Halliday, I don't always choose my words very well. Nowhere in the world are prisons nice places, but eight months in an Iraqi security-police jail would be an exceptionally bad experience. You would not be disposed to forgive the person you considered responsible.'

'You seem to know all about it. Who told you? I'm sure he didn't.'

70

'The story was in the Cairo newspapers at the time. It's the first item in our BND dossier on you.'

'What that story said was that I was accused of attempting to bribe a government official and of smuggling gold to compromise a member of the Muslim Brotherhood. Don't tell me you believed it.'

'Do *you* still believe all you read in the papers?' His sudden smile and the faint chuckle that went with it were somehow cheering. 'Besides,' he said, 'a section of the Arab press outside Iraq carried the story with the added information that you were a CIA agent. The clamp-down on that came from the Iraqis themselves. We wondered why. Usually they are ready to blame the CIA for everything bad, from a measles epidemic to an earthquake. Why would they neglect a real chance of compromising the Agency?'

'There was egg on some very important faces. They'd been so busy netting the little fish - me - that they let the big one get away. Their security brass boobed and there had to be a face-saving cover-up. I didn't enjoy that. They had to pretend that I was a big fish until the fuss had died down and they could throw me back.' I broke off. He had begun to nod understandingly. The man was a trained interrogator and I was chattering. 'What does all this ancient history have to do with Zander?' I asked abruptly.

'The reasons he picked on you to work with him are that you are a respectable journalist and writer and that you also have a private line to the CIA.'

'Nonsense. I have no such thing.'

'You may not like it, Mr Halliday, but the truth is that you have.' He tried without much success to look as if he knew exactly how I felt and fully sympathized. 'You once carried out an assignment for the Agency. Most regrettably that fact is public knowledge. You choose to speak of it as ancient history, but think. Using highly unconventional methods, Zander is able to draw the Agency's attention to you again. As a result, your former case officer has re-established contact with you and now placed you in touch with me under secure conditions. You may dislike him and his employers, with some justification maybe, but I respect them. On Nato's behalf I work closely with the Agency in those areas where our interests coincide. If you think that this re-establishment of old contacts and the making of new

71

has not been anticipated and counted upon by Zander, you underrate him. His methods are, I admit, bizarre, but only when judged by western standards. Prolonged contact with the Arab world often has this effect. Even the most level-headed European businessmen can find themselves acquiring bizarre and convoluted thought habits.'

Pacioli had been fidgeting. Now he broke in sharply. 'You tell us, Herr Schelm, that this man's motive for blackmailing us into this situation is to establish communications with you through the CIA? It makes no sense! What would a gangster of this type want with government agencies such as yours?'

'A sensible question,' Schelm replied, but he kept his eyes on me. 'What do you think, Mr Halliday?'

I had been thinking of Chihani's references to me as an 'experienced' person. Now I knew what she had meant. I shrugged.

'You may be right about his wanting a sort of special messenger,' I said, 'but what messages can he possibly want to send? A man with something to sell to Nato or the CIA – something they could really want to buy I mean – doesn't need special messengers. If it's something worth buying, he'll most likely be a pro who already has contacts. Anyway, Zander's a man used to dealing in billions, according to what I was told. If he has something to sell it must be something quite unusual.'

Schelm nodded. 'It is unusual, for him. And so's the asking price.' He swung around suddenly to face Pacioli.

'Sir,' he said, 'while we were waiting for Mr Halliday to return I suggested that, once you had satisfied yourself that he was safe, you might prefer to leave us. We have, as I am sure you will now understand, confidential matters to discuss.'

Pacioli's face tightened. 'Are you ordering me to go?'

'I am trying to spare your feelings, Sir. You have heard a description of the persons who attacked Mr Halliday here in this room. You said nothing, but your face told me that the description fitted also the persons who were seen to attack your driver and injure him so shamefully. So, you have confirmation that they work for Zander. You would like, naturally, to give this evidence to your police and set them on to Zander. It is my duty to advise you that you would be wasting your time. From what you have also heard in this room you will realize that I am here with the knowledge and permission of Italian colleagues in Nato intelligence. We have at present no intention of disturbing the gentleman in his safe house, even if we could find it. You see, Sir? There is nothing that I shall be saying here that would not distress you.'

Pacioli hesitated, then stood up. He took no more notice of Schelm. To me he said: 'As I was leaving the office my secretary handed me English translations of all the expert opinions on the subject of the Nechayev memoirs that we have received to date. The latest has just come in.' He drew a folded wad of papers from an inside pocket and handed them to me. 'You may find them instructive. Goodnight, Mr Halliday.'

I saw him to the door, helped him on with his coat and said that I would call him in the morning. He was too polite to tell me not to bother.

Schelm was clipping the end of a Petit Corona when I rejoined him. 'A good man, that,' he said, 'a kind-hearted man. In my trade, unfortunately, kindness of heart is not a quality for which there is much demand. It tends to hinder rather than help.' He held the cigar up so that I could see the length of it. 'This won't take long to smoke and I'll try to be gone before it's finished.'

'Would you like a drink?'

'Not if you have to order again from below. Just let me tell you where we stand with Zander.' He paused, to light the cigar, and also probably to decide how best to make what he had to say sound bland and matter-of-fact. Finally, he pointed with the cigar at the papers Pacioli had given me. 'Let's start there,' he said, 'with opinions, expert and not so expert, of the Nechayev memoir. For Zander it served a multiple purpose. It backed up his operational cover story that he was writing a definitive work on the subject of terrorism. It gave Syncom-Sentinel and Mr McGuire something tangible, something that sounded academically interesting, with which to approach you through your agent. And, most important of all, it provided the means of making a long, complex and highly secret proposal to the United States government without going through State Department channels and without compromising the proposer.'

'Then the memoir is definitely both a fake and a forgery?'

'Parts of it are certainly faked. Parts of it are certainly forged. Whether or not the whole thing is faked and forged is another matter. Both paper and inks as well as writing styles are right for the period from which they pretend to come. Pacioli's museum friends and their laboratory findings were definite about that from the start. But that applies also to the parts that are known to be faked. It seems likely that fly-leaves from old books were used as stationery. That's a common trick in these cases apparently. But neither the faking nor the forging was the work of amateurs. The people Zander employed knew their jobs. When you come to the text of the main body of the memoir, well, I found it difficult to arrive at a decision. I think you may too, if you ever get around to reading it.'

'In what way difficult?'

'Well, it's so very boring. That makes it feasible, I suppose. If faked, it's ingenious. At least I thought so, but then I'm not a literary man. You probably know that Dostoevski based a lot of his novel *The Possessed* on Nechayev's life and on the evidence given at his trial for murder. What the faker has done, according to the CIA's expert, is to paraphrase Dostoevski, borrow from the writings of Bakunin and Ogarev and mix it all together with a pseudo-romantic love story. It fooled the first expert, again according to the CIA, because he put too little weight on Dostoevski's known fascination with Nechayev and too much on the fact that there was a period of months during which Bakunin and Nechayev collaborated. In a collaboration, as you know only too well I'm sure, the question of who wrote what can always be debatable. The second expert was more cautious. He didn't say that it was a fake, but he couldn't quite believe in the mixture. So, he called it a contemporary pastiche. Only the CIA expert, the one called in to examine Mr McGuire's photocopy, spotted the anachronism that was the key to the document as a whole. It lies in the six passages written in Fayet shorthand. They constitute the document within a document, the hidden message. They are the bits you couldn't read.'

'They're in some sort of code or cypher?'

'No, they're in Esperanto. That particular shorthand is ideal for rendering Latin phonetics and they're the kind that Esperanto uses. Yes, you can say that Esperanto in an old French shorthand is in effect a code, but it is a code that is very easy to break.'

'Those first two so-called experts didn't break it.'

'Be fair. If you're an expert on nineteenth-century Russian manuscripts under pressure to authenticate what looks like, and really may be, a very interesting find, why should you start thinking about Esperanto? The CIA expert had a different brief. He'd been told to treat the whole document as suspect and look for hidden messages. The first thing he spotted was the anachronism.'

'I'm sorry. I don't get it.'

'Esperanto didn't exist as a language until eighteen-eighty-seven, five years after Nechayev died in prison. So, he wouldn't have known it. So, we take all these shorthand passages, add them together, transcribe them, translate them and we have a long message from Karlis Zander.'

'Saying what?'

'In the copy Zander chose to give you tonight, not very much of interest. From the little Esperanto I've picked up in the last few days, I'd say that your copy's padded out with nursery rhymes. Mr McGuire's copy had Esperanto passages that were totally different. It's more than possible, we think, that his was the only copy with the real message text in it.'

'The real message being what?'

The ash dropped from his cigar and he scooped it away tidily. 'Well, let me see. It begins with what soldiers call an appreciation, that is an analysis of a military situation, and then it goes on to make certain proposals for solving the problems that have been shown to exist.'

'Couldn't you be a little more specific?'

He smiled pleasantly. 'That depends on whether or not you're going to telephone your agent in New York and tell her the deal's off. Before you make up your mind, however, there are one or two things I should point out. Under your existing agreement you were to be paid fifty thousand Syncom dollars for doing a piece of work that was never worth doing. The nature of the work has now completely changed. It has become well worth doing. It would be well worth doing, let me tell you, even if you were being asked to abandon your editorial cover and do it for nothing. I must also tell you that, for reasons that are probably obvious to you by now, you are, for the few days we are asking you to help us, in a key position. *Zander* chose you, we didn't. If *we'd* asked you, you'd have refused. But Zander asked, in his roundabout and dishonest way, and you accepted. Now, you can invoke the forgery clause in your contract, shrug your shoulders and walk away. We hope you won't do that. I'm not begging you to co-operate because I think that would embarrass both of us, but I am most seriously asking you to do so.'

The smile I gave him was polite I think. 'I don't have many finer feelings, Herr Schelm. You can't be appealing to my patriotic instincts. Why shouldn't I walk away?'

He stared at me blankly for a moment, Then he said: 'I see. Fifty thousand dollars and the thanks of people you have been taught by experience to dislike and despise are not enough. Unfortunately we have nothing more to offer.'

'You could try me with a little information. No, I don't mean secret information. Call it job description. For instance, how dangerous could this be? And, if you're claiming that it's not dangerous at all, who's the enemy Chihani's so worried about?'

. He hesitated, wondering how truthful he might have to be, before he answered. 'Very well. I'll tell you about the people who have contracted to kill Zander. They call themselves Mukhabarat Zentrum. As you probably know only too well, *mukhabarat* is the Arabic word for a secret intelligence service. The *zentrum*, I suppose, is a cosmetic addition intended to suggest that this is a legal group with an official headquarters. For the sake of convenience, most European police forces and Interpol bureaux use the code abbreviation Rasmuk and record its activities in their files on organized crime. How would I describe Rasmuk? Well, it is secret, or tries to be, and it is an intelligence service of sorts. In truth, it is an international gang, working only under contract and for big money, in the fields of extortion, intimidation and murder. That code name for it is a reference to its history. When you worked as a newspaper man in the Middle East did you ever hear of a strong-arm organization called Rasd?'

'The Palestinian Mafia, you mean?'

'Originally it was mostly Palestinian, but it wasn't to begin with a Mafia-style thing. Rasd came fresh and raw from the refugee camps. It began as an undercover disciplinary force of zealots set up to track down and punish those who had been sent on missions abroad and then betrayed the cause. Most of these betrayals involved stealing or otherwise misusing funds contributed by the faithful. Some of the traitors were executed. Others were forced to repay more than they had stolen. Then, quite logically, Rasd itself took to fund-raising. Ultimately, it too became corrupt. It bought into nightclubs, gambling casinos and brothels. All in the decadent west, you understand. Soon it was making huge profits and spending them on high living.

Naturally, this was very bad for the Palestinian image and morale. Eventually, the PLO cracked down. Some heads rolled. Rasd was denounced and discredited.'

'But not entirely disbanded, I seem to remember.'

'Not entirely, no. After the purge it ceased to be an accepted Palestinian group and most of the liquid assets were seized by the PLO accountants. However, not all the assets were taken because ownership of some things was effectively concealed. There was real-estate for instance. This remained in the hands of the elite, if I may call them that, of the non-Palestinian dirty-job staff. During the mid-seventies Rasd had managed to recruit undesirables of a dozen nationalities. There were Cypriots, refugee Hungarians, Maltese, Moroccans, Egyptians, a very cosmopolitan collection. One *Paris Match* writer called it " a devil's brew of all the talents". The only thing they now lacked was skilled top management. The new team came to them from my country.'

'Does that trouble you?'

He smiled. 'I should have said *via* my country, not *from* it. The two men in question are Croatians. They came to West Germany some years ago to work. Their permits described them as skilled welders. In truth, they were skilled black-marketeers and smugglers. Where those two came from in Yugoslavia criminals have to be highly skilled or they don't survive. My country must have seemed easy for them at first. When it became less easy they moved south, taking their German women with them. In Rome they found the remains of Rasd waiting to be picked up by men of ability and imagination. They saw the possibilities. Rasd became Mukhabarat Zentrum and started looking for a new class of business.'

'In the Middle East?'

'That's where the market is, *and* the kind of money their services command. They had two changes of name in fact. For a while they called themselves the Democratic Liberation Executive, but they must have soon been told, or realized from prospective customer reactions, that the name sounded too idealistic and unbusinesslike for the market they were in. So, they settled on Mukhabarat Zentrum. We prefer our six-letter codename Rasmuk. To Rasmuk, I will tell you, the contract to kill Zander is worth twenty million Swiss francs.'

'Who's paying?' I asked.

He stubbed his cigar out. 'Unfortunately, Mr Halliday, that we don't know.'

'Even though you know the contract price?'

'That's right. The Italians have managed to penetrate Rasmuk, but not yet as deeply as they would like. These things take time. So, Mr Halliday, I am sorry. *I* can't promise you anything like the joys Zander was hinting at when he sent you that postcard of the Hotel Mansour.'

'I don't think I follow you.'

'I think you do. The Hotel Mansour? That's where the Iraqi security police arrested you, wasn't it?'

'So what is it *you* can't promise me?'

'Iraqi heads on a platter of course. The sweet taste of revenge that Zander talked about in his letter and McGuire was briefed to offer more explicitly when he interviewed you.' He threw me an ugly look as he levered himself up out of his chair. 'I'm not so simple, Mr Halliday, as to suppose that it was the offer of a fifty-thousand-dollar fee that led you to accept Zander's invitation so promptly. You have some old scores to settle. You must have seen in this Zander book a possible opportunity, perhaps the one you'd been waiting for. Iraqi government involvement in world terrorist movements and adventures has been notorious for years. If Zander had really meant to start speaking out, giving case histories and naming names, you could have had the time of your life writing in your own personal list of candidates for public damnation. Your meeting with him this evening must have been a disappointment to you.'

'I've been disappointed before.'

'No doubt. For Zander, of course, the consequences may be more serious. He'll have to re-think his retirement plan completely and I don't believe he can do it in the time.'

'Retirement plan?' I thought that his English had finally let him down. 'You mean the deal he's trying to set up?'

He had picked up a bottle with some water still in it and was refilling his glass. An impatient movement of his hand slopped water on the table. He put the bottle down with exaggerated care.

'I said retirement plan, Mr Halliday. I *meant* retirement plan. I am not, however, talking about pensions and cottages in the country. This retirement is from a field of battle on which he has fought successfully for years, and it is very far from being voluntary. Why, suddenly, must he retire? Why, suddenly, is someone willing to pay Rasmuk prices to have him killed? No doubt the answer is that he has been too long in the field, that he has made too many enemies and that they have at last succeeded in combining against him. We can't be sure. All that concerns us is that he has had his day, that he knows it and that he seeks a guarantee of lasting safety for himself and his family of a sort that only the west can give. In return he offers something that we might find of military value to us. Might or might not. The offer itself, if real, is certainly of interest. At any rate, both the offer and the ability of his patron to deliver what is offered must be carefully evaluated.'

'If he's as rich as I'm told he is, I should have thought that he could have bought his own safety.'

He raised his eyebrows. 'In a fortress buried in some South American jungle? He is not a war criminal. Is he any kind of criminal? I would find it hard to say. Is he more a criminal than any other sharp business man or soldier of fortune?'

'The FBI might think so. About the Italian police I wouldn't know.'

He chuckled. 'Oh come now, Mr Halliday, you're not as naïve as that. In your profession you must have met lots of very rich self-made men, as rich as or even richer than Zander. They always tend to regard themselves as a little above the law, wouldn't you say? Zander's no different in that respect. The unusual thing about him is his vulnerability. He's very much the family man I gather. He's had three marriages. His first wife died, the second was killed in the Algerian war. Both had children of whom he is very fond. He also has adopted children. His third wife, with her two children by him, is at present in America, illegally and in hiding according to your old friend. They are in hiding so that they can't be taken as hostages. He has been on the run for five months now, ever since the contract on him was put out to Rasmuk. Do you think that a man like he is could accept such a state of affairs – separation from his wife and young children, being holed up in safe houses, rooms in third-rate hotels with exercise bicycles and sun lamps for company? This proposition, this bargain he has managed to put together from a distance and by manipulating old associates is his way back to freedom and family. Or so he thinks. That's the message he sends with his proposition. You ask about the dangers. For him, the next few days will be critical. To deliver what he has promised he has to show his face and run a few risks. Anyway, that was how he planned it. He assumed, of course, that you would automatically respond favourably to an official request for co-operation.' He shrugged. 'Since you don't feel able to . . .'

I cut him short. 'No, Herr Schelm. You're not having me in floods of tears over the Zander family. What I asked you about was the possible extent of the danger to *me*. What risks are you asking *me* to run?'

He stared, then sat down again and took a sip of water. 'All right,' he said, 'I'll do my best. Rasmuk have only one interest in you. You're here to see the man they're being paid to kill. They've no reason to disbelieve your cover story. You're a professional writer brought here at Pacioli's expense to see Zander about a book he's writing. Obviously, though, they'll try to use you to find him. Miss Chihani's job is to see that they don't succeed. Your only task for us would be to maintain communications between Zander and my people, to act as our liaison man with him and his people for a few critical days, a week at most. Naturally, you would take care to stay clear of any possible line of fire. Miss Chihani seems a very capable person. How did she justify to you her actions here this evening?'

'She wanted me out before enemy surveillance could become one hundred percent effective. Or words to that effect.'

He nodded. 'It might have worked very well for a first meeting if you had been briefed in America as they had hoped and expected. If you had been, of course, Zander would know by now how his proposal had been received and whether all his planning was going to pay off.'

'Whereas now he'll have to wait until tomorrow or the next day.'

He looked at me sharply. 'No jokes please, Mr Halliday.'

'I wasn't joking. If it's not all that dangerous I may as well take the whole fifty thousand.'

'There are going to be no changes of mind?'

'I don't anticipate any, but I'm still curious to know why the CIA don't want to deal direct with Zander.'

'I know that you distrust your old CIA friend but what he told you was quite true. In the Persian Gulf these days they are very sensitive. Even the little potentates have very big egos. If you knew the number of those who would be outraged by the idea of an American government agency even *listening* to what Zander has to propose, you would see why it must be done this way. This way, when the story is leaked or we are seen to be negotiating, the CIA and its masters can place their hands on their hearts and deny all. "Don't forget," they will be able to say, "the southern flank of Nato lies far south on the Tropic of Cancer. If some of our Nato allies choose secretly to conspire with the man known as Karlis Zander, to make secret military and naval preparations suggested by him to help protect their oil supply routes, how were we to stop them?" '

'I see. Is that what Zander has to sell?'

So then he explained what the deal was. After that he told me what our initial reply to the Zander proposal was to be and how he wanted it delivered. If, when that stage was over, we were still in business, arrangements for the high-level meeting that Zander was insisting on could go ahead. If there was anything about the details of those arrangements that I didn't like I should say so in the messages I would be sending.

It was quite late by the time we finished, but as I went with him to the door I remembered something and paused.

'Since you've appointed yourself my new case officer,' I said, 'maybe I'd better know what the old one is saying about me these days.'

He looked puzzled. 'I don't think I quite ...'

'He said it to you in German just as he was leaving. I caught two or three words of it. I'm only curious.'

'Ah yes. I remember.' He pursed his lips and thought hard before he went on. 'The German idiom is very different, you understand, but I'll do my best to translate. He said: "Dieter, don't say I didn't warn you. The son-of-a-bitch hasn't changed a bit." '

SIX

It was exactly noon when Chihani called. She wasted no time on idle courtesies.

'All telephones are insecure, Mr Halliday, especially the one you are using at this moment. Remember that, please. Are you alone in your room?'

'Yes.'

'Have you read the typescript?'

'Yes.'

'*All* of it? Every page?'

'Those parts of it that I couldn't read for myself have now been thoroughly explained to me. Okay?'

'*When* were they explained?'

'Last night when I got back here. Do you want to know who did the explaining?'

'*No*! Offer no information. Just answer my questions and listen carefully. I have only one instruction to add to those you have already been given. You should have your passport and your room key with you. Everything else is as instructed. Do you understand?'

'I guess so.'

She hung up.

Malpensa, the older and least fog-prone of Milan's airports, is forty-five kilometres north of the city along the autostrada to Varese. Taxis, according to the hotel doorman, were in short supply at that time of day. Happily, though, he commanded the allegiance of the driver of a Mercedes limousine. Simply to oblige the doorman, this faithful fellow was ready to postpone his lunch in order to take me wherever I wanted to go.

The fare asked was exorbitant but I only offered a token protest. The Mercedes would be easier on my developing bruises than a compact cab of the kind I had ridden in the night before. Besides, I needed the reassurance of a little comfort. Five hours' drugged sleep and a starch-rich breakfast with lukewarm coffee had restored my ability to think clearly. It had also clarified my recollection of the patient skill with which Schelm had persuaded me into foolishness. Specific misgivings had soon followed.

Schelm's description of the original Rasd gang had been reasonably truthful. He hadn't tried to soft-pedal it or play down the efficiency of the dedicated maniacs who served it, but I happened to know that the organization had never really been as fresh and raw as he seemed to think. I had heard of it first when I was working in the Lebanon and Beirut was still the Paris of the Middle East. Rasd's European base then had just moved to Rome and its assassination squads were beginning to be spoken of with awe as well as respect. Their characteristic way of doing business had been to accept a hit contract and then approach the prospective victim to see if he wanted to pay a bit more than his enemy had offered and so be allowed to keep his life.

The possibility of those bright, experienced Croatians, those clever crooks who had turned Rasd into Rasmuk, deciding to stop selling such profitable labour-saving options seemed remote; as remote as the possibility of Zander's having rejected one if it had been offered to him. The hubris of the rich can, of course, render them absurdly touchy, but for a non-Arab businessman operating at the highest levels in the Persian Gulf there could be no loss of face at all in buying protection for himself and his family. Zander's defensive tactics were far more demeaning. The reason for them could only be that he had had no alternative, that holing up in an Italian safe-house-cum-office had been the only way the man had had left of staying alive and, to a limited extent, in business without compromising his family's hide-out in America.

The price on the Rasmuk contract was also disturbing. When I had been in the Lebanon it had been common knowledge that Rasd had been offered the gold equivalent of twenty million Swiss francs to assassinate Colonel Qaddafi, the Libyan head of state. The Rasd hit teams had turned the job down; not, however, because the price was too low, but because the Colonel himself was one of their most valued clients, a constant user of their various services and a prompt payer too. Times had changed, of course, but, even allowing for inflation, twenty million Swiss was still a big fee for that kind of job; and Zander was no head of state. If that was the agreed price for killing him someone had to be very serious about wanting him dead; serious enough, and powerful enough too, to be able to persuade the top management of Rasmuk that this was one contract that no one was auctioning off to the prospective victim. Who could the someone be?

I didn't believe in Schelm's old-enemy theory and he hadn't sounded all that convinced by it himself. Revenge may be sweet, but only if it carries a reasonable price tag. Besides, if any group of Zander's known ememies – former business rivals or cheated associates presumably – had suddenly clubbed together to put out a multi-million-dollar hit contract on him there would be nothing secret about the names of the club members. Every gossip in the Middle East would have had the story. This was different. This contract had to have a political motive behind it. For instance, the Iraqis' so-called 'Arab Charter' was a specific prohibition of just the kind of defence development programme that Zander was now busy touting on his patron's behalf. My old jailers, the *mukhabarat* in Baghdad, would certainly have been ready to kill him in order to put a stop to it. The hit contract, I maintained, would have gone out the moment the first whisper of what he was up to, of what he had been commissioned to do, had reached their ears.

Schelm had been patient with me but firm. He wished that I could have been right; it would in a way have simplified his task if Zander and I had been sharing a common enemy; but unfortunately I was wrong. In looking for the political motive behind the hit contract I was making sense, but I could stop looking in the direction of Baghdad. Had Iraqi intelligence known what was in the wind, it would not have been Zander they would have gone for but his patron, the personage we had agreed to refer to, respectfully but discreetly, from now on as 'The Ruler'. And the Iraqis would not have gone to the expense of employing Rasmuk. They had their own trained assassination squads always there ready and eager to go to work for the glory of it alone.

That, I had to admit, was true enough. So, who had been ready to pay that twenty million for Zander's head? There was only one possible answer left. You had to start thinking about and looking among The Ruler's princely friends.

The sovereign state now known as the United Arab Emirates is a confederation of seven sheikhdoms lying on and off the southern shores of the Persian Gulf. Before federation they were known as the Trucial States and were British protectorates. In the old days, before the oil was found, the richest of them, then

Dubai, made its money mostly by smuggling gold to India for foreign traders. Now, since the oil, all that has changed. Even the small local populations of desert nomads, fishermen and oases farmers, who used to live at a bare subsistence level, now have, on paper anyway, higher per capita incomes than West Germans or New Yorkers. They have a great many other things now, too, including some that nit-picking outsiders insist they neither need nor want – four international airports and fifty banks, a satellite communications system and a European pro-soccer manager, skyscraper office buildings and vast sports arenas, an aluminium smelting plant and a great many of the worst, as well as the most expensive, modern hotels in the world. The confederation has other claims to distinction. It may be the only Arab country to have its own chapter of Alcoholics Anonymous, and among its many thousands of self-employed foreign residents are some of the wealthiest and most brazen crooks to be found anywhere.

And, of course, it has its seven princely Rulers.

Some of them are educated men who try to use their yearly billions wisely and for the benefit of their subjects. They build roads and have plans drawn for medical clinics. But things are not easy for them. Their forefathers were pirates and their own fathers often secured the titles they now bear by murdering relatives and close friends as well as envious and ambitious neighbours. Such patterns of behaviour tend to persist, in thought if not always in deed, and the ability to write classical Arabic, read the *Wall Street Journal* and use a pocket calculator modifies them only slightly. If the murder of a fellow Ruler in order to express disapproval of his political or social goings-on is now thought an unseemly form of response, the murder of his favourite man of affairs instead might well be one of the acceptable alternatives. The employment of a notoriously expensive team of assassins for the job could serve as a delicate brotherly expression of regret for the inconvenience caused.

Trying to spot the Rasmuk tails in Milan's lunch-time traffic proved to be a waste of time, but as soon as we reached the autostrada I picked three of them up immediately. There were two in a car and one on a motorbike. They kept their distance and I saw no signs of any back-up team. There were no tricks. They went through none of the standard old-pro routines, such as passing and then tailing from in front for a while, that are supposed to fool the inexperienced quarry. They just followed, keeping their distance. They didn't mind if I noticed that I was being tailed, but weren't making it easy for me to get to know their faces.

In the west most passenger airports get extra busy on Fridays. Malpensa, which carries long-haul international traffic, can become badly congested. It was so that Friday. Standing by the Malpensa–Milan bus-ticket counter in the main hall was not nearly as easy as Chihani had made it sound. It is one of a small group of counters planted right in the centre of a concourse which is not particularly spacious anyway. I found that if I stood close to the counter the clerk tried, quite rightly, to sell me a ticket for the bus, or I was elbowed away by someone who did want a ticket. When I edged along towards the counter beside it I had to fend off the attentions of a car-rental salesman. If I stood clear of the counter I became an obstruction to be cannoned into or brushed aside by hurrying travellers with glassy eyes and bruising hand luggage on their way to the departure gates.

The tail who had been on the motorbike was the first to follow me inside. I could identify him by his crash helmet. But I knew that one of the men from the car must have come in after him because the crash helmet visor kept turning from me to someone I couldn't see who was on the far side of the check-in lines somewhere under the Air Ticket Purchase sign. I had no way of discovering what he was doing there and not much time to wonder if it mattered. Just as I was dodging, for the second time, a small boy pushing a baggage trolley in circles, I saw Chihani's stubby girl assistant marching briskly towards me from TWA's special check-in area.

She was wearing, of all things, a light straw stetson with a high-curl brim, a denim vest and a red-gingham shirt over jeans. A tooled-leather bag completed the ensemble. She looked like an overweight child dressed up for a school play. As she passed me and I turned to follow she issued sharp sotto voce orders out of the corner of her mouth nearest to me.

'Oo-it me,' she said. 'Queek, queek. Oo-it me. Come.'

For several confused moments I thought that she was telling me to hit her. That was how it sounded. Luckily, she supplemented her verbal orders with gestures so I was able to get the right message. 'Oo-it' meant 'with'. She was telling me to walk with and beside her and not to waste time gawping.

'Queek, queek,' she said again.

She herself was practically running by then. I glanced back and saw the crash helmet starting after me. He did not get far. An empty invalid chair propelled by the armlock boy wearing an Alitalia cap and shoulder-boards took him in the back of the legs and sent him sprawling. I saw no more of him. My companion was still squeaking 'Queek, queek' but with a new note of urgency in her voice. I looked down and realized that she had been trying to thrust a boarding card into my hand. We were approaching what a sign said in English was International Departures Gates 1-10 as well as passport control and there was a notice warning that boarding cards must be produced with passports. I just had time to see that the card she had given me was for a British airline flight before I had to show it with my passport. Then we were through and facing a security check where a one-handbag-per-passenger rule was being strictly enforced.

I had no bag to be searched so all I had to do was walk through the body-check frame. My escort joined me on the other side after retrieving her bag from the counter.

'Where now?' I asked. 'London?'

'Us be still.'

She was anxiously scanning the passport control channels which could still be seen beyond the security-check area behind us. After a moment or two we saw the boy with the wheelchair appear on the far side. He gave us an unobtrusive little wave and then turned towards a door with the wheelchair symbol on it alongside some lavatories.

'He has passkey. Us go. You follow. Queek.'

She was away again, whipping off her cowboy hat as she went. Facing us across the departure lounge were the boarding gate doorways. She seemed at first to be heading for the duty-free shop, then suddenly she veered away towards a door with a small glass porthole in it and a sign above saying in four languages that it was for AIRPORT PERSONNEL ONLY. She gave the door a tentative push. It swung open. The boy in the Alitalia outfit was on the other side with his hand on the passkey ready to relock the door behind us the moment we were through.

'Follow,' he said.

We were in a passage, with office doorways on one side and the duty-free shop storerooms on the other. There were background sounds of aircraft noise, an unanswered telephone ringing and the clatter of a teleprinter. At the end of the passage there were two or three steps down. That was the way we went. At the foot of the steps the passkey unlocked another door.

Beyond it we were in the open air. To the left was the steel gantry that carried the overhead walkway to the airport restaurant and also served to house aircraft service vehicles. To the right, away from the main tarmac, was a stretch of asphalt marked out with yellow lines for use as an employees' parking lot. The jets of a plane about to taxi out to the runway began to scream as we walked smartly away between the parked cars.

Our general direction was towards an open gateway in a chain-link fence, but I saw that we were going to have to come right out into the open to reach it. We made an odd trio. It seemed unlikely that, with no crowds around, the boy's Alitalia uniform alone could get us through unchallenged when security people spotted us. But I had done Chihani an injustice. As we were about to leave the shelter of the parked cars, a red Alfasud moved out of one of the parking slots on the far side and then backed up at speed to meet us. She herself was driving.

By the time she reached us she had the passenger door wide open and the two kids quickly scrambled through into the back seats. I got in beside her. As she drove out slowly on to the airport perimeter road she listened to a voluble report from the back. It appeared to satisfy her. She nodded approval, but she wasn't passing up the chance of delivering a homily for my edification.

'You saw the enemy, Mr Halliday? You saw how close they came to you?'

'I saw three of them. That second man who came in after the guy with the crash helmet? What was he trying to do back there?'

She consulted the kids before she replied. 'Almost certainly trying to buy a flight ticket and check in. The moment they saw that you were bound for the airport they must have feared that they were going to lose you. A ticket to stay close to you was their only chance. They think quickly. You see why our security must be so strict?'

'Did you know that passengers have to have boarding cards as well as passports now?'

'Of course. It is a new airport security rule.'

'Were those real boarding cards or do you keep blanks for use on these occasions?'

'With this enemy,' she said sharply, 'you use a new trick only once. Certainly the cards were real. The time of that British flight to Manchester happened to be right for us. There was a Warsaw flight that for time would have been even better but one would have needed Polish visas to get boarding cards for that with any of our passports.'

'Still, Manchester must have cost quite a bit.'

She began to suspect that I was putting her on. 'They were stand-by economy class tickets,' she said crisply. 'Now, please, we shall all smile at the security police in a friendly and untroubled way. Yes, even you, Mr Halliday.'

We were approaching the perimeter-road checkpoint. The striped barrier was down and two uniformed men peered at us intently through their cabin windows. We coasted almost to a standstill, with Chihani smiling winningly and flourishing a piece of official-looking plastic at the men watching her, before the barrier went up and we were allowed through.

I pointed to the plastic. 'Is that genuine too?'

'No, this is a Polaroid copy of a pass we borrowed a few days ago from one of the duty-free shop people. I thought we might have a use for it. We borrowed his key for a little while too. He was cheaper than the economy fare to Manchester.'

Once clear of the airport service road she began to drive fast and away from the autostrada. Soon, we passed an old red-brick factory with the name CAPRONI spelled out in huge letters along its road frontage. A few hundred yards beyond it she turned on to a minor road with dirt shoulders flat enough to park on. She gave a series of orders to the back seat as she ran off the road and stopped.

'Out please, Mr Halliday.'

I obeyed orders smartly. 'What now?'

'Change of plates,' she said and went to unlock the hatchback.

They were well drilled. The boy, who had already discarded his Alitalia props, jacked up the car and went through the motions of changing a wheel for the benefit of passers-by. The girl changed the plates. Chihani covered her while she worked by leaning against the car and studying an opened-out road map. Italian car numbers are prefaced by initials denoting the place of registration. We had been wearing TO for Turin. Now we were switching to GE for Genoa.

'What's the point?' I asked.

'Those people who were trying to follow you are under strict discipline. They will not dare to return with a simple report of failure. They must at least be able to show why and how they failed. And they are not fools. They will already have figured out our exit route. So, they will also have found that the airport security police we passed at the checkpoint record all vehicle movements in and out. For those police it is a very boring routine, and they are not well paid. Do you think they will refuse a man with ten thousand lire in his hand a glance at their time sheet?'

'I guess not.' I thought she was crediting the enemy with faster reaction times than they probably possessed, but refrained from saying so. Her arrangements for losing the tails I had brought from Milan had worked. While I might not be an enemy target, I would, for a few days anyway, be spending time in the target area. I should be praising not carping. 'The two kids did well,' I said. 'The orders you gave them can't have been easy to carry out. They had to use their heads.'

She nodded. 'They were trained by the patron. He trained me too. We think as one. It's all the same with us.'

'By the patron you mean Mr Zander?'

'Of course. You had better know their names. That is Mokhtar tightening the wheel nuts. The girl we call Jasmin.'

'That's not her real name though?'

'Oh, we never use real names.'

'Is that language you speak between you some kind of Arabic?'

'You must know very well that it isn't.' Then she shrugged. 'I don't see why you wish to know but, in fact, it is a Berber language.'

Five minutes later we were on the move again.

At first we headed for a place named Busto Arsizio. Then we turned towards the A8 autostrada and took a northbound on-ramp. A sign said that we were bound for Sesto C and Arona.

'It is along here,' she said, 'that they would pick us up if we still had the Torino plates. All they would need would be two men with their eyes open and a little luck.'

I didn't argue. 'Where are we going? Whereabouts is the safe house?'

I asked expecting another need-to-know lecture. To my surprise she gave me an answer. 'Stresa on Lago Maggiore.'

'Who picked that?'

'It was a collective choice. Communications are very good. We are near an international airport. The Swiss and French frontiers are both within easy driving distance. There are even fast trains if you want them. It is a prosperous petit-bourgeois little town. What appealed to the patron, though, was that it made him laugh. The very name.'

'Sorry. I don't get it. The joke, I mean.'

'Stresa was where two of the most absurd international conferences of the nineteen-thirties took place. In 'thirty-two, fifteen great nations met to agree on economic collaboration for all Europe. And they left thinking that they really *had* agreed. Then, in 'thirty-five, France, Great Britain and Italy – calling themselves The Big Three if you please – met to co-operate in preventing the Nazis' re-armament of Germany. He thinks that, with Mussolini presiding, that must have been the most absurd conference of all. I don't know. I wasn't born.'

'Zander was only a teenager himself. His family was probably pro-Nazi at the time. Does he still find international conferences a joke?'

'He thinks the world would do better with secret diplomacy.'

'Lots of professional diplomatists have the same idea.'

'You think it's wrong?'

'No. I just don't think that secrets of any kind have much chance of being kept any more. Not for long anyway. You're the security expert. What do you say?'

'Some secrets can be kept for long enough.' Her lips tightened. 'They *must* be.'

'I guess so. What's Stresa like these days?'

'Oh, it's picturesque.' She didn't sound as if she cared though. Her mind was still on secrets.

Sesto C, which turned out to be Sesto Calende, was not at all picturesque. The same went for Arona. However, I managed to identify the 'corduroy road' of the night before. It was an obsolete box-girder bridge over a creek near Arona. The bumps were either clumsy expansion joints or, more probably, steel humps put down purposely to make the traffic cross very slowly.

Soon, on our right, I began to see Lake Maggiore as strips of blue between the high walls of the massive old villas which line the lake shore. When we reached Belgirate, Chihani took the CB radio from the glove box and passed it over her shoulder to Mokhtar. He went through the reporting-in routine for her. The only difference from the night before that I could make out was in the answering voice the other end, a man's this time instead of a woman's.

Stresa looks a bit like Cannes before the days of high-rise developers and show-biz festivals. Although it has suffered one or two architectural misfortunes, including a convention centre, and the Corso Umberto Primo now serves as a parking lot for far too many package-tour buses, the prevailing style is still *belle époque à l'italienne*. The souvenir shops are still behind and away from the florid grand hotels that overlook the lake and its enchanted islands. Just before we made the left turn on to cobbles I caught a last glimpse of Isola Bella. Then, we were in what seemed to be an oldish and not very desirable residential section. Buildings were being demolished. Just short of the railroad tracks we turned into a street which had in it a plumber, an upholsterer and a TV repairman occupying what had once been shops, a cabinet-maker who stacked his lumber in what had once been a garden and an automobile spare-parts stockist in what had once been a livery stable.

It was a dead-end street. Set behind tall railings at the end stood a glum old building still showing the outlines on its stucco façade of the ornate letters that had once been fastened to it. ALBERGO DORIA, said these rust-stained ghosts, *senza ristorante*. We were back at the safe house.

There were a pair of gates in the railings. As we bumped up over the sidewalk and into the courtyard, I saw that, fixed to a hardwood panel on one of the gates, there was an engraved brushed-bronze plate. It declared solemnly that this was now the Pax Foundation's INTERLINGUA INSTITUTE OF COMMUNICATIONS. It made the rest of the place look even shabbier.

'What's the Pax Foundation?' I asked. 'Does it really exist?'

'Certainly it exists. It was registered as a non-profit organization in the State of Delaware eight years ago. It supports the Institute and grants annual scholarships to foreign-language teachers from the developing countries, especially North Africa. The founder believes that the teaching of modern languages, in particular those of the west, is of the first importance. Languages first. Science and technology then follow more easily because the books concerned are no longer closed.'

'By the founder you mean Karlis Zander or Dr Luccio, I guess.'

'Why not? The cause of educating the young is very dear to him. He keeps an office here, as you saw.'

'Still, now that it's doing duty as a safe house, I take it the Institute doesn't have any student teachers in residence at the moment.'

'Obviously not. That is another count against the enemy. For the last intake of students we had to make other arrangements. It is a pity that the founder chose Italy. We would have been more secure in Switzerland.'

'But also more closely supervised. Right? How can you be sure that the enemy won't connect the founder with the Foundation?'

We had climbed out of the car. She tossed the key to Mokhtar and thought before she answered.

'How could they? The founder's name in the legal records is none of those that you or they have heard. Here our status as a foreign charity is long-established.' She had begun quoting from the book again. 'Our visitors, both students and others, have always been very quiet and well behaved. We cause no trouble and we give no offence. We buy all our supplies and services from the local people and we pay cash. But we remain private and dull. You looked at the old sign marks on the wall. Yes, we could paint them out. With paint we could make everything outside look much better. We would also attract attention and arouse curiosity. You know, before this became a bad hotel sixty or seventy years ago, it was the weekend villa of a Milan silk merchant. What happened was that the last of the big hotels put up below spoiled his view of the lake. They say that he died of a broken heart. We don't want old stories like that revived because we make it look like a villa again. Better that it stays looking like the bad hotel that nobody wanted at the end of an uninteresting little street.'

As she led the way in I had a sudden suspicion about that book from which she kept on quoting. She was writing it herself.

The fat girl with the blue glasses was not on duty. At the reception desk this time was a more imposing figure. He was handsome, stern-looking and fiftyish. With his dark grey suit he wore an immaculate white shirt and a pearl-grey silk tie. He glanced carelessly at me and gave Chihani a curt nod.

'You've taken your time,' he said in French. 'He has been asking why you were not here. Lunch has been kept back. What happened? Did you have problems?'

'No problems, Jean-Pierre. Mr Halliday had to hire a car and chauffeur. He was twenty minutes late. It is Friday remember.'

Jean-Pierre turned his attention to me. 'Are you carrying any kind of arm or weapon?' he asked. His English was good but careful.

'No,' I said. 'Would you like to search me?'

He had a petulant upper lip. It twitched impatiently. 'I ask only to save us both from embarrassment, Mr Halliday. We have metal detectors in the penthouse entrance hall. Now, you brought your hotel room key with you I think. May I, please, have it?'

I handed it over. He passed it to Chihani, dismissed her with a casual wave and then came out from behind the desk. 'Come this way, Mr Halliday, please.'

He behaved, and indeed looked, rather like the martinet manager of a very grand hotel who has taken personal charge of the arrival of a distinguished guest. The only thing immediately wrong with that picture became visible when he lifted the hinged section of the desk counter to come through. On the shelf just below the counter was a sawn-off pump gun and an open box of 20-gauge ammunition.

I had been ready for the stairs again, but he ushered me instead through a curtained archway on the far side of the small lobby. In its hotel days the room beyond must have been a lounge or writing room. It still had the flowered wallpaper. Now, it was furnished as a classroom with twelve or fourteen desks, a blackboard on an easel and a record player with twin speakers. An opening behind the blackboard led to a short corridor. At the end was what looked like the door to a small closet.

He unlocked the door with a serious-looking modern key and swung it open. Inside there was a wrought-iron gate and an elevator of a kind I had believed long extinct, even in Europe. It was shaped like a birdcage with room for two slim persons one of whom had to operate a large control lever. He opened the gate and motioned me inside.

I looked at him doubtfully and was favoured with a chilly

smile. 'It was installed before the house was a hotel,' he said. 'At least, that is what I am told. It is said that the owner suffered a cardiac crisis. The hotel used it for breakfast service to the rooms. We have had it checked. The engineers were surprised and proud to find it safe.'

I stepped in. The floor dropped with a thud. It wasn't a big drop but it was startling.

'That is normal,' Jean-Pierre said, 'a safety device.'

He joined me, closed and locked the outer door, shut the gate and operated the lever. We rose shakily, passed two steel-faced shaft doors and stopped at a third. It had a wide-angle peephole, two locks and a bell-push that could be reached through the elevator gate if you knew how.

It was the family man himself who unlocked the steel door to admit us.

SEVEN

THE first surprise was his appearance. Gone was the terry-cloth robe. Today he had decided to dress up.

He was wearing a dark-blue silk shirt, well open at the neck to show the gold chain with louis d'or medallion, white gabardine slacks with plaited patent leather belt to match and black crocodile loafers. The buckles on the loafers were just small enough to suggest that the metal they were made of might really be gold. He looked like an aging playboy who has just spent a small fortune on the Via Condotti or is all set to make a large one in a Beverly Hills boutique.

The second oddity was the decor. Number 17 below, the office and gym, had been good-quality functional. On the top floor a different kind of designer had been at work; the kind who designs interiors for such things as caravans and tries to make them appear to be what they are not. What the designer had tried to make Zander's 'penthouse' look like was a mountain chalet.

As a way of turning a clutter of small rooms under a low mansard roof into one apartment the idea had probably sounded good, especially to a man who needed a bolt-hole in a hurry and for a longish stay. No walls would have to be demolished or replastered. Most of the new interior could be prefabricated from ply-backed panelling and standard 'built-ins' and then installed without fuss or exterior mess in a few days. Stock items, from the plastic floor-tiles to the false roof-beams, would be used throughout. The sketches for it might even have conveyed an impression of cosiness. The thing itself had all the charm, and something of the smell, of a cheap furniture showroom. Zander's expensive finery was almost absurdly out of place there. He seemed to know it and the eyes above the simper warned that comment would not be welcomed.

His attempt at brisk amiability did not quite come off. 'Today,' he said as he raised his hands in greeting, 'we don't have to talk about an old book of memoirs, eh my friend?'

'So I understand. Was it all faked or was part of it real?'

'Perhaps, when we get to know each other better, I will tell you. Well now, come in both of you.' He led the way through a doorframe that had obviously been put there to conceal the metal detectors Jean-Pierre had mentioned. Beyond was a bar leading into a dining room.

In the bar he paused. 'Shall we eat before we talk?' he said. 'Guido has worked hard on an ossobuco for us.'

'Whatever you say, Mr Zander.'

'Good.' There was a brass bell on the bar. He tinkled it and then strode through into the dining room. The spray-finished rustic table was laid for three.

'Jean-Pierre is joining us,' Zander explained. 'He is the Pax Foundation's European director and in charge of all our operations here. You may speak freely before him. It's warm up here today, Mr Halliday. Would you like to take your jacket off?'

'I'm okay, thanks.' And I was. He was the one who was feeling the heat. What he wanted was not his lunch. What he wanted was to know what sort of a reply I was bringing him without having to ask me for it. There was a smell of food coming from his private kitchen now. I began to feel hungry. 'There's one thing,' I said. 'I didn't get Monsieur Jean-Pierre's full name. If he's in charge of your operations here I think that fact should be included in the initial telex I shall be asking you to send for me later.'

Jean-Pierre had been opening the wine at a waxed-pine side table. He swung around instantly.

'My name,' he said, 'is Jean-Pierre Vielle, but it would be most mistaken to involve the names of the Foundation and its European director in negotiations of this character.'

'Yes, yes, of course,' Zander said.

'The name of the Foundation stands for peace, patron.'

'I am aware of it, Jean-Pierre.' Zander was sounding a little testy. 'But we shall discuss all these questions later, no doubt. Now, please, let us sit down and eat. You, here on my right, Mr Halliday.'

The food was served by the girl with the blue-tinted glasses and Guido the cook, an intense-looking young man who perspired a great deal and muttered to himself incomprehensibly as he fussed over us. Neither of them was a skilled waiter and both were clearly scared of making mistakes, but they managed. The food was good, the wine drinkable. No coffee was served. When the plates had been cleared, Zander told Vielle to open a second bottle of wine and put it where we could help ourselves. Then he sat back with his hands raised, scrubbed-up and ready to make the first incision.

'Well, Mr Halliday,' he said, 'I presume that if the reply to the set of proposals I have made had been negative in character you would not be here. No?'

'I guess not.'

'So, it would be interesting to hear from you now the terms of the acceptance. However, before we get to that, I need the answer to a question of critical importance. With whom am I dealing? Until I know that there is no point in your saying anything. Agreed?'

Schelm had warned me about Zander's negotiating techniques. In the Gulf, apparently, they were regarded as brutal and lacking in finesse. They were also greatly feared. In the west they had more often, though not always, caused amusement. They were predictable. He always began by seizing the initiative, whether he was in a real position to do so or not, and assailing his opponents with bluster and meaningless rhetorical questions. The way to counter this was to ignore the questions and stick firmly to your own script. Zander would then appear to become entirely understanding and reasonable. That was when you really had to start watching out.

So, I began by sticking to Schelm's script. I even took out a page of notes I had made – Schelm had called it an *aide-mémoire* – to make sure that I got it right.

I said: 'The terms of the reply I am instructed to make to you, Mr Zander, is not exactly an acceptance.'

'If it's not an acceptance,' he snapped, 'why are we wasting time?'

'Mr Zander, the reply I am instructed to give is as follows. I quote. "We are sufficiently interested in the proposals you outline in your confidential memorandum to discuss them further, providing that certain questions that arise can be answered satisfactorily." Unquote.'

The arms dropped and the eyes chilled. 'If that is not a total and complete rejection it is dangerously close to it,' he said carefully, then suddenly his voice rose. 'Let us stop this nonsense, eh? Eh? Let us *stop* it. Who is the fool who writes this pompous rubbish? Who am I dealing with? Speak. Who have the CIA put up to front for them on this operation? Don't you *know*?'

'The CIA are not involved, Mr Zander.' I went back to the script. 'I am liaising between you and Nato's Combined Intelligence Services Bureau. They are not fronting for anyone except themselves. You may choose to recall, though, that the USA is a member of Nato.'

Vielle gave a sarcastic little laugh. '*Tiens*! Such secrets! We are privileged.'

Zander silenced him with a glance. 'At what level, Mr Halliday, am I supposed to be communicating with Nato Combined Intelligence Services? The cleaning woman? The office boy? Do you know?'

'Initially this liaison is with the Director of Combined Intelligence. If the proposed preliminary meeting with The Ruler takes place the Nato representative will be the Military Deputy to the Commander Nato Strike Force South. The Commander is an admiral. His Military Deputy is a lieutenant-general.'

'Would he be given decision-making powers?'

The way they both seemed to be watching the movements of my throat now instead of just listening was making me feel quite uncomfortable. The time had come to obey the other set of orders I had been given, the one that permitted me to use my own judgement about the degree of politeness with which I made certain crucial points, but enjoined me to make them firmly, clearly and early on in the proceedings even if I had to shout to make myself heard. I poured myself a little wine to give me time for a quick re-cap and then sat back in my chair with a small but plainly exasperated sigh.

'Before we start talking about decision-making, Mr Zander, in fact before we even get to the point of negotiating what might eventually call for decision-making on a subject of such delicacy, Nato will want straight answers to some very important questions. They will want the air cleared, Mr Zander.'

Vielle jumped in again. 'Have you been given plenipotentiary powers?' he asked.

'No, of course I haven't.'

'Then the messenger is merely giving his own opinions of what his masters are thinking.'

'My opinions don't come into it.' I turned to Zander. 'I've been told to give you verbal replies to your written proposals. Do you want to hear the replies or don't you?'

The eyes were glittering angrily but he shrugged. 'Low level exchanges on matters of high importance are usually a waste of time. However, if you have been told to deliver messages you had better let us hear them.'

'Right. Now, to begin with, it is noted that your principal in this – The Ruler as we have agreed to call him – wishes to enter into a defence pact of a special kind with the west, if not with the United States directly then with one or more of America's allies. Specifically, he is offering to let this ally put a military and naval base on territory under his personal, princely control. This territory is adjacent to the Strait of Hormuz and is known as Abra Bay. The work of building such a base would, of course, be observed both by Soviet surveillance satellite and by Soviet reconnaissance flights from their air bases in South Yemen. According to you, The Ruler believes that, in the early stages of the project at any rate, the real nature of it could be concealed by a cover plan involving the construction of container-ship docking facilities in Abra Bay and extensive warehousing facilities to service them on Abra Point. Right so far?'

'A desalination plant would also have to be built.'

'That's understood. What has to be clearly defined is the area of agreement. The Ruler considers that such a base, operating under air cover from the reactivated RAF base on the Omani island of Al Masirah, would do much to offset the recent Soviet build-up in Ethiopia, Socotra and South Yemen. I am to say that The Ruler's opinion is shared and that the Nato planners concerned are ready to respond to The Ruler's suggestion in the friendliest and most affirmative way. The request for a prompt and decisive response is also well understood.'

Zander was staring critically at the cuticle of his right forefinger. 'At least they are not complete fools.'

'They're not fools of any kind, Mr Zander. As I said, they want clarification on some points. And, before we go any further, they have certain reservations to make.'

'About the cover and deception measures, no doubt. What don't they like?'

'The measures wouldn't work and even if they could be made to work they would be undesirable. In the Gulf strength should be displayed not concealed.'

The eyes smiled a little. 'I agree. I told The Ruler that they wouldn't like his cover plan. It's a minor point. What else don't they like?'

'When I mentioned reservations, Mr Zander, I wasn't referring to minor points.'

'What major reservations can they have? Reservations about what?'

'For one thing, about *your* acting for The Ruler in the matter.'

The eyes went blank. 'I do so at his personal request.'

'That is understood. You have acted for The Ruler on many occasions, in business transactions. The difficulty here is, as you must realize, that any serious discussion of the granting of military base facilities at Abra Bay, or anywhere else in the United Arab Emirates, would normally be conducted in the first place through diplomatic channels involving the UAE's Foreign and Defence ministries and then between heads of state and governments. There are six other Rulers in the UAE. What would be their view of a deal of this importance done unilaterally and behind their backs?'

'They will welcome it.'

'When the west came looking for bases in the Gulf a couple of years ago Abra Bay wasn't on offer. Nowhere in the Gulf was on offer.'

'The Gulf peoples wished to remain aloof from the super-power confrontations. They wished to be what your press calls non-aligned.'

'What's happened to change their minds?'

Vielle snorted his share of their joint exasperation but Zander only raised his hands and glared. 'You can ask me that?' he demanded. 'With Soviet encirclement of the Gulf now complete? With their missile ships covering the sea lanes? With Cuban and East German assault troops deployed in the Yemen? You don't call these things reason enough for minds to be changed?'

'No, Mr Zander, I don't. There's nothing new about them. These build-ups you're talking about began years ago when there was a Shah in Iran and before Afghanistan became a Russian colony. The fact that some of the pro-Soviet ground troops and technicians in the area are now Cuban and East German is something of a change, maybe, but it's a change without much of a difference. Cubans and East Germans tend to get on better with the local people than the Russians do, that's all.'

'You are deluding yourself, Mr Halliday, or you have allowed others to delude you. Are you not aware that new chemical and biological weapons have been introduced into the area? Would you not call that a very considerable change?'

'I might. How considerable would depend on how long their presence has been known. And how new is new? New to whom?'

'New to The Ruler and deeply offensive to him.'

'So, it's *his* mind that's changed. But how about the minds of his six colleagues? You say that they'll welcome the Abra Bay deal. In that case, why is he acting independently? You see the reason for our concern I'm sure. We in the west now buy more oil from the UAE than we bought from Iran, even when it was in full production. Our relationship with the UAE is a highly sensitive and important one. So, we ask again. Why, in this very serious matter of Abra Bay, must we negotiate in the way you propose? First, you answer, because Abra Bay lies in The Ruler's traditional family territories and so he has been deputed to act for all. That we can understand. But why, if he is acting for all, must we meet to confer with him in the hole-and-corner way you specify in your proposals? What is there to be said or discussed in this Austrian house of his that couldn't be more comfortably and securely said in one of the UAE embassies or at some agreed conference site on neutral ground?'

He rolled his eyes at Vielle. 'And your all-wise, all-knowing Nato masters no doubt wonder also why The Ruler calls upon me, a man with a price on his head, to act for him in a matter of such delicacy.'

'Yes, they do wonder a bit about that. Of course, you've acted for him a great many times before on matters of business. But why, they wonder, does Zander take this on? If a base at Abra Bay is to be built, the contracts wouldn't be of the kind he is used to handling. They would be no-nonsense cost-plus defence contracts. So, "What's in it for Zander?" they ask.'

He looked astounded. 'They ignore the request I make in section five of the presentation?'

'They feel that it must be incomplete. You ask for United States or Canadian nationality.'

'*Plus* the protective documentation and assistance normally given a Soviet defector to the west following debriefing. Don't forget that.'

'A man of his wealth? Can he be serious? That is all he asks? To get Rasmuk off his back? These are their questions, Mr Zander.'

'Then they know nothing about Mukhabarat Zentrum and I am dealing with fools,' he snapped.

I said nothing and waited. After a moment or two he took a sip of wine and then massaged the back of his neck. The eyes calmed down. He said: 'The Ruler understands very well my desire for peace and tranquillity. It is a desire he shares. You ask, "Why Austria?" Do you know Judenburg in Styria and the hills just north of it?'

'I've driven through there, I guess, on the Klagenfurt road. I can't say that I recall it as one of the beauty spots of Austria.'

'In the Middle Ages there were silver mines worked for over two centuries in that region. The house that The Ruler has bought stands over the main entrance to one of those old mines. It was built in the last century by an Austrian doctor who was also an amateur archeologist. He spent many years of his life exploring the mine-workings below the house and made a little private museum of the artefacts and relics that he had found. He died in nineteen-fourteen. A grandson who inherited the house and land allowed it to decay. The land was useless for farming. For safety reasons the mine entrance was sealed. Then, twenty years ago, an important discovery was made at another old silver mine not far away at Oberzeiring. The air in those mines there is very pure and free from pollens. At Oberzeiring they began using the mine for the treatment of certain kinds of asthma, bronchitis and sinusitis. The patients go to the clinic above the mine and then descend for a certain time each day for treatment. The Ruler himself suffers from sinusitis. At Oberzeiring he found a treatment that worked. He looked at this other mine with the house above it. The owner was only too glad to sell to someone with the capital needed to re-open the mine and make all safe. In place of the old house The Ruler means to build a modern clinic where people from the Gulf may go and be given treatment free of charge.' He paused thoughtfully and then added: 'Of course, The Ruler has a number of anxieties and problems. Sinusitis is only one of them.'

'Yes. I was told to ask about The Ruler's anxieties. Are they taking any particular form at present?'

'As I told you, the introduction of chemical warfare weapons into the Gulf has been a source of great concern to him. But let me deal once and for all with your side's reservations about the protocol for this conference.' He raised his hands and examined them as if to check that they were perfectly clean. 'There is,' he went on finally, 'a truth that you must grasp and hold on to. It is this – that you in the west, with very few exceptions, always fail to understand the Arab mind. That is why your business men need persons like me to interpret for them. To interpret not merely words, but attitudes and states of mind. The English I speak is different from yours. You'll have noticed that.'

'Yes. You speak British English, Mr Zander, with some other sort of accent in there, but essentially British English.'

'I learned it from a British officer with whom I worked many years ago in Jordan. He was a good soldier, as I also was then, very good at training men for war, for the battlefield that is, not the barracks. But he was also a scholar, an Arabist. He taught me about the desert Arab, and he taught me about men like The Ruler. I didn't need teaching about your kind. I had already learned all I needed to know about the west. He taught me the Arab mind. You have probably been told that The Ruler is a crazy man. Am I right?'

'I was told that he can sometimes be eccentric and that he worries a great deal about his health, particularly about the consequences of getting old.'

'His neurotic fears of impotence? Did they have a laugh behind their hands about those? Did they tell you about his strange adventures at La Clinique de la Prairie in Switzerland?'

'No. They didn't mention that he suffered from sinusitis either.'

All quite true. What Schelm *had* said was that The Ruler had been diagnosed as a paranoid schizophrenic, but was unlikely to become as dangerous a case as his father had been. The old Sheikh had achieved a certain notoriety in the Gulf, and deeply embarrassed his British protectors, by killing a most respectable and very important Egyptian business man. The unfortunate Egyptian had been wearing a Brooks Bros suit instead of the white *dishdasha* robe when he was presented to the Sheikh at an audience. It had been the Sheikh's belief that only Englishmen wore suits. His suspicions were aroused, understandably perhaps when it is recalled that as a child he had seen four senior members of his family assassinated during public audiences. Anyway, what happened was that, when the Egyptian had reached into his jacket pocket for a letter of introduction he had brought with him from Cairo, the Sheikh had immediately pulled a gun and fired. He had been an excellent shot and the British army Smith and Wesson revolver he had used had left the Egyptian's head unrecognizable. The Sheikh's son, The Ruler, was less trigger-happy but given to strange fancies and certain habits that in some western capitals had led to trouble with the police.

'He has great personal pride,' Zander said, 'as they all have. They are dignified and very sensitive men. The Ruler is not one of those with great mineral wealth on his personal territory. He shares, of course, in the collective wealth of the Confederation, but his personal spending power is not in the billions. This is understood by his brother Rulers. So what do they do? Among those people for whom dignity is more precious than life there can be only one answer. They express their fraternal understanding in a practical way. The Abra Bay project will be of benefit to all. It will provide a defence umbrella for the Confederation under a unified command that they badly need. They have now come to realize the truth of this. The balance of superpower in the Gulf must be adjusted in the west's favour and to the Gulf's lasting advantage. Your Nato experts know this as well as I do. And yet they raise these petty questions of protocol. Fraternal understanding, that is the answer to them. Why should his brothers deny The Ruler the privilege – his by *inherited right*, I must remind you – of negotiating the future of Abra Bay? Eh? Well, they are generous and they are wise. They do not deny him. He goes with their blessings, and with God's.'

'How about Saudi Arabia's blessing? Does he have that too?' I asked.

That had been one of the questions Schelm had most wanted answered. The Ruler, he had argued, must have had at least tacit UAE approval of the Abra Bay proposition. 'Without it,' he had said, 'not even this irresponsible wild man would have dared make such an approach. Why have they let him loose? It can only be because they fear that when the Saudis hear about it they will object. They may not like the idea of a foreign base at Abra Bay. If they don't, then they'll pressure the Americans into killing it. Letting The Ruler do the preliminary talking may be a face-saving device. If all goes well, the UAE will give it the nod and take over. If the Saudis don't like it and say so very strongly, there will only be The Ruler to look foolish. If we knew whether or not the Saudis had been consulted, it would help us to decide how to handle The Ruler if the price he's going to ask is too wildly extravagant. Please, Mr Halliday, try to find out for us.'

So, I had tried. I had asked.

Zander's reply was to stand abruptly and fill his lungs as if the effort of sharing the atmosphere with a person capable of asking so grossly impertinent a question had suddenly become too much for him. 'Jean-Pierre,' he said, 'will you take the wine into the living room, please? We must see if we can persuade our friend here to recall his own words. He wasn't going to ask questions, was he?'

'No, patron. He was going to give a verbal reply to our written proposals.'

'Exactly. He had a message to deliver. This way, Mr Halliday.'

He led the way into a room with a large tiled chimney-piece, rustic chairs with blue-rep seat cushions, a lot of bilious-looking wood panelling and wrought-iron standard lamps with parchment shades.

The two of them went on with their cross-talk act as if I were no longer there. I sat down in one of the nastier chairs.

'He did not claim that he had been given plenipotentiary powers,' said Vielle.

'Not directly, no. We must give him that.'

'On the other hand . . .'

'Very true,' said Vielle. 'On the other hand he *has* been a professional journalist.'

'And so has the old-pro journalist's habit of assuming, or pretending to assume, that *his* request for information is always the lesser mortal's command,' Zander said slowly and solemnly; 'to be obeyed *like that*!' And he snapped his fingers quite loudly.

There was a pause. They seemed now to be expecting me to rejoin the conversation. I let them wait a bit longer and then said: 'What a really ugly room this is.'

Only Vielle looked surprised. Zander's eyes smiled slightly and he nodded. 'I use it as little as possible,' he said. 'I regret to have to tell you, also, that your bedroom has something of the same style. The designers' salesman called it folklorique. However, there are compensations. Up here on this floor, everything mechanical works properly, including the plumbing. Your clothes and other things will arrive from Milan shortly. We shall do our best to make you comfortable.'

'Who's taking care of the hotel bill?'

'The hotel will charge Pacioli. That was the arrangement.'

'So, I can begin drafting the telex you're going to send for me. Right?'

'I expect you would like to go down to the office to do that.'

'No hurry, Mr Zander. They'll be standing by from five o'clock. It's only four. I'd like to go back for a moment to those wise, generous brethren of The Ruler's and the mission they've entrusted to him. He goes with their blessings, and God's, you say to shape the future of Abra Bay. Okay. But I still don't understand why he has to go to an old Austrian silver mine in order to meet Nato representatives – if we get that far. Are his sinuses giving him trouble? I mean what's the thinking on it?'

'He goes there because it is his property,' he said firmly, 'and because it is a logical place for him to go. He has been to Austria a number of times during the warmer weather to consult with the engineers restoring the mine to safety and the architect planning the clinic. This next meeting was arranged a month ago. Of even greater importance, we here may think, is the fact that the mine and the clinic project enable us to satisfy our own stringent security needs. We have a secure means of making the journey there. Your principals can attend the meeting incognito without risk. I suggest they have papers saying that they are foreign medical men. You asked for neutral ground. What could be more neutral than Austria? Further, it is entirely suitable for the television interview cover story that you will be providing.'

I made a stop sign. 'If we may hold it right there for a moment, Mr Zander. I need some clarification. The story is that I'm interviewing The Ruler for American television about his wonderful new treatment centre and clinic. The reality is that we rent the transportation and name of a regular TV location unit and use that to get us all safely to and from the rendezvous. I've got it right, yes?'

'Exactly. We use the apparatus of a conventional news-gathering operation as our cover.'

'Where will this outfit be coming from?'

'France. But don't worry. Simone has checked thoroughly. All these European mobile TV units are virtually the same. In the small truck or van which carries the equipment there are two technicians, one for the camera and one for the sound, plus a helper who is usually the driver also. In the accompanying car is the director, a production assistant and possibly a writer or interviewer if this is not the director himself. Some of these units belong to networks or TV production companies but many are freelance. They are all members of a new and highly privileged class. They go very much where they please, back and forth across frontiers, and often into places and zones where ordinary persons would be stopped. Their medium protects them. As long as you are in a vehicle with the name of a TV station or channel or company on the side, all that a policeman or official wants to know is the name of the programme that is being made so that he can tell his wife. It is excellent cover. Do you not agree?'

'Who'll be riding in the car?' I asked.

'Myself as director, you as the well-known American interviewer and Simone as driver, still photographer and script assistant.'

'Will Jean-Pierre be coming with us?'

'He will be in charge of the equipment truck. Why do you ask?'

'If you're going to try to pass him off as a technician, he'll need a beard and a pair of old jeans.'

Neither of them thought that worthy of comment. There was a silence as Zander poured out the last of the wine. Then he said: 'Have you any constructive observations to make on the plan, Mr Halliday?'

'You could have problems with the local press and radio. The story may not be new, but sending in a television unit to get coverage always creates a bit of excitement. There's another thing. As you say, the on-site interview is a conventional news or current-affairs operation, but supposing Vienna likes the idea of foreign interest in the story enough to want to see the interview and maybe use some of it. How do you say no? It's their country.'

'The interview is in English for use in America.'

'They could still want to see it. Who cares if it's in English? They can always do a voice-over track in German. It would be embarrassing if they found out that you had no interview to show them.'

'We would simply say that the matter had been referred to New York for a decision. As for the local press, The Ruler's own personal entourage will be well accustomed to dismissing them.'

'I see.' It was clear that he wanted to hear no more on that subject so, for the time being, I let it go. 'Where is this mine of his?' I asked.

'In the hills twenty kilometres from Judenburg. It is a very beautiful part up there. However, we will stay a short drive away at a Gasthaus near St Veit. On the night before the meeting that is. Your negotiators should stay in Velden, as advised in my plan. There are plenty of tourist rooms to be had there and among tourists they should not be noticed. You can report to them there from the Gasthaus if they want to see you personally. At present all we have to do is to confirm the date and the time of the rendezvous. That had best be a little before their audience with The Ruler. I propose Tuesday morning next at eleven.'

And we could take it or leave it. I said: 'Yes, Mr Zander.'

Drafting the telex message I would send to Schelm was tricky, and not only because I had to remember the code-words needed to authenticate the message and how they were to be included. On my pocket stratch-pad it came out like this:

LINDWURM FROM BOB. SITUATION AS YOU FORECAST. BRIEFING QUERIES ASKED BUT NONE UNEQUIVOCALLY ANSWERED. ONLY FRANK EXCHANGES POSSIBLE BETWEEN PRINCIPALS. SILVER PRICE UNCHANGED. RENDEZVOUS PROPOSED FOR 11.00 HRS AT SITE NEXT TUESDAY. OUR PARTY WOULD ARRIVE IN THE AREA MONDAY EVENING IN TIME FOR PERSONAL REPORT TO YOU; IF THIS IS OKAY WITH YOU REQUEST YOUR LINDWURM HOTEL PHONE NUMBER SOONEST. SUGGESTION FOLLOWS. STRONGLY RECOMMEND PROVIDING BACK-UP 16MM AND/ OR VIDEO TAPE UNIT TO SATISFY POSSIBLE GENUINE LOCAL CHANNEL OR NETWORK INTEREST.

I glanced at my watch. It was nearly five. 'No one can read my writing except me,' I said. 'I'll have to type it. I'd like to go down to the office now, if that's okay.'

The elevator only had room for two. Vielle said he would use the stairs. In the elevator, Zander said: 'Are we to be allowed to read the message?'

It was the first really silly thing he had said, and the first hint I had had of the strains he had been managing so well to conceal. I answered as casually and carelessly as I could.

'Oh yes, of course. I can't operate a telex machine anyway. Someone will have to do it for me.'

'Jean-Pierre often works it. Where is the message going to?'

'Ulm in West Germany. I'll put the station number on top.'

When I had typed the message I handed it to him and watched him read. He didn't like any of it much, that was evident, but he objected strongly only to the last sentence and my suggestion that there should be a back-up unit. 'It is absurd and unnecessary,' he protested.

I shrugged. 'You may be right. It can do no harm, though, to see what the other side thinks, can it?'

He hesitated, then nodded and Vielle went to work. We sat and watched him.

In my trade, the private attitudes I have towards clients during our work together often change radically and sometimes suddenly. Respect for a man's honesty can within the space of minutes turn into admiration for the skills with which it is counterfeited. Pomposity may be endured for days before the shyness it conceals is at last plainly seen. Such changes, of course, are quite natural. You may start by accepting the client at his or her own valuation, but that is rarely the way you will end. Likes and dislikes have little to do with it. You are reaching for insights and, although those you gain may not invariably make the job easier, there is always a good chance of your being given a surprise of one sort or another.

Zander was certainly not a client, but some thought-processes can never really be switched off. As we sat there listening to the telex sounds I had a change of mind about him, or at least the beginnings of one. I had begun by fearing him. For someone with my mental scar-tissue that would be understandable. But then, that afternoon, he had puzzled me. Now, ever since that odd question of his in the elevator had, so to speak, lifted the edge of the wrapping, I had been getting an idea of what might be there to find if I could worm my way a little further inside. All I had to do was to ask him the question that I ought to have asked Schelm.

'Mr Zander, how did you find out that Mukhabarat Zentrum had been commissioned to kill you?'

He raised his eyebrows and stared. He was trying to look mildly surprised, but his eyes were giving him away. The question had jolted him and he was playing for time before he answered. 'I thought that you had been fully briefed,' he said after a pause.

'Maybe they skipped that bit.'

'They were probably keeping strictly to the operational brief I gave them. But they must know all about the attempts on me. The first was made six months ago in Paris. Two young punks with a pistol that jammed. I was leaving Jean-Pierre's office with him. I kicked in the ribs of the one carrying the pistol. We tried to make the other one talk, but all we got was the usual story. They'd been offered the money, taken the first half and been given the pistol. They didn't know who it was they'd been working for. We gave them to the police. The second attempt in Rome could have been more serious. The grenade the girl threw exploded all right, but she was too anxious to get rid of it before it burst. I just had time to roll clear and got off with a little damage to an eardrum. This was right outside my Rome hotel rooms. She was lucky to get away. Two weeks later The Ruler sent for me. It was he who gave me the warning from his intelligence sources that Mukhabarat Zentrum had agreed to take over the contract from the incompetents for a huge price. He had also heard that they meant to go for my family as well as me.'

'Did he know who was paying this price?'

'I knew better than to ask. To that kind of question not even The Ruler could get an answer that wasn't a lie.' He gave me a sly, sidelong look. 'Why should it matter to you? Just imagine that it is the Iraqis who are paying – *if* they get results.' He waved the thought away. 'With The Ruler, anyway, I had more important matters to discuss.'

'Abra Bay?'

'That was the most important, yes.'

Vielle turned his head. 'Reply coming, patron.'

We went over to the machine and waited. The reply read:

BOB FROM LINDWURM. YOUR REPORT NUMBER ONE RECEIVED. MEETING DATE TIME AND PLACE APPROVED. PHONE NUMBER MONDAY LINDWURM AREA CODE PLUS 26557. REFERENCE YOUR SUGGESTION AGREE DESIRABILITY GENUINE BACK-UP CREW. COULD NORMAL PERSONNEL OF RENTED EQUIPMENT BE HIRED TO JOIN AT RENDEZVOUS WITHOUT COMPROMISING ESSENTIAL LINDWURM OPERATIONAL OBJECTIVES QUERY. STANDING BY.

Vielle had an objection. 'Lindwurm is the code-name of the operation,' he complained. 'Why do they use it as a telephone number?'

'Lindwurm means dragon,' said Zander, 'and a dragon is the city emblem of Klagenfurt. Velden, where they will be staying, is in the Klagenfurt area. So, they are using Lindwurm there to indicate the telephone prefix Mr Halliday should use. *There* I see nothing wrong with the message.' His eyes glared into mine.

'What I dislike is that they so quickly agree with you about this change of plan. Did you perhaps already discuss it with them at your briefing last night?'

'No. I was only given a general outline of your proposed plan. Now, looking at it close to, I can see a weakness. I think it should be corrected.'

'And I don't agree that the correction is necessary.'

'That's because you don't know how people in the television business think and behave. I don't know much, but I know more than you do. For instance, if you think that a TV news or current affairs producer in Vienna is going to accept, quietly and without argument, your telling him that some person in New York must give permission before he can be allowed to see an interview just shot right there in Austria, you're dreaming. He'll want to know who in New York has the say-so. If you lie, he'll know it in a matter of minutes. If you're evasive it'll be just as bad. Either way he'll believe he's on to something hot. Before you can do anything more about it your cover will be blown and The Ruler very seriously embarrassed.'

'You are overstating, Mr Halliday.' But the eyes were flickering.

'I could be understating. Look, Mr Zander, let's at least consider the other side's proposal. What about this French outfit you're renting all the equipment from? What's the deal with them?'

The eyes searched mine for signs of treachery before he answered. 'We take over the two vehicles and basic equipment on Sunday.'

'Where?'

'They will deliver it to Geneva,' said Vielle.

'Why can't you do a supplementary deal for the technicians? Hire them to go separately by car or train to Klagenfurt. Pick them up and take them to the mine site Tuesday afternoon when the private talks with The Ruler are over or recessed. We set up quickly then and shoot some real footage. Not much. I ask The Ruler a few stupid questions and get some wise, golden answers from him. Finish. Your cover's watertight. You're in the clear. Why not?'

Zander looked at Vielle. 'Your opinion, Jean-Pierre?'

Vielle shook his head. 'It is too late now. The two technicians who matter will not be available. They have taken their share of the front money we paid and gone to Mexico for a vacation. It seemed good that they were uninterested in us and pleased to go. It will be the drivers who deliver to me in Geneva. Only the producer will be with them to take care of the business angle.'

'Then we'll ask the other side to help out,' I said and sat down again at the typewriter.

'What do you intend to say?' Zander asked.

I thought for a moment. 'How about this? "Normal personnel not available. Request you arrange for German, Swiss or Austrian freelance unit film or videotape interview at rendezvous Tuesday afternoon." There's no need to say anything about security. They'll be well aware of the problem by now.'

He nodded, so I typed out the message and Vielle began sending again. Zander sat down at his desk and stared at me across it as if he were trying to formulate a rather tricky question.

'You have impressed me, Mr Halliday,' he said at last.

'Oh?'

'You saw what you considered, because of your special knowledge of television executives' business behaviour, to be a flaw in our planning. You pointed it out. You also argued with some persistence your case for its correction. Why? You have been hired to act as a go-between for a few days, to support a cover story about a television unit making an interview with an Arab who has bought property in Austria. If those who hire you don't know enough to make this cover story work properly, why should you care? It's no skin off your nose.'

'No, that's right. It isn't.'

'Can it be that you wish the operation to succeed?'

'As you yourself say, I've been hired. As Miss Chihani reminded me quite forcibly last night, I'm being well paid to do a very small piece of work.'

The eyes laughed at me. 'That's no answer, Mr Halliday. There's no craft-pride for you in what you are being asked to do for us. No! All the same, I begin to think that you are wishing us to succeed, and not just to defeat old enemies who still trouble your sleep.'

'No?'

'No. Otherwise you'd have talked about them to me, asked about names that I might know and who hated me in Baghdad. Instead, you think of ways of improving our chances in Austria.'

He sighed deeply and then held up his hands for a good look at them. 'I don't know why,' he went on slowly, 'but I think you are *with* us. Is that possible, Mr Halliday? Is it possible that you are truly with us, that we have enlisted you?'

I thought for a moment of Pacioli's driver and of saying what I thought. Then I decided not to try fooling myself. Zander was right up to a point. I wanted the operation to go ahead. I didn't want it to fail because it had been bungled. On the other hand, I wasn't exactly 'with' him in the way he meant it.

The men and women who have interested me most professionally have been the hard cases, the survivors. I have not often liked them, but that hasn't seemed important. Zander was beginning to interest me very much. The reason was that I now had a hunch about him. Even the little I knew of his history made him, by any standards that had more to them than simple endurance, a considerable survivor. He had had physical strength and plenty of courage, of course, but it had been his wits that had really counted, his wits and his ability to adapt to cultures utterly foreign to those of his youth and early manhood. It had been a remarkable performance. What I suspected, though, was that he was now a survivor for whom the care of time was becoming hard to ignore. He had started to falter. It does me no credit to say it, but that was why I had become so curious about him. I wanted to see how he would manage and what would happen if he were to stumble and then fall.

He was still waiting with the simper on his lips and the question in his eyes for me to swear allegiance to his cause. I smiled regretfully.

'No, Mr Zander,' I said, 'I haven't enlisted. I think I may have become what that British officer friend of yours would have called a bad sport. I just don't like being on a losing side any more. If there is any way, any way at all, in which I can help you not to lose, you can rely on me completely.'

By then Schelm's reply telex had begun to come through. It read:

BOB FROM LINDWURM. YOUR NUMBER TWO RECEIVED AND UNDERSTOOD. BACK-UP UNIT WILL BE FOUND AND DIRECTED TO REPORT TO US NEAR RENDEZVOUS AT TIME TO BE ARRANGED. KINDLY ADVISE EARLIEST YOUR EXPECTED DEPARTURE TIME TOMORROW AND REPORT FROM YOUR SUNDAY NIGHT-STOP LOCATION WHEN YOU REACH IT FOR POSSIBLE COMMUNICATIONS CHANGES. ACKNOWLEDGE.

EIGHT

WE left for Geneva on Saturday afternoon, travelling in two parties and by separate routes out of Italy. Chihani took Mokhtar and Jasmin in the minibus along with all the larger bags and Guido as driver. They were going north by the alpine road to Switzerland and took off immediately after an early lunch.

Zander and I went in the Alfasud with Vielle doing the driving, and I was glad to see that my remark the previous day about TV crews' appearance had borne some fruit. Vielle wore a knitted alpaca golfing cardigan over a yellow shirt the cut of which suggested that it had been borrowed from the fat girl with the blue-tinted glasses. Zander had entered into the spirit of the occasion by wearing a suede jacket with gun-pads on both shoulders and a white silk roll-neck sweater. I wore what I usually wear and felt overdressed, even for an interviewer.

Our route was easier and we left an hour later than the others. We went south to Novara and then took the autostrada north to Aosta via the Ivrea turn-off. We entered Switzerland through the long St Bernard tunnel. At the Italian end of the tunnel they glanced at the outsides of our passports but the Swiss didn't even bother to do that. Both Zander and Vielle had French passports I noticed.

The motel chosen for our first night stop was just short of Geneva near Coppet. Chihani's party had arrived ahead of us and had already checked in. There was a brasserie with a bar attached to the motel and it was arranged that we would meet Chihani in the bar as soon as we had freshened up. However, she had something to ask first. 'The young people,' she said had spotted a discothèque on their way in and had requested permission to spend a couple of hours there. She thought they should have it. They would be back soon after eleven.

Zander agreed. 'They have worked well these last days,' he said. 'Why should they not enjoy themselves? Perhaps Mokhtar will see a little Swiss girl he fancies.'

Where the older ones were concerned, however, Chihani was applying a different set of rules. We were sitting in the bar drinking white wine when the fuss began. Vielle started it by reminding Zander of a good restaurant they both knew in Geneva.

'Cuisine de minceur,' he explained to me eagerly; 'sauces of great elegance. You too would like it, Mr Halliday, I assure you.' He turned again to Zander. 'Why don't I call for a table, patron?'

I already knew that Vielle disliked Chihani and had guessed that he was jealous of her relationship with Zander, whatever that was, as well as the authority Zander had delegated to her where matters of security were concerned. It was also clear that the table Vielle was proposing to reserve would be for three. She wasn't included in the invitation. But I don't think she even noticed that. Her reaction came straight from the book.

'No! On no account, patron. Why take needless and absurd risks simply to please your stomachs?'

Zander glanced for a moment at Vielle then looked around the bar. There was nobody else drinking and the barman, who doubled as a waiter in the brasserie, was away attending to the cheese sauce for the raclettes. We were more or less free to speak our minds. Vielle lost no time in doing so.

He began with the leaden sarcasms which are the characteristic first stages of a French loss of temper. 'I beg your pardon, Madame. Please excuse me, Madame. I was completely unaware that I had taken the liberty of addressing you upon any subject at all, much less consulting you about the restaurant at which I am proposing to have dinner with friends. Please forgive me, Madame. I certainly had not the slightest idea that you might suppose that I was asking for your permission to do something, or seeking your valuable opinions on *anything*!'

Chihani was not even looking at Vielle. She had been watching Zander. With a flick of her hand she invited my attention as she replied. She was very cool and sure of herself.

'Patron, you are here under an alias and travelling on a passport that is good but not perfect. Your face is known in Geneva. In the restaurant mentioned it is well known. The chances of your being recognized are high. That place is much used also by senior journalists with expense accounts. Mr Halliday could easily be recognized and questioned about his presence in Geneva instead of New York or Pennsylvania. It would be friendly questioning, no doubt, and he could make up a story, but how does he introduce his table companions? As Monsieur Iks and

Monsieur Igrek? No. The elegant sauces can wait for another day. We should dine here, simply and discreetly, and then go quietly to our rooms.'

'Madame is so kind to issue orders for our comfort,' Vielle began again savagely, but she cut in on him by rapping the table with her glass.

'The orders are not for your comfort,' she snapped; 'they are for the security of the operation. That is the responsibility I have been given. If you yourself, Jean-Pierre, wish to go to this restaurant there is nothing to stop you. Telephone for a table and a taxi. If *you* are recognized it doesn't matter. You have your own name and passport and nobody will care why you are there. There could be a dozen reasons, all banal. Okay, off you go. Bon appetit. But do not ask me to compromise the operation.'

Vielle was pink with fury. 'Madame,' he said, 'I ask nothing at all from you except your silence and ...'

He paused to choke a little and Zander moved in smoothly. 'All the same, Jean-Pierre, there's probably something in what Simone says.'

He spoke ruefully and consolingly, but I could see that he was enjoying himself. Among the tycoons I have known at all well, the umpiring of disputes between rival subordinates has always been regarded as good healthy fun. And if a senior subordinate is being attacked by a comparative junior, so much the better. The stakes are higher. There is more raw emotion. Blood may flow.

'There is *always* something in what she says,' Vielle said bitterly. 'That something is the attempt to assert herself. How? By trading on family affections and by reducing every problem, even that of choosing a restaurant, to one of security. And she has the impudence to talk of responsibility to me, your colleague for twenty years.'

Zander's eyes were laughing merrily. 'But it *is* her responsibility, Jean-Pierre. It has been delegated to her. My dear old friend, you agreed yourself to the arrangement.'

'Perhaps,' Chihani said kindly, 'Jean-Pierre feels that I have become obsessed with the subject, that I have become too serious.'

It was a neat little trap and Vielle fell into it face downwards. 'No, Simone, I feel that you are serious only as a way of making yourself important.'

'Are you suggesting that *we* – I don't mean you, Jean-Pierre,

I mean those of us whose lives are at risk – should *not* be serious about security?' she asked and glanced at Zander. 'Shall I telephone for a table, patron?'

But he was tiring of the game. He turned to me. 'You have said nothing, Mr Halliday. Have you any thoughts on our security?'

I had, but they were not primarily about restaurants. Chihani's analysis of the risks in Geneva had reminded me of one security risk we were preparing to run of which she was not yet aware. The day before, while I had been persuading Zander that we needed a back-up TV unit to protect our cover with the Austrians, she had been with Mokhtar and Jasmin in Milan distributing largesse to her stooges in the hotel and retrieving my baggage. That morning, when Schelm had telexed the news that a freelance Dutch unit just finishing a job in Yugoslavia would be joining us at the Lindwurm rendezvous on Tuesday, she had already left and was on the road. The change of programme was not a serious one, maybe, but someone ought to tell her about it. Vielle wouldn't. Perhaps Zander would. Meanwhile, she was making more sense than the self-indulgent Vielle. I said so firmly.

'As far as I am concerned, Mr Zander, it would be the height of folly to go to that restaurant. Miss Chihani is dead right about my being recognized there. I know of at least four old friends who could be there on a Saturday night and all at one table. Two of them at least would be glad to see me and want to know what I was doing in Geneva. It would be very difficult for me to think of a lie to tell them that either would believe. I'll settle for the brasserie here.'

Vielle sighed gustily, but Zander overruled him and that seemed to be that. It wasn't quite.

I was in bed trying to work out the time in Bucks County and wondering whether I ought to take the sleeping pills right then or wait and lie there awake for a couple of hours, when I heard a key being inserted very quietly into the lock of my room door. The key turned. The door opened slightly.

This was disconcerting because I had locked the door from the inside, checked to see that it was in fact locked and then put my key on the dresser. I thought how much things must have changed in Switzerland if, even there, you could now get mugged in a motel room. I also wondered what there might be within reach, aside from a spare pillow, with which to defend myself. There were no bedside lamps, only wall brackets, and the intruder was inside now. The door closed softly.

'Awake?' It was a whisper.

'Yes.'

The shutters were closed and the curtains drawn. It was very dark. I sensed rather than saw her move towards me and stop.

'I wished to thank you for speaking in support of me this evening,' she said; 'you were of the greatest help.' She still spoke in a whisper.

'I simply said what I thought. You were quite right. Jean-Pierre was quite wrong. Stupid too. Do you collect passkeys everywhere you go?'

'Here there is no need. At the desk in places like this there are always two keys in the box of a double room.'

It took me a moment or two to realize that she was stepping out of her pants, that she had recently showered and that the soap she smelt of was not the bain-moussant supplied free by the management. When she had the rest of her clothes off she slid under the sheet beside me. Nothing more was said. There seemed to be nothing much more to say. I was being rewarded for good behaviour.

It must have been about eleven-thirty when the young people returned from the disco. They sounded as if they too had enjoyed themselves. As soon as they had quieted down she dressed again and left. I had no trouble at all in getting to sleep.

The arrangements for picking up the French television unit vehicles had been made by Vielle's Paris office, from which, I gathered, most of the various Zander organizations' European purchasing was done. The pick-up was to take place at ten-thirty in the visitors' parking lot of the Palais des Nations. There, the French producer would be paid cash in West German marks for the balance of the rental and receive a post-dated cheque in Swiss francs, drawn on the American Express International bank's Geneva branch, as a returnable deposit. He would be providing the vehicles and equipment plus insurance Green Cards endorsed with the names of additional authorized drivers. At ten o'clock Vielle set off, carrying a bulky briefcase, with Chihani driving him in the Alfasud. The young people followed in the minibus.

The Alfasud returned at noon. Vielle was driving and in a

very bad temper. According to him, the French producer had exhibited the shabbiest kinds of petty greed and gross bad faith. The little crook had tried to jack up the agreed rental price, he had reneged on the agreed conditions of the deal by removing most of the camera equipment and he had had the effrontery to question the validity of the post-dated cheque in an attempt to get more cash. Vielle had had to remind the fellow that a word to good friends in Paris could ruin him, not only as a freelance film-maker but in certain physically humiliating ways as well, before sense had been seen. It had all been very time-consuming. However, the unit vehicles were now in a drivers' rest area off the eastbound lanes of the autoroute near Begnins. The minibus was in the parking garage at Cointrin. The sooner we began to make up for lost time the better.

The unit vehicles were a Citroën van and a Peugeot station-wagon. The van had had a conversion job done which gave it three fully-reclining passenger seats that could be used as bunks. Stowed behind them, in compartments and lockers and slings, were what looked to me like the usual paraphernalia of a mobile television film unit: the scuffed camera and film-magazine cases, the tripods, the photoflood projectors and stands, the accessory bags, the junction boxes and the heavy-duty cables. On the roof was a rack carrying a collapsible rostrum and a pair of step-ladders strapped over it. A nest of red-plastic traffic bollards was roped to the ladders. On the sides of the van was a logo featuring a stylized bird design and the words *ORTofilm TV ORTofilm* lettered in black on an orange ground. Below this, in very small letters, was the corporate name – Productions Radio-TV Ortofilm S.A. Paris. The station-wagon's sides bore the same legends. It occurred to me that the word Ortofilm had been put together because of the first-glance resemblance of its first syllable to an acronym used by the French state broadcasting services.

'How do you think it looks?' Zander asked.

'Convincing. It looks like the real thing. Why shouldn't it? It *is* the real thing.'

'Yes.' He pointed at the camera cases. 'Unfortunately those are empty. We must hope that the Austrians don't examine us too closely.'

'There's no law against not having camera equipment. If they get curious you could say you're going to rent it in Vienna.'

'Could we rent it?'

'I don't know. Probably. Why not? Are your papers okay?'

'Oh yes. All of us except you have French passports. We will hope to be taken for what we must seem to be, a television unit from Paris with an American journalist going to shoot a news interview in Austria.'

'Where are we going to stop tonight? You won't forget that I'll need telex facilities?'

'You'll have them, Mr Halliday. And I hope *you* won't forget that I shall expect your Military Deputy to the Commander Nato Strike Force South to be given a name. I have to be able to assure The Ruler *before* any meeting takes place that he will not be dealing with some impostor, some underling.'

'All that is understood. You'll get the name.'

'I hope it proves to be the right one. Tonight, I think, we will stop near Zug. Then we shall cross over into Austria in the morning. On Monday mornings there tends to be less traffic. Ah, here now is Simone.'

She had been to garage the Alfasud with the minibus at Cointrin and driven back in the station-wagon with Guido. It was by then one-thirty. Zander decided that we would give lunch a miss. Too much time had been lost. The station-wagon, with Simone driving, would lead the way under his command with me in the back. The van would follow us closely. Beyond Berne, perhaps, when we were well on the way to Zürich, we might stop for coffee and sandwiches.

We made two stops, in fact, and at neither did we eat or drink anything. The first was in an autoroute service area where there were gas stations, drink-dispensing machines, a self-service cafeteria, a store selling novelties and a lot of parking space. For some unfathomable reason the place seemed to be popular with local Sunday drivers and their families. Both store and cafeteria were doing brisk business, but a lot of the people there had just parked their cars and were strolling around in the sun as if the place were a beauty spot.

When we drove in we pulled over to one of the gas stations to fill the tanks which the French producer had neglected to top up after his drive from Paris. By the time we had filled both tanks and the spare cans a crowd had gathered. To begin with they just stared, then they started peering inside the van and asking questions. Vielle headed for the toilets. Zander had to field the questions – they were mostly in German anyway – and he became a centre of attention. He hadn't expected this and he didn't like it. When we started to move towards the cafeteria the crowd followed. As soon as he realized this he turned back. He had had enough.

'We can't stay here,' he said to Chihani. 'Tell Jean-Pierre. Unless anyone else wants to go to the toilets we leave at once.'

When we were back on the road he turned around to face me. 'Are they all crazy here?' he demanded.

'What were they asking you?'

'Crazy questions. What is the programme we are making? What is the name of it? Is it for the Swiss and German chains or only Suisse Romande and France? That one expects. I say it is a documentary about asthma. I could have saved my breath. They go on and on. Where have we come from? Where are we going? What does Simone do? Is she an actress? Am *I* a star? Who are you? Why are you wearing a tie when I am not? They do not listen to what one is saying, you understand. They only want to talk and show you their stupid faces. The parents are as bad as the children. Are you an American? What part of Germany do I come from with that strange accent? Why do I have Arabs working for me? Yes, even that. One of those people heard Mokhtar speaking to Jasmin and thought it was Arabic. Are you a famous star who used to be in cowboy films or are you the cameraman? Am I Monsieur Ortofilm himself? Here we are, not far from Zürich, and there are crazy people walking about.'

'You've just been meeting the public, that's all, Mr Zander. You should be pleased.'

'What do you mean? Pleased about what?'

'To the uninitiated we must look like members of that new and privileged class you were telling me about.'

'I am looking for cover, not exposure to the half-witted.'

'You'd better get used to the idea that in this case the two things go together. You've been lucky this afternoon, Mr Zander. Now you know better what to expect, and you found out in a place where it didn't matter what anyone thought or said about you and your reactions. Call it a dry run.'

'A what?'

'A performance before a camera that's running but with no film in it. A combat exercise with everyone firing blanks.'

The eyes hardened. 'No one ever learned about combat by firing blanks,' he said and turned away from me to look ahead. 'Perhaps it's as well,' he added sombrely, 'that there's only one more battle to be fought.'

He was silent for a long time after that. I guessed what was happening. He was a man used to success. A lot of careful and complex thought had gone into this operation and it had worked splendidly, so far. All of a sudden, though, he was having to accept the fact that there might be a flaw in his phase-three planning and that, somewhere along the line, he must have made an error of judgement. Now he was trying to identify and locate it. Then, he would either retrieve or neutralize it. But where along the line was he to look?

There had been truth in what he had said about television units. Many of them, including on occasion some of the freelance teams, often enjoyed nowadays the sort of freedom and prerogatives once granted only to the accredited correspondents of great newspapers. Mobile units with access to the world's networks and satellite picture-transmission systems could be invested during time of crisis with an even headier importance, a kind of supranational status. These were the crews before whom the modern Nechayevs liked to act out their crudely-scripted tales of villainy unmasked, righteous anger unleashed, innocence redeemed through the cleansing fires of violence and of mob-rule justice seen to be done. On those occasions, with millions watching, such crews and the equipment they operated became sacrosanct.

Zander had understood this, of course, but he had only understood it from the outside, as a member of the audience. Yes, he had made some guesses about how it felt to be where the camera was, but they hadn't been good enough. What he had seen as the elements of a secure cover – the TV logos, the indulgent customs men, the helpful officials, the protective police – were really the trappings of something quite different. They were the things that would make even the normally incurious person turn a head. The real crews were aware of the intense interest they aroused and were for the most part professionally indifferent to it. Our mixed bunch of phoneys could only look sullen or smirk with embarrassment.

On the outskirts of Zürich we came to a big filling station without a parking area or coffee shop. Zander told Chihani to pull into the forecourt and top up with gas. Then he got out and walked back to the van. He and Vielle spoke briefly before heading for the station manager's office and, I guessed, a telephone. I saw Chihani watching them, but when she had paid for the gas she made no move to join them. Instead, she got back into the car and turned around to face me.

'It was the questioning that surprised me,' she said. 'Were you expecting that?'

'No. Of course it's Sunday afternoon. Those people back there had nothing better to do. But I don't think that's the whole story. The questions, some of them anyway, were pretty stupid, yes. But people really aren't all that stupid. We were doing it.'

'Making them stupid?'

'No, but we *were* giving them a feeling that we weren't quite right. And we weren't. We were all wrong. Do you know what a real unit would have done? Locked their vehicles and gone to get their coffee and sandwiches. A few people would probably have collected. They would have been ignored. All anyone who asked a question would have had for an answer would have been a stare or a shrug or a "comprends pas". If anyone persisted the crew would talk between themselves so as to exclude him. We not only answered questions and kept on answering them but the young people chattered away and giggled as if they were on a picnic. No wonder the questions became stupid. *We* were stupid. I suggest that when we stop next time the young people pretend to be asleep. At other times they should keep their heads down. On no account should they appear to be enjoying themselves. Jean-Pierre should drive the van and try to speak nothing but French.'

'I will tell the patron.' She smiled slightly. 'It is very unprofessional. You must be suffering.'

'I'd be suffering more if I thought this particular cover was your idea. I don't think it was.'

'I was against it. It was good cover for you, but not for us. But then I am sometimes wrong. I was against making the attack on Pacioli's bodyguard. I thought it was ...' She shrugged.

'Brutal and unnecessary?'

She looked surprised. 'No, I thought it mistaken. Coercive action should always be direct. The Syncom man in Rome was permitting the delay. He should have been the one who was hurt.'

'I'm told that prolonged contact with the Arab world tends to complicate thought processes. Yours seem straightforward enough.'

She gave me her sidelong look. 'I'm not an Arab and only half Berber. You are thinking of the patron. He is the one who likes the desert Arabs. He can even sometimes like The Ruler.'

'You don't and can't?'

'There are civilized men down there,' she said, 'but he' – she made a gesture with her left hand as if she were shaking drops of water from her finger-tips – 'him I always prefer to avoid. The patron knows this.'

'Did the patron tell you that we're going to be met on Tuesday somewhere near the rendezvous by a Dutch television unit, a real one?'

She stared. 'What are you talking about?'

As I told her she pursed her lips and drew deep breaths. Then, with a brief snarl of disgust, she went back to the book. 'A cover story requiring skills or abilities not possessed or not easily acquired by the person or persons using it is inherently weak. The good cover requires almost no pretence.'

'I'm sure you're right.'

'And over-elaborate cover tends to be self-defeating. I do not blame you for this complication, my friend. You thought correctly. It is better than having trouble with the Austrian media. Where is the Dutch unit now?'

'On the way north from somewhere in Yugoslavia. I don't know exactly where. But I have another suggestion to make. Want to hear it?'

'Very well.'

'Why don't we leave Jean-Pierre, the young people and all this junk we're driving around? We leave them somewhere in Zürich and then fly to Vienna tomorrow. There, we rent a car and drive to the Gasthaus near St Veit where the patron said we'll be staying before the meeting. Then we'll be all set for the rendezvous with no problems.'

'Impossible.'

'Why?'

She was very patient with me. 'Because that is not the plan agreed in advance by The Ruler. Even a request for minor changes would cause deep suspicion. You don't know him.'

'You're making him sound just like his father.'

'Oh, you have heard of that one. Well, this one would not pull his own gun and shoot us, I think, but your friends would not see him. He would disappear with his entourage in a private jet to London or Paris. Another meeting would take many weeks to arrange. The patron could not consider such a basic change of plan.'

'Honey, there are two parties to this negotiation. Why should The Ruler call all the shots?'

'No reason, if the other party doesn't mind forgetting Abra Bay for a while.'

'Aren't *you* forgetting something? How about this Dutch unit that'll be arriving and the interview I'm going to do? You don't call that a change of plan?'

'The only change will be that the camera he sees will now have film or tape in it. Before, it would only have been a – what did you call it?'

'A dry run?'

'That's it. A dry run after the secret meeting so that there appears to have been a simpler explanation than the real one for all the coming and going.' I was leaning forward with my elbows on the back of the front seat beside her. She reached over and patted my hands. 'My friend, you must not make the mistake of thinking that these people automatically respond to sane voices talking good sense. Only a few are sane and sensible men. Sometimes, I think, not even the patron is wholly sane.'

She said the last few words so casually that the oddity of them didn't really register with me for a moment. By then she had opened the driver's door and was getting out. Zander and Vielle were returning to the van and Zander was beckoning to her.

They all got inside the van and remained there for some minutes before she and Zander came back to the station-wagon.

'I have decided that we shall divide our forces,' he said to me as he climbed in. 'Divided we shall attract less attention. Simone has told us of the criticisms you've made about behaviour and discipline. Your points have been noted and your advice will be taken. Jean-Pierre will drive the van and the young people will remember their new orders. They will go for the night to a motel on the other side of Zürich near the airport. We, the three of us, now have reservations at a hotel in the same area. It is one of the new convention places and has telex. Jean-Pierre will join us by taxi so that we can confer later.'

He said nothing after that until we reached the hotel.

It had a new look, that of a pile of supermarket egg-boxes made of concrete instead of papier mâché. It had newness of another sort too. Once you had checked in you were on your own. You found your own room, carried your own bag, fixed your own drinks and found your own pillows in the closet. There was no room service. If you wanted anything that wasn't in your room you called the desk and they told you where to go find it. That way I found someone who was prepared to rent me a cubicle with a telex machine and show me how to work it.

I called Ulm and gave the name and number of the hotel. In return I was given again the phone number I was to call in Velden when I reached the Gasthaus near St Veit plus the name of the person I was to ask for. I was to ask for Herr Kurt Mesner. Please acknowledge.

Zander had come to think of me as *his* man, not theirs, and he monitored these exchanges jealously. He also became impatient. 'Who cares what noms de guerre they are using?' he asked irritably. 'Ask them for the name *we* want, the name we need to know.'

I did so not because I was obeying him but because that happened to be the next item on the list of things to do that Schelm had given me for my aide-mémoire.

LINDWURM FROM BOB. REQUEST NAME OF SENIOR NEGOTIA-
TOR.

The reply came back immediately.

BOB FROM LINDWURM. NAME OF NEGOTIATOR IS NEWELL.
REPEAT NEWELL. ACKNOWLEDGE SHOWING YOU HAVE
SPELLING OF NAME CORRECT.

I did as I had been told, then looked at Zander. 'Does the name mean anything to you?' I asked.

'I will soon know when Jean-Pierre gets here. Where *is* he?'

'Trying to get a taxi from a motel near the airport on a Sunday, I imagine. What do you want me to reply?'

'Say I will telex acceptance or rejection within an hour.'

'Why should you reject? On what grounds?'

'If this Newell is not a lieutenant-general on the staff of Nato as you have led me to expect, I shall reject. And if we have not among the identifying photographs of senior Nato personnel in our dossiers a picture of this Newell so that I shall know it is he the moment I first set eyes on him, I shall reject. The Ruler will be trusting me to vouch personally that this man is who he says he is.'

I wasn't going to use the word 'rejection' though. What I sent was:

BOB TO LINDWURM. NAME BEING CHECKED. WILL CALL BACK WITHIN HOUR IF ANY QUERY. OTHERWISE NOT.

Vielle arrived, with his briefcase, ten minutes later and was hustled upstairs by Zander. Each room had a locked refrigerator stocked with small bottles of wine, liquor and soft drinks which the occupant could get at by using the room key and agreeing to accept the charges on his bill. Chihani and I were instructed by Zander to gather bottles of whisky and soda from our refrigerators and join him.

By the time we got there Vielle had the card on Lieutenant-General Sir Patrick Newell, KCB, CBE, DSO, MC, out of the Nato file and Zander was studying a photograph of the man. Vielle was reading aloud from the card.

'Born: 1931. Educated: Wellington College and Royal Military Academy, Sandhurst. Joined Royal Regiment Fusiliers, later transferring to The Parachute Regiment. Service in Korea, Malaya, Cyprus, Aden. There are promotions with dates and three small initial letters – p.s.c.'

'That means he passed the British Staff College course at Camberley,' Zander said. 'What else it could mean about him I don't know.'

'There are various appointments and commands he has held listed here. I don't understand the meaning of some of these abbreviations.'

'Surely,' I said, 'the only one that matters is the last one. Military Deputy to Commander Nato Strike Force South.'

Zander looked up. 'That one you won't find. These details are from published sources. Military Deputy is another way of saying Nato Military Committee Intelligence. Nato don't publish the names of senior officers with appointments that involve reporting confidentially to the Military Committee and Council.' He looked at the photograph again and then passed it to me. 'Interesting face. There is a soldier, but you can also see the English gentleman.'

Chihani was handing me a drink. She peered down over my shoulder to see the picture.

It was a black-and-white shot, probably taken during an army exercise in Germany. He was standing by an armoured scout car talking to another uniformed man who was mostly out of focus in the foreground, and he had a map-case propped against the car's turret. The General wore a beret and a British field-service sweater. I could agree with Zander that the face below the beret was that of a soldier and that he was possibly English, but I didn't think he looked any kind of a gentleman. It could have been that the man in the foreground, the major he was tearing strips off, had attempted to excuse some inexcusable foul-up by telling an even less excusable cock-and-bull story, but to me the General Newell of that photograph looked a foul-tempered, vindictive, sadistic, any-man's-army bastard.

'A strong face,' Chihani said. 'Very good bones. And those lines about the eyes. He smiles a lot. One can see.'

I felt suddenly that it had been a long day.

NINE

WE had an early breakfast in the hotel coffee shop, then Simone sent Zander and me back to our rooms. She would pay the bills and do any talking that was necessary. From now on, strict security controls would be applied. For instance, there would be no dawdling in the lobby to buy papers or for any other reason. She would get the station-wagon from the car park and stop outside in a convenient spot. Then, and only then, when she was ready for us, would we be told by phone to come down with our bags in our hands and embark.

While we were still in the hotel Zander did as he had been told, but as soon as we were on the road again and heading east, he wanted a report.

'No problems,' was all she said.

'What sort of an answer is that? They did not notice *this*?' He banged the door beside him with his fist. 'The television name on the side?'

'Of course they noticed it. It caused great interest. The manager asked me who you both were.'

'What did you tell him?'

'I said that you were temporary production assistants to a French producer-director at present making package-tour travel commercials for an American airline, and of no importance in the company.'

'Good,' he said and then repeated the word. '*Good*.' His tone lacked conviction. He did not like being described as of no importance, even for a sound security reason. He must, I thought, be longing very eagerly now for the moment when a meeting of minds on the Abra Bay project would free him both from his past and from the attentions of Mukhabarat Zentrum.

At the Austrian frontier we had no trouble, but half a mile beyond it, in the frontier town itself, we ran into trouble of a peculiar kind. The road forked and there was resurfacing in progress on the main through section to the right. At the fork a small, hand-painted sign announced an UMLEITUNG but had no arrow directing traffic into the detour. Instead, there was a cardboard sketch-map below the sign. This looked as if it had been done by a four-year old experimenting with finger-painting in a play school. The message it conveyed was that there were two ways of getting through – straight ahead or via the detour. On the straight-ahead road the map had a box with four wheels travelling along. On the detour road there was a box with four wheels travelling and a bicycle. So, if you were travelling on four wheels, it seemed, you had a choice – go straight on over the ruts and loose rocks or save your tyres and go with the bicycles along the smoother road out of town.

Most went straight ahead. The police were waiting to pounce just around the bend about a couple of hundred yards beyond the 'map'. Cars with Austrian plates were turned back and directed to the detour. Straight on was for trucks only it transpired. Those of us with foreign plates were lined up along the shoulder of the road while the police proceeded to collect fines. They seemed to be going through a familiar routine. As each driver was directed to pull off the road the cop would yell *'Passport'*. Then, when he had the driver's passport, he would yell *'Fined one hundred Schillings'* or, as we had French plates, *'Amende de cent Schillings'* and then walk away. The driver had to buy the passport back by paying the hundred Schillings. Some argued that the sign was misleading, as Simone did, but argument got you nowhere. They ignored it. A Dutch driver ahead of us had no Austrian money and was obliged to cash a travellers' cheque at a change booth across the road from the police trap, where the con-man operating it was paying twenty-five percent below the going rate. Luckily, we had Austrian money with us.

'Pay, Simone,' said Zander, 'and let us be on our way. Yes, it is a racket and they could only get away with it in a frontier town where there are always foreign tourists in a hurry. Have you noticed that there are no men or machines working on the road? Very interesting. They do not mind if we notice. They don't care what we think of them as police. Let us pay and go.'

She paid the hundred Schillings and received a scribbled receipt with her passport. She passed the receipt to Zander who glanced at it, snorted with amusement and passed it back to me. It was headed *Organstrafverfügung* and was an official, numbered receipt for ten Schillings. The signature, of course, was illegible.

'Welcome to happy Austria,' Simone snarled as she wrestled the station-wagon back on to the 'detour'.

'Why be angry?' Zander asked. 'They gave you an official receipt. And don't forget your history. Austria has often been nearly as anti-Semitic as Russia.'

'What has anti-Semitism to do with it?'

'To those policemen, maybe, all foreigners look Jewish.'

'Patron, you are talking nonsense.'

'Perhaps,' he said dreamily; 'but think for a moment of Judenburg. Do you know of any other country in Europe which would call a place Jewstown and never, even in the second half of the twentieth century, trouble to change its name?'

'The Ruler should feel very happy here.'

'Oh he does, my dear. He has even begun to forgive them for the fact that the founder of modern Zionism was an Austrian Jew.'

I was watching his eyes through the rear-view mirror and he caught me doing so. The eyes twinkled. If he enjoyed teasing her, he was also beginning to enjoy disconcerting me.

'No, Mr Halliday,' he said, 'I am not a Jew. Nor do I belong to an ethnic minority. No. For me there is a special kind of undesirability, a special category. I am every country's, every people's bloody foreigner.'

'Everyone's bloody foreigner? That phrase sounds as if you learned it from your British officer friend, the Arabist scholar.'

'Of course I did!' The eyes lit up in triumph. 'And it was old-fashioned even then. He told me so himself. But I still like it, though your version may be better. Everyone's bloody foreigner,' he repeated, and then burst out laughing.

That was the first time I had heard him laugh aloud freely at something that really seemed to delight him. It was a strange sound though, more like that of quiet weeping.

We had arranged to meet up with Vielle's party at Feldkirch and they were already there when we arrived. The van had been waved through the police trap and they had had no problems at all. The young people were behaving circumspectly and Vielle himself had made a useful discovery. The van had a well-insulated food and drink locker. With ice from their motel rooms and a quick marketing expedition in Feldkirch while they had been waiting for us, we had supplies that would make us independent for the day of the tourist stopping places. By eleven we were in Innsbruck. From there we headed for Kufstein before starting to work our way south through the mountains and the tunnels. We reached Villach at five and were at the Gasthaus Dr Wohak an hour later.

I never found out anything about Dr Wohak except that he was dead and that it had been he who had made an attractive hotel out of a cluster of nineteenth-century farm buildings. It had an imposing porte-cochère style of entrance into a central courtyard with two smaller courtyards leading off it. The walls were of stone, a grey stone but one with a lot of life in it. After the prettiness of the Tyrol the whole place was very refreshing.

The desk clerk spoke English. As soon as I was in my room I called down and asked him to get me the Velden number. The answering voice was that of a hotel switchboard operator.

'Herr Kurt Mesner?'

'One moment, please.'

'Mesner.' It was Schelm.

'We've arrived.'

'Then we should have a little chat, you and I. Perhaps you would join me for dinner. If I sent a car for you in, say, an hour, would that be too soon?'

'No, but our friend has become a little possessive.'

'We can become possessive too. Tell him that the senior negotiator wishes to see you for identification purposes well in advance of any meeting. Their side insisted on a name and a face he could identify. So now we're insisting on the same thing. If he is difficult, tell him that.'

In the event I had to tell Zander nothing more that day. I freshened up, changed and was thinking of going down to the bar, when there was a sharp knock on the door. It was Simone. She pushed past me without a word and quickly locked the door behind her.

'We have troubles,' she said a trifle breathlessly.

'The local press? I told you they'd be around.'

'It is not the local press. Much worse. It is radio and television.'

'Already?'

'The manager here likes publicity. The moment he sees a television unit he becomes excited. Then he discovers that you are an American journalist.'

'How?'

'From visas in your passport. So then he asks Jean-Pierre, who has been acting here as the French boss of Ortofilm, why we are here and what we are going to do. Jean-Pierre gives him the agreed cover story. We are here to interview The Ruler at his famous health mine for an American TV network.' She threw up her hands. 'It could not have been worse.'

'Did Jean-Pierre forget his lines?'

'He said what had been prepared for him to say.'

'Then I don't follow you. What's gone wrong?'

She sat down abruptly. 'Too many things have gone wrong, and The Ruler hasn't thought it necessary to let us know about any of them, even though they compromise the conference rendezvous that *he himself* selected.'

'What kind of things?'

'There are so many.' She stood up and began panthering around the room as she ticked them off on her fingers. 'First, there is a law in Austria controlling the putting up of new buildings in the mountains and high valleys. This is to protect the natural beauties, the – what do you call it?'

'The environment.'

'Yes, that. A new house may only be put up where an old house has been. So, when someone wants to build in the country-side where it is beautiful he buys an old house first.'

'Which is what The Ruler did.'

'But not to put up an ordinary house.'

'Ah, I see. The authorities are objecting to his plan to build a clinic instead.'

'No. What the authorities object to is his refusal to submit what he plans to do for their approval. Secondly, he insists upon importing French mining engineers to supervise the work of restoring the deep mine workings, of installing electrical pump-ing equipment and of making it all safe. Third, he will no longer permit official inspection of the mine. Fourth, he has employed so far five architects for the clinic above the mine. Four of them he has discharged. All of them have been foreigners, one Italian, three Germans and the latest who is Swiss. Nothing is yet known of his design, but one of the Germans who was fired has talked to the German press. What he said was that what The Ruler wanted was not a clinic but a sort of palace. He also said that what might look very romantic in the middle of a desert would at Petrucher look highly offensive and absurd.'

'Petrucher? Is that the name of the village?'

'No, it is the name of the mine. Johannes Peter Petrucher was the amateur archeologist who bought the disused mine and built the house and museum that The Ruler is going to pull down. The nearest village is two kilometres away. The Petrucher is quite isolated. I have seen photographs. It is a lot of trees and this old building on a hillside. It is certainly not a great beauty spot.'

'But the authorities are behaving as if it *were*, because this foreigner, The Ruler, refuses to go by the book and submit a set of plans before he builds. Yes, I see. I'll bet he could have submitted any old set of plans at the start and then quietly modified them later. But I guess that's not The Ruler's way.'

'Didn't the patron tell you about pride?'

'He's not in the Gulf here. Why don't they take him to court?'

'He employs five Viennese lawyers. In addition, he retains a professor of law who has represented two Gulf members of OPEC before the International Court on questions involving Human Rights.'

'What have Human Rights to do with this?'

'The Ruler claims that the government of the Austrian province of Steiermark, that's Styria, is invading or attempting to invade his privacy. In particular, he refuses to acknowledge that the media, whether press, television or radio does not matter, have any right whatsoever to question him, his servants or other employees, or his legal representatives on the subject of his personal property wherever it may be. He has refused all requests for statements and interviews. It has caused a great scandal and the matter has even been raised in the Federal Council in Vienna. Why is this oil sheikh being allowed to defy the law? If he has nothing to hide, why does he remain silent and reject legitimate questioning? Can it be that this clinic he says he wishes to build is to be used for quite other and immoral purposes? The whole affair has caused much suspicion and, in some political quarters, great anger.'

'At which point we arrive and announce casually that *we*'re all set to do what nobody else has been able to do, namely, interview The Ruler for television. I see. That's really great! How does the manager react?'

'With delight, of course. He telephones the local radio station. They telephone the Austrian radio-television service in Vienna. ORF it is called, Österreichischer Rundfunk. Then, ORF telephones back. They have found out that you are a professional writer who is known. So, *you* are to be interviewed. At once.

Tonight. There is a current-affairs interviewer on the way to do the preparatory work. An ORF mobile television unit will soon follow. You see the problem?'

'There's no problem. It'll be one of those non-interviews. Sorry I have nothing to tell them. I don't know The Ruler. That's why I'm here. To meet him. Yes, I'd heard he was having trouble over this health-mine of his. Anything they can give me on that I'll be glad to have.'

She gave me a shrewd little smile. 'Ach so! But if you are not interviewing him about the mine scandal, Herr Halliday, what could be the object of your interview? What else is it that America cannot wait to learn about from the lips of this interesting Arab personality?'

'The Ruler is seen as an increasingly significant figure in Gulf politics.'

'That is what you will give them to quote? That is what you will actually say into their microphones?'

'I'll try to make it sound a little better than that, I guess, but it's all I've got until I've actually met The Ruler.'

'It is still too much.' She had stopped fooling and was looking quite fierce. 'There must be no publicity.'

'Look,' I said, 'there's a car on the way from Velden to take me in there to dinner. If there's an interviewer and a unit on their way from Vienna they could be waiting here when I get back. There'll probably be phone calls too, any minute now, from the radio people. I can't say nothing. No story, gentlemen, and no comment? Believe me, it doesn't work. They just get mad at you. You have to give them *something*.'

'Your name must not be publicly mentioned while the patron is here.'

'Because Rasmuk might be listening in Italy?'

'Because they might be listening *here* of course.'

The phone rang. I was going to suggest that she'd better answer it, but she snatched it up before I could speak.

It was the desk to say that a car from Lindwurm had arrived for me. I told her to say that I would be down and then thought for a moment.

'Where's the patron?' I asked finally. 'Keeping discreetly to his room?'

'No. He has already been summoned by The Ruler to report in advance of the conference.' She took a folded envelope from her shirt pocket. 'He left you a note with orders for tomorrow.'

I stuffed it away without reading it. 'Will he be coming back tonight?'

'I don't think so. The Ruler has a chalet that he and the entourage use when he visits the Petrucher mine to meet the architects and engineers. The patron will stay there. We are instructed to meet him with the vehicles and crew at the Petrucher in the morning. Not later than ten, he said.'

'Maybe it's as well that he won't be here. You and Jean-Pierre are going to have to handle the ORF people and any other media characters when they get here.'

'You said that there is no way.'

'There's no way of dodging the problem. We may be able to postpone it. Jean-Pierre should begin by telling the ORF man *off the record* that I'm on a network assignment from New York to do an interview with The Ruler. Why me? I'm a political writer and interviewer who happened to be nearby in Italy working on a book. Which network? Jean-Pierre's sorry but he's not saying. Why? Because, although the network has been *promised* this interview, previous experience with The Ruler has made them cautious about accepting his word. The ORF people will certainly buy that. So, Jean-Pierre goes on, until he knows firsthand that The Ruler has actually kept this promise, his orders are to say nothing. And, in the same context, he should emphasize that any careless talk about the interview before it has actually taken place could kill the whole deal. If the interview *does* go according to plan, however, *then* he'll be able to talk business. He'll have to clear it with New York, of course, but there seems to be no reason why, if they want to, ORF shouldn't process the film themselves right here and run off their own print.'

'Will they believe him?'

'Probably, if you help. You must be acting as the research assistant on this project. You should have picked up the local interest story about the goings-on at the mine and be thoroughly enthusiastic about it. The network will *love* it, and you too for finding it. So, if you were really working on a story you'd just come across about a crazy oil sheikh who wants to build a desert palace in the Austrian alps, do you know what you'd be doing?'

'Tell me.'

'You'd be picking the ORF people's brains. You'd be trying to get every last scrap of information that was going. You'd be greedy. You'd want to know in detail about this Austrian law. You'd want them to suggest awkward questions that you could feed me to ask instead of all the bland political stuff I have at present. You'd be going on and on. You'd be boring them. You'd also be making them start to worry. If you're going to be feeding me their best questions, I'm going to be taking the credit too, see?'

She had brightened up. 'Yes, I see. Counterattack where they keep their vanity. I will do my best. What time will you return?'

'I don't know. Not very late I would think. If they want to know where I am, say that I took a taxi and went off looking for a bar where they serve my favourite brand of American whisky. You could be bitter about me. You're the one who's been doing all the work. I'm just the slob who gets paid top money for asking the questions you write. They won't mind believing that. With luck, they'll have believed Jean-Pierre and simply be hoping to get their hands on the film. But let him do his talking first. I'm assuming he'll go along. Do you think he will?'

'Yes, if I tell him that these suggestions come from you. He may possibly enjoy himself.'

'As long as he doesn't look defensive. You should look stern and suspicious.'

'That I can do.'

I smiled. 'Yes, I know.'

The car Schelm had sent for me from Velden was an Avis rental driven by a saturnine young man who spoke only six words during the trip. He asked me if I was Mr Halliday and then told me please to get in. I assumed that he was one of Schelm's junior operators.

The forecourt of the hotel Schelm was staying at in Velden was entered through a splendid baroque archway. The hotel beyond, though, failed to live up to the promise of that approach. It was trying hard to look as if it had once been the noble house whose archway stood in front of it and still unwilling to admit that it had been a hotel from the start. It was, however, far more comfortable than the noble house would have been. It had a nice expensive feeling, and the people who ran it seemed not to have heard of the term 'self-service'. Schelm's room was large with space enough for comfortable armchairs as well as a bed and a drinks tray on a side table.

As he was mixing me a drink he motioned with his head towards a door connecting his room with the next. 'The General will be joining us,' he said. 'If you don't mind, Bob, I'd like him to hear what you have to tell us from the beginning. It'll save you from having to say things twice and we do have a lot of ground to cover before the meeting tomorrow.'

'What's he like?'

'Charming, and I'd use a different word if I really meant that he was a light-weight charmer. You'll get on well together. Zander had a dossier on him I assume?'

'Published material only, and not very much of that.'

'Did it mention that he spent a couple of years as an adviser in Oman and that he speaks fair Gulf Arabic?'

'If it did, they didn't read that bit out to me. All I was actually shown was a black-and-white picture they had of him.'

'I see.'

He went to the connecting door and opened it without troubling to knock first. 'Bob's here, Patrick, if you'd care to join us,' he said.

General Newell in colour and out of uniform looked very different from the picture I had been shown the night before. He was of middling height with a swarthy complexion, greying, slightly untidy dark hair and, as Simone had been quick to note, an attractive pattern of laugh lines around his eyes. Clearly, unless you happened to have seen that other reading of his face, he was far too relaxed and kind-hearted a man to tear strips off anyone. He also looked remarkably healthy for his age. The suit he was wearing was at least fifteen years old and still fitted him well. It was one of those London suits, navy blue pin-stripe with vest, that always looks as if it may at some time have been slept in but never as if it has just been pressed. With it he wore a striped shirt a bit frayed at the collar points and a blue tie with a small knot.

As we shook hands he said: 'Glad to meet you, Bob.'

'Thank you, General.'

'Heard a lot about you, of course. One thing though.' He hesitated and then decided how he would say it. 'I'm taking the liberty of calling you Bob because that's your message name for this operation. But I have a suggestion. If you call me Patrick and we stick to first names all round, it'll make it easier when we go downstairs to dinner. We can go on talking a little shop if we want to without the waiter taking too much of an interest because one of us is a general. What do you think, Dieter?'

'Good idea. Now, first things first. Bob has been shown a photograph of you that they're proposing to use for identification purposes. We don't want any foul-ups, Bob. Would you have recognized Patrick from their picture of him?'

'The upper part of the face looks the same. The lower part is nothing like. In the picture they have, Patrick, I'm sorry to say, you look as though you are about to tear some unfortunate major to pieces with your bare teeth.'

He nodded amiably. 'I know the picture you mean. Some press photographer took it up near Lauenburg. Bad habit losing your temper. I used to think I'd broken it, but it still creeps up on me again once in a while. Pity they had to get *that* picture. When there are photographers about these days I always try to keep my mouth shut.'

'I'll warn Chihani. She's the security expert. She liked your eyes anyway. They are what she's going to look at.'

'Then that's settled,' said Schelm. 'Now, Bob, we've only been here a couple of hours, but the word's already around among the hotel staff here that there's a French television unit in the neighbourhood and that The Ruler is to be interviewed in his old silver mine. It looks as if your request for a back-up crew was more than justified.'

'Even *with* the back-up crew, this rendezvous tomorrow is going to be about as private and secure as Central Park,' I said. 'You've heard about the public row that's going on over this clinic he wants to build?'

'We'd picked that up before we came.' He handed the General a drink. 'We wanted the rendezvous changed, of course. We tried and were refused as late as Saturday morning, before you left for Geneva. Did they tell you that?'

'No, but that doesn't surprise me. Zander feels that he's *enlisted* me – his word – that I'm on his side now and working for his success. He wouldn't want me to get worried at this stage, just before the battle.'

'*Are* you worried? I mean we'd like success too, though not necessarily his version of it. Do you think you can cope with this PR complication? And, in particular, can you be sure of keeping us out of it?'

'Your best way of keeping out of it would be to get yourselves a couple of press cards. The Austrians'll be elbowing the foreign competition right out of it. This is their story. Can I cope? I guess I'll have to. So far, the trouble all seems to be coming from the television people.' I gave them a quick run-down on what had happened at the Gasthaus and on the instructions I had left with Simone.

'Will it work, do you think?'

'If Vielle co-operates. Unfortunately, those two don't get on well.'

'You don't know why?'

'They're both worriers, I guess. Vielle's worrying about his dignity all the time. She's worrying about security.'

'Maybe, but it's not just that, Bob. She's the boss's daughter.'

'Zander's?'

'By his second wife, the one who was killed in the Algerian war. His name would have been Brochet then. Those young Berber hoodlums are his children too, but adopted. He trained them. I'd have given you this background stuff before, but it's only just coming in. We've had a lot of people digging. The family in America, by the way, has Spanish as its second language.'

'Well, at least you've explained Vielle and his jealousy.' I drank some Scotch and decided that I had a need to know more. 'On the TV situation,' I said, 'the best way out is for me to get an interview with The Ruler, turn it straight over to ORF and hope that they'll be grateful enough to be nice about all the lies they've been told. What I'd like to hear about now is this Dutch back-up crew. Who are they? When do they get here?'

Schelm consulted a notebook. 'The name of the company is Viser-Damrak TV Film' – he spelt it out – 'and they are based in Eindhoven. The director is Dick Kluvers. I don't know exactly how that is spelt. They are night-stopping in Trieste and will be here by noon tomorrow. They will report to one of my people here in this hotel for instructions and guidance to the location. What you have told me, however, about the ORF situation makes me think that we may have further problems.' He stood up. 'Patrick, may I use the telephone in your room? There is something I must check.'

The General waved permission. Schelm shut the connecting door behind him when he left us.

The General eased himself lower in his chair and gave me a friendly smile. 'Nice chap, Dieter. Gives one the impression that he's good at his job. Probably is, too. You must find this Zander fellow professionally interesting. I know I do.'

'You mean how did a good soldier like that get into the murky work of doing business for people like The Ruler?'

'Oh heavens no! Good soldiers can get into all sorts of murky jobs. Like this one, for instance, the job I'm in. The good soldier Zander happened to get into a war of liberation on the winning side and made useful friends. That part's easy. No. What I couldn't see, at least at first, was how he ever *became* a good soldier. From Abwehr to senior Warrant Officer in the Legion is quite a long step. How did he take it? And *why*?'

Without thinking I parroted the explanation my agency friend had given me on the day I had received Zander's letter. 'All he knew was soldiering.'

The General stared as if I had taken leave of my senses. 'Well, he couldn't have learned it in the Abwehr.'

'According to my sources he was sent to a special infantry training school.'

'Special infantry training, my foot. It was a spit-and-polish unit that specialized in ceremonial drill for guards of honour. One of those places where they went poncing about in boned black-calfskin boots. You can see why he'd be thought suitable. He's a Baltic-German who's proved his loyalty to Führer and Fatherland by escaping from the Soviets to join the fight for glory. He's also, no doubt, a good-looking lad of the right Aryan complexion. You don't learn soldiering in those places. Eventually, of course, they found a better use for him and his languages. That's when they sent him for signals training. When he joined the Abwehr they put him to monitoring enemy signals traffic. Later he was used on POW interrogation. That's not exactly a desk job, but it's certainly a sit-down one. Care to hear my theory about how he became transformed into a soldier? You might even be able to check with him on it if you get a chance.'

'He's not a man who likes talking about himself, or answering questions.'

'If my theory's correct, he wouldn't mind talking about the Russian winter of 'forty-four and 'forty-five in the least. You don't believe me? Think about it. The Wehrmacht was falling back all across their northern Russian front into Poland. The Russians were already in East Prussia. The Germans weren't taking prisoners for interrogation, so what was Zander doing? Don't forget, he's still a youngster in his early twenties and he's an NCO with a confirmed rank. After three years in his job on that front it would be *Feldwebel* I'd say. Well now, the German army was desperately short of reserves by then and the drafts that were being sent to them were of doubtful quality. There were the too-old and the too-young, returned wounded, tired men and demoralized men. Don't forget, either, that the Russian front was a punishment posting by then for units accused of misbehaviour or insufficient enthusiasm for the war elsewhere. So, the German commanders did what army commanders always do when they get hard-pressed for effective manpower. They weed out the young and the fit from specialist units, lines-of-communication troops and non-combatant services and use them as reinforcements, usually to fill out mixed drafts of old soldiers and new who haven't yet had time to get to know each other. Know what I mean?'

'I know.'

'Then you'll also know about long retreats, I dare say. Must have seen it as a war correspondent. They bring out the best and worst in men. And, paradoxically, it's in retreat that some men find their talent for leadership. I don't mean leadership in a race for safety, but the kind that turns headlong retreat into a rearguard action and withdrawal with light casualties. I think that's what must have happened to Zander. I think that in those last few months he found in himself qualities as a soldier that he hadn't known he possessed. He found the secret of leadership at combat level. He found that he could command obedience, make men do things they were afraid to do, by making them believe that *his* respect for *them* was something really worth having. It was the confidence he had gained from that discovery that took him to the Legion. He knew his job, so he went looking for work, this time with a possible winner. I'll bet you that was how it was.'

'You may be right. I've been looking at him as a skilled survivor. As a soldier he's only been on losing sides. First the Russian front, then Dien Bien Phu. He's done better as a civilian. Until now, anyway.'

'Has he said anything about this silver mine nonsense? Does he believe it?'

'Naturally, he gives The Ruler's version. This is a miracle treatment for asthma, bronchitis, sinusitis and a few other things. It's been working at Oberzeiring.'

The General looked at his drink as if he were wondering why he bothered with the stuff. 'I asked an MO in Brussels about it,' he said, 'and the fellow was very anti. He said that if what your asthma really needs is a regime of regular eight-degree Celsius temperatures, ninety-five percent humidity and water dripping down your neck, the place for you is Liverpool on a wet Sunday in March. He comes from Liverpool.'

'How about the success rate at Oberzeiring? Did he have any explanation for that?'

'Unsympathetic. A lot of asthma, he said, is psychosomatic. Back-to-the-womb therapies can succeed for a time, especially with elderly patients who've tried everything else.'

'Does The Ruler really have sinusitis, I wonder?'

He gave me a look. 'So you've asked yourself that one, too, eh? And if he hasn't got sinus trouble, what use has he for that old mine? Any ideas?'

I had, in fact, the beginning of an idea, but just then Schelm came back from his telephoning.

'I have an apology to make, Bob,' he announced. 'I hope you will find it acceptable.'

'What's gone wrong?'

'According to you, Simone Chihani's security plan calls for absolutely no mention of your name and whereabouts that could enable Rasmuk to trace Zander.'

'You had the same idea yourself back in Milan.'

'Yes. But I should have given orders on the subject. There has been a leak, small but you had better know about it. We found that getting the back-up TV crew you asked for was more difficult than we expected. It was the shortness of the notice we were giving. Eventually my people found this Dutch crew in Yugoslavia who were going to be free. The trouble then was getting them to do the job. They've been working in the Yugoslav mountains on a documentary film and living rough for over two months. They'd had enough. Money was no argument. They had to be persuaded. We told them that the footage they'd be shooting would be for international release.'

I sighed. 'Through an unnamed American network?'

'That at least was avoided. However, in the course of persuading them, your name was mentioned. That's what I wanted to check, whether your name was actually used. It was and I'm sorry. I don't think the leak's a bad one, but they are undoubtedly out having a few drinks in Trieste this evening. It only needs some bar fly who deals in gossip to get them talking and we could be in trouble tomorrow.'

The General broke in sharply. 'What's on offer, Dieter?' he demanded. 'What choices are you giving the man? Are you asking him whether or not he'd like to pull out because someone on your staff is a name-dropper? I wouldn't. He might say yes, and to hell with being considered a spoilsport. If that Dutch unit were to bring a Rasmuk killer squad trailing in after them tomorrow, it wouldn't only be Zander who got hit. I'd sooner put the question to Bob this way. If a bunch of home-sick Hollanders go out and get stinking in a Trieste night club, which language are they more likely to end up gossiping in – Italian or Dutch? That's assuming that most of them won't end up speechless anyway. I'd say Dutch. How about you, Bob?'

'I don't think it matters all that much,' I said. 'But then, I've had a day or two to think about the threat-to-Zander problem.'

'And we haven't?' Schelm inquired curtly. 'Or are you saying that if we can blow the man's whereabouts to a Dutch television crew, we're perfectly capable of blowing it to Rasmuk direct?'

I shrugged. 'It's no good getting mad at me, Dieter. I'm the one who asked about the risks. Remember? You're the one who described them to me. I think you misread the evidence.'

The General intervened again. 'I hope you're not going to go cryptic on us, Bob? You're going to tell us how the evidence was misread, aren't you? My desire to learn is just as keen as Dieter's I assure you.'

'Your teeth are beginning to show, Patrick,' I said. 'I'll tell you exactly what I mean. Through force of circumstances I've been looking at the evidence from a different angle. I need to know something, Dieter. How far back do you go on this whole deal? How long have you been involved, you personally?'

'Almost a month. Naturally, I've had access to a lot of research. What do you need to know about?'

'The time when the contract to kill Zander was put out to Mukhabarat Zentrum. You told me then you didn't know who was paying.'

'I still don't.'

'Do you know who it was who told Zander that Mukhabarat Zentrum had accepted the contract, who it was who tipped him off?'

'No.'

'Do you know about the two attempts to kill him that failed?'

'I've been told about them. They didn't seem relevant to this operation.'

'I can see that they wouldn't. They were both outstandingly amateurish. The first time it's a couple of kids with a pistol that jams. The second time, it's a girl with a grenade that's thrown the moment the pin's out so that he has time to roll clear. Must have shaken him though. I think that Rasmuk – or Mukhabarat Zentrum as he insists on calling it – organized both those attempts.'

Schelm was watching me carefully now. 'Why should you think that, Bob?'

'Because immediately after the second attempt The Ruler sent for Zander and warned him that he must take no more risks, that Mukhabarat Zentrum had accepted a contract to destroy not only him but his family too.'

Schelm's drink slopped. 'The *Ruler* told him?'

'That's what Zander said and I believed him. The warning came via The Ruler and Zander reacted promptly. That's when he went out of circulation and sent his family into hiding. Kids with grenades can't do him much harm, only soften him up a little maybe, but Mukhabarat Zentrum is different. So, that's when he went to work in secret for The Ruler, setting up the deal for Abra Bay.' I paused. 'Mind if I have another drink?'

Schelm took my glass. 'You're not trying to tell us, I hope, that there's *no* contract out on Zander. There you'd be quite wrong.'

'I'm trying to tell you that there are some unusual clauses in the contract.'

'Go on,' said the General.

'Last Friday, when I went to Malpensa as instructed, I was tailed. Miss Chihani, very efficiently I thought, lost the tail.'

Schelm handed me a fresh drink. 'So you've already told us.'

'What I didn't tell you about was the tailing operation. I'm important to them, right? I'm the one who's going to lead Rasmuk to the Zander hide-out and a quick killing. Well, they had three men on the job, three men who made themselves very conspicuous moreover. They had no back-up team that I saw. Now, whether more men would have helped against what Chihani had planned is beside the point. I thought it was common knowledge that a thorough tailing job calls for minimum teams of eight working in shifts. What's the matter with the all-powerful Rasmuk? Don't they know this? Do they have a manpower or cash-flow problem?'

'What's *your* answer, Bob?'

'I think they were simply going through the motions so that Zander and his people would continue to believe that they were under *immediate* threat. That way he would remain isolated and out of free circulation during the run-up period to the opening of the Abra Bay negotiations, the talks about talks that are due to begin tomorrow. The moment The Ruler tells you to sit down facing him, Patrick, Zander will become expendable. After that, Rasmuk can do their killing any time they like.'

'Oh Christ!' said the General softly.

But Schelm had still to be convinced. 'You say we misread the evidence.'

'Or had it misread for you. Dieter, when you briefed me the other night you told me that, according to the experts, not even The Ruler was crazy enough to make this approach to you about Abra Bay without the tacit approval of his UAE brothers. Well, I think your experts misread him, I think they credited him with too much sense. They were wrong. He's made the approach without any approval except that of his own peculiar ego. However, to protect himself against the wicked slanders of enemies – and all men of true worth have enemies, remember – he's dreamed up a beautiful lie. It goes like this. Here he is in Austria, quietly treating his sinus trouble and talking to architects about the clinic he wants to build for his people, when an American television reporter arrives with a camera unit to interview him about the project. The interviewer had been expected. What had not been expected was the arrival with him of three other persons in no way concerned with television. The first of these, my brothers, was a man no doubt well known to some of you. He is the European entrepreneur who calls himself Zander among other names. Such men have their uses and he has served me on occasion. Normally though, he does not enter my house uninvited. The two men with him he introduced to me as a West German senior diplomatist and a British lieutenant-general both at present in the service of Nato. The laws of hospitality obliged me to receive them. Judge of my surprise, then, when these Nato officials proceeded to put to me a secret proposal. They wish, they say, to discuss with me the building of a great port and other facilities on territory of mine at Abra Bay. They speak of the vast benefits that such an enterprise would bring to my poorer people. I listen politely and, I hope, with dignity. I say that I will give the matter thought, but make no promises. Then, without a moment's delay, I report to my brothers this thing that has happened and seek their fraternal advice on behalf of my people.' I looked from Schelm to the General. 'Who's to know that that's not the way it happened? Only one man who would be believed in the UAE – Zander.'

'*We* might be believed,' said Schelm.

'If Patrick's committee decides that it wants Abra Bay you'll keep your mouth shut, Dieter. And you'll see that I do too.'

'What about The Ruler's entourage? If you're right, he'll have to have all of them killed off as well.'

'I wouldn't worry too much about the entourage, Dieter,' the General said. 'They'll be well-trained non-observers. I don't suppose you've ever seen a man have his tongue cut out. They, almost certainly, have. The victim makes some very strange noises, believe me, and quite often he goes on making them for a long time before he bleeds to death or chokes. If Bob's right, Zander's the only witness The Ruler has to fear. He knows that The Ruler cheated on his princely brothers and he'll know exactly how the cheating was done if he ever gets to be questioned. He also probably knows what The Ruler will be asking for as his personal under-the-counter sweetener.' He glanced at me. 'Have you any ideas about what that might be?'

I thought. 'One of The Ruler's current anxieties is about chemical and biological warfare substances which might hasten his decline into impotence. He may ask for special protection. There'll be a huge instant cash demand too, I guess. I doubt if Mukhabarat Zentrum likes giving extended credit. Otherwise, I can't think of anything in particular that he might want.'

Schelm had been swirling a piece of ice around the bottom of an empty glass. 'If you're right, Bob,' he said, 'and maybe you are, do you think Zander has seen it this way?'

'Until quite recently, I think, he only had a nagging suspicion and was taking care. As I told Patrick, Zander seemed to me like a skilled survivor. But he's a survivor for whom time is running out, who's losing his self-confidence and wondering if he has begun to depend on luck rather than his wits. On the way to Zürich yesterday he talked of having one more battle to fight. Today, he was in a funny sort of mood. Now, I think, he's finally faced the fact that he was set up.' I took the note Simone had given me out of my pocket and handed it to Schelm. 'It's from Zander. His daughter gave it to me just before I left to come here. I read it on the way. It's handwritten by him. He likes to print with a felt-point pen.'

In response to a nod from the General, Schelm read it aloud. ' "*It is essential if our conference tomorrow is to succeed that the nature of my modest personal rewards for initiating this project and bringing the parties concerned to the negotiating table is* NOT *repeat* NOT *described or alluded to in any way at all. Kindly convey this in the strongest terms when reporting to your colleagues.*" Well, that seems to clinch it.'

The General grunted. 'He doesn't want The Ruler to know that, if his luck holds, he's getting the defectors' vanishing-cream treatment for himself and his family somewhere in North America. Don't blame him. Is that how you read it?'

'Yes,' Schelm said; 'but I can't help wondering what he *has* told The Ruler that he's getting from us for his trouble.'

'I can tell you that,' I said. 'Peace and tranquillity. The Ruler was very sympathetic when Zander told him that. I guess he thought that, for poor old Zander, peace and tranquillity could only mean money.'

The General threw me a cool look. 'Sure you're not making that up, Bob? Sounds a bit literary.'

'If you mean a bit fancy, I agree. But peace and tranquillity were Zander's own words for what he wants. He's not a simple soldier, Patrick, any more than you are.'

Schelm smiled. 'Bob's a little short-fused. I did warn you, Patrick.' He glanced at his watch. 'It's really time we went down to dinner, but if nobody minds I'm going to have another drink.'

However, when he reached the drinks table he just looked down at it. 'Why,' he asked us, 'did The Ruler have to cheat? We sold the Saudis a complete biological and chemical warfare defence system. The UAE could have one for the asking. The Ruler could have one all to himself. What is it he wants that he believes he can get from us only by secret unilateral dealing and dangling bait like Abra Bay?'

'I met some weird ones down there,' said the General, 'but this chap sounds very far gone indeed. Obviously, he must know that there are some things we're *never* going to give him, no matter how many Abra Bays he has to offer. Have you considered the possibility, Dieter, that what he wants may be something that he's just read or dreamed about or seen in a film about goings-on in outer space?'

Schelm slammed ice into his glass. 'Something that doesn't really exist, Patrick? I wouldn't mind that at all. If he wanted an expensive toy we could make it or fake it for him. But I don't think The Ruler goes in much for toys.'

'What about the silver mine?'

'That's no toy, Patrick. You've said as much yourself. No, I'm afraid there are only two basic things that The Ruler wants – a long life for himself and instant death for his enemies. What Bob's been telling us shows that we haven't taken this madman seriously enough. He doesn't care who he has to kill in order to get what he wants. And I'm sure of one thing. You may say that there are some things that we're *never* going to give him. I agree. But for Abra Bay, it's in the death department that we're going to be asked to go shopping with him.'

TEN

I WAS driven back to the Gasthaus by the driver who had brought me. On the return journey he didn't utter a single word. That suited me. I had much to think about and to remember, but, this time, no aide-mémoire to help me keep track of it. Schelm on security had begun to sound remarkably like Simone Chihani Zander.

From the time we had gone down to dinner, the only moment of light relief – at least, for me – had come with the coffee. The General had been talking about the way he intended to handle the meeting with The Ruler. He would try to say as little as possible and encourage the other side to be as talkative as possible. He had checked on The Ruler's command of English and been advised that it was grammatical and spoken with a good accent, but limited – 'has a Mayfair vocab'. The Ruler and Zander would undoubtedly use Arabic between themselves. The General would pretend not to understand and hope that the pretence would be believed.

'Now, about you, Bob,' he went on. 'How well do you speak it?'

'All I know is what you need in an Iraqi prison.'

'How much is that?'

I thought for a second or two and then gave him a sample.

His jaw dropped slightly and he glanced furtively around the restaurant to see if anyone had turned a head. No one had, it seemed. He looked at Schelm. 'Did you understand that, Dieter?'

'Not a word.'

The General lowered his voice. 'What he said was this, more or less. "The only way you'll empty your bucket before we say you can, spy, is to drink all the piss and eat the shit yourself." Or words to that effect. I'm not much good with their slang.'

'Seems pretty clear,' said Schelm.

'I can give you more of the idiomatic stuff if you like,' I said helpfully. ' "Stand with your heels against the wall, son of filth, and remain still until you're told to move. If you fall down or begin to shake too much, we'll have to think of something else for you to do with your legs." '

'Thank you, Bob. I think we have the message. Your accent's very odd I must say, even for Iraq. I don't think you'll understand more than a word here and there when The Ruler and Zander are talking. If you do understand something, just don't react to it. All right?'

'Sure, Patrick. I don't think that problem's going to arise, though, do you? I don't think I'm going to be allowed into that meeting any more than Jean-Pierre is. The last thing The Ruler's going to want is extra witnesses.'

He raised his eyebrows. 'Aren't you forgetting your own scenario? There can be as many witnesses to this meeting as the place will hold. The Ruler's story's going to be that Zander set it up to oblige his Nato friends and paymasters without any advance permission from him on the pretext that it was to be a simple television interview. We may know that story isn't true, but why should we announce the fact? Even if The Ruler managed to cheat us, make us look idiots, there'd be nothing for us in denouncing him. Besides, who would believe us? Zander's the only one who could really spill the beans and he's not going to be around much longer. He'll either be dead, or elsewhere. The latter I'm inclined to hope. He may not be a simple soldier, but he has guts.'

'Will you offer to take him with you?'

'Yes, if he looks as if he might accept the offer. If he asks for a ride we'll certainly give him one back to Germany with us. What happened after that would be up to Dieter's office of course. But he probably won't want to leave without his own people here and risk reprisals against them. His original plan called for maintaining the Ortofilm television unit cover.'

'That could already be blown.'

I hadn't known how right I was.

When we were within sight of the Gasthaus I told the driver to stop and that I would walk the rest of the way. He nodded and switched off the lights as he pulled in to the side of the road. I said, 'Danke' as I got out. He raised a hand in silent acknowledgement. As I walked away he did a slow U-turn before switching on the lights again. He could not have made my return more unobtrusive.

I had noticed earlier that there were two entrances to the Gasthaus. If you already had your room key you could go in through the car park entrance and straight up the stairs, avoiding the lobby. So that is what I did. The sight of a Mercedes with an ORF press permit on the windshield parked alongside the Ortofilm vehicles was good for a few moments of self-congratulation.

They ended at the head of the stairs. The Gasthaus was one of those hotels with alcoves in its corridors. Each was furnished with ladder-back chairs and a small table with a potted plant on it. As I reached the first alcove and turned towards my room, a shock-headed young man in a silver-buttoned blue blazer and grey slacks rose from one of the chairs.

'Mr Halliday,' he said, 'my name is Christian Rainer. I am from ORF current affairs Vienna. I would like a few words with you, please.'

'I was on my way to bed, Herr Rainer.'

He nodded as if he had known that I would think of nothing better to say. 'Yes. However, I still think you should spare time for a little talk. It could be to both our advantages.'

'If it's about the interview I'm booked to do tomorrow, I doubt if there's anything useful I can tell you. You've spoken to Monsieur Vielle?'

'And to Madame Chihani. I would suggest that we went down to the wine bar to talk, but it is closed now. May I suggest instead my room?'

'If you have something to say that won't keep, Herr Rainer, why don't we just sit here for a couple of minutes?'

'Very well.' He sat down again. 'But I am afraid that what I have to say is likely to take more than two minutes.'

I sat down facing him. The chairs were as uncomfortable as they looked. 'You could try editing it,' I said.

His clear brown eyes examining me across the potted geranium informed me that he was a top producer not an errand boy and that he wasn't taking cheap cracks from freelance reporters, no matter how venerable they might believe themselves to be. 'Have you worked with this Ortofilm unit before?' he asked brusquely.

'No.'

'We have. They worked on two short assignments for us in Belgium. We had bad experiences both times and will not use them again. Nothing to do with the technical quality of the work. The crew is good. It was their management. The English word is "tricksy" I believe.'

I nodded. Vielle, too, had found the Ortofilm management tricksy. 'So, you're not using them now. Someone else is. What's the problem, Herr Rainer? Has Vielle started being tricksy?'

'No, Mr Halliday. Monsieur Vielle is just incompetent. Are you aware that he doesn't even know whether he will be shooting on film or on video tape tomorrow? He does not know whether, if he is asked to shoot film in the mine itself, he has enough lamps to light the job. Finally, he says that you will be directing the interview as well as conducting it. One may do a sidewalk interview that way perhaps, but in a situation such as this, where the subject is a difficult and controversial foreign personage, the interviewer, even the most experienced one, needs help. You can consult with the director about *how* the interview should best be shot and what should be covered for technical purposes, but one cannot just leave it to the camera and sound men. However good they are, it is not fair to them. They have their own jobs to do.'

Every word he said was true but it was time to stop the flow. 'You're quite right, Herr Rainer,' I said. 'Monsieur Vielle is an accountant, not a production man. But that's not the worst of it. You said that the Ortofilm crew was good. Well, I found out just three days ago that the good Ortofilm crew you spoke of is at present in Mexico, of all places. What we have here is an Ortofilm B team. I wasn't prepared to accept that and I told the people who are paying me that I wasn't. For contractual reasons, apparently, they can't fire Ortofilm. Besides, Ortofilm's researcher, Madame Chihani, is extremely good and has done most of the preparatory work. What I have insisted on, though, is another unit, with a director, to shoot the interview.'

'ORF would be glad to help there,' he said quickly. 'You can use one of our units. There would be no problem.'

'There would be a considerable problem, Herr Rainer. Your unit wouldn't be allowed near The Ruler. Nothing I could say would alter that. The most likely effect would be that The Ruler would ban me too and cancel the interview.'

'"The Ruler", Mr Halliday? Is that what you call him?'

'The idea amuses you? He *is* a ruler so why not call him one?'

'Do you know what kind of a man this is?'

'The idea of interviewing the man is to give television viewers a chance of seeing the man for themselves. Whether they also see what kind of man he is depends on several things. How shrewdly he handles himself I don't know. He's made a habit of avoiding publicity.'

'For good reason. Where are you getting your competent unit from?'

'Holland. Viser-Damrak of Eindhoven. The director is a man named Dick Kluvers.'

'I know him. Very good. But he and his unit are in Yugoslavia, making a documentary. This I know for a fact.'

'It was a fact, Herr Rainer. They finished shooting down there a few days ago. They're in Trieste tonight. They arrive here tomorrow at midday. The film you get will be technically competent. You need have no fears on that score. I take it that Vielle has asked you to handle the processing? And you've agreed? Fine. Then, if you'll have a car standing by here from, say, four o'clock tomorrow afternoon, Kluvers will see that you get it as soon as it's all in the can. We'll want a first look at the answer print of course.'

'You can see it in Graz.'

'Splendid. I'll leave you and Kluvers to get it all together.' I started to go, but he reached over and put a hand on my arm.

'Surely you are going to tell me something of the questions you will be asking him, Mr Halliday?'

That really deserved a brush-off. I tried, though, to stay reasonably cool. 'Herr Rainer, how do I know what questions I'll be asking him? I don't do interviews by reading questions off a clip-board. I brief myself as well as I can on the subject. I talk to him for a bit before there's any filming. Usually a pattern for the interview begins to take shape. In effect, I try to get the subject to interview himself. I do as little talking as possible and ask a minimum of questions.'

If he had noticed that I had suddenly begun to steal lines from one of the highest-paid interviewers in the business, he gave no sign of having done so. He merely nodded. 'You said, I think, that you found Madame Chihani a very helpful researcher. I, too, found her very receptive and quick to take a point.'

'I'm glad of that. But I'm sure you're too experienced to believe, Herr Rainer, that a squabble between The Ruler and an Austrian government department over a building permit for a clinic is going to hold the interest of an American audience for very long. They'd sooner know where he stands on defence ties with the west. I don't want you to feel disappointed with what you see.'

He took his hand off my arm and we both stood up. He said: 'I haven't asked who it is who's employing you to do this interview, and I won't. If the real object of it is a public relations exercise for the benefit of this Ruler of yours and a big corporation like Syncom-Sentinel is footing the bill, then you will certainly be wise to let him interview himself. If you are hoping to produce something of more social value as well as news interest, you will have to ask him at least one question awkward enough to loosen his tongue.'

'You have a suggestion of course.'

'Of course. It goes like this. Here in Austria, Mr Ruler, you are building a clinic for the treatment of respiratory diseases. Am I right? Good. And do you know that some people here are saying that it is not really a clinic at all, but a huge private fall-out shelter? And that there are others, even less kind, who say that what you are building is not merely a fall-out shelter, but a *fortress* designed solely for your exclusive personal use during World War Three? How would you answer such accusations, Mr Ruler?'

'Herr Rainer,' I said gently, 'if I were The Ruler, or even a minor politico, I'd have to begin by saying that you weren't asking questions but making a speech.'

He actually blushed, 'I can assure you, Mr Halliday, that, under normal circumstances, I would say the same thing to one of my own reporters who behaved so. I was simply trying to describe briefly some of the reasons for local feeling against this man.'

'Are there other reasons?'

'He employs no Austrian people.'

'What about the security guards at the mine? Doesn't an outfit in Vienna take care of that?'

He sniffed. 'Ex-policemen with pistols and riot control equipment, tear gas. There was talk of student action against the mine property a few months ago. Nothing came of it, but the guards remained. You cannot consider that as employment for Austrians. What I am speaking of are the professional workers. The architects, the engineers, the experts and specialists that he has brought in have all been foreigners. One asks why.'

'Is it illegal these days, Herr Rainer, to build a fortress in Austria?'

'It is when you call the structure a clinic for the treatment of respiratory diseases and refuse to submit building plans for permissions from the proper authorities.'

'How do you expect him to employ Austrian labour when he has no permission to build? If I were The Ruler, I think I might suggest to you that much of this hostility towards him is a response to his race. The local bigots don't like oil sheikhs. As for this World War Three fortress talk, that sounds to me as if it's based on nothing much more serious than gossip.'

He gave me a mocking little bow. 'A very good attempt to make me mad, Mr Halliday. If Syncom-Sentinel selected you to pretty up this really most unpleasant image, they chose well. For a moment you almost convinced me that you believed what you were saying. And you're quite right about there being a lot of gossip. Unfortunately, it is based on a great deal of extremely hard evidence. Ask Madame Chihani for the sources involved. I gave her all the details. They may surprise you. I have a room here and I shall be waiting myself to receive your film for processing tomorrow. Right now, I will not keep you any longer from your bed. Please sleep well, Sir.'

I said goodnight and went along the corridor to my room. There was no need for me to use my key. As I reached the door, Simone opened it from the inside.

'You heard all that?' I asked.

'Yes. I brought up some wine before they closed the bar. I thought you might be thirsty. It should still be cold.'

'Thank you, Simone, I'm afraid you've had a rough evening.'

'Jean-Pierre had a worse time. He strongly dislikes feeling stupid and that man was not kind to him. He is right about the evidence against The Ruler too. A French engineer has been talking. The Ruler wants a fall-out shelter that he can defend against anyone who wants to share it with him, even a mob of local people. The patron knows about all this, of course. It was he who arranged for the supply of the special pumps and other equipment to dry out the deep flooded parts of the mine. Anyone who tried to get into that clinic when The Ruler had need of it would die on the fences, or perhaps before reaching them. I don't want to think about it. What happened at the meeting in Velden? Is everything all right?'

'It was all very friendly.'

She handed me a glass of wine. 'Are they ready to give the patron what he has asked for, and for all of us?'

'Oh yes. There was no argument about that. There are some technical problems, but we'll have to iron those out.'

'But there is total agreement in principle?'

'Absolutely.'

'That is what matters.' She began to climb out of her pants.

'As I said, it was very friendly.' I sipped at the lukewarm wine. 'The chief negotiator is a modern professional soldier. I think that he and your father are going to like one another.'

She was suddenly motionless, half out of her pants and standing on one leg. 'By my father you mean the patron?'

'They said he's your father. Isn't he?'

'We will continue to call him the patron, please.'

'Security?'

'Mostly habit perhaps. But yes, security also.' She went on undressing.

'They were puzzled,' I said, 'about the security situation here. In particular about your insistence on the need to keep my name off the air.'

'Didn't you explain to them that Rasmuk must not be told that you are here?'

'No. I explained that Rasmuk already know where we are. They know because The Ruler will have kept them posted. When did the patron realize that it was The Ruler who was paying to have him killed?'

She threw her pants across the room and sat down on the bed. 'Who told you?' she demanded.

'No one. I figured it out. I should have thought the patron would have seen it too.'

She shrugged. 'He refused for a long time to admit it to himself, or to me. Now he knows for sure, yes, but now it is safer – safer for us all – to pretend that we don't know. The longer they think we are sheep who do not know the way to the slaughterhouse and cannot read the signs the better off we'll be. There's more chance of surprising them.'

'When did *you* suspect?'

'When The Ruler changed the rendezvous. It was to have been at a villa near Stresa. Then, suddenly, it was here. There seemed to me no sense in the change. Gradually I began to reason, perhaps as you did, but more slowly and unwillingly. There was only one person who could believe himself to be safer with the patron dead. The patron himself would not listen to me at first.

He listened to Jean-Pierre who has never even set eyes on The Ruler. But we were all slow. Even knowing The Ruler as we do, it took us weeks to believe it of him. The only precaution the patron took was to make his price for Abra Bay sanctuary for us.'

'The possibility was discussed this evening of giving the patron immediate personal protection tomorrow. All he'd have to do is ask for it.'

'What kind of protection?'

'A ride back with them into Germany. There, he would be given top security treatment, the best.'

'What did you say to them?'

'They said it for me. They said that as it was a ride only for him they didn't think he would accept, because he would be leaving you and the young people at risk as hostages. I said that I didn't think he would be persuaded to change his mind. Was that right?'

'He would never go alone leaving us. Jean-Pierre is safe. So is Guido and those back in Stresa. They are not of his personal family, of his blood. But he will insist that the four of us go together into any safety that is offered.'

'It's difficult. Austria is neutral and properly touchy on the subject. These Nato people are here unofficially and because The Ruler wouldn't meet them anywhere else. Even offering the patron a ride to the German frontier and German protection is stretching things a bit for them. Their passports don't show who they really are. Effective protection for the four of you would involve an armed escort to a helicopter that would be landing and taking off without proper clearances in the corner of some field. A shoot-out with Rasmuk could be a distinct possibility. They can't risk having to explain shenanigans of that sort to the Austrians.'

'That is understood by all concerned, including The Ruler. It was understood from the beginning. The Ruler said that he feared high-handed behaviour on the part of the CIA in other places. Yes, my friend, you may laugh, but only a little. Rasmuk can be high-handed anywhere it chooses.'

'Does the patron still believe that the Ortofilm cover is going to see us through?'

'He knows that it won't, and he blames himself for thinking like a lazy old man. He sees now that Ortofilm is worse really than no cover at all. The Ortofilm vehicles can be used to identify us as the target group. All The Ruler has to do is tell his chief secretary to make a telephone call just as we leave him tomorrow. What do your people have to suggest?'

'A rendezvous just outside Austria. A place where they could set up one hundred percent protection. They could do that with a phone call.'

'Where outside Austria?'

'Tarvisio in Italy. It's about an hour and a half by road from here. But we'd have to make it on our own.'

'And from the Petrucher, the moment we leave, we will have a Rasmuk hit-team with us.'

'They're not going to start anything anywhere near The Ruler. They'll bide their time.'

'But not for long. *They* don't mind offending against Austrian neutrality.'

Later, when we were lying quietly in bed, I said: 'Have we plenty of money available?'

'What for?'

'Why couldn't we charter a helicopter?'

'I called the charter companies this evening. There are two of them and there is an airfield not far away from which they will fly us anywhere we like within range.'

'Well then . . .'

'Unfortunately, the airfield is three kilometres north of Klagenfurt. So, we would have to drive not only seventy kilometres back from the Petrucher, but also a further fifteen kilometres beyond to reach the airfield. Charter aircraft are not permitted to land at unauthorized places without special clearances that we could not obtain. In any case, what do you think that the Rasmuk team would do when it saw us approaching an airfield or an open space where a helicopter could come in to pick us up?'

'Move in for a quick kill?'

'I think so. Have you any other ideas?'

'A possible, but I'd better think some more about this one before I try it out on you. Tell me something. How do you think The Ruler is now thinking about this television interview I'm going to do? I mean, you said that he doesn't like changes of plan. How did the patron sell him this one? How completely has he accepted it? Obviously, it's still needed as window-dressing to cover his big meeting in the back room. But how is he going to be approaching it? Will he now expect this interview to be real, false or a mixture? Could you make a guess?'

She stared up at the ceiling. 'I will do better. I will tell you precisely. If the preparations for the filming and the interview are made with the greatest of ceremony and seriousness, with him at the centre and all ears attentive to the slightest sound he makes, then he will consider the occasion real. Does that help you?'

'Very much.'

'Then let me qualify it. For how long does a boy enjoy playing with a toy machine gun? I will tell you. Only for as long as the bangs it makes are loud enough to make the particular game he is playing seem real. The Ruler is the same.' She turned her head to look at me. 'Don't think too much. Better get some sleep.' She smiled. 'And to save you from bad dreams, I will tell you something highly confidential. In the Ortofilm van we have hidden four good assault rifles and plenty of ammunition. We brought it all with us from Stresa.'

'No dreams, you said?'

'No *bad* dreams. My dear, it was always possible that we would have to fight a Rasmuk team for our lives, and kill some of them. Now, that is what I think we shall have to do.'

She somehow made it sound like mixed doubles on a grass court in May but I could think of no acceptable way of saying so. As soon as she had gone I went to the bureau drawer and dug out a folder of Gasthaus picture postcards and stationery that I had seen there earlier. Then I sat down and wrote a letter to Christian Rainer.

The first page went like this:

Dear Herr Rainer,

I am writing this at one in the morning and will have it delivered to you by hand at breakfast time.

Since our conversation earlier, and having heard what Mme Chihani had to tell me, I have felt obliged to re-think my approach to the Petrucher interview. I now believe that you are right and I was wrong.

This man who avoids all media contacts does so protesting that his privacy must be preserved and that personal publicity is offensive to him. His real aim, clearly, is to avoid the kind of unsympathetic questioning in the face of which he might have to choose between maintaining the silence of guilt or attempting to defend the indefensible. However, faced with an interviewer like the American Halliday, billed in advance as sympathetic, he might well be led into putting his case as he sees it with that blithe lack of inhibition that often tells the truth without the teller knowing it. It can make exciting television. The respectful, head-nodding interviewer with a few carefully-worded leading questions has often succeeded where more abrasive inquisitors have failed. Thanks to the time difference between here and New York, I have been able to reach my producer there and secure his approval of the new line I propose to take.

Unfortunately, there are practical difficulties of which I was unaware when we talked earlier. I am told that our unit, and its vehicles, are now under strict surveillance by an international security agency (not Austrian) newly employed by this paranoid Ruler and that the surveillance will continue during our stay in your country. Under the circumstances, I think it would be advisable to change the arrangements we made for delivering the film to you for processing. Ideally, it should be made to appear to those keeping tabs on us that ORF tried to get the film and failed. This will spare you the inconvenience of having The Ruler's lawyers in Vienna trying to retrieve the film by court order before you have had a chance to air it. So, the Ortofilm unit (with the film shot by the Dutch unit on board) will leave the Petrucher mine as soon as possible tomorrow afternoon and head directly for Italy via Villach and the Arnoldstein frontier post. I propose to make the actual delivery of the cans to you in the following way.

By two I had finished. Then I called Barbara in her New York apartment. I wasn't worried about Rainer checking on my long-distance calls. They had direct dialling from the room and all he would be able to check on, if he took the trouble, was the amount of the phone charges on my bill.

To Barbara, after small talk, I said: 'You'll be interested to know that tomorrow I'm going to do a television interview with an oil sheikh who's bought himself an Austrian health-mine.'

'A what?'

'Never mind. Are you still friends with that producer who got burned over *First of the Week*?'

'Reasonably. I've always maintained that it wasn't entirely your fault. He's with Public Service television now and leads a better life.'

'Would he like something for nothing?'

'Robert? Is this you speaking or those memoirs?'

'It's nothing to do with the memoirs. All he has to do is take a call from ORF, that's Austrian television in Vienna. The man calling will be a current affairs producer named Christian Rainer. Here's what he'll say.'

It was two-thirty before I got back to bed.

Breakfast came at seven-thirty and I gave the room waitress the letter to deliver to Rainer's room. He called within minutes.

'A very pleasant surprise so early in the morning, Mr Halliday.' He said it very cautiously though.

'I'm glad you think so. How about the delivery arrangements? Will you go along with them?'

'If you really believe that they are necessary. But first we shall have to be more businesslike. I must know now who is your principal in New York.'

'Okay. As I told you, I've already called and explained the situation. It's a PBS project and the producer in charge will be expecting a call from you this morning New York time. I'll give you the name and number in a moment. Meanwhile, he's given me a message to pass on. He wants the processed film airmailed to him by the fastest route you know, and he doesn't care whether *I* get to see a run-through or not. He wants it in his hands as soon as possible.'

'I understand perfectly.' And he did. If the situation had been reversed, the processed film in his own cutting room would have been what he would have wanted, and the hell with any other interested parties.

'He suggests,' I went on, 'that you sort out the business details and accounting when he has the film.'

'Very well. I will make arrangements, then, to play our part in your delivery plan. May I say something personal, Mr Halliday?'

'Sure.'

'You will not take it amiss, I hope, if I tell you that the reports we have had on you as an interviewer have been, as they say, mixed.'

'Mostly bad you mean?'

'Mostly, though not all. What I have to offer is a thought for you. I have noticed that some interviewers who work for me do better when they don't rehearse. I think you may be like that.'

'Do you think it's the same way with persons being interviewed?'

'I am sure of it.'

'Then what's your guess about The Ruler?'

'No need to guess. He has been silent. The first difficulty will be to persuade him to start talking. If you succeed, then you will have trouble stopping him. You may need a great deal of film. Tell Dick Kluvers that from me.'

There was one more bridge to cross. Sitting with Simone and Jean-Pierre in the privacy of the Ortofilm station-wagon, I told them what I had arranged with Rainer.

'It could postpone the battle for a little while,' Simone said calmly. 'In these matters, later is usually better than sooner. I say it is a good idea.'

'Only the patron can decide,' Jean-Pierre said heavily.

'Okay. Let Simone call him then. They can speak Berber. I'll bet nobody in The Ruler's entourage will understand what they're saying.'

'Out of the question.' His face had become white and pinched. 'When he is with The Ruler we wait to be called, as the patron himself is called, like dogs. To call the patron at this moment would be to tell them that we have understood their treachery.'

'Then we'll have to decide without calling, like sensible men and women who'd rather not be sitting targets. Listen to me, Jean-Pierre. If we had armoured personnel carriers instead of the Ortofilm logo to protect us, I'd say come along too. But there's no reason for you and Guido to take these risks. You stay with the van and you follow us only as far as the frontier. Then, you stop. Agreed?'

He looked me in the eyes. 'And what is *your* position now, Mr Halliday? Which way home do *you* intend to go?'

'I'm being paid to act as a go-between and to do a television interview with The Ruler. I shall arrive with Ortofilm. Obviously, I should leave with Ortofilm.'

'You could leave with your Nato friends,' Simone said. 'There would be nothing to stop you accepting a ride from them, and nothing embarrassing for them in offering it.'

'My arrangement with Rainer is that I hand over the film to him personally at the frontier.'

'Very well. If we get as far as the frontier and your handing over of film, then you can leave us.'

'I'll see how things go and decide later.'

'I think not,' Jean-Pierre said firmly. 'You ask me to accept decisions in the patron's absence and I agree in principle. But where and when you leave us will be something the patron himself must decide. Now, it is after nine and time we went.'

'I have to call Velden first.'

'The bills are already paid. Is it absolutely necessary?'

'Yes. I'll use the pay phone in the lobby. Yes, I'll be as quick as I can.'

Schelm listened to my plan for getting to the frontier in one piece without marked enthusiasm, but he didn't try to discourage me.

'It could work,' he said. 'I hope it does.'

'Can't your friends on the other side move a bit closer to the border than Tarvisio?'

'I've already asked them to. You told me that the Ortofilm station-wagon is distinctively marked and easy to spot. What is arranged is that the Carabinieri will set up a temporary road block on a straight bit just north of a village named Coccau-alto. It's barely four kilometres from the frontier and that's a busy road. They're doing us a big favour. What the driver of the station-wagon must do is this. It's a winter sports area and there's a small road off to the right just there that in the season leads to a chair lift. As soon as the driver sees the Carabinieri's halt signal he's to pull off the main road into the narrow one and stop.'

'What then?'

'All persons in the station-wagon will be taken immediately to the Carabinieri barracks. What happens to them from there need not concern you, Bob.'

'How many Carabinieri will there be and what sort of transportation will they have?'

'I don't have that sort of detail. Why do you want to know?'

'Jeeps would be no good, and some of those panel trucks the Carabinieri use are quite flimsy. I'd hate to be inside one that was being shot at.'

'The Carabinieri's anti-terrorist squad is one of the most experienced in Europe. Anyway, if you have any sense, Bob, you'll be on your way back to Milan by another route. Nobody's going to be shooting at you. By now, I would think, Pacioli probably has a second cheque waiting for you.'

'My agent takes care of the cheques, Herr Mesner. I'll see you later.'

The manager was at the desk and most affable. He refused to let me pay for the call. I said that if there were any way in which I could casually mention the Gasthaus Dr Wohak in the course of the press and radio interviews I would be doing, he could count on me to seize the opportunity.

Mokhtar and Jasmin were sitting in the back of the station-wagon chewing on something pink. They looked bored. The last couple of days had been no fun at all for them. Their special skills had not been called upon. They had simply had to look solemn and keep quiet. The only candy bars obtainable locally were not the kind they really liked.

'There's something I forgot,' I said as I got into the front passenger seat beside Simone. 'You said that you had rifles and ammunition hidden in the van. It'll only be going as far as the frontier.'

'I didn't forget,' she said. 'It's all in here now. Under the baggage behind the back seat. The young people cleaned the rifles early this morning. Can't you smell the oil?'

I found, now that she'd mentioned it, that I could smell gun oil. I had thought it must be the smell of the local candy.

ELEVEN

THE valley of the river Pölstal runs north from the Klagenfurt–Vienna road three miles west of Judenburg. Today, it is mostly pasture-land with wedge-shaped plantations of black pine on the hillsides, but in the twelfth century a stretch of fifteen miles or more centred on the town of Möderbrugg had long been a mining and industrial area. For how long no one can be sure, but, as the floor of the valley once carried a busy Roman road, the outcrops in the limestone hills of silver-bearing lead and zinc ores must have been known about before the Dark Ages and long before the skills needed to exploit them were available locally. Probably it was men from Saxony who eventually provided the skills. They were the great mining experts of the early Middle Ages. In the fourteenth century, however, there was extensive flooding in some of the deeper mines. By the fifteenth, most of the accessible wealth had gone, and with it went the families of the miners, the smelters, the cupellers and the silversmiths along with those of the less skilled, the ore-millers and the workers *mit Schlegel und Eisen* who had once made the valley ring. The neat green and brown landscape through which we now drove looked as if it had been modelled as scenery for an expensive toy train set.

The approach to the Petrucher property was along an inconspicuous turning on the left hand side of the road between Unterzeiring and Möderbrugg. Simone passed without seeing it the first time and we had to go back. The only signpost was a small poker-work board nailed to a sapling. It said: PETRUCHER – *Zutritt verboten*.

The lane beyond was steep and winding with tall, thick hedges on both sides that made it impossible to see more than a few yards ahead. We went up slowly over a dirt surface that had been deeply rutted by heavy trucks. Then, as we came out of a hairpin bend, the lane widened and we were on asphalt. We were also faced by closed gates in a high fence with barbed-wire coils along the top and notices forbidding entrance, warning of dangers and threatening penalties. Three security guards in grey uniforms and a snarling dog peered at us through the wire mesh. One of the guards consulted a piece of paper and then nodded to the others. The dog handler persuaded his charge to back off a little so that his colleagues could open the gates. Then we were waved through. The dog started snarling again as the van followed us.

'Jean-Pierre will not like this,' Simone said. 'He is afraid of dogs trained to attack.'

'I don't much like the look of that one myself. What's worrying me more, though, is being out of touch with the patron for so long. Who's going to tell those characters on the gate to let the Dutch unit in? What about the arrangements I've made with Rainer? Who's going to tell him about the Carabinieri?'

It was Chihani who answered. 'Dealing with these Nato persons has made you officious,' she said snappishly. 'All you have to worry about at present is your interview with The Ruler. You address him, by the way, as Your Highness.'

Where the patron was concerned, I noted, Jean-Pierre wasn't the only one who could be jealous. 'Just plain Your Highness? I'll remember that,' I said.

Now I could see the steeply-pitched roof of the Petrucher house above a screen of trees. Then the driveway swung sharply left and we were in a bull-dozed clearing occupied by two of those long, narrow temporary buildings that contractors bring in for use as offices, canteens and changing rooms on a construction site. Beyond them was a row of parked cars. The big Buick with Zürich plates had to belong to the Swiss architect. An Opel and a Taunus, both with W-prefixed Austrian plates, were probably used by the security guards. A little apart stood three white cars, all brand new. Two were Series 7 BMWs, the third was a Mercedes 600 limousine. All three had temporary Z-plates from West Germany. Another guard with a dog signalled to us to park alongside the Buick.

I could see all the house now. It stood on a rocky ledge at the foot of a hillside to which it seemed to be clinging. It wasn't in fact, but Simone, who had found out all about the place, had explained the effect. Nearly all the old mines in the valley had begun as small open-cast operations on hillside outcrops. Then, when the ore veins had been followed, the original holes in the ground had become what miners called adits, level passageways into the hillsides. The sinking of shafts from the passages had been the third stage, and that had always been when the problems of drainage, ventilation, hauling and underpinning began. So keen had Dr Petrucher been to explore the ancient wonders of his mine that he had built his house on foundations set back into the wooded hillside. This had enabled him to have the mine adit right in the main living room. As a result, of course, all the windows had to be in the front of the house. To a man who had felt so strongly about his hobby, however, this would have been a small price to pay. His wife must either have been very fond of him or else a little bit dotty herself.

To the left of the main house there was a small annexe on the end wall of which someone, Petrucher's grandson perhaps, had once painted the word MUSEUM in Gothic lettering. It was still just visible. As Simone finished parking and switched off, the guard with the dog moved back to make way for his superior, a martial figure who wore a highly-polished officers' sword belt on which to carry his revolver holster. He said something to me in German which I didn't understand. It was Simone who answered and interpreted.

'The patron wishes to see me in the house,' she said as she climbed out. 'You and Jean-Pierre can stay here or have a seat in the museum. It's as you choose, but there must be no wandering about. The young people stay with the transport.' She repeated the instructions so that Mokhtar and Jasmin could understand them and then went over to the van to speak to Jean-Pierre before telling the security captain with a nod that she was ready to be shown the way.

I got out of the station-wagon and went across to Jean-Pierre.

'Coming to see the museum?' I asked.

'Thank you, no.' He glanced meaningfully in the direction of the guard with the dog. 'There are two of those beasts here, perhaps more. The men with them think they can control them, but I have seen what happens when something goes wrong. There is a lot of blood and everyone says it has never happened before.'

'Some people feel the same way about seatbelts in cars – that they can sometimes turn out to be dangerous, I mean. If there's anything worth seeing in there I'll tell you about it.'

The museum was a large square room with stone walls, two casement windows, a heavy wooden door and a tiled floor. There was a kerosene lantern hanging from the ceiling. It didn't look as if it had been cleaned or lighted recently, but there was kerosene in it still. It gave the room a faint smell of times past.

The exhibits were mostly in two glass cases. Others, too large or heavy for the cases, stood against one of the windowless walls.

I looked in the glass cases first, where every object had a yellowing label beside it and a description written in sepia ink. One case contained nothing but skeletons that had been found in the mine. These were mostly of small mammals – cats, dogs and rodents of various sizes – but there were one or two birds and an incomplete human skeleton as well. I tried hard to read the label on that one but the writing combined with the German defeated me. The other case housed the artefacts. They too had been recovered from the mine workings and were, not surprisingly, nearly all miners' hand tools without their wooden helves. There were picks, shovels, hammers and wedges all arranged in what I soon gathered was chronological order. Dr Petrucher had assigned the picks, for instance, *circa* dates covering three centuries. At first I could not see how it had been done. The picks, apart from small differences in sizes and the way some of them curved, all seemed identical. The differences could have been accounted for simply by saying that not all of them had been forged by the same toolmaker. Then I noticed that beside each date card was a coin. In another part of the case there was a whole collection of old coins. Dr Petrucher's system of dating had been based on sound archaeological thinking. If you find an object, such as a coin, which can be dated with reasonable confidence, then it is *probable* in most circumstances that other objects found with it will be of the same period. I approached the rest of the exhibits more respectfully. Against the wall I found parts of an old windlass, a small iron sled and an ox-hide bucket. The German word for ox is *Ochse*. That's how I knew it was ox-hide.

The most interesting exhibit, however, was Dr Petrucher's attempt to make a map of the mine. It hung high up on the end wall and I had to stand on a chair to see it properly. It looked like a cross-section drawing of a huge sponge. The Doctor had been something of a sketch-artist too, and around the outer edges of the sponge he had done drawings of how he had thought those old miners must have looked when they were at work. In the lower galleries, it seemed, they had generally worked lying prone in minute tunnels or on their sides hacking away beneath the limestone overhangs. The only standing room in the sponge was in the higher galleries where the winching-up of the baskets filled with ore had been done or at the foot of the ventilation shafts sunk from the hillside above. There was also a drawing of a drainage pump consisting of a lot of scoops or dippers mounted on a long revolving chain the bottom loop of which stayed under water in a deep sump. And Dr Petrucher had tried to figure out the size of the workings, though the difficulty of making estimates that would be any better than rough guesses had clearly bothered him. However, his medical training had taught him how to make guesswork sound good. He admitted that it was guesswork but made the admission in Latin. *Magnitudo quod cogitari potest*, he had written coyly in a delicate little scroll above his estimates. Translated from the Latin, they were: *Greatest measurable depth* – 280 metres, *Greatest width* – 400 metres, *Volume of air within when unflooded* – 8 million cubic metres, *Volume of air within at maximum (1904) flooding* – 2 million cubic metres.

'And what do you make of it all, Mr Halliday?' Zander asked.

I had left the big door open to give myself more light, but even so he had come in very quietly. His hands were in the scrubbed-up position, which I now recognized as an indicator of fast thinking in process, and the eyes were smiling up at me. The thing that startled me was that he was wearing a shirt with a tie and a beautifully cut grey mohair suit.

'What do I make of this mine? It looks to me like a sponge,' I said.

'Think of it as a lung, Mr Halliday, and all will become clear.'

I climbed down from the chair. 'Simone has put you in the picture? You agree with what's been planned?'

'I think you have done very well indeed, Mr Halliday, and worked very hard for us. I said we had enlisted you. You see now? I was right. The idea of using the Austrian television people as a kind of escort was very cute.'

'Cute you say? You mean you don't think it'll work.'

'Up to a point, I think it may work quite well.' The quality of the simper made it less patronizing than it sounded.

'If it works to the point of getting us as far as the Italian frontier in one piece, I'd say that it had worked amazingly well.'

'Perhaps,' he said absently.

'Perhaps what?' I was getting annoyed.

'Perhaps they are not planning to make the kill in Austria. In their place I would not try it, I think. For them a clean getaway is most important.'

'Then we don't really need an escort? Is that what you're saying?'

'No, no, Mr Halliday. The escort will be most useful. It will tell them that we believe we need one and that we think we understand their intentions. We shall be taking up what they will see as a natural defensive position. Don't worry. You have no reason to reproach yourself.'

'I wasn't reproaching myself.'

'Good, good.' Further discussion of plans for dealing with a Rasmuk hit-team would have bored him. He changed the subject with a flutter of hands. 'Right now, what is important for your interview with His Highness is that you understand the special significance for him of this mine.'

'Significance as a fall-out shelter you mean.'

'Significance as a nuclear fall-out shelter, certainly. But also its value as a defence against biochemical warfare substances.'

'I only asked because the other day, Mr Zander, you were selling the place as a clinic like Oberzeiring.'

He brushed that away with the edge of a hand as I had seen him brush away other awkward or unwanted trains of thought.

'That was the other day,' he said. 'Now you must have the facts. First, consider the site. Austria is now neutral and most unlikely to suffer a direct attack. All dangers to her in the final World War will come from the devastation of her neighbours. The prevailing winds in this part are westerly, so here, on the eastern slopes of the hills, fall-out of all kinds is likely to be received in smaller amounts. Now, for the mine itself. You were looking at old Petrucher's ideas about its size. What had occurred to you? Why were you interested?'

'I was thinking that if there hadn't been a fairly high silver content in the ore, nobody in the Middle Ages would have bothered to scratch it all out. Their smelting processes must have been pretty wasteful.'

'But there *was* a lot of silver there and they *did* dig the ore out and there had been much more there to take than Dr Petrucher ever thought. The workings, now that they have been pumped dry at the deepest part, have about forty percent more air in them than Petrucher's calculations indicated. I told you to think of it as a lung, Mr Halliday.'

'Yes, you did.'

'Very well. When the final World War breaks out and the two sides have begun to use nuclear and biochemical weapons on the grand scale, how will you try to meet the threat?'

'By getting drunk, I'd say.'

'I am being serious, Mr Halliday. Would you perhaps seal yourself in protective clothing and then, when the filters in the face mask ceased to work, try to hold your breath?'

'Who's joking now? I guess a cold water diving suit with plenty of air bottles would help, if you didn't mind giving up eating and drinking.'

'And for as long as your supply of fresh air bottles lasts, yes that would help. How long shall we give you? A week?'

'Thanks. But it's not enough, is it?'

'No. Six months at least you would need before harmless and easily breathable air once more became available. This mine here would give you and twenty of your friends or servants an ample supply of safe, easily breathable and uncontaminated air for a minimum period of eight months.'

'How does it do that?' I pointed at the sponge on the wall. 'What comes in through the ventilation shafts? Contaminated air? No, because you'd shut them off presumably. What about the pumps? What keeps them running? Emergency generators? Where does the air and gas to keep them running for eight months come from? How about breakdowns? Do you have spares?'

But he was flapping his hands at me. 'Please, please, I am asking you to think of it as a lung. With the pumps below now keeping all the workings empty of water, the mine has drawn the equivalent of a deep breath, a breath consisting of nearly twelve million cubic metres of pure air. Now, the great emergency arrives. It could be tomorrow. The electricity fails. The pumps stop. Slowly, very slowly, the deep parts of the mine will begin to flood again and, as they slowly flood, the water will start pushing air out of the mine up through the ventilation shafts. They will have non-return air valves and filters on them, of course, as a precaution, but with the mine gradually flooding the flow of air will always be steadily *out*. The whole mine will be like a lung breathing out, but, because of its great size, taking eight months to do so. Even if mains electricity is restored quickly, the pumps will remain silent. They will be silent so that the pure underground water from the deep springs can continue to flow in, displacing the fresh, clean air and forcing it into the upper galleries for men to breathe.'

'Whose idea was this? The Ruler's?'

The simper became bland. 'The Ruler has a most ingenious mind, as you seem to have realized rather quickly, but in the areas of science and technology it works only superficially. He bought the mine as a simpler kind of refuge from germs and chemicals that might attack his princely virility. He proposed to do much as you suggested a moment ago. Shut the ventilation shafts and rely on his stores of food, bottled water and aphrodisiacs to see him through. These more interesting developments were suggested by the mining engineer I first found to advise him.'

'The one who's been shooting off his mouth to the media?'

'No. He left because he disliked the uses to which his work was to be put. He believed that story about a clinic. When he found it wasn't true, he resigned. But he made no scandal. The man who followed him was different. You must not think that there was anything very remarkable or original about this engineering idea. It is only making gravity work for you. Think of a dry dock. First, you pump out the water so that you may repair your ship. Then, when you want the ship to float again, you stop the pumps, open the valves and let water return. The Ruler, though, had difficulty sometimes in understanding this. A moment came when this second engineer treated His Highness with insufficient respect. He was fired. He bears a grudge.'

'What did he do? Tell The Ruler he was stupid?'

'He said, and in the hearing of others, that His Highness knew less than nothing about hydraulic engineering. Very foolish. What satisfaction can there be in stating the obvious simply because of a loss of temper. In fact, His Highness had been trying to understand why others could not do with other old mines what he was doing with this one.'

'Don't tell me he was beginning to think of civil defence for all.'

'No, he was thinking that there might be profit of some kind in selling the idea to his brother Rulers. In fact, very few old mines could be used in this way. When they cease to be maintained, most of them soon collapse. It happens that a few of the old limestone workings in this area are more like natural caves.'

'Is there any chance of my having a quick look down below

before the Dutch unit gets here. If it's at all possible I'd like to shoot the interview below ground.'

'That may be possible, but there's no chance of your going to look now.' The blandness had gone. 'His Highness is being very careful today. To reach the mine entrance you would have to go through the room in which he confers with the architect. You would meet and that would be wrong. He will only meet you when I bring you in for an audience, accompanied in the background by the Nato representatives, before his chosen witnesses, the Chief Secretary and the Financial Counsellor. You understand?'

'Sure. Nothing's been pre-arranged. It's all a big surprise.'

'Yes, Mr Halliday.' He gave me a hard look. 'And we do or say nothing to contradict that impression. He is all-wise and all-knowing and we treat him with the respect he considers due to him.'

'Ignoring the fact, for the time being, that he's an all-time murderous son-of-a-bitch. I see.'

'No you *don't* see, Mr Halliday.' The eyes glittered into mine. 'We don't ignore it. We *forget* it. That way I may improve a little my family's chances, and mine, of staying alive. As long as he thinks we are still innocents we have a small chance. We could still, perhaps, surprise them. But only if we seem innocent. Innocence, remember, is respectful. Your disapproval, your detestation of treacherous behaviour is unimportant and, at present, inconvenient. You will forget it please.' He glanced at his watch. 'I hope your Nato friends are not going to be late.'

'They won't be late for another quarter of an hour, Mr Zander. Let's not start biting our nails just yet. You ask me to forget something. Right. But don't you forget, please, that I have an interview to do later. And it's going to have to be a much more serious job than the quick, easy question-and-answer session that we talked about back in Stresa. I have to get The Ruler talking and I don't want to hear too much about hydraulic engineering. I want to show the kind of man he'd like you to think he is, and then let you catch a glimpse of the real Mr Slyboots underneath.'

'I wish you luck, Mr Halliday.'

I didn't respond to his smile. 'You can do better than that, patron,' I said. 'What do you think he's going to ask for Abra Bay? What kind of a price and in what currency? Fighter planes?

Tanks? A flight of custom-fitted Boeings? A private aircraft carrier? The moon?'

He thought about it. 'I think that the asking price will be impossible, yes, but how impossible and how far negotiable towards the possible, I really don't know. As you know, I am no longer wholly in his confidence. Besides, what I, in my old-fashioned way, might consider impossible might be seen in a different way by younger minds. They might believe that, providing proper precautions are taken, almost any price may seem to be paid.'

'*Seem* to be paid?' I was sure now that he knew what the asking price was to be.

The eyes saw that I had understood and smiled. 'Hydraulic engineering is not the only subject on which His Highness can display ignorance. If the conjuror is clever enough His Highness will believe for a while in magic. But let me warn you. Don't think he's simple. It you start asking questions about Abra Bay, if you so much as mention it in the presence of this television unit, you will get no answers and no interview. Talk about the mine, talk about his frustrated plan for a clinic, talk about sinusitis if you like. Then you may get answers.'

Outside, the guard dogs had suddenly started barking. Zander looked at his watch again. 'I think your friends may be a few minutes early,' he said and went outside to see if he was right.

I followed slowly, shutting the museum door behind me.

Rainer had said that he thought I might be one of those interviewers who do better when they don't rehearse. Well, it was an interesting theory, and it seemed to me, just standing there wondering if I should lock the door or leave that for one of the security guards, as if I now had the perfect opportunity to test it. At that point, I didn't even have a good first question to ask The Ruler when the camera started rolling. Once I had identified him for the viewers, we might both sit there staring at one another and clearing our throats. Perhaps he would end up by getting bored enough to start interviewing me. How would nice clever Mr Rainer like a reel or two of that?

Simone and Zander were standing beside the Ortofilm station-wagon with security guards on either side of them. An elderly steel-grey Porsche with Schelm driving was coming up the track from the lower road. The car had Belgian plates. It stopped beside the station-wagon. Schelm and the General climbed out slowly looking around as they did so. Simone turned and gave me an exasperated look. I was neglecting my duties. I went over and made the introductions.

'Miss Chihani and Mr Zander, allow me to present General Newell and Herr Mesner.'

The General smiled politely at Simone and gave Zander a friendly nod. Zander responded with a stiff little bow. I wondered what the General was making of the simper. Schelm was puzzled by it and so, when he spoke, sounded irritable.

'I assume,' he said after a short silence, 'that Mr Zander accepts Mr Halliday's statement. We are not going to have arguments about everyone's identity I hope.'

'No, that should not be necessary.' Zander let him see the eyes harden for a moment. 'The fact that your name is not Mesner but Schelm doesn't matter at all. General Newell is certainly genuine. You agree Simone?'

'Quite genuine.'

'Then I suggest we go up closer to the house so that we are seen to be present and waiting. His Highness has his architect with him at present, but that audience won't last much longer and we have questions of protocol to discuss. We go this way, General, if you please.'

He and the General fell into step beside one another as the rest of us trailed behind them up the slope to the house. 'And how is His Highness these days?' I heard the General ask. 'Does he still have that Landru beard of his?'

'A Landru beard, General? What is that?'

'You must have seen pictures of Landru. Before our time, of course, but he was very famous. A French mass-murderer who killed a lot of women for their money. Guillotined eventually, and quite right too, but it was an interesting face. Big sad eyes and this long black beard that seemed to hang down as if it were fastened to his ears with wire loops. Know what I mean? Like His Highness's beard used to look.'

'A real beard that looks false? Ah yes, I understand. So many beards look like that I think. His Highness was advised recently to shave the upper lip. He seems to like the result. But I was not aware that you had met him before.'

'I haven't met him. I just saw him once a few years ago at Cairo airport. He had a Lear jet and a Belgian pilot. There was some sort of row going on I was told. How long did that Belgian last?'

'About three weeks. He was inclined to question orders. The current plane is a Caravelle Super B and the pilot is a Pakistani.'

'Who doesn't question orders?'

'Who is more tactful in his approach. When the orders are not to his professional liking he always seems able to ground the plane with mechanical faults. This is far enough for the moment I think. The personal bodyguards all speak English. It will be better if they do not share our thoughts.'

The two Arab bodyguards we had been approaching were now about fifteen yards away from us flanking the bolt-studded main entrance door to the house. They looked like soldiers wearing cheap civilian suits that were too tight under the arms because the alterations fitter hadn't been told about the machine pistols they would be cradling in front of them all the time they were on duty. Now, as they levelled the guns at us and prepared to go through the routine of telling us to halt and state our business, Zander spoilt it for them by turning his back on the levelled guns and indicating with a gesture that the rest of us should do the same.

'Ex-Arab Legion with UAE passports,' he explained quietly. 'Well-trained up to a point and fairly steady when they have been given simple orders that they understand, but can get trigger-happy. That very dark-skinned one with the bright blue tie claims that he is a bilingual lip-reader. He's almost certainly kidding himself, but I've never had a chance of testing him, so when he's around I'm always careful.' His eyes beamed at the General and his raised hands seemed almost to be blessing him. 'Well now, it is good to meet with you at last. I gather that your discussions last night with Mr Halliday were, as the communiqués say, full and frank.'

'We also talked this morning,' Schelm said. 'I have arranged for the Dutch crew to be here as early as possible, around noon. If they have to be kept waiting it can't be helped. Our Italian friends will be as near to the frontier as they can, but I'm told that you understand their difficulties, and ours, in this peculiar situation.'

Zander bestowed on him a lesser smile, the kind that I had merited once or twice. 'Yes, Herr Mesner, I understand. A little later, though, I would like to discuss the difficulties in greater detail with you. Meanwhile, to business. This is the agreed protocol for your audience. His Highness is expecting only one set of visitors today. It consists of Mr Halliday and his television crew. Understood? Mr Halliday will be received first in the presence of the Chief Secretary and the Financial Counsellor. Refreshments will be served. During that period I shall request permission to introduce you, General, and you, Herr Mesner, as honoured strangers of my acquaintance who seek an audience with His Highness. They have private and confidential proposals to make to him of some urgency and are hoping that his presence here in Europe will excuse to some extent the unorthodox nature and crude European informality of their approach. His Highness will express amused surprise. I shall persuade him that there could be nothing lost by humouring such eccentricity and that these strangers and their proposals might serve to pass the time while preparations for the important business of the day – the television interview – are made by Mr Halliday in consultation with the Chief Secretary and the Financial Counsellor.'

'Supposing they decide that one of them can deal with me and that the other sticks around to hear what the eccentric strangers have to propose?' I asked.

'Neither of them decides anything. His Highness gives the orders. They obey. Their orders for today are to take Mr Halliday down and show him the upper gallery of the mine. That's the place where patients of the new clinic will be treated as soon as the Austrians come to their senses and stop all this nonsense about building permits. They, and you, will be told when it's all clear for the three of you to return. That will be when His Highness has finished telling the General what he wants and the General has asked all the questions he knows he's going to be asked when he reports back to his Committee – those questions he can think of while he's still in shock anyway. The refreshment, by the way, will be mint tea.'

'Who starts the ball rolling, about Abra Bay I mean?' asked the General.

'I do,' said Zander. 'The moment Mr Halliday and the two officials are out of the way, you'll be brought in. I'll introduce you. His Highness will have no difficulty in stating his terms. And there'll be no beating about the bush. You'll forget I'm there. So will His Highness. My last act will be to perform the introductions. After that I'll be superfluous. I might be told to suggest the best channel, from *his* point of view, for further direct talks between you and him. I shall suggest a senior member of Syncom-Sentinel's Gulf management. If I were you I'd reject that suggestion and propose one of the Benelux ambassadors in Abu Dhabi.'

'And if he agrees, what then?'

'He won't agree to anything immediately, General. You'll be asked to withdraw for a while so that *he* can consider *your* proposal. Later, you will be recalled so that arrangements for a further meeting may be discussed. I shall not be present and you will probably be told to break off all contacts with me. You will be asked what my price was or is.'

'Halliday gave us your message about that,' Schelm said. 'All we tell him is that it involves a great sum of money. Right?'

'Thank you. I shall have another, but minor, request to make, but we can leave that until later, until after your first audience. We shall have to wait, of course, while Mr Halliday does the television interview. I shall leave with him.'

'Not with the Dutch? Wouldn't it be safer to do a quick switch?' The General had clearly taken to the good soldier Zander.

'No, General, I shall leave with Mr Halliday and my family. The Dutch have been explained by telling the truth. Our unit was incompetent, the Dutch are acceptable to the Austrians. This has been agreed with the Chief Secretary. There should be no thought of other possible changes of plan.' He glanced at his watch. 'We shall be summoned at any minute now. Keeping the architect there talking is only a way for His Highness to avoid seeming eager.'

'What do we do while you and Halliday are received?' Schelm asked. 'Just wait here?'

'You might stroll up and down admiring the view beyond the parking lot. He won't let Mr Halliday keep him long. You are the ones who can deliver his heart's desires. Believe me. Ah yes! See? Here we go, and right on time.'

The big front door had opened and the architect emerged. He was square and plumpish and carried a tube of plans. The man who followed him out to the steps leading down was grossly fat and wore an Arab head-dress with his grey suit.

'The one wearing the keffiyeh is the Chief Secretary,' said Zander.

As a statement it was not completely irrelevant. The fat man could have been the Financial Counsellor or some other court functionary of consequence, but Zander had said it breathlessly as if it really mattered.

Hurrying past us on his way to the car-park the architect muttered a polite greeting in German. By pretending to respond to it I was able to turn a little so that I could see what was happening in Zander's eyes. I at once wished that I hadn't. The simper had become a hole in the face and the narrowed eyes were those of a predator, ready to kill and perhaps eager to do so. It was easier to look up at the bulk of the Chief Secretary.

He was still considering our group and identifying those in it. Then, after a moment or two, he pointed a forefinger at Zander and made a beckoning motion with the thumb cocked above it.

'You may bring the American, Robert Halliday,' he said.

TWELVE

A HOUSE built against a wooded hillside with the adit of an old mine as its central feature and all its windows on the front is bound to have some drawbacks as a place to live in. Dr Petrucher, or the wretched architect working for him, had solved the basic problems by placing the rooms in two straight rows, one up one down. He had connected them all laterally by doors – two to all rooms except those at the ends – and vertically by an iron spiral staircase in the kitchen. There was, remarkably, a bathroom, but to get to it from the living room you had to go through three downstairs rooms to the kitchen, then up the staircase and back through two bedrooms. That, however, was a later discovery. My first impression of the interior was that I had entered the back lot movie-studio façade of a Styrian hunting lodge which had been stacked, rather carelessly, against a section of the mock-up used for shooting fights to the death on mountain ledges. In the entrance hall a huge slab of bare limestone that was part of the hillside jutted out of the rear wall masonry at head height so that you had to walk around it to get to the living room.

Outside the door we paused. The Chief Secretary was a heavy breather and sweated a lot. He mopped his face with a king-size handkerchief and then peered at me over it. 'I am assured,' he said, 'that you are carrying no weapon of any kind, Mr Halliday. Is that correct?'

'Quite correct.'

'When His Highness first acknowledges your presence at an audience, you should bow your head.'

'I'll try to remember that.'

'Then follow me.' He scratched on the door with one of the rings he wore and waited. I caught Zander's eyes on me. They were telling me in no uncertain terms not to play the fool. If His Highness's Chief Secretary said that I should bow, then I should do so. It was my piddling bloody dignity that I should forget.

Inside the room a small bell tinkled. The Chief Secretary opened the door with a flourish. 'Your Highness,' he announced, 'in accordance with your instructions issued to your French purchasing agent in the month of Shawwal, he has brought for your consideration the journalist and television reporter Mr Halliday.'

When I hesitated, wondering if I could make it sideways around the Chief Secretary's belly, Zander nudged me forward and the Secretary withdrew slightly to let us pass.

'Be careful of the step,' he murmured.

There were, in fact, two steps: the curved, ankle-breaking kind. It was a preposterous house, but this one room was the reason for it. At the far end there was a big fireplace; set in the left wall was the entrance to the mine adit. Framed in a massive stone architrave and protected from the outside world by a pair of sheet-steel doors, it dominated the room. The stonework was obviously part of the old house and had been decorated, probably by the monumental mason who had done the local grave-yard work, with a simple pattern of scrolls and curlicues. It was chipped here and there and vandals had attempted to gouge initials and other messages for posterity on the more accessible parts, but it had lasted well. The steel doors were clearly a very recent addition with two welded hasps on them and serious-looking modern padlocks.

The Ruler had placed himself to receive us standing between the fireplace and the mine entrance, and he was wearing full Arab dress for the occasion. Both robe and head-dress were all white. However, the light from the two windows was good and it was possible to see the glint of the gold threads that had been woven into the black silk *aqal* resting on his high forehead. To a tall, bearded man with a good posture and not too much flab, the Arab robe made from expensive materials can be very flat-tering. From the other end of the room, The Ruler looked most impressive. It was only when you drew closer, when you saw the handsome face with its petulant upper lip and its eyes plead-ing that no one had ever quite understood him that you had the first series of second thoughts.

Psychopaths, of course, can be good playactors and are not easy to evaluate if all you have by way of evidence are the lines they can shoot and the faces they can pull. But, for me, the really strange thing was that someone as shrewd and experienced as Zander should ever have found it hard to believe that the man now standing there looking dignified and gracious could be a treacherous, murderous, unconscionable son-of-a-bitch who in-tended, at the earliest convenient moment, to have him killed.

Even the security-conscious Simone had boggled for a while at the idea. Perhaps, because he had been so easy to despise, they had neglected to remember how dangerous the mad and bad can be. Perhaps Schelm had put his finger on the trouble when he had said that prolonged contact with the Arab world could induce bizarre thought habits in those who came from the west. And perhaps, too, as the outsider who had happened to hit upon the truth because he had known so little about the facts, I was giving myself credits for good thinking and ability to see the obvious that had not really been earned.

As we approached him The Ruler did not even glance at Zander. To me he said: 'Welcome, Mr Halliday, to the famous Petrucher mine.' The accent was British, the tone of voice light tenor.

I managed to make the required bow without overdoing it. In The Ruler's shadow a small man in black – the Financial Counsellor I guessed – snapped his fingers quietly and an off-duty bodyguard came in from the hallway carrying a two-tiered silver tray suspended on thin chains. Both tiers had little cups of mint tea on them. The Ruler sat down in a high-backed armchair at the head of a long table and indicated with a gesture that the rest of us should also be seated. When we were all at the table and the tea had been served The Ruler gave me a cool nod.

'Now, Mr Halliday,' he said, 'we will hear your request.'

What in hell was he talking about? What request? My eyes went to Zander for help, but he was staring respectfully at the halo space above The Ruler's head. Obviously, I was being given some sort of test, perhaps to see if I could do mental somersaults without falling over. So, remembering Simone's advice about ceremony and seriousness, I did the best I could.

'What I have to say, Your Highness, is offered more in the nature of a suggestion rather than a request. As the Chief Secretary has just reminded you, your order to obtain my services was given several months ago. The idea that there might be a use for them here was clearly already in Your Highness's mind. My suggestion, or interpretation, is that, in your far-sighted way, you had already anticipated the political difficulties that might arise from your decision to build a clinic here for your subjects' health and welfare. A television interview exposing the absurdity of the difficulties placed in your path here, a short film made available freely to the Public Service television network in

America as well as to the stations of Austria's neighbours, would have a powerful effect. You would *control* the propaganda situation here.'

'Control? How?'

'The Austrian public looks at German and German–Swiss television as well as Austrian. ORF would not dare to refuse your interview prime air time, nor to edit out the parts they didn't happen to like. And, in case you should think that American audiences are not interested in Austrian clinics, permit me to draw Your Highness's attention to a factor in this equation that your modesty may have concealed from you. Today, the Arabian Gulf is of unique world importance. Yet, who from the Gulf states do they see and hear as spokesmen? Low-voiced and pro-west Saudis nominated by factions within OPEC. When, they must ask, do we get to hear from a man with an independent voice? What sort of men are they who rule these distant desert lands? Let them see and hear *you*, Your Highness.'

He was silent, and for several moments I thought that I had laid it on too thick. After all, I was there simply as a cover story invented by Zander and he knew it. So what was all this heavy-handed stuff about independent voices from the desert? The two men he really wanted to talk to and get down to business with were still cooling their heels outside.

Then he nodded curtly. 'Yes, Mr Halliday, what you say makes sense. I agree with it. Unfortunately, I have other, and quite unexpected, business to attend to at this very moment.'

Zander decided that it was time now for him to lend a hand. 'If I may be so bold, Your Highness. The unexpected business is, as you remind us, urgent. But need the two conflict? Mr Halliday's unit is arriving now I understand. But they will have their technical preparations to make. That will take time. And another thing. Mindful of the impact the film is certain to have on Austrian government opinion, Mr Halliday has requested that the interview should actually take place in the upper gallery of the mine itself.'

'He could do this?' The Ruler turned to me. 'You could film me in the upper gallery? Actually in the mine?'

'If there is mains electricity there, Your Highness,' I said, 'we can also film the interview there. I can also promise you that if, while you transact your urgent business, someone responsible in your entourage can give me and the technicians access to the upper gallery so that lighting and other preparations can all be made in advance, we shall be waiting for you whenever you are ready to make your person available.'

There was another long silence before he began to give orders in Arabic. I knew just enough to know that they were orders, but could not follow the meaning. Then, suddenly, he stood up and sailed out of the room without another glance at me.

Of course, the moment he had risen there had been a quick scramble around the table to get up and follow. 'What's gone wrong?' I asked Zander. 'We seemed to be moving along quite nicely.'

'Nothing's gone wrong, so far,' he said. 'You're just not used to the way autocracy works. He liked your pitch, so the orders have been changed. Now, he will receive the strangers I have brought with me in another room. After that little ceremony the Chief Secretary and the Financial Counsellor will be at your disposal with keys to the mine. Just stay here a few minutes and they'll come back for you. Tell them what you want done and, as soon as you can, get that Dutch unit busy. You promised instant service. You'd better be ready to deliver it. See you later.'

I sipped lukewarm mint tea as I watched the next moves from a window.

After a brief interval Zander and the Chief Secretary came out. The latter then summoned the General and Schelm to an audience with His Highness using the same stentorian tones he had employed earlier. The bodyguards stood aside to admit them, but became tense again when the dogs set up another commotion beyond the car-park. I assumed that Dick Kluvers and the Viser-Damrak outfit had arrived. After another wait I saw them climb up the hill. They parked alongside the Ortofilm vehicles. They had a slightly bigger van and a smaller car. Both were a lot dirtier than our stuff. A man with a lot of greyish-blond hair and an old track suit – Kluvers obviously – got out of the car and stared at the Ortofilm truck with Jean-Pierre and the young people in it. I was glad to see Simone slide out of the station-wagon to intercept him. Jean-Pierre would have put his back up and the last thing I needed was a bad-tempered director. I didn't see any more of the encounter because, just then, the Chief Secretary and the Financial Counsellor returned from the meeting in the other room to put themselves at my disposal.

The first thing, I said, was for me to be shown the upper

gallery of the mine. No problem. The Chief Secretary had keys and proceeded to unlock the steel doors. Beyond them was a sort of vestibule with a sizeable switchboard on one wall and a lot of plans and drawings on the other. The Secretary began flipping switches and then unlocked the door beyond. He opened it with something of a showman's flourish.

There was a blaze of lights coming from below, but the thing of which I was most immediately conscious was a complicated tangle of steel scaffolding and girders. Then, as I moved forward following the Secretary, I began to see the shape of it all. At the entrance we were in a cave, the floor of which was covered with ridged steel plates and more or less level. Then, the cave became a largish cavern with a ceiling of rock. This ceiling was supported by slanting girders all grouted into the rock with mortar. The next thing you came to was the mine shaft. It wasn't vertical but zigzagged down through a cage-like arrangement of rock-face supports which also carried flight after flight of steel stairs.

'This was all done by His Highness,' the Chief Secretary said proudly.

'But with a little help, I guess. Is this the upper gallery that was spoken about as a location for the interview?'

'Oh no, Mr Halliday. That is down the stairs. There are one hundred and ten of them. That is where the pure, clean air is.'

'I see.' I thought for a moment. Where we were standing there was quite a bit of echo. Down below there might be even more. There was also an almost continuous sound of dripping water, the kind that drove sound recordists into deep depressions. Suddenly, another sound was added – a high-pitched howling that seemed to come from the centre of the earth.

'What's that?' I had to yell to make myself heard.

'The special pumps below,' he shouted in my ear. 'They switch on automatically when the deep sumps become full from the springs below.'

'Can they be switched off for an hour or two or is that impossible?'

He beckoned me back to the vestibule and pulled a couple of circuit-breakers on the switchboard. The howling stopped instantly. 'Those pumps keep the deep sumps dry,' he explained, 'but they can be switched off for days before any harm is done.'

'All the same,' I said, 'that may not be the only problem we have shooting down there in the upper gallery. Just now I saw the film unit arrive with Mr Kluvers in charge. I would like him and his technicians with us when we go down to the gallery. It is they who will have to decide in the end what is technically possible and that way we will save time.'

'I will see that they are brought,' the Financial Counsellor said promptly and hurried off to do so. I had already noticed that he did not share the Chief Secretary's enthusiasm for the mine. Why, I could not be certain, but I could well understand. Claustrophobia and fear of deep holes in the ground were only two of the many valid reasons a person might have for disliking the Petrucher. My own reason, at that stage, was the immediate prospect of having to persuade Kluvers and his crew, tired from a rough assignment in Yugoslavia, that it was going to be worthwhile, in order to interview The Ruler effectively, for them to toil up and down one hundred and ten slippery steel stairs carrying lamps, cables, tripods and all the rest of their equipment instead of using the museum.

While we waited, the Chief Secretary entertained me by explaining the principal features of the mine workings in their modern form. He used the charts and plans on the vestibule wall to illustrate the various points. I didn't listen as carefully as I should have done. I was wondering how to make the museum look more interesting. I was still wondering when Dick Kluvers arrived with his camera and sound men. All three spoke good English. Kluvers was agreeably businesslike.

'I don't understand any of this,' he said. 'When we check in at Velden, as instructed, there's a guide and a guy named Rainer waiting there for us. Rainer's from Austrian television and going to process the film. But he's not paying us. And New York's not paying us. A bank in Munich is paying us, in cash. Is that the deal you have?'

'No. I'm being paid by Syncom-Sentinel and by cheque.'

'My deal's better then.'

'Yes, I guess it is. Right now, though, we don't have too much time to talk deals. If it's okay with you, I'd like to see if we can shoot this interview down the mine in a place they call the upper gallery. I think there may be too many problems, but I'd like you to see it before we start on the alternatives.'

'What kind of problems?'

'Dripping water noises and echo mainly, but there may be others. There's mains voltage power down there.'

The cameraman grunted. 'But can you get at the power? With all that dripping water about I mean. In damp mines they tend to keep the high voltage stuff sealed away so that damn fools don't get killed doing things they shouldn't.'

The Chief Secretary intervened to reassure him. 'There are specially protected outlets in the gallery. They are used to plug in the heaters His Highness needs sometimes for his hands and feet. No doubt your lights would serve to keep him warm instead.'

'Why don't we just go down and have a look?' I said. 'Then we can decide.'

The journey down the stairway to the upper gallery was interesting but unpleasant. The interesting aspects were provided by the limestone walls and the curious shapes they made. There were, too, strange holes in some of the walls. They were smooth and angled like chutes. According to the Chief Secretary, they had once been the crawl holes used by the miners to scratch out every last scrap of silver-bearing ore that could be carried away to the crushing mills. The mills had been across the valley. That was why no slag heaps had been left. Petrucher had written all this down. We should read it. The unpleasantness of the descent was due to the damp, the cold and the mud. The General's doctor friend in Brussels had been right, I thought. If all this was good for bronchitis and asthma, the Austrian traffic police could be good for high blood-pressure.

Kluvers' thick shock of hair was immaculately clean and he didn't like muddy water dripping on it. Clattering down the third flight he muttered that the whole thing was ridiculous, but he kept on going. It was on the fifth flight that we had our first look at the upper gallery.

The lighted part was a space about twenty yards long and four wide. Within it, beyond an iron grating at the foot of the stairs, was a hardwood floor made in sections and resting on steel joists. Amazingly, the floor was quite dry When we got down there we could see why. The rock roof of the gallery had been given a slightly curved false ceiling made of a corrugated plastic material. In the gallery all the drips were carried away to drainage ducts running along the sides. Standing in the centre of the floor were four clinical-looking reclining chairs. One of them, larger than the others, was obviously The Ruler's. Of more immediate importance was the fact that under the plastic false ceiling there was much less echo.

'This would not be too bad for sound,' Kluvers said.

'You'll still hear the dripping,' said the sound man. 'It's all around us. We're not very deep here. Where does the water come from?'

'It is last winter's snow from the hills above,' the Chief Secretary explained. 'It takes many weeks to melt and filter down to here. In two months it will be much drier.'

The cameraman was examining the power outlets. 'We could light it,' he said. 'Does that tunnel beyond here have lighting of any kind? We don't want a black hole in back.'

The Secretary pressed a switch and showed us the tunnel at the other end. If we could shoot there, the pictorial values alone would be worth something. Kluvers evidently thought so too.

'We can explain the dripping background sound by showing the drips back on the stairs. The problem is going to be getting the equipment down here.' He looked at the mud on his shoes. 'What does this sheikh use when he comes down here? Gum boots?'

The word 'sheikh' had made the Chief Secretary wince quite noticeably. 'His Highness the Emir,' he said stiffly, 'uses the lift, naturally, when he wishes to visit the upper gallery. I use it myself normally. For a man of my age those stairs are a great trial. But I assumed that you would be interested by the drama of the old entrance, the romance.'

'You mean there's an elevator here?'

'I *told* you, Mr Halliday,' he sighed. 'I showed it to you on the plan. In the old ventilation shaft that the engineers call Up-Flow B. The stairways and steel scaffolding and girders went in by the main entrance in the house. The engineers simply removed the old wooden structures and supports that Petrucher had installed and replaced them with steel. But when it came to the big pumps and other heavy equipment, His Highness would not allow the old entrance to be enlarged or damaged. The lawyers advised against it too. So, the contractors installed a kind of lift, a hoist they called it, in the Up-Flow B shaft.'

'I'm sorry,' I said. 'I thought you were talking about some sort of block-and-tackle arrangement. Where is this hoist? How do we get to it?'

'Along the tunnel there where I put the lights on. And above, it comes out at the top of the shaft behind the museum. I will show you.'

A hoist it was, slow, noisy and a bit scary when all you had to protect you from the reinforced concrete on the shaft walls was a single handrail. But it made Kluvers' day.

'We can be set up and ready to go in less than an hour,' he said. 'How do you want to shoot it?'

I remembered Simone's briefing. 'It's to be done with the utmost ceremony,' I said. 'That big chair of his must be treated as a throne. His Highness must be left in no doubt that he is addressing the entire world, and that the world is listening with bated breath to every word he says. I shall grovel unobtrusively before him on one of the smaller chairs. We must be very careful of his dignity. I don't want your cameramen sticking light meters or tape measures under his nose or trying to make him move again once he's already set. Let's be ready for him in advance. I'll act as stand-in if it'll help. When we're shooting and you want to reload, just touch my arm. I shall tell him to ignore the camera, so if he goes on talking while you're reloading don't worry. My problem's going to be to start him talking freely. Keep the clapperboard as quiet as you can. I don't want to give him any reason or excuse to decide that he's tired or bored or being treated with insufficient respect and consideration.'

'Who does he think he is? *What* does he think he is?'

'That's what I'm hoping he'll tell us. One other thing. I don't want to try hanging a mike around his neck. I think he might feel that it spoilt the princely image. Use a short boom or a stand. It doesn't matter if it's seen.'

'I can't wait to meet him.'

The reason we had been able to speak so frankly was that the Chief Secretary had left us alone for a moment. He was having an argument with the camera and sound men who wanted to relieve themselves. They could not understand why they were being asked to climb in through the kitchen window to get to the spiral staircase that led up to the only bathroom in the place, instead of going through the front door and up the stairs there like civilized beings. When it was explained to them that there were no other stairs but that there were toilets in the temporary buildings below the car-park a fresh difficulty arose. The sound man shared Jean-Pierre's fear of attack dogs. In the end I had to persuade the Chief Secretary to order the uniformed security people to kennel all the dogs for as long as we remained there.

It was a peculiar sort of battle to have won, but from then on

I had the crew on my side. That turned out to be a real plus. They were ready to help me make things go smoothly with The Ruler. Meanwhile, Simone had established good relations with the handyman-driver of the Dutch van and, with Jean-Pierre's agreement, a pooling of food and drink supplies for lunch had been negotiated. Soon we were all drinking Italian wine out of Austrian paper cups and eating sandwiches of both nationalities. I almost forgot about the real reason for our being there. But not for long.

About two o'clock I saw the main door of the house open and Zander came out with the General and Schelm. They stood there for a moment before they were joined by the Chief Secretary. There was a brief discussion, then Zander looked around, apparently for me. I stood up and he beckoned. As I approached the group, the General and Schelm moved away. There was a suggestion in the way they held themselves that their session with The Ruler was something that they did not want to talk about, even to each other.

When I reached Zander I said: 'Everything okay with those two?'

'I told them they'd be in shock for a while. I don't think they took me as seriously as they should have done. Chief Secretary, you have orders for Mr Halliday?'

The Chief Secretary cleared his throat. For some reason, Zander's presence was now making him feel nervous. 'Yes,' he said to me, 'I have proposals. His Highness has retired to take a little food and to rest. Your unit director seemed to think that the interview could be filmed in the upper gallery after about an hour's preparation there. Was he exaggerating?'

'No. In fact, I think the preparations could be made sooner if necessary.'

'No. His Highness said an hour. Make your preparations on that basis please.'

I looked at Zander again. He nodded blandly. 'As I said, Mr Halliday, everything so far goes according to plan. The Chief Secretary agrees with me, I think.'

The Chief Secretary was looking more uneasy than ever, but managed a shrug.

'Okay,' I said, 'we'll be ready in an hour.' But I couldn't help glancing again at Schelm and the General and was opening my mouth to ask a question when Zander cut in sharply.

'No, Mr Halliday. Those gentlemen have serious things to think about and perhaps discuss. You can't help them. Best if you leave them alone. You do what *you* have to do. Get your TV interview.'

The eyes, too, were telling me in no uncertain terms to mind my own goddam business. So, I shut my mouth, nodded and went back to the car-park.

'We have forty-five minutes to get it all set up,' I said.

'What'll he be wearing?' asked the cameraman.

'When I saw him earlier he was in full Arab dress as worn by a man of rank.'

'All *white*, you mean? With the black head-band? No colour at all? Can't you tell him to wear a suit and the head-dress like the fat man who showed us the lift?'

'If I try and tell him anything at all, there'll be no interview.'

Kluvers intervened. 'It's the face you want, isn't it? The face and the head-dress?'

'That's right.'

The cameraman looked perplexed. 'You don't want even to see him walking in? We miss all that interesting background?'

'Let's talk about the foreground first,' I said. 'What I need is a full head and shoulders to begin with, enough to see that he's sitting in this curious chair. Then go in gradually as close as you can get. We want to see the hairs on his face, the eyes, the lips, the teeth and the tongue as well as hear what he has to say, if anything. When we're through with him, or he's through with us, use the backgrounds when you pick up the cut-away footage of me listening to him and asking two or three of the questions that worked, if any.'

'Rainer said we may use a lot of film.'

'I hope he's right. We may end up using very little. Either way, I think we should get moving.'

Kluvers got to his feet. 'You hear what he says. Let's get the job done. With luck we should be able to pick up our money in Munich tomorrow and be home the day after.'

They made three trips in the hoist. I got a sweater out of my baggage, then climbed down to the gallery by the stairs so as to keep out of their way and watched them set up. I also went on trying to figure out a way of handling the interview. First, of course, I would introduce him, explaining who I was and where we were, in the bowels of a disused, thousand-year-old silver mine in the province of Styria, Austria. A little bit about why we were there, then I would ask my first question. 'Your Highness, I would like to begin by asking you this . . .'

And at that point my mind would go blank.

Until around three o'clock, the chore of acting as a stand-in, so that the cameraman could light the occupant of the big chair and the sound man work out his problems, helped to keep the worst of the anxiety at bay. It also kept me warm. According to the Chief Secretary, the temperature in the upper gallery at that time of year remained at, or just below, nine degrees Celsius, night and day. There was no wind or discernible draught to make the air seem colder than it really was, but it was still very chilly. In my house the thermostat would long ago have switched on the heating.

At three o'clock I moved over to the seat from which I was going to do the interview and started looking at my watch. Five minutes later the whine of the hoist in Up-Flow B began as it started for the surface. Only this time it wouldn't be bringing down cables and lamps. According to Simone, The Ruler's only good habit was that of punctuality. Unless a person or group was to be kept waiting intentionally, he was rarely more than a quarter of an hour late for an appointment. The hoist was silent for a moment or two and then began to descend.

The moment we saw him in the tunnel I heard the cameraman swear softly and start to change his lighting. The Ruler had discarded his Arab robes, including the head-dress, in favour of a blue suit with a vest and dark tie. Someone must have told him about the aversion of television to certain colours because he was wearing a blue shirt too. In fact, the blue-shirt rule for those to be interviewed is, with modern equipment, a thing of the past. Against The Ruler's sallow complexion, however, the pale blue would have been a good choice of colour anyway. The thing that drew my attention most, though, as I went forward, bowing, to escort him to his television throne, was the high colour on his cheeks. I also noticed that the Chief Secretary waddling behind him was looking anxious. I began to think very quickly indeed.

Kluvers and I had earlier discussed the possibility of using make-up on our subject and decided not to risk it. The Ruler was quite capable of regarding a proposal to use make-up as a suggestion that he was unmanly. Only if he began sweating in the heat of the lamps would someone suggest a little powder to take off the shine. The idea that he might himself decide to use make-up had not occurred to us. Now, though, as he came into the spill light from the photo floods, I could see that the flush on his cheeks wasn't make-up. He was just excited about something, or by something.

It certainly wasn't the prospect of being interviewed for television that was turning him on. When I went on with the ceremonial of introducing Kluvers particularly and the rest of the crew generally, all any of them received was a vague nod. As Kluvers invited him to sit in his chair for a last quick check on the lighting, he turned to the Chief Secretary and said something in Arabic. I knew enough to get the drift of what he said. It was an order to the Secretary to tell him every twenty minutes what the time was. For me, there was only one possible explanation for the way he was looking and behaving. He had had a fix of some sort.

It was at that moment that I decided to fall back on one of the crudest of the old interview gambits. If the person being interviewed has any sort of rank, you try pushing it up. If he's flattered enough to let it go you've won an advantage; if he promptly corrects you, you have something with which to start the ball rolling. The only risk you run is with someone who is prepared to make you look, and feel, foolish by remarking that you obviously haven't checked your basic facts. With The Ruler, I decided, that was a risk it was fairly safe to take. So, when the cameraman said 'rolling' and the handyman-driver snapped the clapper-board on 'Petrucher interview take one', I began introducing The Ruler not as 'His Highness the Emir of', but as 'His *Royal* Highness the Emir.'

For a while I thought he was going to let it pass. But no. When I began the only question I had managed to think of to lead with, a banal inquiry about his reasons for buying the mine we were sitting in, he put a hand up to stop me.

'No, Mr Halliday,' he said. 'Please hold your horses. Not *Royal* Highness.'

'My apologies, Sir. I had no wish ...'

But he cut me off. 'Our family is ancient and noble, but not royal. We leave that dubious honour to the kingly dynasties.'

'Such as that of the Saudi royal family, Your Highness?'

But he saw the pitfall. He wasn't going on record as describing

195

the Saudi royal family as dubious. 'No, Mr Halliday. I was thinking more of the Iranian Pahlavi dynasty,' he said and began to smile. 'The father of the second and last Shah was a donkey-driver who could not read or write, who became a soldier, who overthrew the dynasty he had been paid to serve and ended by calling himself not only Shahanshah, but also Vice-Regent of God and Centre of the Universe. Now that, I think, was very royal.'

He had begun to snort with amusement as he said it. Then, he coughed once, tried to swallow and suddenly went into a parox-ysm of laughter.

THIRTEEN

It went on for nearly a minute. I saw Kluvers, who was crouching beside the sound man, making signs asking me if I wanted them to cut, but I shook my head. He then made a pill-swallowing sign, raised his eyebrows and rolled his eyes at the man with all the lights on him. I shrugged. By then it was obvious that The Ruler was on a high of some sort, but of what sort and how it had been induced there was no way of telling. Maybe we would find out. At that stage it really didn't matter. We had some interesting footage. Now, the tone of the laughter was becoming less maniacal and beginning to subside into a breathless cackle. Finally, it stopped as abruptly as it had started. The Ruler began to get his breath back, lick his lips and finger his tie.

The Chief Secretary had sidled over to me. 'His Highness sometimes finds in the world too much to laugh at,' he whispered. 'This film will, of course, be edited with discretion.'

'Of course,' I said. And it *would* be edited with discretion. But if he thought that Rainer, or any other producer, was going to leave that rich sample of The Ruler's finer feelings about the mighty fallen and the death of kings on the cutting-room floor, he was going to be disappointed.

The Ruler himself, still flushed but more or less composed, now announced that he was prepared to continue. 'But please, Mr Halliday,' he added, 'please don't make these American jokes about dynasties. My sense of humour cannot stand it.'

'I'll remember that, Your Highness. Perhaps we could talk about this old silver mine. You bought it, I understand, so that you may replace the house above with a clinic and so that the old mine workings may be used, as those at Oberzeiring are now used, for the treatment of respiratory diseases. Is that right?'

'For bronchitis and so on. Yes.'

'Are those diseases particularly prevalent in the dry, warm country of which you are The Ruler?'

'They are prevalent, in one form or another, in all countries. That, surely, is common knowledge.'

'Perhaps not as common as it should be, Your Highness. I am simply trying to use your special knowledge to inform viewers in many countries. You yourself suffer from sinusitis, I believe.'

'And allergies. The two, in my case, are mixed.'

'How many medical doctors have you in your entourage, Your Highness?'

'None at present. In due course, when I am permitted to build the clinic in the way I wish, patients will be referred to the clinic in the customary way.'

'At Oberzeiring there are some conditions for which this particular kind of treatment is contra-indicated. Do you intend here to follow the same medical policies?'

'Contra-indicated? My English is not perfect I'm afraid.'

'Broadly speaking, Your Highness, contra-indicated conditions are those in which the treatment would do more harm than good.'

He tried a jocular smile that didn't quite come off. 'I would hope not to do harm, Mr Halliday.'

'Your Highness, would you regard a patient with right-sided heart trouble, or acute liver disease, or advanced emphysema, or tuberculosis as suitable for treatment in your clinic?'

He thought carefully before he delivered his verdict. 'For advanced emphysema I would think it very good, and perhaps for TB too. About the liver disease I am doubtful.'

'At Oberzeiring, Your Highness, *all* patients suffering from the diseases I have mentioned are regarded as *un*suitable for treatment of this kind. Didn't you find that out when you went for treatment there? Weren't you examined by a doctor?'

'You forget. I was being treated for sinusitis and allergies. Obviously, you have been talking to the doctors there.'

'Your Highness, all the information that I have just repeated was obtained from a small give-away leaflet about Oberzeiring that I found in the desk of my hotel room. How did you hear about Oberzeiring?'

'From a doctor in Switzerland. I have been grateful for the cure, of course, but my own medical interest, the subject that I have studied intensively, though naturally as an amateur, is the central nervous system.'

'That would seem an unusual field of study for amateurs, Your Highness. Does one of the difficulties about the permit to build your clinic here hinge on the fact that it will not be supervised by any Austrian medical authority?'

'My lawyers in Vienna have mentioned that. This, however, would be a private clinic.'

I thought he was going to elaborate, but he didn't. So I let it go. It seemed to me that I had already more than fulfilled my obligation to Herr Rainer. Having an amateur student of the central nervous system in control of a clinic of any sort was on a par with having an amateur brain surgeon on the staff of a general hospital. There were just a few more things that I wanted to clear up for my own satisfaction.

'You must know, Your Highness, that there are many in this province, and in Vienna, who simply do not believe in your good faith. They don't believe that you really intend to build a clinic.'

'Of course I know this. And I am constantly reminded of it.'

'This refusal to believe seems to have been based originally on *your* refusal to submit plans for the proposed rebuilding above ground to the regional planning authority. Would you care to explain your refusal to our viewers?'

He wagged a finger at me. 'No permission was required to spend the large sums of money I have spent here below ground. This was a derelict mine, largely flooded, and, where not flooded, dangerous because of rotted wooden structures almost a century old. I changed all that. I put in pumping and other machinery, the newest and best. I put in steel and concrete. I made the place safe and usable. We are sitting safely in it now. No one lifted a finger to stop me. Yet, when I propose to replace a derelict and ugly house with a modern structure designed by a known and respected architect, I am refused permission.'

'But, Your Highness, how can they grant permission if you will not submit your architect's plans?'

'My plans are for a clinic. If they refuse to hear first what my lawyers have to say about the need to replace a smallish structure with a slightly larger one, what can I do? How can I explain anything to a faceless bureaucracy?'

I switched the attack to another front. 'No doubt Your Highness is aware that a former employee of yours, an engineer, has made statements claiming that your intention here is not the one you have announced. Your true intention, he says, is not to build a clinic but a private fall-out shelter for your family and entourage.'

He had been waiting for that one. 'Former employees who have been discharged for inefficiency,' he said with a smile, 'often attempt to slander their former employers.'

Kluvers was warning me that they were going to have to reload. I gave him an okay sign, but went on talking as if nothing had happened. We had used up a lot of film on the laughing fit but I didn't want to stop the flow; though, at that point, there seemed only a few more questions for me to ask, and for him to answer or, more likely, to evade.

'In what way was he inefficient, Your Highness?'

'He knew nothing at all of hydraulic engineering, even though in that he was supposed to be an expert. He made gross miscalculations.'

I remembered that this particular man, a French engineer, had been the one who had lost his temper with The Ruler and told him, in the hearing of others, that *he* knew nothing about hydraulic engineering. The Ruler was not the first employer to denounce those he had fired by accusing them of his own deficiencies.

'Miscalculations in an enterprise such as this, Your Highness, could be expensive I imagine.'

By the time he had given me a string of figures to show just how expensive it had all been, we had reloaded and the camera was running again. The second clapper-board was slipped in so unobtrusively that The Ruler didn't seem to notice it. Doing an interview with someone who is completely self-absorbed at least makes some things easier.

'You see, Mr Halliday, what his ignorance cost me? And yet he persisted in blaming me. The man is insane.'

'Still, a lot of people, journalists and civic leaders, seem to have believed him. There are those now who are making a political issue of it.'

He leaned forward unexpectedly and I heard the cameraman's sharp movement as he reacted to keep The Ruler's face centred and in focus. I hoped he had succeeded. The cheeks were pink again and the lips twitching with excitement.

'Do *you* believe him, Mr Halliday?' he asked. 'Do *you* believe that I am stupid enough to build a nuclear fall-out shelter three thousand kilometres from my palace on the Gulf?'

'Your Highness, I don't think that questions about stupidity or good sense are relevant in any general discussion about civil defence against nuclear attack. Still, the idea of your using this mine as a nuclear fall-out shelter does seem strange, I admit.'

'More than strange, I would say. If there is to be a nuclear war, we may receive, I am told, half-an-hour's warning. How do I get here from the Gulf in thirty minutes?'

'The same thought has occurred to me, Your Highness. But as I've said, sense doesn't really come into it. On the subject of how a nuclear war might begin I've heard all sorts of different scenarios. I've heard it said that the start of *any* major war involving the superpowers, even if to start with they're only using tanks and planes in the old-fashioned ways, will be a clear warning to anyone with access to a fall-out shelter of any kind to run for it as fast as they can. *Or* fly to it. I'm trying to be objective, of course, and on this subject one can't be. The nuclear warfare threat takes different people in different ways.'

'How about you?' he demanded. 'How does the prospect of nuclear war take you, Mr Halliday?'

'Your Highness, I'm afraid that I am one of those who don't give it much thought. If there is a nuclear exchange between the superpowers, even a limited one, most of us in the populated areas of the west will be dead or dying within the first hour.'

'Even if the initial strike is a pre-emptive one on the other side's first and second strike capabilities?'

'I don't know much about current targetting policies, Your Highness. I don't know who gets it first, the silos or the cities or the submarines. I do believe, though, that, in any nuclear war, those who survive the first few hours will be the *unlucky* ones.'

'I agree. But I don't think you're going to have your nuclear war, Mr Halliday. I think that the balance of terror will hold up. The Soviets and the Americans will go on glaring at one another and the fringe bomb-makers will look nervously over their shoulders. It is the new conventional war that I fear.'

'Helicopter gun-ships and napalm, Your Highness?'

'Those are the weapons now of the rural, colonial wars, the Third-World bush campaigns. Mostly, that is. When I speak of new conventional war I mean the chemical kind. *Not* the biological. Biological fall-out can be as deadly as nuclear. The new chemical weapons are controllable. With them, you can kill your enemy without running the risk of killing yourself. You can kill where you want to and then clean up the mess, make it all safe again. All you need is the know-how.'

'Both sides in World War Two had the know-how, Your Highness. Yet, neither side used poison gases or chemical weapons of any kind, even though they manufactured them.'

He snapped his fingers disdainfully. 'I am not talking about such things as phosgene. They were toys. I don't even consider tabun as coming within the category of modern chemical warfare weapons. What I am speaking about is . . .' He broke off with a coy inclination of his head. 'But no, perhaps it is better if I don't speak about such things. I have no wish to frighten anyone.'

'We here, Your Highness, have no wish, of course, to pry into secret matters or to cause alarm. I am sure that you, in your position as Ruler, hold many secrets that it would not be safe or in the public interest to reveal. That is clearly understood and I would not presume to press you to confide in us.'

The pomposity worked. I could almost see the wish to impress me and the uneasy feeling that it might be better to change the subject battling inside him for the next word. He was excited about something and wanted to spill it all to someone who would listen sympathetically. I think he had completely forgotten that there was a film camera with a sound track running. He was looking for a way out of his difficulty. Suddenly, he thought he saw it.

'Of course,' he said carefully, 'not all these matters are secret. There is much that is common knowledge. For instance, have you heard of the group of organophosphorus chemicals called anti-cholinesterases?'

'I can't say that I have, Your Highness.' I was watching his face intently, though, and had a feeling that if, at that point, I stopped and waited for him to explain he would get cautious again. So, I threw him a small joke at my expense. 'Let me try and guess, though. Would I be correct in saying that they are, where human beings are concerned, contra-indicated?'

He didn't get it instantly, but when the bell rang I thought we were going to have another bout of hysteria. However, it turned after a few big laughs into snickers. 'Oh my God, yes,' he said eventually. 'Very much contra-indicated. The American and British armed forces call them nerve gases and pretend not to recognize them as weapons for the battlefield. That is all my eye and Betty Martin, naturally – bullshit you would say – and they have stockpiles of one gas they call Sarin. They call it that because the chemical name is very complicated. Sarin is just a code name. They call the Soviet version of it Soman. That is supposed to be even stronger and more terrible. Why they should need anything stronger, I don't know. They both attack the central nervous system. It is thought that a single one-milligram droplet of Sarin inhaled will paralyse a healthy adult and cause death in less than a minute. But it doesn't have to be inhaled. Contact of a droplet with any part of the body will cause death. The death is just quicker if it is inhaled.'

'You say that these nerve gases are *thought* to be so deadly, Your Highness. Yet you have studied the central nervous system yourself quite extensively. Are you telling us that there may be some doubt about the military value of these gases? Are you not *certain* that they are deadly?'

He hastened eagerly to set my mind at rest. 'Oh absolutely certain, Mr Halliday. There have been tests. Sarin and Soman have both killed large apes, sheep and other test mammals pretty well instantly. Spasm, paralysis, death. That is the sequence. It is with human beings that we are lacking the controlled test results. So far, the only information we have about the effects on human beings has come as the result of accidents. And the information has been very sparse. Both in the United States and Britain the authorities were very successful in covering up. There were only leaks of information which were of little military value and of no use to the scientific mind at all. The major accident at the city of Sverdlovsk in the Soviet Union was too big to cover up. Over a hundred people were killed by windborne droplets and many more made seriously ill. Soviet propaganda tried to say that it was a virus epidemic but no one believed that. It was a manufacturing accident. Yet again, no scientific information became available.'

'You say that these substances can be absorbed through the skin? Does that mean that gas masks don't work?'

'Only complete covering will protect you, Mr Halliday, a special suit, something that can be sealed and later washed down to decontaminate it. The new tanks are being made with this need in mind, I believe. You need something that can be sealed for a time until it can be cleaned off with the proper chemicals.'

'How about a pressurized plane. Could that be made safe?'

He pretended not to have heard that. 'The best thing, of course, is an antidote.'

'There are antidotes? They already exist?'

'In secret, obviously, and they have not yet been tested on human beings. You must understand that substances like Sarin and Soman are invented chemicals, like modern insecticides.

They are not found in nature. But, what can be made with chemicals can be unmade with other chemicals. Again, it is the know-how.'

'I see, Your Highness. So, apart from sealed containers and people in sealed suits to wash the poison off for you from outside, protection will be chiefly a matter of having the right antidotes and knowing that they are still right, that the enemy hasn't switched to some nastier droplets that you don't know about.'

'You are forgetting one thing, Mr Halliday. With antidotes, one must also know how exactly to use them, at what points and with what precautions one must apply them.'

'Realistic tests must be made.'

'That is obvious. You cannot teach apes how to handle antidotes.'

He was getting tired. It was nearly time to wrap it up.

'Your Highness, in the course of your personal researches into the mysteries of the central nervous system in mammals, you must have witnessed some of these tests. When a one milligram droplet of Sarin, for example, is inserted into the mouth of a large ape, what exactly happens? Can you tell us?'

He warmed to my appetite for eye-witness information. 'Yes, Mr Halliday, certainly I can tell you, though you will not expect me to reveal where I was privileged to see these demonstrations.'

'No, of course not.'

'Well, the droplet is squirted into the mouth with an instrument that looks like one of those scent atomizers that western women carry in their handbags. Only it is at the end of a long rod and, naturally, is not made of gold. The one milligram is squirted. No sound. For a moment, nothing. Then, every muscle in the body seems to contract as they go into that state that the doctors call by some name of their own. Not spasm, though that I think describes it too.'

'Fibrillation? Is that the medical word?'

'Yes, that's it. Fibrillation. The animal falls down, of course. Usually it starts to vomit and excrete at the same time. Then there are convulsions, a lot of that. The interesting thing is that the actual cause of death is usually simple asphyxiation. The muscles which control the lungs just cannot go on working.'

'Of course, you have no way of telling whether or not human beings would react in exactly the same way.'

'Not yet, no.'

204

'A painful death, would you say, Your Highness?'

'A little painful perhaps, but very quick. All over in less than a minute.'

'Thank you, Your Highness. What you have had to tell us has been both instructive and helpful. I'm sure that viewers all over the world will be grateful to you for allowing them to share your thoughts on some modern problems of living, and dying, that affect us all.'

I signalled to Kluvers to cut, waited until I had heard him say the word and then went forward quickly to shower The Ruler with congratulations. The Chief Secretary, I noted, was looking worried. That was understandable. The Ruler, also understandably, was looking pleased with himself. The ordeal was over. He had survived. He was being praised and flattered. The misgivings, if he ever experienced misgivings, would come later, when he tried to remember what it was exactly that he had said, or when the Chief Secretary plucked up courage enough to give him some quotes.

'When will it be shown?' he asked.

A standard question to which he received one of the evasive answers which are also more or less standardized.

'The film should be processed and flown to New York within the next few hours, Your Highness. After that it's up to the current affairs producers and the programmers. I'll see that you're kept informed.'

The crew had switched the lamps off and started moving everything around for the set-up we were going to use on the pick-up shots. The Ruler must have concluded that they were getting ready to go. With a gracious nod all round, he rose from his chair and prepared to leave. The Chief Secretary drew me aside quickly.

'His Highness has another appointment above in the house,' he said. 'You will not be seeing him again. But before you leave, Mr Halliday, I would like to see you. This interview was, as we both know, a contrived occasion not to be taken too seriously. Your personal assistance in all this entitles you to a supplementary honorarium. I should not like you to leave without it.'

'Whatever you say, Chief Secretary.'

He hurried away along the tunnel to the hoist. The Ruler was already there and becoming impatient. I turned to find Kluvers looking at me with a very odd expression.

'Is that what you were commissioned to do?' he asked. 'A hatchet job?'

'Did you think that any of the questions I asked him was unfair or irresponsible?'

'I think that the only person allowed to ask that man questions should be a psychiatrist.'

'There are lots of people who would agree with you. They don't say it aloud though. Have you heard of some businessmen who call themselves Mukhabarat Zentrum?'

'The murder gang, you mean? Rasmuk?'

'His Highness has them on a multi-million retainer at the moment.'

That shook him. 'We should never have taken this job,' he said bitterly. 'We should have gone straight home.'

'Going straight home is still going to be a problem for some of us,' I said. 'How about getting the rest of the job done?'

'We're almost ready.'

'Did Rainer tell you that I'll be handing the exposed film over to him for processing?'

'Yes, and I gave him a list of our credits. That all right with you?'

'Sure you still want to be associated with me?'

He grinned. 'I didn't say it was a lousy interview. I just thought it frightening. I wonder how much of it will actually get on the air.'

'So do I. Incidentally, I'd like the two cans packaged separately and numbered one and two. Okay?'

'No problem.'

'And I'd like a little extra help from you in the packaging area.'

'What kind of help?'

He sighed a bit when I told him, but he agreed.

We did the pick-up shots the way the cameraman had wanted, against a background of wet limestone walls and dripping steel staircases. Of the questions I had asked The Ruler during the interview, I only changed the wording of one when we came to do the shot of me asking it. That was the one question he had deliberately ignored, and I wanted to show why he had chosen to ignore it.

On the subject of protection against nerve gas attack, I had asked if a pressurized plane could be made safe. No reply. Why?

Because he himself had a private plane that was pressurized, a Caravelle Super B according to Zander. So, I changed my question to: 'How about a pressurized plane, like the private Caravelle that you have, Your Highness? Couldn't that be made safe for a few hours during a nerve gas attack?'

It was cheating, I admit, and Kluvers rolled his eyes to show what he thought of my standards of professional ethics, but he didn't try to stop me shooting the revised version. He just asked, when it was done, if there would be anything more. When I said that we could wrap it up, he nodded and told the crew to get moving.

Only then did I see Simone on the stairs. She had been up on the fourth flight listening to the interview. Her thin clothes were damp and she was shivering, but at first she didn't seem to be troubled by her discomfort, or even aware of it.

'If that interview is ever shown,' she said, 'he is finished.'

'Does that bother you? He's planning to *kill* you, *and* the patron, *and* the young people.'

'He's planning to try, yes.' She was beginning to realize that she was cold and I led her over to a section of the gallery where the lamps had left behind them a patch of warm air.

'Did the patron know,' I asked, 'that his price for Abra Bay was their letting him run nerve gas tests on human beings?'

'Originally, no. But the patron knew that The Ruler was fascinated by these weapons, so he did what you did just now, only more gradually. He asked loaded questions, he debated a little and he encouraged The Ruler to get excited enough to talk. At one time the patron thought that The Ruler was only frightened and that all he really wanted was the secret antidotes. But that was only a hope. He wants the gases themselves. He wants the power to kill as if by magic.'

'Obviously, Nato will turn him down.'

'Because he gives indiscreet interviews in front of television cameras? Perhaps. If so, he will try the Russians.'

'Offering *them* Abra Bay? That's crazy. None of his co-Rulers would stand for that.'

'You don't understand, my friend. Abra Bay was bait for the west. And it brought them to the table, didn't it? They will have to think about the price, no doubt, but they will think very carefully and unemotionally. And it won't be gentlemen like your handsome General Newell and your civilized Herr Schelm who make the decisions. The Ruler would have to think of a different bait for the Russians. Or maybe a different approach altogether. A frank and simple offer of the testing facility in return for a little friendly and neighbourly pressure on neutral Austria to let him keep his floodable old mine and build as he wishes to build above it? Yes?'

'By testing facility you mean human guinea-pigs I gather. The prisoners in his jails?'

'They'd sooner be dead anyway. And they wouldn't care who killed them.'

'How do you know that Nato wants these tests done?'

She smiled wistfully at my innocence. 'My dear friend, every-one concerned with chemical warfare is always wanting human animal tests done. The difficulty is that nobody wants to be *responsible* for doing them, or even requesting the facilities. You see, just investigating unfortunate accidents doesn't tell enough. There are always officious doctors interfering, trying to save life. If small experiments are tried, as there were in the Yemen, they turn into propaganda gifts for the other side. And The Ruler was right about one thing. Testing antidotes, which may have critical reaction times, is not easy to do with animals. You cannot tell them exactly what they must do to be safe, not in a way they understand.'

Kluvers came over. 'We're about ready to go,' he said. 'We'd better give you the film in our truck, don't you think? Safer?'

On the way up in the hoist, I told Simone what I had arranged about the film. She seemed pleased. 'You are learning,' she said. She almost laughed.

When we came from the top of the hoist behind the museum we could see Zander down at the car-park talking to Jean-Pierre. As he had predicted, The Ruler's second meeting with the General and Schelm was taking place without him. Simone went to report. I stayed with Kluvers and watched the film packed in the way I wanted. When the packages had been labelled I went to the door of the truck.

Simone had done as I had asked and Jasmin was standing by the station-wagon with my raincoat rolled up under one arm and her tooled-leather bag slung over the other. I signalled and she came over. I took the raincoat. Two of the packages we had made up, and boldly marked with a 1 and a 2, went into the raincoat side pockets. The other two, similarly but less boldly numbered, disappeared into the tooled-leather bag. I had opened my coat out as if to refold it so that nobody higher up near the house could have seen that last move.

As Jasmin returned to the station-wagon and I shook hands all round with the Dutchmen, Simone joined us on the pretext of doing the same thing. But her goodbyes were mainly for show. She patted the packages in my raincoat pockets and managed to look smugly satisfied as she did so. She also had a message to deliver.

'The patron says that we must leave soon. It is nearly four o'clock and we should do what we have to do while there is still plenty of daylight.'

'Let the Dutchmen go first to see what happens. Five minutes. Okay?'

'All right. Agreed. The more secure they feel here the better.'

We said goodbye to Kluvers and the Viser-Damrak crew all over again and watched them go down to the gate. There, they were stopped by the security guards and there was an angry-looking argument accompanied by a lot of arm-waving and pointing in our direction. Kluvers and his crew had to wait by the gate while the security captain came up to harangue me in German.

Zander was with us now. 'This security captain here,' he explained, 'has received special orders from the Chief Secretary. The film of the interview you had with The Ruler is to be held for censoring.'

'It was to be released by me personally to ORF, the Austrian broadcasting service, for processing.'

'It will be released later after it has been censored.'

'It can't be censored before it has been processed,' I bawled angrily. 'I demand to see the Chief Secretary.'

Zander obligingly translated this too. The security captain beckoned to me and we walked back up to the house. The two bodyguards on duty stiffened as we approached. Clearly, they spoke no German and didn't much care for the security captain anyway. However, when he made signs indicating that I was to remain there while he went inside to make a report, they let him through.

I stood there for several minutes before the Chief Secretary came out. He looked at me, and spoke too, as if he had never seen me before.

'We want the film,' he said. 'His Highness's orders. It is his property. It will not be allowed to leave these premises. You will hand it over immediately.'

'It is to be processed by ORF, Vienna. That has all been arranged.' I hugged my raincoat protectively to my breast.

'It will be processed as we decide. Hand it over immediately.' He came down the steps to confront me with his stomach. 'I would not like to have to use force to compel you to return His Highness's property.'

'This is Austrian territory, Chief Secretary, not the Gulf.'

'And the film still belongs to His Highness. No more nonsense please, Mr Halliday. You were employed and have been paid. If you don't want to give me the film you shot, I will have it taken from you.'

I hesitated a moment longer, then shrugged and gave him the package marked 1.

He took it, ripped off the paper to see that there was indeed a 16 mm film pack inside, then held out his hand again. 'All of it, please. There is a second magazine. I saw the cameraman put it in the camera.'

With a sigh I emptied the other raincoat pocket and gave him the package marked 2. 'Where are you going to get it processed?' I asked as he tore the wrappings off to check again.

'That is no business of yours, Mr Halliday. You have been paid. Now you may go.'

I started to do so, then turned. 'Just a word of advice, Chief Secretary,' I said. 'Don't try to burn it. That kind of film doesn't burn easily and makes a bad smell. If you want to destroy it quickly, just open it up and let the light in. My regards to His Highness.'

I started down again and this time kept going. I didn't think that the Chief Secretary would know enough when he opened the cartons to realize that the film I had given him hadn't been exposed.

From the car-park the security captain signalled an okay to the gate below. The two Dutch vehicles promptly restarted and drove out as the gates opened. From the security captain I received an amiable nod. I, too, could go now if I wished. My friends as well. Discipline had been enforced, and everyone knew it.

'The station-wagon will go first,' Zander said. 'Jean-Pierre will follow. We will keep close together until we see what we have to deal with. Where are we to to expect these ORF friends of yours, Mr Halliday?'

'At the junction with the lower road. There's a wooden sign saying that it's Petrucher territory a few metres this side of the road. We should watch for that, I guess. We'll be turning right towards Judenburg. They will have an ORF camera-car waiting to stay ahead of us and a heavy ORF location truck to stay right behind us. Near Judenburg, when we get to the main road, we'll make a sharp right and head for Klagenfurt. This side of Klagenfurt we pick up the Autobahn to Villach. Rainer will be in the camera-car. His orders to his drivers will be to keep us boxed in, as if they're preventing us from getting away with something they want. If any other car tries to pass or get in between his vehicles and ours, it's to be squeezed out. That means a lot of tail-gating, lousy driving of all sorts and maybe some bumps or a graze. If ORF don't mind, why should we?'

'Where do you propose to hand over the film?'

'At the frontier. It's just beyond Arnoldstein at a village called Thöl.'

'Well, we'll see if we can get that far. Simone, you drive. And don't let the Austrians bump us too much.'

We all got in and followed the Dutchmen down the track past the temporary buildings to the gates. They still had them open for us but the dog-handlers were out again with their charges snarling and trying to snap at our tyres as we went by.

'Jean-Pierre at least will be glad to see the road again,' Zander said. 'Poor fellow. Why should he be frightened of attack dogs? They can be killed so easily by someone who has good shoes, knows how to use his feet and is not frightened.'

We lurched slowly down the lane to the lower road. As we approached it, a bright blue ORF limousine camera-car with a reinforced roof and a flashing amber light on top backed up, blocking the turn completely. We jolted to a standstill, I wound down a rear window and looked out. The man beside the camera-car driver was Rainer. I gave him an okay sign and he raised a hand in acknowledgement. Then the camera-car moved forward and we followed. Jean-Pierre in the van was only a couple of yards behind us. The ORF location truck that followed him looked enormous.

Driving in convoy, especially when the vehicles in it have

widely different powers of acceleration and braking, is not as easy as a good armoured division on the move can make it look. Even with our little convoy of four, the concertina effect was noticeable from the start. Then Rainer decided to take it slower – a steady fifty kph – and we got on better. By the time we reached the reasonably straight bit beyond Unterzeiring the drivers were all beginning to get the hang of it.

The Rasmuk team picked us up, with no trouble at all, near Judenburg as we turned on to the road to Klagenfurt.

FOURTEEN

THEY were in a beige Citroën CX with Vorarlberg plates, and the first we heard of them was a long horn blast as they tried to pass the ORF truck and failed to make it. The road through Neumarkt and Friesach south to Klagenfurt is a main road but not a very modern one. There are stretches where fast traffic can pass the slow stuff, but not many, and a lot depends on the slow stuff being kind enough to co-operate. The ORF truck at the rear of our convoy was being unkind and unco-operative. It was also making playful little efforts of its own to pass the Ortofilm van, or pretending to make them. The Citroën team made three abortive, and increasingly noisy, attempts to pass the truck before deciding that they would have to bide their time.

It was Zander who identified them positively as the hit team and not just a group of four impatient Austrians. After the first horn blast he said something over his shoulder to the kids riding with me. Jasmin rummaged under the seat where the ammunition boxes were and came up with a leather case containing one of those telescopes that look like half of a pair of big binoculars. They are called, not surprisingly, monoculars and people who go in for target shooting or who have only one good eye prefer them to binoculars. Zander checked the eye-piece adjustment carefully.

There were quite a lot of bends in the road and it was possible every now and then to see the Citroën edge out from behind the truck. Finally, Zander said: 'I know the front-seat passenger. He's a man named Raoul Bourger. You remember him, Simone?'

'I remember him only too well, patron.'

He turned in his seat again and balanced the telescope on the head-rest for a longer look at the occupants of the Citroën. 'Bourger's father,' he explained to me, 'was a *pied noir* killed in the Algiers street fighting of January 'sixty. The boy, Raoul, was fourteen then. During the next year he killed four officers of the gendarmerie. He alone, though there were witnesses to the killings. The thing became an open secret.'

'But he wasn't caught?'

'Oh, he was well protected. Then he tried to kill himself, but the gun he used misfired.'

'He didn't try twice,' said Simone briskly. 'There were those who doubted that he had really tried the first time.'

'You were jealous of the attention he received, my child.'

'How could a nine-year-old girl be jealous of a fourteen-year-old Nechayev?'

He grinned. 'You were jealous, child. Don't pretend you weren't. Nine-year-old girls often are. Anyway, I wasn't the only one who tried to help him. Many of us tried. He would just smile politely. He hated the lot of us, of course, because his real father was dead and we who didn't fight the battles of the streets were alive.'

'He might smile politely to your face,' she retorted, 'but behind your back he would mimic your sympathy. You can be mimicked, you know, patron. A Nechayev manqué, that's what he was. A pretty young con-boy killer, but without the other one's intellectual pretensions or his knack of political phrase-making. You would have adopted him if his mother had let you.'

'That is a lie, Simone, and you are impertinent.'

In her anger she was beginning to take her eyes off the road. I tried to cool them both down. 'So it came to this,' I said. 'Having failed, or tried insufficiently hard, to kill himself, he went back happily to killing other people. A typical success story of our time. Right?'

Simone contented herself with a nasty little laugh.

Zander sighed. 'Friends and relatives gave the family money and saw to his education,' he said sombrely. 'Later, he went into business.'

'What kind?' I asked. 'To start with I mean. Do concerns like Rasmuk have a bottom of the ladder, or do youngsters of proved ability get the stock options right away?'

He lowered the telescope then passed it to Mokhtar so that he too could have a look at the Citroën before he turned to me. His eyes told me that he wasn't going to waste words on my cheap sarcasms.

'Mr Halliday,' he said, 'revenge isn't a lasting pleasure. It isn't nearly as sweet and satisfying as it's said to be, not even for fourteen-year-old boys with blood-feud grudges to nurse.'

'You didn't favour me with that solemn thought in your letter to me on the Baghdad postcard.'

'Did the hint of revenge that I offered make any difference to your thinking? Did it influence your decision to accept?'

'It set off a few day-dreams, of course. The person whose thinking it influenced was the police chief. Was it for him, or someone in authority like him, that you put it in?'

'Simone's idea. We had to remind authority of your past.'

'You did. The police chief even gave me a kindly warning. He said that some sweet things can be bad for one's health.'

'Revenge can be fatal.' He retrieved the telescope and gave it to me. 'Have a look. It helps to know the enemy's face.'

But from where I was sitting I found it almost impossible to hold the telescope steady when the Citroën became visible on the bends.

'How would you describe Raoul Bourger?' Zander asked.

'I think he has a black moustache. I think the driver has one too.'

'They've all got black moustaches,' Simone said impatiently. 'When the sun catches them, even I can see that, just in the mirror.'

'Did you notice how many black moustaches there were in The Ruler's entourage?' Zander asked as I gave him back the telescope. 'Some would like beards, but The Ruler reserves that mark of virility to himself. Of course, he has no other proof. No children. Just a beard. Anyway moustaches are the new thing. In some Middle East circles these days, black moustaches are absolutely de rigueur, and if the real hair is a little brown or red it is dyed.'

'Patron,' Simone said, 'I know you believe that on a day of battle it is best to talk only nonsense, but don't you owe it to Mr Halliday to talk a *little* sense. He has come a long way with us. He is entitled to know where the road leads. Rasmuk was not mentioned in his contract.'

He polished the telescope with his handkerchief while he thought about it, then had another look at the enemy behind us. 'You know why I selected you in particular for this task, Mr Halliday? You don't still have any illusions?'

'You tell me. I had old links with the CIA that could be re-activated by sending cute letters and package bombs through the mail. I'm a freelance who could be tempted with an offer of fifty thousand dollars for doing very little work in a cause that would appeal to a child's tit-for-tat conception of justice. And I knew enough about the mechanics of making television to fit into that too-easily-blown cover story that you had manufactured in one of your least-inspired moments. I don't think I'm the one who should be worrying about illusions at this stage, Mr Zander. If that's a Rasmuk hit team back there, the exact colour of their moustaches seems to me as unimportant as the brands of after-shave they're using.'

Obviously, he hadn't heard a word of my last few remarks. My reference to television had started him brandishing the tele-scope as if it were a rubber truncheon. Now, he raised his voice over mine. 'I have already conceded defeat on the television cover question,' he yelled. 'You were right, as it happened, but *only* as it happened. We would have had no trouble at all, no serious trouble, except for two obstacles. The first was the unexpected trouble with the Austrian authorities over The Ru-ler's plans for the Petrucher mine. But that could have been overcome had it not been for the second obstacle – *you.*'

'You've lost me, patron.' And he had. The fact that I couldn't see his eyes, even through the rear-view mirror, put me at a disadvantage.

'My original specification,' he said, 'made it clear that the go-between should not only know something about television prod-uction, and be known as an interviewer, but also that he should be a weak performer. Not totally incompetent, but consistently third-rate. You fitted the specification like a glove.'

'It's always good to be paid a graceful compliment.'

He ignored that. 'Until,' he said, 'today. Today, when you should have been at your worst, you were at a totally unprece-dented best. One can only ask why.'

'These accidents happen.'

'They shouldn't happen. They add to our burden of responsi-bility. May I remind you of your own words in Stresa. You were justifying the inclusion of this back-up unit. You were to ask The Ruler a few stupid questions and get from him some wise, golden answers. Wasn't that what you promised?'

'I'm sorry. I didn't know The Ruler so well then.'

'It was permissible to get him to talk about his troubles with the Austrian authorities but, according to Simone, you then proceeded to run rings around him. Very cleverly you showed him up as a rich, autocratic pretender to medical knowledge he doesn't possess. You exposed him as a dilettante who should not be allowed to open an unsupervised clinic of any description in Austria or anywhere else. Golden answers, eh?'

'It was unrehearsed. The man dug his own grave.'

'You didn't have to bury him in it. You didn't have to manipulate his state of high excitement and emotion, to lead him on until you had him talking his lunatic head off about matters that are supposed to be deeply secret. You were disgracefully irresponsible.'

'Are you worried about Kluvers and his crew?'

'They have no film evidence. They have no dangerous background knowledge. You could talk and be believed just as we could talk and be believed. That is why there is a four-man Rasmuk team back there waiting to see what they can do about killing us when we get off this narrow road with trucks to protect us and on to the Autobahn.'

'You mean that I'm now on the hit list too, like the rest of the family?'

'If you have not already been added to the list, you soon will be. Yes, even those butchers back there may already have been told. They use their radio a lot. I blame Simone for conspiring with you behind my back.'

'Nonsense,' she snapped. 'The world needs to know that The Ruler is a homicidal maniac and a public menace. But how can it know if there is no one about with guts enough to record the evidence?'

'Clap-trap, Simone, and you know it. The Ruler has no real power, merely nuisance value.'

'You are beginning to think like an old man, patron. These days, mere nuisances can start wars.'

I intervened hastily. She was beginning to take her eyes off the road again. 'Aren't you both forgetting something?' I asked. 'The Chief Secretary believes that *he* has the interview film.'

Zander said: 'Ha! Do you think he took your word for it that he has the real film? Let me tell you something. If it hadn't been for that Austrian security captain, no film at all would have been allowed to leave the compound. There would have been a body search of everyone, including the Hollanders. But that Austrian was scared. He had seen the ORF trucks waiting down on the road. That flashing light of theirs can only be authorized by the police. He thought that you or the Hollanders might make an official complaint.'

'So I *have* done something right. I arranged for those ORF

vehicles to be there with their flashing light. You should be grateful, patron. You should be thanking me. Instead of golden answers you get golden deeds.'

My impudence seemed to please him. 'All right. A thousand thanks, Mr Halliday. But don't forget this. One of those BMWs is already on its way to the nearest colour film processing laboratory. The Chief Secretary will know soon enough that you tricked him. You'd better start doing some quick thinking. What was your plan for today? I mean your plan for handing over the film?'

'When we get to the frontier, or close to it, we'll have to stop. When we do I'll get out and hand Rainer the package marked with the figure 1. That's got most of the Petrucher stuff in it. That's the stuff he really needs.'

'What about the second package? Keeping that for yourself?'

'I was thinking of giving it to you and Simone.'

'To us? Why?'

'You're defecting, aren't you? From the Gulf anyway. I thought defectors always took along a little something with them, something to make their hosts feel warmer and better-disposed towards them.'

Simone's quiet chuckle clearly annoyed him. 'We are being given political asylum. That is all,' he said testily.

'Still, the General should be grateful. That second reel of interview could make his job a whole lot easier. I mean the job of persuading this Nato committee he reports to that The Ruler is not a man to be trusted with anything more lethal than a fly whisk.'

'Perhaps. Though I don't think that the General I spoke with today will need much help from us. Let us hear more about *your* plan. When you have given this Rainer his film, taken your valises from behind you and are standing in the road with them, what then? I am assuming that we shall all still be alive by then. But let us suppose that most of us are. What will you do next?'

'Ask Rainer for a ride to Vienna, I guess. From there, I'll get a plane to New York. I may have to change at Frankfurt, but I should make Kennedy by breakfast time tomorrow. I'll rent a car to drive home.'

He had turned round on his seat to face me. 'You won't make it, Mr Halliday, not any of it.'

'No?'

'Well, you might just make it as far as the airport at Vienna, but there'll be someone from Mukhabarat Zentrum waiting for you there. They'll have seen you hand over film to ORF and they'll have reported by radio to The Ruler. Even if he hasn't yet had a lab report on the blank film you gave the Chief Secretary, he'll be taking no chances with you. Think carefully, Mr Halliday.'

'Are you inviting me, patron, to stay with you and this group?'

'You would be well advised to do so, yes.'

'And, if we make it, are you suggesting that I ask for political asylum in my own country?'

He looked at Simone. 'Is that what I was suggesting to him?'

'No, patron. But you don't make it clear what you *are* suggesting. To us he has been very helpful. You yourself admit it. I think we should speak more freely to him about his own position. We have nothing to lose by frankness.'

'Possibly not.' He picked up the telescope and had another look at the enemy. 'Speak more frankly then. Go ahead.'

Her eyes I could see through the rear-view mirror. They smiled slightly at mine. 'Mr Halliday,' she said; 'about this film you are giving to ORF. Clearly they will make much of it. But when? How soon?'

'Hard to say. It's a hot story. On the other hand, they won't have any pick-up footage. That's all at the end of the second can, the one they're not getting. They'll probably dig up some stills of the mine. They may even have one of me. And then they'll have to do a very careful German translation, record it and dub it as voice-over. I'd say it'll be twenty-four hours before they get it on the air.'

'By then, The Ruler will have been told that the interview you did wasn't destroyed. One way or another he will know. What he will not know is whether both parts of the interview are to be used on the air. His lawyers in Vienna will no doubt be active, but what will The Ruler himself be doing?'

'Using his private plane to get the hell out before the Austrian press gets after him again.'

'Meanwhile, ORF will be denying quite truthfully that they know anything about a second reel of film. All they have is what you gave them.'

'So Mukhabarat Zentrum gets further urgent instructions,' said Zander. 'If they missed you at Vienna, they're to nail you in New York or Bucks County.'

'Patron,' Simone said sharply, 'it was *me* you asked to advise Mr Halliday if you remember.'

'My child, I was only stating the obvious.'

'Mr Halliday can see the obvious for himself.'

'I wouldn't bet on that,' I said. 'What's the obvious way out of the spot I'm in? I mean the easy, painless one.'

'Oh, there is no obvious way out.' She smiled. 'You have to take a chance. Only one, and I hope it will be painless, but it is a chance. After you have handed over the first package of film to Rainer, you stay with us. You may have some uncomfortable moments later, but you will not necessarily be killed.'

'Not *necessarily*?'

'Probably not. My friend, we are not infallible. If you go with Rainer you will certainly be killed. Possibly at Vienna as the patron says. Why are you surprised? The patron is under a sentence of death for *serving* The Ruler. You have done the same man a serious injury. You have shown him as he is. What mercy can *you* expect? None. But if you stay with us and take a chance, the odds are better. And you must be ready to win. This is very important. You take the second package of film and you put it in your pocket. Not in your luggage but in your pocket. And if it is too large to go in a suit pocket, then tear an inside pocket and carry it inside the lining. If our plan for today works out, you will then be able to call on your good friend Herr Schelm for a little practical help. He will not, I think, refuse you.'

'What sort of help? I like him personally but, on anything to do with his job, I doubt if the milk of human kindness flows in any quantity that you could really see.'

'He might find it very convenient to do as you asked. All you are asking is that he makes copy prints of the film in package two and arranges for them to be sent privately to the Foreign Ministers of the UAE and Saudi Arabia and all Nato ambassadors in the Gulf capitals. Or, if he doesn't want to involve Nato, you could use your television connections in New York.'

I thought for a moment. The first can wouldn't be of much interest to the PBS producer, but with the second lot of footage added he would have something to build on. A feature on chemical warfare with sequences showing a crazy oil sheikh holed up in an old silver mine that he had converted into the world's safest fall-out shelter would be pretty interesting any-way. If you stirred in the hysterical laughter bit and the full close-up of the man smacking his lips over the convulsions of his nerve gas victims just before they stopped fighting for breath, you'd have some fairly sensational television. You'd also have an old international issue – the Geneva Protocol on CB warfare of 1925 – freshened up a bit to appeal to youthful palates.

'What makes you think,' I asked, 'that The Ruler's going to like all that adverse publicity?'

'He'll dislike it intensely, of course.'

'Then why should he tell Rasmuk to forget about killing me?'

'He won't have to. By then, he'll be the one on the defensive. Rasmuk doesn't like clients who run up huge bills they are suddenly unable to pay. What his fellow Rulers will decide to do about him is yet another matter. They'll sometimes suffer fools, but not the kind who make their follies public and disgraceful.'

'The sillier I make The Ruler look, then, the better I make it for you. Yes?'

Zander brandished the telescope at her. 'You see, Simone? A little frankness, you said. We have nothing to lose. The next minute the fellow is telling us that he can solve all our problems with television propaganda. He has become our saviour.'

The telescope was pointing at me now. I leaned back to avoid it. 'That's not what I said or meant, patron, and you damn well know it. What I said was that anything that discredits The Ruler takes some of the heat off you.'

The eyes surveyed me almost pityingly. 'You really know nothing about my world, do you? When The Ruler is discredited, the first question to be asked will be, "who showed our brother the steps, the way down to this dangerous path?" And the answer decided upon will be that I was and am the guilty one. As for Mukhabarat Zentrum, they will have a serious public relations problem to face. It is now too widely known, you see, that they accepted a contract, for a top price, to kill me and my immediate family.'

'Known by whom?'

'By everyone who matters in Gulf business circles, and by

some who don't matter at all. I suspect that they have been penetrated by an undercover police spy. Even your friend Herr Schelm seems to know, and he also knows the price. An intelligence officer! If *he* knows, anyone could know. Do you think that Mukhabarat Zentrum can permit a failure on their part to occur so publicly. Who in future would pay their prices after a fiasco like that? Simone is right about their greed, but only partly. The fact that The Ruler may, in any case, now be unable to pay them all he owes is of minor importance. Their reputation is on the line. To murder me and my family *without* the certain prospect of a final payment might be a very good prestige move for them. It would demonstrate to those who matter that, even when others let them down, Mukhabarat Zentrum always goes on acting in good faith. u want a prophecy, Mr Halliday?'

'I'd prefer reassurance. For instance, I'd like to be told, with a reasonably convincing smile, that the General's backroom Nato committee isn't going to play footsy with The Ruler because of Abra Bay. But prophecy will have to do, I guess.'

'Very sensible, Mr Halliday. The buck has passed. What Nato does is Nato's business. Let's concern ourselves with ours. I'll prophesy this. If Mukhabarat Zentrum's people don't kill me today, they will not kill me at all, nor any of my family. There! What do you think?'

'I've heard cheerier forecasts.'

'Listen, Mr Halliday. If they fail with me today they will have to wait and start thinking again. When they find that I and my family have totally disappeared and no longer exist except as memories, they will claim responsibility. Who will there be to dispute their claim? You? Herr Schelm? General Newell? I don't think so.'

'Talking of me, patron, what's your reading of my chances?'

'If they fail to kill you today, they will find it convenient to forget you. No one could ever hear of that failure and hold it against them. And, the moment your interview receives publicity, here or anywhere else, you would be, if still alive, doubly safe. Simone is right about that. They don't like accepting those contracts that are obviously motivated by someone's desire for personal reprisal, even from clients who can afford to pay top rates. When the policeman can see a motive he will go to the client with awkward questions that the client may feel he has to answer. Mukhabarat Zentrum considers that class of business as beneath it. In that area, at least, I can be reassuring. A calm mind helps, though I *have* heard it said that one can be too calm for safety. Have you ever found that?'

'I'll tell you tomorrow.'

'Quite right. It's today that matters. So, let us be serious. What do you now see behind us?'

I looked and saw, as expected, the Ortofilm van. 'The same scene. Nothing's changed.'

'Look again, carefully.'

'Guido's driving the van now. Is that what you mean? I don't see Jean-Pierre.'

'He got out when we stopped for the road repair block at Neumarkt. He's quick for his age. I doubt if anyone noticed.'

'I gather that there's been a change of plan.'

'Not an immediate change, Mr Halliday, and please don't think that I am ungrateful for the arrangements you made for our safety. They have been a great help in enabling *us* to choose where we will stand and fight instead of the enemy. What we will have is not a total change of plan, but certain modifications. Jean-Pierre knows my mind. Before you left the Gasthaus this morning he made some contingency arrangements that he thought I might like to have available. It was a natural thing for him to do. We have worked together for many years remember.'

'Yes. What's the first modification?'

'I want us to make the stop where you will hand over package number one of the film to ORF's Mr Rainer before we get to Arnoldstein. Just after Villach there is a bridge over the railroad. We will make the handover two hundred metres beyond the bridge. Do you have a stop signal arranged?'

'Three quick flashes with the headlights. But why there? What for? We could get ten kilometres closer to the Italian frontier than that, *and* still keep the ORF escort.'

He made one of his giggly jokes. 'We shall have the Mukhabarat Zentrum escort instead.' When Simone sighed loudly, he said: 'Don't worry, Mr Halliday. They won't dare to move against us just there.'

'That means, I take it, that the real problem is going to be blasting our way through a road-block on the way down to Tarvisio.'

'Oh, I wouldn't like to have to do that.' He sounded quite

223

shocked by the idea. 'We would have two enemy teams to contend with then, one behind and one in front. No, no! Let us first worry about the Autobahn to Villach.'

'What about our rifles and ammunition?' asked Simone. 'The rifles are clean, but should we not have one loaded and ready to fire?'

'Leave all that to me. I will have a rifle and one magazine where I can reach them quickly. But if there is an incident, if they try to play games with us on the Autobahn and the police become involved we must not be seen to be armed. Now, we are coming to St Veit. When we stop for a traffic light, Mr Halliday, you and I will change places. But very quickly, please, when I give the word.'

'Okay.'

'And it would be a good idea for Jasmin to give you both parcels of film now,' he went on. 'You should hide parcel number two before we get to the Autobahn.' He spoke in their private language to Jasmin who at once handed me the packages.

Ripping the lining of an inside pocket while you are wearing the coat of which it is a part proved to be difficult. In the end, Mokhtar lent me a murderous-looking flick knife so that I could cut the seam. 'I don't see why I have to treat a good suit like this,' I complained.

'You'll see,' Zander replied. 'And you had better give me the other parcel, the one for ORF. It will be safer in the glove compartment. We don't want you dropping it when we change places. Are you carrying your passport on your person or is it in your briefcase?'

'It's in my other inside pocket.'

'Keep it there. What about your money, your credit cards?'

'They're making an uncomfortable bulge in the same place. Why?'

'You will need them on your person.'

I rarely respond well to being treated like a backward infant, but on that occasion I meekly handed over the ORF package and checked to see that my passport, travellers' cheques and credit cards were where I had said they were. Zander could be maddening, but he had a way of commanding obedience that was hard to resist. No doubt the General would have been able to tell me why.

We went through St Veit without hitting a single red light and

Zander began to get fidgety over the delay in our changing places. We were in the outskirts of Klagenfurt and only two kilometres short of the turn-off for the Villach Autobahn before we had to stop for a big crane transporter backing out of a building site. Almost before we had started to slow down Zander had his door eased open and was telling me to do the same. In fact the whole change-around took less than ten seconds. The manœuvrings of the crane transporter held us up for a full two minutes.

Zander spent them extracting one of the rifles, which were rolled up in what a customs man making a cursory inspection of the baggage would have taken for a piece of camping equipment, and in re-arranging the boxes of ammunition. My knowledge of small arms is pretty well limited to those used in the wars I have covered as a reporter. I *think* the rifles they had that day were Armalite AR 15's, the kind that fire smallish bullets with high muzzle velocities. Marksmen don't like them because they aren't very accurate and you can't really aim them at anything over two hundred yards away. At any range up to six hundred, however, those small bullets can do terrible damage to a human body. Not even the entry wound is a clean hole. The Colt magazines they had each held twenty-five rounds. That I know because the information was plainly stencilled on the boxes they were in.

The Klagenfurt–Villach Autobahn is mostly four lanes with steel dividers. It goes to six lanes for short distances where the on and off ramps join it, but on the west-bound lanes that we were using, Rainer's plan for dealing with any attempts to interfere with the Ortofilm vehicles proved to be simple. As soon as we got onto the Autobahn, the ORF camera-car, its roof-light still flashing, moved out into the fast lane, and stayed there without increasing its speed. I looked back and saw that the ORF truck had done the same thing. The furious horn blasts which now pursued us were not from the Rasmuk Citroën but, quite evidently, from regular Autobahn users. Five-thirty was the beginning of the evening rush hour, and workers from Klagenfurt factories and offices with suburban homes in the Wörther See area were in a hurry. Clearly, the Rasmuk team had long ago realized that ORF, for strange reasons of its own, was providing Ortofilm with an escort. A radio check with whoever was controlling the Rasmuk operation had probably elicited orders to maintain contact and report progress towards the frontier.

Zander was impressed by the way ORF was using its muscle. 'This Rainer of yours,' he said, 'must be an amusing fellow.'

'Not particularly amusing, but very determined. He means to have that film and he'll stay with us until he gets it. All the way to the frontier if you want.'

He ignored my last remark. 'Well, he's given Bourger and his team an anxious time. That is helpful. An anxious opponent is always more liable to make mistakes. Is there anything in this briefcase of yours that you particularly want to keep?'

'There's a thick address book there that I'd rather not lose.'

'Jasmin can take that in her handbag. All right?'

'Okay. If you say so. I gather you mean to ditch this thing we're riding in.'

'I am making sure that if we leave it to be destroyed we take what we need with us. You have also here the Nechayev memoir.'

'You were going to tell me about that some day.'

'I bought the original manuscript several years ago from a dealer in Basel. He did not put a high value on it. It was among what he called his political ephemera – old letters and other documents of passing interest to specialists. He suspected it of being a forged pastiche done ten years or so after Nechayev's death. One of Pacioli's so-called experts had the same idea. I believe it, though, to be genuine. I was almost ashamed to use it as bait in that way.'

'What makes you think it's genuine?'

'Nechayev has always interested me. Are you one of those who believe that soldiers and men of affairs are incapable of serious thought?'

'What I was really asking, perhaps, is why you picked on Nechayev as a subject for serious thought. Why not Kropotkin or Malatesta? Nechayev was just a wild man.'

'Simone would agree with you, but Professor Arnold Toynbee didn't think so. Have you read his correspondence with Daisaku Ikeda?'

'I've never even heard of it.'

'And you a man of letters! Ah well. Toynbee compares Nechayev with Robespierre and Lenin. All made the ethical and intellectual mistakes of believing that violence is a justifiable means when the end you have is the ultimate welfare of mankind. Robespierre and Lenin lived long enough to see, but not to admit, that the earthly paradises they had created were merely two different kinds of terror. If Nechayev also had lived, he too might have been on that famous train that arrived in Petersburg in nineteen seventeen. But he would have been there *instead* of Lenin. Don't worry about the memoir, not this copy. I will send you another, better-translated. Now, we are getting to Villach and must be alert. There is a loop road, eh Simone?'

'We are on it now. The Autobahn stops here. We have about three kilometres to go.'

As she spoke, the Autobahn divider ended and we were on a two-way road with traffic going in both directions and a common centre lane for passing. The ORF camera-car at once moved over into the position dead ahead of us that it occupied before the Autobahn. The big truck that had been running interference alongside our van dropped back into line. A swarm of angry small-car drivers at once seized the opportunity to snarl by, but there was no sign of the Citroën. Zander had the telescope out though and, after a moment or two, reported that the Citroën was tucked in behind the ORF truck.

'Bourger is in no hurry,' he remarked. 'He awaits developments.'

We were in a fringe area of small factories and lumber yards on the outskirts of Villach. I noticed that the signposts were becoming more frequent and beginning to point towards Arnoldstein, the frontiers and a special customs clearance depot for big commercial vehicles.

'Slowly, Simone. Slowly and steadily,' Zander warned. 'We don't want them to think that we don't know where we are exactly.'

'You're getting excited for no reason, patron,' she said. 'I know exactly where we are. We're just coming to the railroad bridge. We can't just stop anywhere here, no matter what the map says. The road's too narrow.'

Beyond the bridge there was a street with old apartment blocks and small stores on either side of it; then came two gas stations, then there was a truckers' café with a big parking lot in front of it.

'There,' said Zander.

She flashed the headlights three times and pulled off the road. I saw Rainer turn his head quickly as his driver stopped and began to back up towards us. When they stopped again, Rainer said something and the driver switched off the roof light.

'So far so good,' said Zander. 'Now, Mr Halliday, he's *your* friend. Go give him the film he wants and thank him for his very efficient help. Tell him we can look after ourselves now.'

'*Can* we look after ourselves? Nothing's changed so far that I can see. We still have a Rasmuk hit team sitting on our tail. Your memories of Raoul Bourger as a teenage killer don't make him sound like the kind who mellows over the years. Has the fact that you once knew him made you change your mind? Does it look now as if, after all, you may be able to do a deal and *buy* yourself off the hook?'

He still disliked my disrespectful habit of asking him direct questions. 'Mukhabarat Zentrum has no use for hit teams of mellow personalities, Mr Halliday,' he said. 'You leave my job to me. Yours is to get rid of your television friend there smoothly and without fuss. I wish to part company with him here. Right? Take your time. No hurry. But get rid of him.'

'Whatever you say, patron.'

I took the package of film from the glove compartment and climbed out. Even from a distance of eight or ten yards, I could see that Rainer was deeply suspicious of me and the unexpected stop we had made. That very morning I had asked him for an escort all the way to the frontier at Thöl. Now I was stopping when I was nearly there. To fill up with gas? No. I'd just passed a couple of gas stations. Was I stopping for coffee? A last cup of the real Austrian-style brew with cream? Absurd. No, I had to be trying in some cunning way and for some disreputable reason of my own to renege on our deal. Or maybe I'd just failed to get a foot of film and had been postponing the embarrassing moment when I would have to admit it. Well, whatever the bad news was, he wasn't about to make it easy for me to break.

'Where's this international security agency you made such a song and dance about?' he asked as I came up to him. 'All I've seen is that Citroën back there that began following us just after Judenburg. What have we stopped here for? They seem harmless enough.'

'That's why we stopped. I don't want you to waste any more time giving us protection. It was getting clear of the security people at the mine that turned out to be the big headache. They tried to confiscate the film.'

'Did they succeed?'

I gave him the package. 'You can tell me when you've had that lot processed. That's His Highness on camera telling you the whole story. I think you'll like it. I took your advice.'

'About the questions to be asked?'

'No. I had my own questions. I meant that I took your advice about not rehearsing. It worked well, I think. I listened, he talked. The results were fairly surprising. It's all there anyway, all that really matters to you. Did you speak to New York?'

'Yes, that's all straightened out. What did you mean by "all that really matters"? Is there more?'

'Pick-up footage, cut-aways, mine gallery background. That you don't get. Sorry.'

'They took it from you?'

'They took two reels of film. I had to give them something. What you have there is what you asked for, plus a lot you didn't ask for. They may be the best bits. The sooner it's in your lab the better, and I'd advise you to move quickly. You *will* have the lawyers after you. That's for sure. But get it on the air right away and they'll have to change their tune. He's blown his own case all by himself. I didn't ask him a single question to which any lawyer could possibly object.'

He had opened the outer wrapping of the package. Now, he made up his mind. He decided, rightly, that I was being reasonably honest with him. He could be reasonably amiable to me.

'I'm glad the no-rehearsal approach worked out,' he said. 'It's always a risk the first time, but sometimes a risk worth taking.'

We shook hands, I thanked his driver for his patience and Rainer picked up the car-radio mike, presumably to tell his truck driver that the escort mission had been successfully accomplished and that they would now head for their respective bases. Then, in spite of everything that Zander had said about my not getting beyond the airport if I tried to pull out on my own, I began to wonder if I wasn't being very stupid, if it wouldn't make complete sense for me to change my mind again right there and, as I had originally intended, ask Rainer for that ride with him back to Vienna.

Zander had been standing beside the Ortofilm van talking earnestly to Guido, but as I started back to the station-wagon I saw him turn quickly. The Citroën had parked behind the ORF truck, but now there was one of the men with moustaches walking towards Zander.

He was in his mid-thirties, with bony, aquiline good looks that didn't really need the moustache to emphasize their owner's masculinity. He wore a stylish Italian suit, only slightly crumpled, and had the sort of naturally graceful walk that knows when it is being watched and is used to admiration. When Zander faced him he raised his hands slightly to show that they were empty and smiled. His teeth were excellent.

I had reached the station-wagon by then and saw that Simone was watching too.

'It's Bourger,' she said. 'That's the big smile he always had when he wanted something that wasn't his. You'd better wait in here with me. Leave them to it.'

I got in beside her. She watched them in the rear-view mirror. Rainer's camera-car roared away back towards the Autobahn and Vienna.

'When you were talking to him just now,' she said, 'and giving him the film, I thought for a moment that you were going to change your mind about taking the patron's advice. I thought you were going to leave with Herr Rainer.'

'I did think about it, yes.'

'Bourger thought you might also. He had a man in the café pay-phone cubicle watching you. If you had decided to go with Rainer, no doubt the fact would have been quickly reported to their Vienna contact. So Bourger waited. Now that he knows you are staying with us and that all the eggs are in his basket, he makes his approach to the patron.'

'Do you think there's still a chance of a deal?'

'If there is a deal offered now I would be very surprised indeed. If the possibility had ever existed it would have been discussed months ago.' She shrugged. 'I can't say that it is quite impossible. With someone like The Ruler involved, anything is possible. But you can be sure of one thing. Whatever Bourger's orders are, he will try to talk the patron into making them easier for him and his team to carry out. You know, I was a very observant child and I saw three things about Bourger. Why are you smiling?'

'I wasn't smiling. I was thinking of you, at the age of nine, observing Bourger. What did you see?'

'That he was very vain, of course, but so was I. There were

two special things about him. He was very – what is the word? – indolent. And he always mistook cunning for cleverness. He never saw that cunning can be learned by stupid people.'

'He killed four policemen without being caught. And he's in business with Rasmuk. He must have something.'

'He has. You don't have to be modest or clever or energetic to be an effective assassin. All you need are certain blind spots in your mind and a feeling for the work. The patron is coming back.'

I opened the door to get out and make way for him, but he motioned to me to stay where I was and climbed in behind us.

'Bourger sends you his regards, Simone,' he reported, 'and he tells me the following. His orders are to see us into Italy. He says, in what he believes is a joking way, that he is to be our shepherd. Trying to be businesslike, he says that his planners had assumed that we would make for Italy. Not because of Stresa, but because they suspect that I may have made a bargain for Nato protection. Why? Because they could not believe that a man of my experience would ever have trusted The Ruler enough to turn my back on him even for a moment. He pretends to be greatly saddened by the situation in which he finds himself with old friends.'

'I can see the tears in his eyes. Is he in radio contact with his Italian team?'

'He speaks as if he is. He must be.'

'Then they are well this side of Tarvisio in the pass at Thöl. Not even powerful transceivers will work on the opposite sides of these mountains.' She looked at me. 'You see? We would meet Rasmuk long before we reached your Carabinieri.'

Zander held up his hands. 'Simone, we need daylight for what we have to do. Pay attention to me. I asked Bourger, in the friendliest way, what his orders were if we were to turn and go north, perhaps to Germany. He said that he would remain our shepherd, but that an already-alerted team from Linz would come down to intercept us. He begged us not to attempt such a journey. I asked him, as if I doubted his manhood, what fire-power he had. He said that, as mere shepherds on land owned by others, all they had were modest revolvers.'

'How modest?'

'Police Special thirty-eights. His task all along, and he repeated this, had been simply to watch and report. He had been given the assignment only because he knew my face and yours.'

231

'Did you believe him, patron?'

'Yes.' But I had turned to watch him and saw the doubt in his eyes, and the hint of fear it brought with it.

'Why do you believe him, patron?'

There was a gleam of defiance. 'He didn't ask me what *we* had. He doesn't want to know anything that he might not want to report to his colleagues waiting to receive us. He doesn't like this assignment. He remembers that I still have friends in North Africa who might not like the hand he had in killing me.'

'You don't think he's bluffing?'

'No. He will do no more than he has to. We shall ignore him and go ahead as we planned. When he has lost us he will have his excuse for doing so, and we shall rendezvous with Jean-Pierre. Now, let's get moving. And remember, you must go very slowly to begin with. Guido knows what he has to do, but doing it will not be easy.'

She said no more, just turned the ignition key and started up.

I was still watching him though. He knew it and didn't like it. 'May I know what this plan is?' I asked. 'Hadn't I better know?'

He turned away and began signalling to Guido in the van right behind us. 'The plan is first to lose our shepherd,' he said. 'If there's anything I want you to do, I'll tell you.'

As Simone pulled out of the truckers' parking lot the Ortofilm van was about ten feet behind us. As she very slowly accelerated it stayed that distance from us. We were coming to a crossroad. A sign pointing left gave the names of a couple of small towns and added the information, in German, Serbo-Croat and Italian, that there was no through-road for unauthorized traffic to the Austrian frontier with Yugoslavia.

The big fork in the main road was half a kilometre further on. There, a huge sign made things absolutely plain to all south-bound traffic.

If you wanted to go to *Italien, Italia, Italie,* via Arnoldstein, Maglern and Thöl, you kept to the right. If you wanted to go to *Jugoslawien, Jugoslavija, Yugoslavia,* via Radendorf and the Wurzenpass, you went to the left. Both frontiers were about the same distance away.

We went to the left, and then, as the road ahead of us narrowed, suddenly began to go faster.

FIFTEEN

At first the van kept up with us. The road there was fairly straight and ran along the floor of a valley with high, steep, tree-clad slopes on both sides. Ahead of us, though, was what looked like an impenetrable wall of mountains. There was little traffic coming from the opposite direction and most of it consisted of small trucks carrying farm produce. If I had not seen the sign promising that the road led to a pass I would have said that we were heading for a dead end.

The valley was narrowing all the time and the gradient we were on was becoming steeper. The van was now fifty yards behind us. The Citroën, with our 'shepherd' in it, was beginning to edge out ready to pass and stay close to us. I wondered how long it would take the Rasmuk team in Italy – by now fully aware, no doubt, of our change of route from a busy, well-policed international highway to a relatively quiet mountain road on which anything could happen – to move their ambush a few miles across the Italian frontier with Yugoslavia. About as long, I figured, as it would take me to fill in the application form and buy a visa at the border. I turned to Zander.

'Apart from reminding you that there'll be no welcoming escort of Carabinieri to greet us on the far side of this frontier,' I said, 'I'd better tell you right now that I don't have a visa for Yugoslavia.'

He took no notice. His attention was concentrated on the van. It was Simone who answered me.

'We're not going into Yugoslavia.' Her eyes went from the mirror to the road and back again. 'We are not going to Italy either. The patron knows this road. He walked it as a prisoner at the end of Hitler's war. Here we will deal with Bourger. Then we will go north to Germany. That is what the patron arranged with your Herr Schelm this afternoon while you were filming. Oh yes, I know. Bourger has threatened us with a gang from Linz, but what does that matter if he no longer knows where we are? North to Germany is the only safe route for us because that is the route they will find it hardest to cover.'

She made it sound matter-of-fact and businesslike, but I didn't think she really believed it, any more than I believed that her father had walked that road as a POW. If he had walked it in nineteen forty-five, it would have been as an Abwehr Feldwebel disguised in threadbare civilian clothes and carrying the identity papers of a non-German foreign worker. He would have been with others following the signs pointing in the direction of an American zone displaced-persons camp.

'How are you going to deal with Bourger?' I asked.

'Make him lose us, of course.'

She tried to sound impatient with my slowness, but couldn't quite make it. Zander caught the doubt in her voice.

'Stop talking and watch the road,' he said sharply. 'We are coming to the first corner and must take advantage of every second.'

The road curled suddenly to the right and then went into a left bend that must have been nearly half a mile long. And it was climbing all the way like a huge ramp. Simone shifted down twice and went up at speed with the tyres screaming. Behind us, Guido moved into the middle of the road and stayed there.

At the top there was a hairpin bend to the right and I found that I could look straight down the hillside and see the van grinding slowly up the ramp below. It was at that moment that the driver of the Citroën tried to bulldoze his way past and both vehicles rocked and swayed as they touched. The Citroën had to fall back though. Zander said, 'Ha!' and went on giving the young people what was, presumably, a Berber running commentary on the action.

Then the Rasmuk driver tried again. This time he swung the car right across the downhill lane and up on to the shoulder there so as to gain height and put impetus into a charge that would take the van in the side and overturn it. Earlier it might have worked, but with that gradient against him he could not produce the kind of impact needed to overturn the heavier vehicle. The van only swerved and Guido returned it instantly to the middle of the road.

Zander went on reporting, but now to the front seat and in English. 'They won't try that trick again,' he said. 'That truck we just passed going down will keep them behind on the bend. Begin now, Simone, to look for the track on your left. There is a stone calvary, an old Bildstock with a pointed roof, in the field just by it. Better watch for that. The track may be long disused ow and hard to see. But it should be only a little over a kilometre now.'

The Rasmuk car had fallen back to let the truck on the down ane go by. I was still wondering if Bourger had decided, after the failure of their attempts to run the van off the road, to wait or a more favourable moment and try again when he solved the problem in a different way.

The Citroën moved up close to the rear of the van, edging out lowly to the left as it did so. Then, Bourger himself leaned out of the front passenger window with both his elbows on the ledge of it. In his hands was a stubby machine pistol of the kind that as a skeleton butt which can be folded around out of the way of the pistol grip. Carefully he eased it forward until he could clamp the barrel casing with his left hand firmly against the windshield pillar. Then, he fired one long automatic burst into the centre of the left rear door of the van.

That was it. I saw the van windshield bursting and a red smear that had been Guido's blue shirt rising in the driver's seat as everything tilted. Then, the van settled back on its springs and an along the edge of the road until it hit one of the concrete snow markers that lined the outer shoulder of the bend. However, Bourger's driver did not bother to wait for that. The moment the van had left the centre of the road, the Citroën had passed it and was streaking after us up the hill.

I looked at Zander. His face was white and pinched and the simper ghastly. 'Guido volunteered,' he said, 'volunteered freely.' When no one said anything he touched Simone's shoulder. 'They've killed Guido.'

'I heard the automatic fire, patron.' Her effort to stay cool and calm was only just successful. She was very angry. 'Our handsome young shepherd told you that they only had revolvers. Did you believe him, patron?'

'No, but I thought they would save their real firepower to surprise us. Jean-Pierre will be upset. He never approved of involving Guido in operations outside the Paris office. But Guido appealed to me. He was ambitious. He wanted field experience.'

'In what?' I asked. 'Gang warfare?'

'In covert negotiation, the kind of business which he knew from his work with us to be the most profitable.'

'All I know about him is that he cooked lunch the other day in the safe house in Stresa. What was his job for you in Paris?'

'He was an accountant, a first-class young man, Jean-Pierre'
right hand on taxation matters. He will be greatly missed.' H
paused as if suddenly struck by the pious banality of what h
was saying, then hurried on. 'What gun was that, the gun Bour
ger had? Did you recognize it?'

'I thought that it might be a Uzi. Hard to say.'

'Yes, it could have been that.'

But he wasn't really wondering about the gun. He was won
dering if we were thinking the same things as he was – that h
had made several gross errors of judgement, underestimated a
enemy of known quality, thrown away a good life uselessly
and asking himself how much our confidence in him had bee
shaken. The young people were chattering excitedly as the
unpacked the other three rifles and he snapped an order tha
shut them up. No loss of confidence in him there. To them, n
doubt, Guido had been of no more value or importance than th
Pacioli driver they had kicked and beaten on their patron'
behalf.

'I can see the calvary,' Simone said. 'There, straight ahead
with the pointed roof. Do you still want me to turn off there?

'Certainly.' He sounded surprised that she should ask.

'They're going to catch up with us now. They'll see us mak
the turn.'

'They may not. Put your foot down. We could still lose them.

'They're faster than we are on the straight and on the corners
They're bound to see us. And there's no effective cover on tha
hillside until we get to the trees.'

'Then get to the trees. If we can't hide ourselves, we can a
least take the high ground before they can get to it.'

The track we turned on to had once been the approach to
hill farm, but that had been long ago. The old wheel ruts beneath
the weeds had been made by carts, not tractors, and the thin
patches of top soil left on the stony slopes below the tree-lin
had been taken over by crabgrass and scrub. Two or three
hundred yards from the road we came to the roofless walls of a
stone barn. Not far beyond stood the brick hearth and chimney
of what had been a wooden house. A tourist authority infor
mation board, with its own neat shingle roof and a trash car
standing by it, gave the traveller a variety of hints, tips and
instructions. Caravans were forbidden to park there and camp
ing was permitted only in designated places. Lighting cooking

fires was forbidden as was shooting without the permission of the Landesfremdenverkehrsamt. A pointing plywood finger showed us the way to a hikers' trail up through the woods, a trail which led to a ridge road (*Höhenweg*, 1063 m) along the Karawanken hills. On the trail and ridge road, bicycles and motorcycles were forbidden. It said nothing about station-wagons.

The hikers' trail ran through the trees diagonally across the face of the hillside. We lurched up past another pointing-finger signpost through a fringe of saplings. From there on, the trees were bigger and grew closer together. The trail was narrowing and becoming a ledge along the contour line.

Simone, wrestling with the wheel, nearly stalled once because she had forgotten to shift down into first, but she recovered. The killing of Guido had shaken her, but only shaken her. If I had been driving, that would have been it. I was by then scared witless and the man we called 'patron' had become, for me, a callous and complacent bungler. The assault rifles the young people were crooning over behind my head would turn out to be useless because they had brought the wrong ammunition or because the firing pins were missing. I knew it. We had been 'followed' ahead by a second Rasmuk team which was, at that very moment, quietly waiting up on the high ground our wise patron had urged us to occupy, carefully positioned in ambush and all set to slaughter the lot of us.

The wagon rocked wildly, side-swiped a tree and stopped. I looked down at the track below and saw the Bourger Citroën turning off the road after us. Simone had been right, our patron fatuously optimistic.

'Attention to me,' he said. 'We leave the transport here and quickly deploy.' To Simone, he went on: 'We also take care to hold our fire until I give the signal. The shepherd should be made to suffer maximum surprise and shock when the sheep turn around and start to bite him.' To me, he said: 'We will all go up the hill, please, well away from our transport. Don't use it as cover. If you will help us carry some of the ammunition, so much the better, but don't try to take anything else. When they reach the hikers' trail, stop moving. Just lie flat on the ground behind the thickest tree you can find and remain absolutely still.'

All four of them had rifles now and there was already a smear of oil on one sleeve of Zander's beautiful mohair suit. I took one of the ammunition boxes, as he had asked, and started off. The hillside beneath the trees was covered with feathery undergrowth above a soft bed of decaying pine needles that was rather slippery. The ammunition box was also heavier than I had expected. After about a hundred yards' climbing I stopped to get my breath and looked back.

The Rasmuk team had stopped by the signs and their driver was turning their car. The other three were already out and looking up in our direction. They were all carrying the same type of machine pistol and had what looked like CB transceiver mikes clipped to their coat lapels. Bourger had a pair of binoculars. He raised them to his eyes.

That started me climbing again. The others were all somewhere ahead of me. I couldn't see them, but I could hear movement still. I struggled up to a small clearing. There were no trees anywhere near me with trunks thick enough to stop bullets that could rip through the bodywork of a van. What I was probably looking for at that moment was a giant redwood. What I settled for instead was a hole in the ground, or rather a shallow depression in it, behind the remains of a foresters' trestle that had at some time been used for stacking cordwood.

Suddenly, everything was very quiet. Peering around I couldn't see any of the others. I couldn't even hear them any more. I even forgot the discomfort of the can of film digging into my stomach. I was already scared. Now I panicked and started to get up.

There was a sharp 'Psst!' from somewhere near me and Simone said: 'Keep your head down.'

'Where are the others?'

'To the right of us. Keep your head down and keep quiet.'

By moving slightly to the left I found that I could see below the trestle without raising my head. Bourger and one of his team were climbing up the hill below the trail towards the station-wagon. They were being slow and careful. I guessed that the other two members of the team were already across the trail and out on the flanks, moving up to get behind us. They knew roughly where we were hidden. They had seen the station-wagon stop on the trail. From that point we could have continued along the trail on foot. They knew that we hadn't done so because from where they were a long stretch of the trail was plainly visible. If we had continued along it we would have been plainly visible too. So, since we weren't visible, we were somewhere on the hillside. All they had to do was narrow the field a bit, then flush us out and finish the job.

Bourger was near the wagon now and went down on one knee to peer under it. It was over at an angle. I suppose he wanted to see if it was still mobile or whether we had run aground on the crankcase. Then he went up close to it and looked inside.

Our baggage was all there but nothing to show that a few minutes earlier there had been guns and ammunition along with it. It all looked – as, I then realized, Zander had thoughtfully intended it to look – as if the killing of Guido had rendered us all witless enough to turn into a blind alley, ditch our transportation and try to hide. Bourger could not know that I had been the only really witless member of our group. Now, he scanned the hillside above and said something to the man with him. Then, he moved out slowly on to the trail and stood there with his arms raised as if signalling a big pincer movement to someone he could see higher up the hill.

Oddly enough, I knew exactly what he was trying to do. It was possible that one or more of us was armed. Men with backgrounds like Zander's, he would have reasoned, often had a taste for hand guns, and that young Berber of his might very well share it. Anyway, he would see if he could draw fire. The chance of his being hit must have seemed to him acceptably small and the rewards for taking that chance worth having. The leader prepared to draw fire himself often has no need to give orders. Once he had fooled us into giving away our position on the hillside all he would have to give his men would be a nod. They would do the rest. It would be a quick, clean, troublefree operation, a credit to Rasmuk and, of course, to Raoul Bourger. The trick of drawing enemy fire has long been a standard infantry tactic. The only time it doesn't work is when it is used against a highly disciplined enemy who also knows about drawing fire and how to turn it to his own advantage.

All the same, I did wonder why Zander hadn't been tempted by that chance of disposing of the whiz-kid assassin there and then. It took me a moment to see why he had held his fire. Killing Bourger and the man with him would simply have warned the other two members of the team that they were up against more than hand guns. They would then have known at once what had to be done. The Citroën had been parked safely behind the stone walls of the old barn. All they would have to do would be to get to the radio in it, call for reinforcements and keep the trail covered until they arrived. The Italian team now waiting across the border could have been with us in less than an hour. We could have stayed where we were or we could have gone for a hike along the ridge road, but there would have been nothing we could have done to get out of that place alive.

No. It was *our* side that was going to have to draw fire, and suddenly I heard us doing so.

Simone was calling to Bourger. She was calling in Arabic so I didn't know precisely what she was saying, but I knew enough to make out the sense of it.

'Brother Bourger?' she called. 'Brother Raoul? How much is Rasmuk paying you to kill us?'

Her voice reverberated strangely across the hillside. If I hadn't seen her climbing up there with only a rifle and her shoulder bag stuffed with ammunition I would have thought she was speaking into a loud-hailer.

The effect on Bourger was startling. He leaped sideways and landed in a crouch which became almost instantly a roll. Then, he had disappeared over the edge of the trail. At the same moment, a burst of automatic fire from his man on our left flank ripped through the low branches of a tree a few yards away.

'Oh, Brother Raoul,' Simone wailed, 'why do your masters wish to take our lives? They will never be paid, you know, never. Why do you risk so much for so little?'

She had moved. I could tell that from the voice. Another burst of fire tore into the trees, this time near enough to shower me with pine needles. Then, I saw Bourger scuttle across the trail directly below us. He was signalling to someone on our left as he went.

Simone laughed. 'Oh Brother Raoul,' she called, 'be careful. Be careful or you will shoot your friends.'

But he already knew about the dangers of cross-fire and was pressing a button behind the CB mike on his lapel.

The two men working their way along the hillside to get behind us must have been very near because, although he spoke quietly into his mike, I could hear his voice quacking through their speakers. One of them was only a few yards above me.

There followed a brief silence. Then Zander opened fire.

I had my head down and was staring fixedly at the trail. That was because the underbrush was very thin and I was afraid that

240

the man above me might see my face if I looked up. So, I saw Bourger die. I didn't see him hit. What happened was that his body landed on the trail as if it had been tossed there by some monster who had no further use for it.

The noise of the firing went on for only about five seconds, I think. Then, there was silence again. From quite near me, through the singing in my ears, there came the double click of a magazine being changed.

'Are you all right?' Simone asked.

'Yes. Are you?'

She got to her feet and pointed up the hill with her rifle. 'Is he dead? We'd better be sure. I'll keep you covered if you'll have a look.'

I scrambled up to the place she was pointing at. The first thing I saw was the man's machine pistol lying on the ground. He was beyond it. Half his head had gone and the blood was still bubbling out of an artery in his neck.

'He's dead enough,' I said. 'So's Bourger. Did you get him too?'

'That was the patron. The young people will have dealt with the others, but we will wait here for orders.'

We stood there saying nothing until Zander called up from the trail.

'Mr Halliday, Simone, we can all go,' he said. 'We will leave our rifles up here for the police to find and take the Uzis down. But quickly, please. We haven't much time.'

'What about the ammunition box?' I asked.

'Leave it where it is,' said Simone. 'Be kind enough to take that Uzi down with you. But pick it up by the sling. We don't want to leave any prints.' She was wiping hers off with the rifle with a handful of paper tissues.

I smeared the handles of the ammunition box before I picked up the Uzi. 'Aren't the police going to wonder how four men with four rifles managed to kill each other and end up in these positions?' I asked.

'Certainly. They are also going to wonder who fired the other kind of bullets, those in the tree trunks here and in the van that Guido was driving. There will be a lot to puzzle them.' That is why we must move quickly now, so that we are not here to help them solve these mysteries.'

I went down to the trail. Zander, with pine needles clinging to his mohair suit, was using a silk handkerchief to wipe the rifle he held. When he saw me carrying the Uzi he nodded to the one lying on the ground beside Bourger's corpse.

'Perhaps you will take that too, Mr Halliday. We will leave them in their car. It will all help to confuse the police inquiries.'

'Aren't *we* going to take their car then?'

'No, I don't think we'll need to do that.' The eyes were weary. He looked strangely old, I thought, and wondered how long it had been since winning battles by force of arms had lost its appeal for him.

I picked up the second Uzi. 'With the Ortofilm van and Guido shot up,' I said, 'isn't the Ortofilm station-wagon going to be an object of special interest to the police on these roads? Things are surely bad enough already without our being picked up for questioning now. ORF will connect Ortofilm with both me and Jean-Pierre. I don't know about him, but I certainly don't want to have any explaining to do right here in Austria.'

He sighed. 'I see that you have lost confidence in our ability to plan, Mr Halliday. I'm sorry that you feel that way, but perhaps it was to be expected. You weren't prepared for casualties. However, let me reassure you about one thing. *Your* anxieties are groundless. We planned for all the contingencies we could. Jean-Pierre will make himself responsible for any explanations to the police that can possibly involve you. Now, please, go down and put those machine pistols with the others. Mokhtar and Jasmin are already below. Wait with them. Simone and I will join you in a minute.'

I did as I had been told. Then, as Simone backed the station-wagon down to the beginning of the trail with Zander guiding her, a big Ford sedan with a rental sticker on the windshield came bouncing up the track from the road. Jean-Pierre was driving it.

He stopped when he saw me. 'Are they all right?' he asked as he climbed out.

'We are, and so are the patron and Simone, but we'll be leaving four corpses behind us. Did you see the van with Guido in it back there?'

'Yes. The police are in charge and an ambulance was just arriving. I could not stop of course. Is he badly hurt?'

'We couldn't stop either, but we saw him hit. They shot him up to get him out of their way.'

'And now they are dead. That is good.'

'I guess it is. Where did you rent this? Judenburg?'

But he had no more time for me. He had seen the patron and was hurrying to confer with him. Moments later Zander was issuing orders. At once, Mokhtar and Jasmin began to empty the station-wagon of our bags and stuff them into the trunk of the rental car. When Zander beckoned to me to join the conference Jean-Pierre's two-suiter was the only piece of baggage left in the back of the wagon.

Zander gave me one of his hard stares before he spoke. 'The following scenario has been agreed,' he said finally. 'It seems reasonable, however, to ask if you have any comments. So. Listen carefully please. After your friend in ORF had taken delivery from you of the film of your interview, we decided to celebrate our success. But without Jean Pierre and Guido. They were left to drive the Ortofilm transportation back to Geneva. Jean-Pierre last saw us in a bar drinking wine. We had spoken of taking the train to Vienna. He does not know if we did, but he resented slightly being left out of the festivities. As a result, he proposed to Guido a minor change of route. Instead of going straight to Geneva via Milan and the Mont Blanc tunnel, they would first make a detour via the scenic route to Ljubjana and Trieste. It was so agreed. Then, nearing the frontier at the Wurzenpass, Jean-Pierre noticed that Guido in the van was no longer following. He stopped and waited. He is not at that stage at all worried. Guido is young. If he has a flat he can change the wheel. Only after an hour has gone by does he begin to think of possible accidents. So then, he goes back. He is as bewildered as the police at what he finds. Have you any comments, Mr Halliday?'

'Yes, it stinks.'

'Why?'

'Where are we at this moment, now I mean? Whooping it up in a bar in Arnoldstein or on a train to Vienna?'

'What does it matter? By tonight we should be in Germany. After that ...' He shrugged.

'What was the time of the train we took? Supposing there isn't a train from Arnoldstein or Villach that we could have taken? Don't forget, please, that I'm not expecting to disappear and assume a brand new identity with official North American help.'

'Neither is Jean-Pierre.'

'But he has answers ready for the questions he's going to be asked. They're not bad answers either. At least they're simple and reasonably convincing. I don't have any that'll stand up for a moment. And if you believe that when the Austrians come asking the FBI for help they aren't going to get some really enthusiastic co-operation, forget it. I've told some unpleasant truths about the FBI from time to time and they have long memories there.'

'You have committed no crime,' Simone said. 'It may be disgraceful that you can't remember how you reached Germany from Arnoldstein because you were in a drunken sleep most of the time, but they can't extradite you for that. Besides, why should they want to inconvenience Mr Halliday, that good man who rescued an Austrian silver mine from the clutches of a crazy foreign decadent? Those four men up there all have criminal records. Clearly, they attacked Guido because they mistook him for someone else. Which someone else? Obviously, the person or persons who attacked and killed them. Mr Halliday could not possibly have any knowledge of such matters.'

'She is right, of course,' said Jean-Pierre, 'though I cannot wait to tell you why. The longer I stay here, the weaker my story becomes. Goodbye, Mr Halliday.' He shook my hand. 'Good luck and bon voyage.'

He didn't say goodbye to the others, he just smiled and nodded to them as he climbed into the station-wagon and drove away. He would be hearing from the patron again, no doubt, but that would be when the heat was off. Until then, he had the Paris office to take care of and, perhaps, the problem of finding a replacement for Guido.

We waited for five minutes after he had gone. Then, we left too.

Where Guido had run off the road the police had flashing-light barriers out and one-way traffic control in operation. We had time, as we went slowly by, to see Jean-Pierre having an animated discussion with the traffic police. The ambulance crew were in the process of moving a stretcher with Guido on it from the shoulder of the road to the ambulance. A young man in a white tunic who looked like an intern was holding up a plasma drip-feed while the loading was done.

'You see, patron?' Simone remarked. 'Guido is not lost to us. Jean-Pierre will see that he gets the best of attention.'

'Yes, I see. Some wounds, even wounds in the back, can look more dangerous than they really are. We may hope.'

He was in the front passenger seat beside her. By the time we reached Villach on our way north, he was asleep.

We drove non-stop to the airport at Salzburg and turned in the rental car. From there, we took a taxi to the German frontier and walked through passport control and customs carrying our bags. No one took any particular interest in us. On the German side there was an all-night café that served snacks. After I had made a phone call, we sat there drinking beer and eating sandwiches.

His long nap in the car had restored Zander. He ate and drank with appetite. My lack of interest in the food did not go unnoticed.

'You look tired, Mr Halliday.'

'I feel it.'

'You behaved with courage. You will sleep soundly.'

'Sure.'

He glanced at a group of truck drivers drinking coffee at a nearby table, but they were taking no notice of us, not even of Simone. He went on.

'That General I met yesterday, General Newell. Did he interest you?'

'Very much. He seemed an able man.'

'He said something curious to me.'

'Oh?'

'He said that I had an unusual smile.'

'Patron,' Simone said, 'I think cars for us are arriving.'

He moved a hand slightly. The cars could wait. 'The General said that I had a kind of smile that he had seen only once before. It was the smile of a warrant officer he had known who was chief instructor at a school for unarmed combat. Curious, eh? He said that soldiers would arrive at the school for courses of instruction and believe that, because the chief instructor had a pleasing smile, they were going to have a pleasing experience. It never happened that way though.'

'No?'

'No. They would find that the smile was a deception. Curious, wasn't it, that he should say such a thing? I have never thought of myself as a man who smiled often, if at all. You should know that much about me by now, Mr Halliday. I almost never smile.

All the same, I liked General Newell. He would be a good man to serve with.' He stood up. 'Yes, Simone, you are right. There are cars here and people looking for us. Goodbye, Mr Halliday. I have enjoyed our collaboration.' He raised his hands, scrubbed-up and ready, and for an instant I thought he was going to offer to shake hands with me.

Then he turned away. Simone and the young people gave me quick little farewell waves and were gone with him. I also received a nod from the man escorting them. He was the quiet one who had driven me from the Gasthaus to Velden and back thirty-six hours earlier. As they left, Schelm came over to the table and sat down facing me.

'I'm glad to see you well,' he said. 'I have a hotel reservation for you not too far away and there's a seat on the midday Lufthansa flight to New York if you want it. I'd suggest you try to make that if you can. Here's the ticket. The Austrian police are reporting a couple of incidents near the Yugoslav border involving four killed and one seriously injured by gun-shot. Local radio is carrying a story about an Italian Red Brigades revenge shoot-out near the Wurzenpass. Do you want to tell me what happened yesterday after you left?'

I told him as briefly as I could. He ran a thoughtful eye over me.

'What's happened to your suit?' he asked. 'You look like a maternity case.'

'It's not a new suit and it's not used to my falling around in it among the bushes on Austrian hillsides. The lining's torn.' I thought again of Simone's suggestion that I might give the second can of film to my good friend Schelm and ask him to distribute copies of it to interested parties in the Gulf. Now, it didn't seem to be such a good idea after all. If, in spite of the asking price and everything else that could be said against it, Nato was still going to flirt with the notion of making a deal for Abra Bay, a can of film showing an interview in which The Ruler exposed himself as a fool as well as a criminal psychopath might be thought of rather as a can of worms. It might easily get lost. I might never see it again. Better to keep it in my own hands. 'Where will you be sending the Zander family?' I asked.

The question outraged his sense of propriety sufficiently to distract him, for the time being, from the subject of my suit and the odd bulge in the front of the jacket. On the way to the hotel near Munich airport that he had chosen for me, I pretended to doze and very nearly did. When he dropped me he said that I should take the shuttle to Frankfurt for the New York flight and that he would send a car for me at ten o'clock. That way I should get at least three hours sleep.

I needed them badly but was determined not to take the risk. Instead, I showered, shaved and changed into another suit. By then, it was nearly seven and I could order breakfast. I checked out at seven-thirty, leaving a note for Schelm to say that I had decided to try for an earlier flight home and that I hoped to sleep on the plane. I reached Frankfurt with two hours to spare. That gave me all the extra time I needed. I checked in for the Lufthansa New York flight with no trouble at all.

At Kennedy, immigration let me through with only a bored nod. Customs, however, were ready and waiting for me with tight-lipped relish.

'Is this all your baggage, Mr Halliday?'

'Yes, that's it.'

'On this declaration you state that you have bought nothing while you have been in Europe. Is that correct?'

'Correct.'

'Have you *acquired* anything while you have been abroad? An article of commerce or a gift for instance?'

'I have nothing. Do you want me to open the bags?'

'Mr Halliday, this is a spot check. We'd like you to step into the office over there and discuss your declaration. No objection to that, have you? If you have nothing we'll find nothing. Right?'

It took three of them half an hour. There was a body search too, though they didn't get really intimate. They only patted me.

'Do you mind telling me what this is all about?' I asked when they had finished. 'And don't give me any more about spot checks. I may not be a reporter any more, but I can still make myself heard. So far I've co-operated. I haven't started yelling about persecution or my civil rights. So, how about levelling with me? What were you looking for?'

The senior man hesitated, then shrugged. 'Laundered money sealed in a can of sixteen millimetre movie film. That's what we were told. Information received. We had to check.'

'Someone's been kidding you. Do I look like a currency smuggler?'

'These days, Mr Halliday, everyone looks like a currency smuggler. You'd be surprised.'

'What would you have done if I'd had a can of exposed film?'

'Held it for examination. As you'd denied having it, we'd obviously have a right to be suspicious. We'd have figured that the tip-off had been given out of spite. If you'd been carrying film we'd have been pretty sure it was porn.'

The following day, Barbara called me to say that the air freight package from Frankfurt had arrived safely in her office with the can of film unopened and quite safe. I asked her to tell the producer so that he could have it picked up and processed.

He called me the following morning. 'It's great stuff, Bob,' he said; 'even better than the first part, but we have a problem.'

'What kind? Legal?'

'Not exactly. Have you heard from our friend Rainer since you've been back?'

'No.'

'Well, an edited version of the first part went out over Austrian network television yesterday. The impact was sensational.'

'Good. Any reactions?'

'Unfortunately, Bob, those people in the Gulf, the UAE, aren't as pleased as you are. They've lodged a formal diplomatic protest in Vienna claiming that an honoured member of their federal council, your Ruler, was tricked into the interview and libelled.'

'No one tricked him into anything. You've seen it. I just asked him a few questions.'

'That's what the Austrians are saying. However, it's not the Austrians we're worried about. They can look after themselves. Did you know that Syncom-Sentinel is one of our biggest and staunchest subscribers?'

'No, I didn't. I thought you depended on the public's generosity.'

'We depend on what we can get. Syncom is generous in a big way. Which makes things difficult. They know of the existence of the second part of the interview, the one you kept back from the Austrians.'

'And they don't want it shown.'

'That's right.'

'So, my bold producer, you're going to come right out and tell them that no multi-national giant can censor you, that you have a duty to the public and that they can keep their lousy subscriptions? Yes?'

'It's not that simple, Bob. They've drawn our attention to an Agence France Presse report that came in last night. It says that His Highness The Ruler has entered a Swiss sanitarium. We've checked it out and apparently it's not one of those places where they dry out rich junkies and drunks and then turn them loose again. It's a private maximum-security hospital for the mentally sick, an expensive but very serious institution we're told. It must have been the silver-mine hassle with the Austrians that tripped alarms in the Gulf. There's also a report in from Abu Dhabi saying that a cousin of his has been appointed to stand in for this particular Ruler during what they're calling his "indisposition". If he'd been a king, I guess they'd have said that the cousin had been appointed to be a regent. But you see the problem?'

'By showing this film now, we'd be persecuting a sick man who couldn't defend himself. We'd be exposing a manic-depressive who's not responsible for his actions and utterances, and is, in fact, hospitalized, to public ridicule and hatred. Is that it?'

'Yes, and I'm sorry, Bob. You did a great job there. Too bad he turned out to be a nut-case.'

'Yes.'

Barbara also thought it too bad. The show might have been good for me, good for business that is. She was consoled, though, by Pacioli's release from escrow of the second instalment of twenty-five thousand.

I heard nothing more from Schelm. That attempt to use his American contacts and the United States Customs Service to kill the Petrucher mine interview by seizing the film had been his farewell gesture to me. About three months later, however, one of the news magazines carried a story about Abra Bay. It was the kind of story intended exclusively for those who can read between the lines. Reports, it said, that discussions had been taking place in Rome between UAE defence officials and representatives of Nato concerning the possible preparation of Abra Bay for use as an emergency naval supply base had been categorically denied in Abu Dhabi.

At the end of that same month I received a picture postcard. The picture on the front was of the Gasthaus Dr Wohak. The message on the other side was brief.

The patron says that I may let you know that we are well. Perhaps, fairly soon, I will be able to write asking you frankly if such news of us is of any further interest to you. S.

The postmark said that it had been mailed in New York City.

It seems likely that, if Zander Pharmaceuticals are still in business, the next communication will be mailed in Miami. It should be here any day now.

Time is taking care of Zander, as it is taking care of me, steadily and, presumably, without much more fuss. His family, however, still has a long way to go. I am really not sure how I shall reply.